Taking Over

"It's about our expansion, isn't it?" Pauline leant over me, almost totally blocking out the light.

"Just as well it doesn't mention *your* expansion," I said, making one of those intimate little jokes that Pauly enjoyed so much.

"I can't wait to get this baby born," said Pauly. "It's getting in the way – literally – of the autumn collection. I can't get within yards of the drawing board."

To be honest, I was a little shocked. As a modern husband, I was naturally quite happy to allow my wife to do her own thing. She's very good at designing clothes, and as long as her hobby didn't come between her and the family, I saw no reason to put my foot down, like my mother said I should.

After all, little Clerihue was very well looked after, now that Mother had moved in with us.

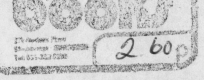

**Also by the same authors,
and available from Coronet:**

SWAPPING

About the authors

Shirley Lowe and Angela Ince met on the *Daily Express* early in their working lives. They have been friends ever since, in spite of collaborating on novels, television scripts and countless newspaper and magazine articles.

They adapted *Swapping*, their second novel, for a BBC comedy drama series, and recently created *Bluebirds*, a major children's television series, also for the BBC. They are currently working on their fourth novel.

They are both married, with children, and live in London; near enough to get in touch when the plot thickens, but far enough apart to stay on speaking terms.

SHIRLEY ANGELA
LOWE & INCE

Taking Over

CORONET BOOKS
Hodder and Stoughton

Copyright © 1989 by Shirley Lowe and Angela Ince

First published in Great Britain in 1989 by Hodder and Stoughton Ltd

Coronet edition 1990

Printed and bound in Great Britain for Hodder and Stoughton Paperbacks, a division of Hodder and Stoughton Ltd, Mill Road, Dunton Green, Sevenoaks, Kent TN13 2YA. (Editorial Office: 47 Bedford Square, London WC1B 3DP) by BPCC Hazell Books, Aylesbury, Bucks. Photoset by Rowland Phototypesetting Ltd, Bury St Edmunds, Suffolk.

British Library C.I.P.

Lowe, Shirley
  Taking over.
  I. Title   Ince, Angela
823'.914 [F]

ISBN 0-340-52812-5

LOCAL WEDDINGS

Pauline Browne married George Jenks, at St. Mary's Church, Hammersmith Road, on Saturday. Pauline, the daughter of Mr. and Mrs. Brian Browne, of Comberton Road, Hammersmith, studied design at the St. Martin's School of Art. George, the son of Mr. and Mrs. Arthur Jenks, of Comberton Road, Hammersmith, is a salesman. The honeymoon will be spent in Padstow.

West London Observer,
15th February, 1981

I can afford anything I want.

When I married George, the "something borrowed" was the cost of the honeymoon. Seven years later I own an idyllic farmhouse in the hills above Grimaud; I can just see my new Mercedes sports car through the waterfall of geranium hedge, my shoulder blades are prickling pleasurably from the most expensive sun in the world, and this evening Marianne has promised me a delicious bourride.

I can afford it all. Armani jackets and cottonwool balls, portable computers and Loch Fyne kippers, and I wonder what Dad would have thought if he could hear me say, "Tobias is down for Winchester, actually," as though we'd been at it for generations?

The only thing I haven't been able to afford very much of, recently, is happiness. Well, you can't buy it, can you? That's what they say. I am in love with someone who only speaks to me over a boardroom table. I think he thinks I'm a clever businesswoman who designs internationally acclaimed clothes. I think that's all he thinks about me.

I came to Grimaud to sort out my life. But all I'm doing is sorting out old newspaper cuttings, as poignant as school photographs. Our wedding, the Bolsover takeover, the time Sybilla nearly sued the Post Office, the day George

5

was arrested at Molesworth . . . I wonder if George remembers it all as clearly as I do?

When exactly was it that I got overdrawn on the happiness account? (Not a particularly good metaphor; I've been spending far too much time with accountants lately.) Back in 1985, I suppose, when George came home, cross, after some board meeting. I was expecting our second child, and George's mother was living with us.

It was about then I realised that George doesn't always tell the truth. And when someone doesn't tell the truth . . .

George and I grew up together. He was the boy next door. Two years older than me, unattainably glamorous. I fell in love with him when I was five. George was Joseph with a stuck-on beard in the school Nativity play and I was one of the angels with a slipping halo. "You did look funny when that white thing kept falling off your head, Pauline." I'd spent the rest of the day glowing because he had noticed me.

I told my mother that George Jenks was my best friend and I was going to marry him when I grew up.

"That's nice, dear," said Mother. She was making a tarte tatin at the time, with windfalls from the big apple tree in our garden. "We must invite him to tea." But she never did.

There was only a broken-down fence between our two gardens; the Berlin Wall, my mother called it. Our families hardly ever spoke to each other, except over the broken fence, an ongoing area of conflict. Every spring, Mother took mournful trips down the garden to inspect her clematis. "Their Russian Vine is suffocating the Nellie Moser again, Brian. Can't you do something, dear?"

And Dad, who would travel a long way to avoid a confrontation, had no sooner hacked his way through the twisting vegetation and pulled his secateurs out of his pocket, than Arthur Jenks would appear on his side of the fence, face flushing belligerently. "That vine is my property, Mr Browne, and I'll thank you to leave it alone."

My parents never actually said the Jenkses were common, because it wasn't a word they used. One Sunday afternoon Mr Jenks lurched back from the Windsor Castle and lobbed a couple of bottles of Watney's Pale over the fence, scoring a direct hit on Mother's plate of cucumber sandwiches. She had picked up the scattered sandwiches and bottles, stowed them neatly into the dustbin and sighed, "Oh dear, I do wish the Jenkses weren't so *uncivilised.*" It was the worst thing she could say about anyone.

Impossible to believe that George, pale and slim, with serious grey eyes and perfect manners, was the child of red-faced boorish Arthur, and Gloria, who thought it was vulgar to laugh out loud.

When I was eleven I watched from behind the curtains in my bedroom as George – the only adolescent in our neighbourhood never to suffer the misery of acne – pumped up the tyres of his red racing bike with the swept down handlebars, and I had erotic fantasies of him pedalling me off to the Wimpy in King Street for an orgy of strawberry milkshakes. I was always hopefully bumping into him in the street, but he never seemed to notice me.

I'd left school, and had been doing Fashion for a couple of years at the St Martin's School of Art, when I kept meeting George on the tube. "What a coincidence," he said, gallantly carrying my heavy art portfolio up escalators and down subways.

We started going out together, and it was at least three months later, between Earl's Court and Baron's Court, before he admitted that our meeting hadn't been a coincidence at all, and he'd gladly spend all day circling the Circle Line for the chance of seeing me. That was the second time I decided to marry George.

"Have you seen the new Woody Allen at the Cannon?" he said, the second time we met. "I was thinking of going this evening."

We saw the Woody Allen and then the latest Tom Stoppard ("Took a long time getting to the point, didn't he?" said George) and we ate pasta at Bertorelli's. Soon we were spending most of our evenings and weekends together, taking long walks along the towpath at Hammersmith, sitting on the banks of Barnes reservoir, watching the swans and talking about what we were going to do with our lives.

"Dad wants me to go into London Transport, but I don't fancy the nationalised industries," said George. He was throwing bits of bread at the swans, but the pigeons kept getting them first. "More opportunity in private industry. I rather fancy myself as a salesman . . ." He looked at me shyly. "What do you think of that?"

I thought he could sell anybody anything. He'd only have to gaze at them with those honest grey eyes and whip out the order book. "I think it's a marvellous idea. But what would you sell?"

"Oh, it's not the product that counts." He straightened his shoulders firmly, as though he was already shaping up to move forty gross of carburettor heads. "Mr Maddox at college says it's the initial approach that matters, the way you soften up the customer. You gain their confidence, you see, Pauline. He calls it the art of salesmanship."

At Christmas, George invited me to his party at Paddington College and I took him along to my New Year's Eve party at St Martin's. Most of the students dressed as an art form in those days, and it was a turn-on to be with someone who cared more about how I looked than whether he'd cut the currently correct number of holes in his T-shirt, or hennaed his hair the precisely right shade of dark red. I loved George in his straight suit, clean white shirt, hair neatly cut into the nape of his neck. I was particularly fond of the nape of his neck.

"Oh, Pauly, I do feel out of place here," he'd said, holding me very close, as the dance floor shook to the inspired gymnastics of the other dancers. "I'm so boring compared with all your interesting friends."

"Who's the Adonis, darling?" Colin Walters said next day, as we were queuing at the coffee machine.

"Hands off," I said. "He's mine."

Colin wanted to be a fashion journalist. He wore his hair

spiky punk, painstakingly shaded pale pink to violent puce, and he was hung about with leather and chains. I saw him in the Caprice the other day. He writes for the *Face* now, buys his three-piece tweed suits from Hackett and wears his hair so fashionably short it looks as though his barber works for the Army.

We were strolling over Hammersmith Bridge when George asked me to marry him. It was one of those grey London evenings, the white gulls circling and swirling above the white-flecked foam of a high tide. I said yes, straight away. And then I told Mum and Dad.

"Oh, Pauline, are you sure?" My mother sat down heavily in the big armchair still wearing her apron, which was something she never did. "I'd hoped for something better for you . . ." She began crying.

"What a thing to say, love." Dad came and stood by Mother, and put his arm round her shoulder. "George is a nice enough lad. I think this calls for a celebration, Pauline. If you look in the dining room sideboard you'll find a bottle of Taittinger. The real stuff, won it at the snooker championship last year. Not my tipple, as you know. I've been saving it for an important occasion like this."

After two glasses of champagne, Mum, looking rather flushed, said, "I really think it's better to have a fling or two before you settle down."

"What are you suggesting, Sarah?" Dad said, giving me a wink.

I lay in bed that night, wondering if Mum was right. Was I making a mistake? I'd never had a serious boyfriend before. Lots of flirtations, the odd pass from one or two of the boys at art school, but I'd never wanted to sleep with anyone, except George. I suggested it once, and he kissed me tenderly. "There'll be time enough for that when we're married, Pauly."

It wasn't, as I later realised in the lumpy double bed at Mrs Tregunter's boarding house in Padstow, old-fashioned respect that had held George back. It was more an anxiety to postpone the moment when I'd discover that he had learned his lovemaking out of a text book and had only got to chapter two. We were both virgins on our honeymoon, and although our bodies seemed to know what to do, our limbs kept getting embarrassingly in the way. We did a lot of fumbling and apologising.

"Oops, sorry . . . that's better . . . oh, I do want this to be good for you, Pauly."

Mrs Tregunter's bed creaked the news of our every erotic move to the other lodgers, who regarded us speculatively over the morning bacon and eggs. Their interest did nothing to help our performance. "Ssh, they'll hear us," will never be a sentence to set the hormones tingling.

We never admitted it to each other, but I think we were both relieved to get home to our rented room in Brook Green, and to a life where sex was an agreeable soufflé in the daily routine rather than the main course.

Before we'd had time to settle into the routine of married life we were moving the toaster, the blue dinner service, the Sheffield plate, the second-hand three-piece suite and the brass bed my parents gave us, out of the rented room in Brook Green and up the A1 to Prescott Avenue, St Neots; two rooms, kitchen, share bath.

George had come home one evening and announced that he'd answered an advertisement for a salesman at Bolsover (St Neots) Ltd, had been up for an interview and landed the job.

"But why didn't you tell me, darling?"

"Didn't think I'd get it, love. Didn't want you to think you'd married a failure."

I hadn't wanted to leave London. My friends and contacts were there, and I'd just started working with a small design group.

"This is a big chance for me," George said. "Well-established company, small sales force, opportunity to move into senior management. You'll soon find something to do, Pauly."

It didn't occur to me to argue. My place, it seemed to

me then, was wherever my husband's work took him. And it had taken him to St Neots.

I noticed the boutique in West Street as I was coming home with the shopping, late one afternoon. It was called Clockwork. Small but stylish. I could see at a glance that the scarlet rayon dress in the window had a dipping hemline and haphazard stitching, but somebody had presented it with a flourish. That somebody was Honor Fletcher, chic, sharp-eyed and, as I later discovered, as tough as old boots.

"Why don't you show her some of your designs, Pauly?" George said that evening. "You made some very nice things at college."

I went in the following day, and had to lurk about behind a curtain in a dingy stock room for half an hour, getting more and more demoralised by the minute, while Honor Fletcher dealt with customers at the front of the shop. She pursed her shocking pink lips doubtfully when I unpacked my samples and showed them to her.

"A little avant-garde for St Neots," she said, "but I suppose we could give it a try."

"Oh, thank you, Mrs Fletcher." I couldn't believe my luck. Less than a year out of art school and already I'd got a shop window for my work.

"My budget is, of course, pathetically small . . ."

"I wouldn't expect much," I said quickly. After all, I'd never made clothes professionally before, only for friends at art school.

"We'll see how it goes." Honor Fletcher hung up my samples and swiftly attached large price tags to them.

I was soon designing and making up about a third of the stock in the boutique, and collecting a percentage on each sale which was, I later realised, a considerable saving on the amount Mrs Fletcher had to pay her regular wholesalers.

I met Julia Mainwaring first a few months later, when she was doing her face in the ladies' loo at the Milton House Hotel. My first Bolsover annual dinner. I knew who she was, of course, I'd noticed her standing next to David

Mainwaring as we came in. He was cradling a large whisky and booming away at a group of sycophants. "Remind me to tell you the one about the man in Barbados who had a tattoo on his . . ." He looked round at his wife. ". . . No, a little early for that, I think." He gave a bark of laughter and everyone surrounding him laughed too, except for Julia Mainwaring, who had obviously heard about the man in Barbados before.

"That's Julia Mainwaring," George whispered, steering me away towards the drinks tray. "She's a lovely lady."

She didn't look very lovely to me. Fortyish, dull hair, a black outfit with a skirt ending at the exact length to make the worst of her ankles; small pieces of antique jewellery in such good taste you hardly noticed them.

I knew George would consider it unsuitable for a junior salesman's wife to surprise the managing director's wife with her face naked, so I started backing out with a polite murmur of apology.

"Please don't mind me," she said, patting on Tawny Beige foundation and leaving a demarcation line under her chin. "I was held up at work this evening, and my husband would rather arrive with a death's-head than miss five minutes' drinking time."

She touched her cheekbones with a powder rouge, ran a blue pencil over her eyelids, deftly applied harsh orange lipstick and instantly aged ten years.

One moment I was staring, rather rudely, at an English countrywoman with a porcelain pale complexion and faded blue eyes, the next at the tart with a heart in one of those vintage Ealing comedies.

I was still watching, fascinated, as she fatally tucked a few appealing wisps of soft brown hair away from her face, pursed her lips appraisingly in the mirror, gave a satisfied nod and turned to speak to me.

"I am sorry, I don't think we've met. I'm Julia Mainwaring." She clasped my hand and smiled warmly. "What a sensational dress!"

"Thank you." It was red velvet and clashed satisfactorily

with my red hair. I'd run it up on my second-hand Singer the previous evening on one end of the table, while George was filling in his order forms at the other end. Cosy. I loved evenings like that. "I'm Pauline Jenks."

"I'm sorry . . . ?"

"Married to George Jenks, one of Mr Mainwaring's salesmen."

"Of course." She obviously didn't know who George was, but why should she? He'd only been with Bolsover's a few months.

I moved towards the loo. Julia Mainwaring was regarding me keenly through the mirror as she washed her hands. "I say, it's awfully rude of me, but where did you get that lovely dress? It's exactly the sort of thing David is always telling me I ought to own and as you can see . . ." She gestured at her black skirt and silk shirt, pulled in at the waist with an unsuitably heavy leather belt . . . "I never seem to have time for serious shopping."

"I made it myself." It was comforting to know that the red velvet didn't look home-made.

"How very clever of you and how disappointing for me." She smiled and moved towards the door. "I suppose I'd better go and do my bit for Bolsover's. I do hope we'll meet again."

"You talked to Julia Mainwaring?" said George. We'd got on to the port and brandy stage by this time, and George was dealing uneasily with an unaccustomed cigar. "Damn thing's gone out again. In the ladies' room?"

"She was doing her face."

"My goodness, Pauline, how tactless. Why didn't you wait outside until she'd finished?"

I saw Julia quite often after that first meeting. We'd just taken out a mortgage on the St Neots' house, and one afternoon – half-day at Clockwork – I went into Cambridge to buy curtain fabric. I was wandering around the Kite, a run-down area of appealing ramshackle shops and cottages which had been threatened with demolition until the conservationists wisely slapped a preservation order on them, when I was stopped in my tracks by a beautiful flower shop. The door and window frames had been stripped down to the bare wood and green paint rubbed into the grain. It was a perfect backdrop for giant tubs overflowing with spring flowers and budding foliage, more like one of those boîtes in Paris than a back-street shop in Cambridge. Flowers were a luxury we couldn't afford, but maybe if I economised on the curtains . . . that gingham in the market was incredibly cheap . . .

The assistant was wrapping yellow spring flowers in yellow tissue paper – not that nasty patterned paper so favoured by florists, I noted with pleasure – when she looked up and smiled. "It's Mrs Jenks, isn't it?"

I spent a harassing few moments trying to remember where I'd seen her before. You don't expect to come across your husband's managing director's wife serving in a flower shop.

"The red dress," she said. Typical of Julia to hand me a tactful clue.

She made coffee and we sat in the back room, where two small girls were busily cutting up the yellow tissue and folding it into darts and boats. They must have been about five, but when you don't have children of your own it's impossible to tell.

"Melanie and Melissa," said Julia, "this is Pauline Jenks."

One child stood up and shook my hand, the other went on snipping and folding.

"Must you mutilate the wrapping paper, darlings?" Julia said mildly. "You've got your picture books."

"I'm bored," said the one who was snipping and folding.

Her sister picked up a book, carefully turned it upside down and sat down, cross-legged, on the floor. "I'm going to read."

You could see they were identical twins, except for the gleam in an eye, the pout of a mouth. "Melissa's just like her father," Julia nodded towards the snipper and folder, "fretful if she isn't kept amused all the time."

I went away with half a dozen bunches of spring flowers

for the price of four and they lit up our dark narrow hall more effectively than any decorating scheme.

"You've not been wasting money on *flowers*?" said George, when he arrived home that evening. "We haven't even got a decent table to put them on." His attitude softened when he heard I'd bought them from Julia Mainwaring. "They do look rather nice on that old chest," he said. "Cheer the place up a bit, don't they?"

I took to dropping in at the Flower Box whenever I went into Cambridge, and Julia always seemed pleased to see me. I suppose we were both lonely, in different ways. I spent most of my time with Honor Fletcher, her carefully made-up eyes calculating the maximum mark-up she could put on my designs, and Julia was too busy to keep up with her friends.

As I got to know the Mainwarings better, I realised that there was very little friendship in her marriage, either. David was the kind of man who was uneasy with women unless they were in bed with him or cooking his dinner. He may have talked to Julia sometimes, but I don't think he ever listened to her.

One afternoon, as we were drinking a companionable Nescafé in the back room of the shop, she told me that David had bought the Flower Box for her as a surprise. "After ten years of marriage, he still doesn't know that I loathe surprises. He said it would give me something to do, now that the twins are at school and off my hands."

We both looked down at the floor, where Melanie and Melissa were wrestling with a small brown terrier.

"Don't do that, silly, you're pulling his tail," screamed one of them.

"I'm not, I'm not, I'm cuddling him," yelled the other.

"Stop it, both of you," said Julia. "We'll be going home soon."

The twins went to the sink at the back of the shop, wrangling noisily and splashing a great deal of water about.

"David rather overlooked the fact that the school day is very short. And then there are holidays and half-terms and measles." Suddenly Julia looked tired. "Darlings, get a cloth and wipe up that water or you'll walk it all over the shop."

"Then, why didn't you . . . ?"

"Say, 'Thank you very much, but I could spend three months in the garden and still not begin to conquer the shrubbery, the study needs painting, the twins demand constant attention and your two will be coming to stay in the holidays?' Oh, I thought about it . . ." She rose as the shop door bell pinged. "It's so much easier to agree with David than argue with him, and I do think florists do an awfully bad job, don't you? Arrogance, I suppose, but I thought I could probably do it better. Excuse me a minute."

She disappeared into the front of the shop and returned with two more children. A fair-haired boy, wearing his school cap and blazer with such easy elegance that it looked like a Paul Smith editorial in *Vogue*, and a scowling small girl. Simon and Alexandra, David's children by his first marriage.

"Have you had a lovely time, darlings?" said Julia, in the bright hostess tone of a stepmother.

"There's nothing to do here," said the girl, sulking at Julia as though she were personally responsible for the dullness of Cambridge.

"Oh, come on, Alex," said the boy. "It was great on the Backs; we had lunch with Father – strawberries and cream – and he asked Parsons to drive us home. I thought you might like us to collect the horrible Mels."

"Horrible yourself," said Melissa.

"How very thoughtful." Julia reached for the children's coats. "Come along, you two, we mustn't keep Parsons waiting."

When I told Julia about my designs for Clockwork, she gazed admiringly at my beige linen culottes. "If they're anything like those trouser things you're wearing, or that wonderful red dress, I shall want the lot. Keep one or two things for me, won't you, until I can get into St Neots."

"Isn't she the wife of the Bolsover managing director?" said Honor Fletcher, as I was sticking Reserved tickets on the things Julia might like. "Lots of money there. Borrow my car, take a selection over to her."

How kind, I thought. And how naive I was. The PJ Range (Pauline Jenks was not, I decided, the most compelling name for a fashion label) was her biggest seller, and it gave her the best profit margin. Julia was soon contributing regularly to that profit.

At St Martin's I'd enjoyed making sock-it-to-them special occasion frocks in glitzy fabrics, but St Neots didn't go in for glitz, and I discovered that the simplest shapes can look elegant enough to go out to a grand dinner if you make them up in really good quality natural fabrics. Julia spent her day changing roles and didn't have the time or the energy to keep changing her outfits to match. It was fun designing clothes that wouldn't cause ribald comment in the market at dawn as she haggled over the price of chrysanths, were respectably okay for client meetings about wedding flowers in the afternoon, and still managed to look glamorous as she entertained potential Bolsover customers in the style David expected in the evening. I didn't realise it then, but I was evolving the fashion philosophy behind Natural Sources.

It all seemed to happen at once. George's promotion. Clerihue. Our business.

"Ask me if anything interesting happened at the office today, Pauly." George had come into the kitchen as I was grilling steaks for our dinner. I had so many orders by this time that we were living on instant grills.

"Did anything interesting happen at the office, darling? Get the knives and forks out, will you?"

"They put me on the board."

I rushed round the table and kissed him. "Oh darling, how wonderful." I might have added, "Why?" but of course I didn't. George was a conscientious salesman but he was still so young, only thirty, and he didn't look like the director of a public company to me. Maybe no man looks like the director of a public company to his wife. I quickly quelled this disloyal thought and kissed him again. The steaks blackened under the grill.

We treated ourselves to a delicious dinner at the Golden Pheasant and then we came home and went to bed. George was high on confidence and excitement. Always, when we made love, he seemed to be holding himself back, as though his father was lurking about behind the bedpost warning, "Watch out, George, or you'll make a right fool of yourself."

That night, though, instinct and a bottle of Chablis took over from intellect, and if there were any voices urging prudent restraint, George was too carried away to hear them.

I lay beside him afterwards, glowing pleasurably and stroking my flat stomach with slow satisfaction.

"I'm going to have a baby."

"When? How do you know? My God, was it all right to . . . well, you know?" George had raised himself on one elbow and was looking at me anxiously.

"Of course it was all right." I smiled up at him and thought what a handsome profile he had. No wonder they wanted him on the board. He'd look perfect in one of those directors' portraits lining the main staircase. ".In roughly nine months from tonight, my love."

"Oh Pauline, *really*. How can you possibly tell?" George lay back on his pillow, quite cross.

I couldn't tell him how I knew. I just did. "Don't you want a baby?"

"Of course I do. But you'll have to go and see the doctor, have tests and so on, won't you?"

"There's plenty of time for that." I started thinking of names, which was much more fun than thinking about medical examinations. "Sarah . . . Emily . . . Tobias if it's a boy. "How about Tobias?" I said to George, but he was asleep.

It wasn't Tobias, of course, it was Clerihue.

"Such a pretty name," George said, coming into the hospital, laden with flowers.

"What a popular girl you are," said Sister, narrowing her eyes at the sight of the bouquets and bunches. "We'll have to see if we can find some more vases."

I gazed at the pink and white baby in my arms, caressed the soft downy fluff on her perfect little head.

"She doesn't look like a Clerihue."

"She's a poem," said George.

I hoped the woman in the next bed, who had called her daughter Cilla ("She's ever so good in *Surprise! Surprise!* Pauline . . .") hadn't heard him. George was fond of quoting bits of poetry and invariably missed a stanza or the rhythm, like those people who insist on singing the wrong words to popular songs. "She's as pretty as a poem . . . a clerihue."

I looked it up some months later and discovered that he'd even got the spelling wrong. A clerihew was a witty, comical verse named after a man who wrote them. It didn't matter. By that time, my baby looked like a Clerihue, and she was certainly comical. With any luck she might grow up to be witty, too.

Julia phoned me the morning after yet another Bolsover dinner.

We were at the top table that year, of course, now that George was on the board, and I was rather alarmed to find myself placed next to Peter Bolsover.

"Nice enough chap, but ineffectual," George had said. "Wouldn't be the chairman if his grandfather hadn't worked his fingers to the bone sixty years ago."

I rather liked him. Tall, slim, a bit of a stoop, grey eyes; not unlike George, but with that touch of natural authority you don't inherit if your father works on the Underground and your grandfather was a hodman. "My grandfather built houses," I've heard George say, as though old Mr Jenks threw up estates like a Wates, rather than carrying the bricks for a local builder.

"How did you manage it, Peter, sitting next to the prettiest girl in the room?" David Mainwaring shouted across the table. He had a large whisky alongside his range of wine glasses and kept clicking his fingers at the waiter as he emptied it. "Keep them coming, waiter, keep them coming."

"Just my good fortune." Peter smiled pleasantly at his managing director but there was a distinctly chilly look at the back of his eyes. He turned to me and said, "I am sorry about that. It's just that you and George are rather a novelty, you see. The rest of us have been sitting around this table together for far too long." I had the feeling that if David Mainwaring didn't hold back on the whisky he wouldn't be sitting there much longer. "Not," Peter added courteously, "that David isn't absolutely right."

Peter's wife, Lady Sybilla Bolsover, shot me a sharp look. She was sitting next to George and talking over his head to someone called Emily Sutcliffe.

"What's come over Julia? She's looking very elegant tonight."

"Wearing one of Pauline Jenks's dresses, I understand," said Emily. "Isn't that right, Mr Jenks?"

"Mmm," said George, who unfortunately had his mouth full of stuffing and cranberry sauce at the time.

"Your wife's a dressmaker, is she?" said Lady Sybilla.

"She is a designer, yes."

"Delightful woman," George said later, manoeuvring the new Rover unsteadily out of the car park.

"Emily Sutcliffe? Who is she, anyway?"

"Finance director's wife, typical American blonde. No, I meant Lady Sybilla."

"I didn't like her much," I said.

So I wasn't totally thrilled to discover why Julia was phoning me. Sybilla had invited us both to lunch.

"Couldn't call you herself, urgent appointment. Manicure, I expect," said Julia.

"Well, I am rather busy." True, but even if I was lolling around on the sofa all day, reading Jackie Collins and eating chocolates, I still wouldn't rush excitedly up to London to be patronised by Lady Sybilla.

"Oh, what a pity," said Julia. "I so wanted you to come. I've been telling Sybilla how clever you are, and she was knocked out by that silk thing I was wearing last night."

"Well, it's very kind . . ." I couldn't imagine Lady Sybilla Bolsover, elegantly swathed in Bruce Oldfield yellow taffeta, popping into Clockwork for a Pauline Jenks original. But maybe a shirt or a skirt . . . ? She spent most of her time in London, but the Bolsover estate was, after all, just outside St Neots.

"Make it Thursday, then," said Julia. "I'm meeting a wholesaler at Nine Elms in the morning, so I'll see you at . . . um . . . 53 Eaton Square. Twelve-thirty."

I hardly ever went into Clockwork by then, so it was no problem getting away. There were so many orders that I'd had to take on a couple of outworkers to help with the machining, and I was a better investment for Honor sitting full time at my sewing machine than helping in the shop. It had occurred to me, more than once, as I watched the customers writing large numbers in their chequebooks, that the time had come to ask Honor for a realistic share of the profits.

George warned me not to rock the boat. "You've got a good job you enjoy doing and Honor has been very kind."

"Kind?" I looked coldly at George. I had to deliver a ball gown, special order for a customer who wanted to wear it that evening, and I decided to speak to Honor then.

"An equal share of the profits, Pauline?" She hung the ball gown on the Sold rail, turned and gazed at me as though I was trying to sell her dodgy double glazing. "A *partnership*?"

I murmured something about most of Clockwork's revenue coming from the PJ Range. "It's not unreasonable, Honor, that I should get a realistic return for all my work."

"*Your* work? My dear girl. You came to me, a raw student. I've moulded you, encouraged you, taught you everything I know, and you talk to me about *your* work.

Where would you have been without Clockwork, Pauline? Where's your gratitude? Now, run along and don't let me hear any more of this."

A butler answered the door at Eaton Square. I'd seen butlers on the stage and in films, of course, but never facing me across a doorstep.

"Her Ladyship is upstairs in the drawing room, Mrs Jenks," he said, inclining his head, auditioning for Jeeves. "She is expecting you."

He led the way upstairs, past marble pillars and a blazing log fire in the hall, (a real fire, not one of those pretend gas things), up a sweeping flight of stairs wide enough to contain the complete cast of a Ziegfield finale, and threw open a pair of double doors.

"Mrs Jenks, my lady."

It was a long walk across the beige carpet and I wished I'd gone in for a bit of power dressing. The black gabardine suit from the current PJ Range would have made a more important entrance than my understated wool dress. Sybilla was sitting on a white sofa. Julia Mainwaring, wearing the gabardine suit – just as well I hadn't dressed up as her twin – was in an easy chair beside another roaring fire, which reflected pleasingly onto a great deal of expensive brassware in the grate. They were drinking champagne.

Sybilla uncoiled from the sofa. "Pauline, you'll need a reviving drink after that long journey." The butler moved towards the drinks tray. "Don't worry, Pedro, I'll deal with it. Champagne?"

She handed me a stylish flute made of such heavy cut glass that I nearly dropped it.

"Come and sit down." Sybilla settled on the sofa and patted the seat beside her. "Shall we have lunch first, Julia, or tell her our plan?"

"Your plan, Sybilla," said Julia firmly. "*Your* plan."

Sybilla's plan was very simple. Or so she said. She had just returned from a trip to India with Peter and, wandering off by herself "to see the *real* India," she'd chanced on a village where whole families worked a fourteen-hour day weaving and dyeing fabrics for Basrawy Specialty Imports of Spitalfields, E.1.

"The most divine fabrics, Pauline." Sybilla waved her champagne towards a sofa at the other side of the room which was draped in rich and colourful silks, spliced with sun-faded cottons and linens.

I could hardly wait to get my hands on them. "They're beautiful."

"Exactly." Sybilla nodded briskly. "They're all natural fabrics, darling, which is why they take colour so perfectly, and Basrawy is practically giving them away. Now," she leant forward eagerly, "if I buy the cloth through Ahmet Basrawy – he's crazy about the idea, I've already spoken to him – you can make them into delicious garments, Pauline, and we can sell them, becoming astonishingly rich in the process."

"We?" said Julia warily. "Who do you mean by we?"

"You, darling. You, of course," said Sybilla. "You've got that nice little shop, prime position, up and coming area, and you know how you loathe rising at dawn to pluck all those flowers, or whatever you do."

"But I don't know anything about fashion," said Julia, "and Pauline's got a new baby . . ."

"You know about *selling*, Julia, that's what matters. And Mrs Thatcher had two babies and still managed to find time to be prime minister. What do you say, Pauline?"

This was considerably more exciting than selling Sybilla a £49.99 skirt. And what a gratifying sock in the eye for Honor Fletcher. "Well, we could try . . ." Better not sound too enthusiastic or I'd find myself working on a mini commission again. "It sounds interesting."

"There you are, Julia, I knew she'd be mad about the idea." Sybilla eagerly topped up my glass. "We all so admire those marvellous things you've been making for Julia, Pauline. Such talent."

"Thank you." I took a sip, which gave me time to think. I had no intention of retiring into motherhood, and this was something I could do from home. But stocking a whole shop? It was tough enough supplying the range for Clockwork. "Even if you kept it to a small coordinated collection, you'd have to cover it in every size . . . it's an awful lot of work."

"Naturally you wouldn't be able to run everything up on your little machine. You make the prototypes, the special orders, and Basrawy's outworkers will do the rest."

Little machine, indeed. I remembered why I didn't like Lady Sybilla.

"You'd need rigorous quality control," said Julia.

"Of course we will, Julia," said Sybilla, a touch impatiently. "I've thought of all that . . ." She enthused on about opening a chain of shops, branching out into mail order, setting up franchises. She just took it for granted that we'd fall in with her plan, and it was look out Benetton before we'd even nodded agreement. "You've done brilliantly with that flower shop, Julia, Pauline clearly has a flair for design and I've got a very good eye for cut and cloth. We'd make a marvellous team."

"Hang on a minute, Sybilla," said Julia. "How about the financial side of all this? Will your good eye be glancing at the balance sheet when it isn't appraising cut and cloth?"

"You're very sharp today, Julia," said Sybilla, which is what I was thinking.

"I'm beginning to feel rather abrasive," said Julia. "As I see it, Pauline and I will be doing all the work and you, presumably, will be taking a third of the profits?"

"Certainly I will. My idea and my initial capital. Unless you, Pauline . . . ?"

"I'm afraid I don't have any money."

"And you, Julia? You must be making a mint out of that flower shop."

"Still repaying David," Julia said. "He put up the money for it."

"Then you need me." Sybilla rose as the butler came in to announce that luncheon was served. "Besides, I've got a ready-made nucleus of customers, all my chums who'll adore Pauline's clothes. And I shall do the PR, sell Natural Sources to the great British public. Natural Sources. How does that sound to you, Pauline, strikes a fashionably ethnic image, don't you think?"

I said it sounded a clever name to me and just right for the Kite, which was knee-deep in peasant pots, wholefood restaurants and dirndl skirts.

"Excellent. Let's go and open one of Peter's better Vouvrays to celebrate."

She'd got as far as the door, when Julia, still firmly seated, said, "I want to make it quite clear that should I agree to move from floristry into fashion I have no intention of doing the accounts."

"But you're so good at . . ."

"No, Sybilla."

"Well, perhaps David . . . ?"

"Far too busy with Bolsover's even to glance at the VAT on the flower shop."

"True. The poor darlings are going through it. Peter says they've never really got back on course since that union trouble."

Since, more likely, David Mainwaring flaunted his £25,000 corporate vehicle at the shop steward, I thought, and only half an hour after making a rallying speech to the work force about lean times necessitating the pulling in of belts.

"What we need," said Julia, over the asparagus quiche, "is a fourth partner, someone with a really shrewd financial brain."

"Better not be Trevor Sutcliffe, then," said Sybilla. "I hear he's practically lost them the Aitcheson Burbank account."

"I was thinking of Emily Sutcliffe, Trevor's wife."

"Emily Sutcliffe?" I said. "She's very pretty, but . . . ?"

"You don't have to have a flat chest and thinning hair to read a balance sheet. It doesn't seem to have done Trevor much good, does it?"

"Sorry . . ." I'd only seen the social Julia before, had no idea she could be so refreshingly crisp.

"Emily did business studies at Harvard. She met Trevor there when he was at MIT. At a rumpus party, or whatever they call it at American universities."

"George says that half the time he doesn't understand what Trevor is talking about." The moment I'd said it I wished I hadn't. Sounded disloyal to George, somehow, but Julia seemed to understand what I meant.

"That's because he's a pure mathematician, more interested in playing with figures than coping with price-earning ratios," she said. "Emily's the practical one. She used to do the accounts for that jewellery shop in South Molton Street, before Trevor joined Bolsover's."

"But do we really want to dilute the profits?" said Sybilla.

"Emily helped me with the Flower Box accounts last week," said Julia, "and spotted, in the first five minutes, that David had overpaid the taxman £250 in the last quarter. I think you'll find she'll save us far more money than she'll cost us."

Julia was right. Emily got Natural Sources off the ground by being one of the first people into the Business Expansion Scheme, and topped up Sybilla's outlay with a useful chunk of equity capital.

BRANCHING OUT

JULIA MAINWARING, 46, wife of local businessman David Mainwaring, Managing Director of Bolsover Engineering (St. Neots) Ltd., plans to open a branch of her successful Cambridge Boutique, Natural Sources, in London later this year. Mrs. Mainwaring's three partners all live locally and are also married to directors of Bolsover.

St Neots Express,
16th May, 1985

"I t's in about our expansion, is it?" Pauline leant over me, almost totally blocking out the light.

"Just as well it doesn't mention *your* expansion," I said, making one of those intimate little jokes that Pauly enjoyed so much.

"I can't wait to get this baby born," said Pauly. "It's getting in the way – literally – of the autumn collection. I can't get within yards of the drawing board."

To be honest, I was a little shocked. As a modern husband, I was naturally quite happy to allow my wife to do her own thing. She's very good at designing clothes, and as long as her hobby didn't come between her and the family, I saw no reason to put my foot down, like my mother said I should.

After all, little Clerihue was very well looked after, now that Mother had moved in with us.

* * *

27

When Pauline and I were driving home up the A1 after Dad's funeral, Pauline said, "Your mother wasn't in a very good mood, was she?"

"One doesn't expect widows to be in a good mood at their husband's funeral," I said rather stiffly. "She was racked with grief." A good way of putting it, I thought.

Pauline gave a rather nasty little laugh. "Racked with irritation at the way your cousins were gobbling up the fish-paste sandwiches. I didn't know they still made fish-paste, did you? And she kept on giving me those funny looks."

"I did tell you grey was inappropriate for immediate mourners."

"I wasn't mourning all that immediately. And if you're honest, George, neither were you. You and your father never really – "

"I regarded him with respect and admiration."

"When Dad was alive I called him Grumpy and I loved him. If you ask me, your mother's quite looking forward to reigning supreme in that house. Did you notice the street's getting all gentrified? I wonder what those houses are worth, now?"

"With a bit of luck we'll get £70,000," I said, thinking how useful it is, being an only child.

"She's not going to sell, is she? Where will she live? In some ghastly old folks' home?"

I glanced at her in real surprise.

"Why of course, Pauline, Mother will live with us. She looked after me when I was small. Now it is my turn to look after her."

"Well, it certainly isn't *my* turn to look after her. Watch out for that lorry. You know she loathes me."

"You've never really tried to get on with Mother, Pauly. And think how useful she'll be with Clerihue, now that you've got regular work."

"She's not getting her hands on my daughter. This is my final word, George, there is absolutely no question – "

I thought quickly. "Pauline . . . Mother doesn't want it mentioned. But she's had to see the doctor . . ."

"Why?"

". . . only a matter of months, apparently."

"Oh, George, I'm so sorry. I suppose we'll have to have her, then. What's the matter, exactly?"

"Something internal," I said evasively. Bit of a white lie, really, but all in a good cause. What the doctor had said was, "Now look here, young man. I've known you since you were in your cradle, so I can speak frankly. Get your mother to lose some weight, or I won't be responsible for the consequences."

So Mother was sitting at the other side of the kitchen table, dipping toast into a boiled egg and feeding Clerihue soldiers with red coats on. And I had £68,000 in the bank, which I saw no reason to mention to Pauline. Mother quite understood that the money should be in my name, to avoid death duties. "Anyway," she said, "money is man's work. Your father always looked after the financial side of things."

"What does it say about me?" said Pauline, taking the paper away without asking. I dared not catch Mother's eye. In her world, the head of the house read the paper first. When he had finished with it, he gave it to his wife to read the women's pages for interesting new recipes.

"Hey," said Pauline, "do look, George. It says I am one of the brightest young luminaries in today's fashion scene. I must phone Julia."

She dashed out, taking the paper with her. Mother popped another soldier into Clerihue's mouth.

"She'll have to give up all that nonsense when the new baby comes, George. We're right out of sponge fingers, how I'm expected to make a trifle for tonight I don't know. And you know I can't get to sleep without my hot chocolate."

"I'll drop in to the Co-op on my way to work. Quarter past eight already, I must –"

"It is not a man's place to buy sponge fingers, George.

29

Your father wouldn't have let himself down, buying sponge fingers. Anyway, the Co-op doesn't have my brand of cocoa. Waitrose in Huntingdon has it. You must tell Pauline to do a proper shopping list. What else did you buy her that car for, if it wasn't to help her run her home? She'll have to go into Huntingdon this afternoon, and perhaps Clerry and I will go with her."

I could hardly tell my mother that I bought Pauline the Renault because she had started asking searching questions about what, exactly, the doctor had said about my mother's condition.

"She's been here for six months and she's never once seen the doctor. All she's done is put on weight, on my housekeeping money, too. I thought she was meant to be delicate? You'll have to give me more, George. And every time I put on the telly she says, 'Disgraceful. I'm glad George's father isn't alive to hear those words.'"

"I know it's difficult for you, Pauly. Old people can be . . ."

"Fifty-eight? That's not old, nowadays."

". . . but she does take Clerry off your hands. And look at all the cooking she does. Leaves you free time for your –"

"All those flatulent puddings? You're getting a tummy, George. And she's absolutely stuffing Clerihue. Why doesn't she pay us anything? With the interest on the house money she must be rolling. I honestly think you've got to put your foot down."

"Tell you what, Pauly, I've been thinking. Time you had a little runabout of your own."

"Could we really afford it? Oh, it would be marvellous."

"Nothing's too good for my Pauly. I've managed to save a bit, one way and another. The garage has got a nice little second-hand Renault, only two five, and you'll find they're very cheap to run." So Pauline got her runabout, and she stopped asking questions.

I hastily kissed Clerihue goodbye. "Be a good girl for Daddy," I said.

She looked at me stonily and said, "A negg," and opened her mouth for another piece of toast.

Pauline was on the phone in the hall, gabbling away. " . . . you must be so excited, Julia. I say, did you see what it said about me? I can't believe it. This afternoon? Yes, of course. Three o'clock at the shop, right. Listen, I've roughed out a few ideas on decor for the new branch, shall I bring them? Hang on a moment. You going, darling? See you tonight."

"I'm afraid there's a difficulty about this afternoon, Pauly. Mother would like to go to Huntingdon, so perhaps –"

"You'd better take her then, George. I can't."

"Can't you have coffee with the girls some other time? You know how Mother lives for her shopping."

"I am not having coffee with the girls. We are having a board meeting. You know board meetings? You have them, don't you?"

Of course, Mother had to come into the hall.

"That child needs to spend more time with her mother," she said. "She's not speaking much, for a two-year-old. I told her that after we go to Waitrose this afternoon, Mummy and Gan-Gan will take her to look at the quack quacks."

"Can't this afternoon, I'm afraid, got a board meeting. I could drop you at the Co-op, on my way to Cambridge."

"The Co-op doesn't have my brand of cocoa, Pauline."

But Pauline was back on the phone to Julia.

"Sorry, Julia, what? Has Sybilla had any luck with the nationals? I mean, long live the *St Neots Express*, but . . . hey, that sounds interesting. Must go, tell me all this afternoon."

"Then it'll have to be you, George," said Mother. "Or perhaps Pauline would be good enough to take me this morning."

"Can't this morning, I'm afraid," said Pauline, (I did think she could be a little more obliging) "Clerihue and I are going to look at some kittens, aren't we, darling?"

"Baby kittens," said Clerihue, jumping up into Pauline's arms.

"And perhaps we might bring one home with us, mightn't we?"

"A kitty for Clerry and a baby for Mummy."

"That's right, my darling angel, won't we both be busy?"

"Kittens!" said Mother, "nasty little dirty things. You're never bringing one into the house with a new baby on the way."

Clerihue buried her head in Pauline's neck. "Hate Gan-Gan," she said conversationally. In my view, she was speaking far too much for a two-year-old.

"I've got a board meeting too," I said, "though not, I am sure, half as important as your board meeting, Pauline, or your cocoa, Mother, or your kitten, Clerihue. Who has moved the keys to my car?"

A bit sharp, I suppose, I didn't usually speak to Mother like that, but I was put out by women's frivolities. I was the one round here who was earning the living, after all. I would have been in quite a mood if I hadn't caught sight of myself in the hall mirror. You get what you pay for, as far as clothes are concerned.

Our board meeting was at three o'clock, in Peter's office. Before then I had to drive to Wellingborough and have a serious talk with Geoff Farnsworth, of Farnsworth Foods at Your Convenience, Ltd. We'd been supplying them with vacuum cut-out auxiliary packaging units since well before my time. And looking at my forward-planning spread-sheet, I saw that they were well due for updating. I rang Geoff to ask him if he fancied a round of golf on Saturday. Did a lot of my selling like that; get to know someone socially and you're halfway there. He had a better handicap than me, so by the time we got to the eighteenth hole, he was usually ripe, as they say, for development.

"Saturday," he said, "there you've got me, George. Can't make Saturday. Some other time maybe. Tell you what, I'll give you a bell towards the end of next week.

No, I tell a lie, I'm in Tokyo next week. Leave it with me, George, I'll be back to you."

"Pauline was saying just this morning that she hasn't seen Susie for ages. Why don't you two come over for a bite to eat?"

"Great idea. Splendid. Better leave the girls to make the arrangements, then? Look forward to it."

"Geoff, while I'm on the line, I think I can tell you in confidence that our people have come up with a modification in thermally activated moisture control that's going to take your breath away. Don't want it to get around, of course, it's still under wraps. But you're a valued client and we'd like you to have first chance."

"Tell you what, George," (Geoff must be doing too much, I thought, he sounded quite tired) "why don't you drop by at, say, eleven tomorrow? Can spare you fifteen minutes, if that's all right with you."

"Eleven o'clock tomorrow, on the dot. Have the old chequebook ready, Geoff; you'll be walking on air this time tomorrow."

When I put the phone down I said to Marcia, my secretary, "You've got to play it subtle with guys like Geoff Farnsworth."

"You know why he's going to Tokyo next week, don't you?" she said, putting away her nail file. "Going to buy packaging machinery. Half what ours costs, and all done electronically."

"Geoff's an old friend of mine. He would have told me."

"Suit yourself, Mr J." She rootled around among a collection of bottles of nail varnish in her drawer, and chose an orange one. "Me and his secretary do aerobics together."

Geoff Farnsworth didn't have fifteen minutes to spare, he had nine. I only hoped all those drinks I poured down him at the nineteenth hole had done something incurable to his liver.

"You've got to look at it from our point of view, old boy," he said. "Those Nips have got packaging units

33

sewn up. You should see their quality control moderating enhancers. Well, I think that's what they're called. Bloody marvellous. We'll be able to cut our work force down by seven per cent."

"I'm afraid I have rather strong views on our Japanese friends," I said. "My father was a prisoner of war in . . . in . . . somewhere in Burma. He never talked about it, of course. Sometimes he used to cry out in the night."

"Water under the bridge, old chap. We're all friends now, commercially. If you've got any spare cash, invest in yen, take it from me. Yes, Barbara? Right, put him through. See you at the Rotary Dance, George?"

To cap it all, when I got back from Wellingborough I found someone had deliberately parked in the slot marked Mr G. Jenks, Sales Director. The perfect end to a perfect day, I thought bitterly, and it isn't over yet.

Having half an hour before the board meeting, I went for a quick snack at the Horse and Hare. As I walked in I saw Peter Bolsover and David Mainwaring in the Saloon Bar. Peter Bolsover, chairman of the board. If I was casting him for television I'd want that chap who played Lord Peter Wimsey. Decent. Ineffectual. Only there because his old Etonian grandfather started Bolsover's back in the twenties. Once or twice recently, though, I'd wondered whether there might be more to him than met the eye. He'd never once patronised George Jenks, Burlington Danes Comp. and Paddington College, and the others did, all the time.

David, of course, would have patronised the Queen Mother, if he was lucky enough to find himself in the same room as Her Majesty. Hail-fellow–well-met, our managing director, but my shrewd Pauline called him the Smiler with the Knife. Nice little phrase, I wonder where she got it from?

I certainly didn't want to get into conversation with those two, they were bound to ask how the Farnsworth fishing expedition went. I nipped into the Public Bar and was ordering half a pint of mild and a cheese and pickle sandwich, when I heard David's blustering voice through the partition.

". . . dreadful little blighter. Why on earth is he a director, that's what I ask myself?" Aha. He didn't like Trevor Sutcliffe, either.

"We've always had the sales director on the board, David, you know that. I've got rather a soft spot for George, myself."

I felt myself going red and started to hum under my breath, which is what I always do when I'm embarrassed.

"He wears suits that are shiny on purpose. Cost a bomb and look like something you see on chat shows."

"He's got his problems, you know. We're all the result of our upbringing."

"That frightful mother, you mean? God knows how Pauline puts up with her. What do you make of Pauline Jenks? Sly little thing, isn't she?"

"A very private person, certainly. Sybilla says she reminds her of a mouse who has signed the Official Secrets Act. Did you see what they said about her in the *Express* today?"

"That's exactly why I wanted a quiet word, Peter. If you ask me, the girls are getting above themselves. A branch in London, for God's sake. Where the hell are they getting the money from? I'm certainly not –"

"As far as I can make out, their bottom-line figures are rather better than ours."

"Of course they bloody are. We're financing them. Who paid for the shop in Cambridge? Muggins did."

"Fair enough. Julia got bored with getting up at four to buy carnations. Sybilla came back from India loaded to the gunnels with piles of faded cotton lengths –"

"Dreadful dyspeptic colours. I like a woman in something vivid, myself."

"No doubt. And then it turns out that Pauline Jenks is a fashion designer."

"And before we know where we are they are selling

Madras blazers like hot cakes and calling themselves Natural Sources. I don't like it, Peter. What's more, I'm bloody not standing for it. Do you know what Julia said to me last night? 'I'm not hungry,' she said, 'can't you get yourself some ham from the fridge?' "

"I think we ought to be rather proud –"

"And when I said I expected rather more than ham after a hard day's work, she said, 'You'll have to wait till I've finished these stock controls, then. I warn you, I'll be ages.' Surely you don't approve of Sybilla spending half her time in London getting press coverage?"

"Sybilla – as you know, David – has always done exactly what she wanted."

There was a bit of a funny pause, and then David said, "Have the other half, shall we?"

"Not for me, thank you. Like to keep alert for the board meeting. Better be getting back, hadn't we?"

They always say eavesdroppers hear no good of themselves. Frightful mother, dreadful little blighter . . . David Mainwaring would pay for that one day.

I was last in to the board meeting.

I suppose I shouldn't have stopped to speak to Ron about my parking spot, but I always think these things should be stamped on early.

"Sorry, Mr Jenks," Ron said breezily, "thought you was out for the day. Only the district nurse dropped by – Mary in the canteen has got quite a nasty thumb –"

"People with nasty thumbs shouldn't be in the canteen. Is that slot marked Mr G. Jenks, or do my eyes mislead me and is it marked Casual Visitors?"

I rather pride myself on my line of sarcasm; gets a point across so much more efficaciously than shouting.

Ron smirked at one of his cronies (and what was he doing, standing around in the car park doing nothing?), walked over to the slot and put his eyes very close to it.

"There, now," he said insolently, "would you believe

it? It says Mr A. Hitler." He and his crony laughed rudely and I left the car park in a dignified manner.

"Sorry if I'm a little behind time," I said, sliding into my accustomed place at the directors' table, "I feel I must mention that the car parking arrangements are giving cause for anxiety. The attendant is unfortunately quite impervious to –"

"Poor old Ron," said Peter, "wounded in the Korean war, you know. In terrible pain most of the time, but never says a word. And his father was my father's batman in the desert. First time I saw my father cry, when he came back from Corporal Taylor's funeral."

"Perhaps we can stop handing out Distinguished Service Medals and get on with the matter in hand," said David.

"I've always found Ron a delightful character," said Trevor Sutcliffe, "so helpful. And a very sound chess player, incidentally."

Typical Trevor. Went to St Paul's, just another London day school, when you get down to it, and the way he talked to me, head of sales and the one at the sharp end, you'd think I was his daily help. And nothing to write home about as a finance director. Always talking about his "Post-Graduate at MIT" (the first time I heard it, I had to go and look it up. Didn't like to ask, everyone else seemed to know.) If you wanted my opinion, the Massachusetts Institute of Technology had done very little for him beyond providing him with that long-nosed vegetarian from Boston. I'd never pretended I liked Emily Sutcliffe, because I didn't. But she could read a balance sheet in the time it took Trevor to take his glasses out and give them that silly wipe.

tries. I'm still not sure how we managed to fight them off last year. But all the indications are –"

"Point of order, Mr Chairman," I said.

Peter smiled kindly at me. "Yes, George?"

"I thought we had agreed – concomitant with current medical thinking – that a No Smoking rule should adhere at board meetings?"

We all looked at Trevor, who already had two stubs in his ashtray.

"Sorry," he said, stubbing out his third. "Trying to give it up."

"You're right, Peter. Somebody's out with a fishing net," David said. "May just be coincidence, Trevor, but we ought to keep a bit of an eye, don't you think?"

Trevor, as was his wont, rose superbly to the occasion.

"Er," he said.

"Oh come on, Trev," said David, "my instinct tells me hounds are on the scent and running."

"What?" said Trevor, and I couldn't blame him. Peter Bolsover went hunting and fishing too, but he wasn't always using daft metaphors to show what a countryman of the old school he was. Didn't have to, of course.

"I think what David means," said Peter diffidently, "is that somebody is buying up parcels of our shares. Some quite small, nothing out of the ordinary. But taken as a whole . . . enough to be . . . quite worrying."

It was time I said something.

"Good sign, isn't it? Shows someone thinks we're worth putting money into."

"I suspect this buyer is . . . possibly a little more intelligent than that," Peter said, so quietly that it took me a second or two to grasp his drift.

"Do you mean you don't think we're worth putting money into, Peter?"

"My dear chap . . . look at the figures. Trevor, would you be good enough to show George our last running spreadsheet?"

"Hang on a moment, Peter." David took out a Romeo y Julietta cigar, almost certainly his fourth of the day and equally certainly paid for by our shareholders. "You're taking rather a black view, aren't you? I admit the last eighteen months haven't perhaps –"

"In the last eighteen months, David . . ." It suddenly occurred to me that Peter had quite a look of his grandfather, whose portrait was glaring down at us. I don't know where I got that idea. The first Peter Bolsover was a right old terror, by all accounts. ". . . our problems have, to use one of your metaphors, accelerated to a gallop from what was previously a jog. We are going to be taken over, and I rather fear we have asked for it."

Trevor's jaw dropped, the most decisive thing it had done that afternoon. I don't suppose I looked shrewdly knowledgeable, either. We both gaped from Peter to David like Wimbledon.

"Rubbish. That strike didn't do us any good, I admit, but –"

"It didn't do our competitors any good, either, but they seem to have risen above it. David do, for once, look facts in the face –"

"That's ripe, coming from you, Peter. You wouldn't know a fact if it stood up and peed."

"Must I remind you that Miss Nelson is present?"

Miss Nelson, so efficiently taking notes that none of us noticed her, modestly lowered her head and turned over a page of her notebook. She'd been David's secretary for ten years, and with the firm for thirty; she must have heard far worse in her time. Still, decent of Peter to try and keep up standards. I thought I'd put in a bit of gentle back-up.

"Now that the subject has been brought under discussion," I said, wishing I could think of shorter sentences, "I have experienced a certain tendency – which I had hitherto accounted for by the depression in the North–East – of a disinclination in some of our long-term outlets to, er, to –"

Peter grinned. "You mean they weren't in when you called, George?"

I smiled back at him gratefully.

"Something like that, yes. Mind you, sales are holding up very well, considering, but –"

"Considering what?" said Peter. "Isn't there supposed to be a minor boom in light engineering at the moment? Had lunch with Granville Levy the other day, cock-a-hoop about some Saudi contract or other. Martin Fishburn's just bought himself a new Corniche, and –"

"I'm not interested in what a lot of yids are doing." Quite uncalled-for, and absolutely typical of David Mainwaring.

"Then I think you should be. If a firm called Levy and Son can sell to the Arabs, I don't quite see why Bolsover's –"

The flab under David's eyes slid malevolently in my direction. Only myself to blame. I should never have supported Peter, of course.

"I was hoping not to have to bring this up. If we have a problem, and I for one deny categorically that we have, it does, I am afraid, lie with our sales force. If force is the right word," he added sourly. Trevor looked pleased and lit a cigarette.

Get in there quick, I said to myself. Don't hang about.

"If it's saleable, we'll sell it. But . . . take those new superheat freeze valves we spent a fortune developing. When I showed them to Cummins, Delairey and Finn (one of our steadiest customers for fifteen years, I don't suppose I have to remind you, gentlemen) their on-floor technology administrator –"

"Their what?"

"The one who makes the machines work. He practically laughed in my face. 'Not still water-cooling them, are you, George?' he said. 'Sell them to someone who's thinking about inventing the motorcar, he'd probably find them quite revolutionary.' That's the kind of attitude my face is forced with, my force is faced with everywhere. And as for back-up; young Edwards came to me practically in tears yesterday. Apparently Accounts . . ." Teach Trevor MIT Sutcliffe to look pleased when I'm right in it, ". . . had forgotten to allow for the roll-over discount when they billed Aitcheson Burbank for those fan belt idlers, six per cent of which, you will recall, were returned as faulty."

"Nobody told me," said Trevor sulkily, "that Aitcheson Burbank was a schedule D-7 on-going. If they had, I would have –"

"Yes, I did. My memo to you of October 10, '84, *which* I happen to have a copy of presently with me, clearly sets out –"

"I'll have a word with Douggie Burbank on Saturday," said David. "He's bound to be at the Cropthorne meet. Trying out my new grey, Peter. Like to hear what you think of him. Cost me the best part of four thou', mind you, he'd better –"

And what did your new horse go down on expenses as, I wondered. Transport? Agricultural research? Social contact with Douggie Burbank? What a set-up.

"I honestly don't think," said Peter gently, "that a few words with Douggie Burbank over a hunting flask are going to solve our problem. Shall I tell you what I think our problem is? I don't think any of us are very good at our jobs."

We all tried to look affronted, and I for one failed. He was right, of course. Managing Director Mainwaring milking the business for every penny he could get. Finance Director Sutcliffe roaming vaguely about among logarithms, Sales Director Jenks having to give himself a sweet sherry in the car before he tried the positive selling bit. And Peter Bolsover, the brightest of the lot of us, so diffident about his family connections that he wouldn't say cheep to a chicken. Until that day. I wondered what had stiffened his backbone? Wasn't there a bit of a clue in that conversation I overheard at the Horse and Hare?

"Some of us certainly aren't," said David, "and anyway . . . we don't want to be too hasty, do we?"

"I think we want to move very quickly indeed. They are blatantly only after our Crown Jewels."

"The most attractive assets of our company, you mean?" I said knowledgeably.

"Which would be unlikely, as I have just pointed out, to include any of us."

"Now, hang on a minute, Peter." David lit his cigar. Trevor lit a cigarette. I got up and opened a window. "I think you are being a shade on the pessimistic side, there.

Was talking to Jeremy Pitkin at Newmarket the other day
– that colt I put him on to is turning out to be quite useful,
by the way – and I got the impression that he was verging
on the sympathetic side . . . icy draught in this room,
someone shut that bloody window."

"You mean he'll offer you a seat on the board if you sell
him your shares, David? Leave the window alone, George.
What's the going rate, thirty pieces of silver?"

"I rather object to your tone, Peter."

"I can't say I'm enchanted by your methods, David. That
useful little parcel of three thousand voting preference that
came into their hands last year."

"What about them?"

"Oh come on, don't give me that fish-eyed look. We all
know they were Julia's."

By the time I got home I had one of my migraines. Mother
buttonholed me about her cocoa, and Clerihue screamed
with excitement and dropped a kitten in my lap. It relieved
itself instantly.

"Do you know what mohair costs?" I shouted, pushing
the filthy thing off. It made a noise and Clerihue cried.

"Now then, George, that's no way to speak to a child.
Of course she doesn't know what mohair costs. Mohair.
In my day women wore mohair. What your father would
say I don't –"

"Where's Pauline? Why isn't she back yet?"

"Don't ask me what her ladyship's plans are." Mother
and Clerihue left the room, taking the animal with them.
High time it went back where it came from, I thought.

I heard Pauline's car drawing up outside and looked out
of the window to see that she had parked it crooked again.
She rushed in, full of exuberance.

"Hello darling, how are you? I say, you'll never guess–"

"I have one of my heads."

"Bad luck. How was your board meeting? Bet it wasn't
as exciting as ours. Sybbo's done amazing work with the
women's pages of the nationals, darling. The *Daily Mail*,

can you believe? And there might be something on *Woman's Hour* . . ."

What had happened to Pauline? She was getting quite . . . hard. Where was the confiding little thing I married?

I remembered cleaning my new racing bike in Comberton Road, with Pauly watching me shyly from her bedroom window. My father worked at Hammersmith Station (he'd have had a fit if he saw the state it's in now), hers was a commissionaire at Olympia. I suppose they had roughly the same income, but that was about all they had in common.

My father didn't approve of books; "You can't eat them and they won't keep you warm," he used to say. The Brownes' house was full of books and music. And people. You could hear her mother laughing through the party wall, sometimes. My mother used to purse her lips and say "Typical!"

I didn't see much of Pauline when I went to Burlington Danes, the comprehensive up at Wood Lane; it was another chance for my mother to say "Typical!" when we heard that Pauline's parents had got her a place at the Sacred Heart High School.

"Sounds Catholic to me," said my father, "I don't hold with it."

"Oh, the local comprehensive isn't good enough for the Brownes with an E," said my mother, "you should have known that, Arthur." The way they spelt their name had annoyed her since the day they moved in, though as I pointed out, it was hardly their fault.

We got together again when we were both students; "St Martin's School of Art!" said my mother. "What that girl needs is a secretarial course that she can earn a living with."

I read Business Studies at Paddington College, which is what my father told me to do. "They're looking for qualifications in Admin. on the Underground," he said. And if I thought it sounded not quite what I wanted to do, I was never one to argue.

Every morning we'd walk to Hammersmith and take the

Piccadilly Line to Leicester Square, where Pauline got off to go to her art college, and I got off to go back to Piccadilly Circus and pick up the Bakerloo for Queen's Park. It infuriated my father. He would never have heard the last of it from the lads at work if they knew that the son of an Underground man took the long way round.

"You want to take the Metropolitan and change at Paddington," he said, "it's only eleven stops that way."

But by then Pauline's carrot-top had turned for me to flames of glory, and her green eyes had art student's eye-liner round them. I'd have gone to Cockfosters by way of Hounslow West for the chance to stand behind her on escalators and shepherd her through the sliding doors. My mother regarded our growing intimacy (not physical, of course; I respected Pauline) with disfavour which deepened to alarm.

"You'll get caught, young man, and don't say I haven't warned you. It would be a fine feather in Sarah Browne's hat to see that flashy daughter of hers hooking a good prospect like you."

And when, in the last year of our studenthood, I told Mum and Dad that I was going to ask Pauline to marry me, Mum cried and Dad took me for a drink in the pub.

"Art students," he said, "there's no need to marry *them* if you want a bit of the other. Know what I mean?"

I put my pint of Mild down and walked out. If I'd stayed I think I would have hit him. We didn't half have a family row when he got back from the pub.

We had to do it in whispers because of the party wall, which made it nastier, somehow.

"You know what I think of that family," hissed my mother, "giving themselves airs and laughing half the night."

"You'll never have any savings," croaked my father, "good money going down the drain for books and paints and that posh classical music they're always playing.

Beethoven indeed. We knew what to do with Huns in the war."

"It's pronounced Batehoven," I muttered, "and it's my life and I'm going to marry Pauline. If she'll have me."

"If she'll have you? Don't talk so far back, lad." My Dad's voice rose and Mum shot him a reproving look.

"Ssh, Arthur. Keep your voice down. Your father's right, George. She'll leap at the cha – . . . you've haven't gone and got her into trouble, have you?"

"Mother! I wouldn't dream of –"

"More fool you," said my father.

"Arthur, I will not have you speaking like that. Not in my sitting room, thank you very much. In that case, George, there's no harm done, and you can put this reckless idea behind you."

"I'm over twenty-one. I love Pauline. She's all I want in life."

We all went to bed then. We were one of those families which if the head of the household went to bed, everyone else had to, too. That way there was no chance of anyone sneaking an extra cup of tea or a late night programme on telly.

"You'll feel better in the morning," said my mother, as if Pauline was some kind of rash that would go away with calamine lotion.

I asked her, and she said yes. We were walking over Hammersmith Bridge and the seagulls were strolling about on the mud, and I loved every one of them. But a little clicking voice at the back of my mind said, "Mum was right. She said she'd leap at the chance . . ."

I had a free afternoon from the Polytechnic, and I'd arranged to meet Pauline off the Underground.

It was early in January, and I didn't fancy her walking home by herself through the dark streets. And I had a surprise lined up for her. I'd found a little old engagement ring in an antique shop. An aquamarine, the man said it was, surrounded by pearls, late nineteenth-century.

I had enough in my Post Office Savings for it. "You're never going to spend your nest egg on a second-hand ring," said my mother, who had slightly come round to the Brownes since she'd heard that his second cousin worked at Harrods. "I wouldn't like them to think we couldn't afford something new." But I knew Pauline would love it.

I got to the station a bit early, just in case, and went into the café opposite to have a cup of coffee while I was waiting. Balancing my coffee and Danish, I slid into a booth opposite two old ladies. They looked at me like all old ladies look at the younger generation and I smiled politely to show I'd never mugged anyone.

The one with the tweed coat and cracked plastic shopping bag said, "Well, I think they ought to be castrated. Simple as that. You've heard about Sarah Browne's daughter, have you?"

The one with the brown woolly cap said, "The art student? What's happened to her? *She's* never been . . ." she looked across at me and lowered her voice, ". . . you know."

"No, nothing like that . . . though Sarah's almost as upset as if she had. Got herself engaged to an absolute wash-out."

"No. And I'd heard she's grown into such a lovely girl. Another art student, is it?"

I couldn't swallow my Danish. I tried to wash it down with coffee and made an unpleasant spluttering noise. They raised their eyebrows at each other and tweed coat said, "The boy next door. Six foot two of good looks with nothing behind it, apparently. The mother's rather a common sort of person, and the father . . . Sarah told me confidentially, mind . . . has got hands that can't mind their own business, if you know what I mean."

"Never!"

"Right old groper. Sarah had to speak quite sharply to him at the Jubilee street party."

I looked over the brown woolly cap and saw Pauline coming out of the station. Supposing I got up and went to meet her and one of them looked round . . . they'd know that I was Son of Groper. If I just sat there . . . Pauline might cross the road, might come in, might sit down next to me and say, "Hello, darling . . . Mrs Tweed Coat, haven't seen you for ages. I bet you didn't know you were sitting opposite my fiancé." Please God, do something. Anything. Make Hammersmith Bridge fall down. Would we hear it from here? My mother . . . *Common?*

Pauline looked round, hesitated, and turned for home. I slid out of the booth and knocked woolly hat's Sainsbury's carrier bag over. Something rolled out of it and tweed coat said, "You wonder where they were brought up, don't you?"

By the time I caught Pauline up I'd resigned myself. She was going to say, "George, let's not rush into anything." And if she did, I'd throw myself off Hammersmith Bridge. With my luck the tide would be out.

Pauline looked up to me in those days. And now she was calling an earl's daughter Sybbo and talking about things I didn't understand.

Source of Irritation?

There was triumph tinged with temperament for Lord Goodrich's lovely 36-year-old daughter, Lady Sybilla Bolsover last night, when she and her three partners brought Natural Sources, their successful Cambridgeshire fashion venture to Primrose Hill, London. Lady Sybilla, married to engineering tycoon Peter Bolsover, whose family firm has been the subject of recent takeover speculation, was fuming about the postal service. 'Nobody is here,' she told me, as crowds filled the boutique, enjoying champagne and blinis with caviar. 'Some very key people did not receive their invitations, and they were posted over a month ago. I shall sue the Post Office,' said Lady Sybilla.

Daily Mail Diary, 10th July, 1985

On the day Mrs Jenks moved in with her walnut suite I remembered what Dad had said as we walked up the aisle together, and all those critical eyes on the right side of the church had swivelled round to appraise my wedding dress ("Made it herself, and they've got such lovely things at Pronuptia . . ."). He'd given my arm a comforting squeeze and whispered, "Remember, sweetheart, you're marrying George, not the Jenks family."

George and his mother, as it turned out, and it was not an ideal ménage à trois.

"You'll need help when the new baby arrives," George kept saying.

"And how much help can I expect from someone who's supposed to be frail?" I kept answering. This conversation tended to bring on George's shifty look.

"What's going on, Pauline?" There was nothing frail about the way she came bustling into the nursery, sensing a scene.

What was going on had started earlier than I would have wished, when Clerry came into our bedroom, carrying Stripey.

"Stripey's puddled," she said, dropping the kitten onto George.

George sprang up, instantly alert. "What's happening, Pauline? Is it your contractions?"

"Stripey puddled," said Clerry, clambering onto the bed and scooping up the kitten.

George reached over child and kitten for the alarm clock. "I told you, Pauline, Mother told you, that cats are nasty insanitary things to have around young children. How many times have I told you to get rid of it?" He squinted at the clock and fell back on his pillows. "Do you realise it's only six forty-five?"

Climbing out of bed, or rather, rolling out of bed, since climbing isn't a practical pastime when you're nearly nine months pregnant, I followed Clerry, sobbing dolefully and clutching her kitten protectively to her, into the nursery. "Where pet? Where did Stripey puddle?"

Not on the vinyl floor, of course, but all over the furry bunny-rabbit rug in the cot. "Stripey will have to sleep in his own little bed downstairs, with his own little litter tray, darling."

"Not getting rid of Stripey." Clerry was still cuddling her kitten.

"Of course not." I gave them both a big hug.

Really, I could hardly believe George's insensitivity. You'd have thought, with all those childcare books he read so avidly and quoted so often, he'd have picked up on sibling rivalry.

Typical of George's mother to loom up when I was coping with a crying child and a wet bed.

"Poor little mite," she said, looking at the sheets, "no wonder she's insecure with her mother working all day."

"It was Stripey, not Clerry," I said shortly.

Grabbing Stripey from Clerry, she smacked the kitten and insisted on rubbing its nose in the wet bunny-rabbit rug. Clerry howled. Stripey, I was pleased to see, dealt Mrs J. a swift right-hander, leaving a nasty scratch an inch below the frilled winceyette.

"Nasty creature!" She dropped Stripey onto the floor,

Pauline

who hastily cringed off towards the door, tripping up George as he came in.

"What on earth is going on, Pauline? I'm chairing a sales conference in less than two hours, you know."

"Where's the Dettol, George?" screamed Mrs Jenks. "I'll have to get a tetanus injection. Someone will have to take me to the hospital."

Clerry sobbed, "Stripey's sorry . . ."

I consoled Clerry, gave George's arm a comforting pat, and smiled weakly at Mrs Jenks. I didn't mention the autumn collection, press show in a week, baby due in two weeks, and likely to arrive any minute if I got involved in another row with that woman.

She cooked breakfast again, of course. Bacon, eggs and didn't I detect the aroma of frying onions drifting up the stairs? I felt my baby move. I also felt sick. I'd never had morning sickness before, but I hadn't had Mrs Jenks frying up every morning when I was expecting Clerry.

"You've got to eat for two, Pauline," she said, avidly eating for three, the scratch on her wrist forgotten.

"Thank you. No." I poured out a cup of weak tea, added a sliver of lemon.

"But Mother went out and bought those mushrooms specially for you." George was really pushing his luck that morning. Twenty-five pence a quarter at the greengrocer on the corner. With all that money in the bank, it wasn't a flamboyantly generous contribution to the family budget.

"Thank you. No." Pushing back my chair, possibly just a shade aggressively, I went into the dining room and tried to concentrate on the new autumn jacket.

"Don't worry, Pauline. I'll clear up the breakfast things and see to Clerry." The consciously virtuous voice followed me into the dining room. And then in an even more audible hissed undertone. "I don't know what the world's coming to, George, I'm sure. Poor little neglected mite. All right, Clerry darling, Gan–Gan's here . . ."

* * *

I'd only just banished Mrs Jenks from my mind and achieved the perfect armhole – the sleeve seam tapering gently into the waistband which flared into a peplum – when Sybilla phoned.

"Pauline? I didn't wake you?"

People who phone you up early in the morning to ask you this question are invariably lolling about in bed themselves. If I had a video phone I would certainly have seen Sybilla, still comfortably cocooned in cream silk sheets, Vitamin E facial cream vibing up her perfect features, daily newspapers (gossip columns rampant) strewn about the bed, sipping a cup of Earl Grey. For Lady Sybilla, in Eaton Square, eight o'clock may well signal the dawn chorus. For Pauline Jenks, in St Neots, it had already been an action-packed day.

"No, Sybilla, it's quite all right." Must be something important for Sybilla to raise a hand to the telephone before 9 a.m.

"Did you see the *Mail* this morning, darling?"

"Oh, Sybilla, not the Madras shirts?" She'd been trying to get a fashion spread on them in one of the nationals for weeks.

"No, darling, not clothes. The opening. *Mail* Diary. Dreadful photograph of me."

Our first London shop. I'd so wanted to be at that opening party. Primrose Hill may not be Mayfair or Chelsea, but in some ways it was better. We'd found a shop in a cobbled courtyard, surrounded by expensive Regency terraces and the sort of delicatessens and chic antique shops that attract women who can afford to splurge on an eighteenth-century armoire or an outfit when they've just popped out for half a pound of smoked salmon.

It had been a mistake to tell my gynaecologist about the launch party.

"Blood pressure's up a bit," he had said, at my last checkup. "Nothing serious, but I'm not having you gallivanting off to London for a cocktail party."

"But . . ."

"Absolutely no 'buts', my dear." He placed the stethoscope on my stomach, and listened intently. "Won't be long now . . . so you be a good girl, put your feet up and get plenty of rest."

"But . . ."

"Especially if you're still determined on a *natural* birth." He said it as though it would be more natural to have a nice, neat Caesarian.

"A photograph of you, Sybilla?" I said vaguely, as the baby gave a determined kick.

"In the *Mail*, Pauline. You are listening? I was wearing that beige tussore dress, last collection. I knew those gathers at the waist were a mistake. I remember saying at the time that pleats would have been more flattering."

Just because she looked so soignée herself, Sybilla was inclined to adopt the role of design consultant. Sometimes it was a help to sound off ideas against someone who understood fashion – Julia and Emily hadn't a clue – but it was getting increasingly difficult not to turn every collection into a personal wardrobe for Sybilla and her friends.

"I'm sure you looked wonderful, as usual," I said tactfully, trying to ignore the creak of the door opening, and George's mother peeking round it in an overly polite, intrusive manner.

"Oh, you're on the phone again, dear . . ."

"Working." I had asked her not to disturb me when I was shut away in the dining room.

"Are you still there, Pauline? Really, it's impossible to talk to you . . ."

"Hang on a minute, Sybilla. Yes, Mrs J?" I couldn't bring myself to call her Mother, as she suggested. I had, after all, a mother of my own.

"Clerry and I are just popping out to the Co-op. I can't find a list anywhere, Pauline."

"That's because I haven't made one." I had also pointed out, more than once, that it was easier to do the shopping myself than think about Vim and pork chops when I ought to be concentrating on how many skirt sections I could get out of five thousand metres of fabric.

"Shall I get some nice stewing steak, then?"

"Whatever you like."

Mrs Jenks withdrew huffily, murmuring that she always made sure her husband came home to a good hot meal after a hard day down the Underground.

I shut the door firmly after her. "I'm sorry, Sybilla. You looked a fright in the tussore dress and it's all my fault."

"No need to jump down my throat, Pauline. I suppose it's that ghastly woman; I can't think why you put up with her."

"She's impossible, Sybbo. She's been frying onions."

"Well, I didn't phone up to talk about your domestic problems. You read the piece, I suppose?"

"George has the *Guardian* . . ."

"Then you won't know that I threatened to sue the Post Office."

"The Post Office? I thought it was all about the new shop?"

"In a way. Only the most embarrassing thing has happened, Pauline. You know I invited Selena and Anne and Joanna . . ." She reeled off a string of Christian names which I knew to be celebrities by the heavy emphasis she placed on each name.

"And they didn't turn up?"

"One or two, because I took the precaution of phoning them yesterday afternoon. Tina and Jane and Sarah, that pretty little singer, and *none* of them, my dear, had received their invitations."

"But I don't understand. Julia put our lists together weeks ago and sent out the invitations."

"That's what I thought, too. So naturally I blamed the GPO, sounded off to Nigel Dempster's leg-man about it, and now it turns out that Julia filed my list in her underwear drawer."

"In her underwear drawer?"

"That's what she said. Phoned me first thing this

morning. Read in the *Mail* that I was threatening to sue the
GPO and suddenly remembered, it seems, that she'd tidied
the list away, people coming to dinner or something, and
had completely forgotten about it."

"Poor Julia." George's mother was no picnic, but Julia
Mainwaring had to contend with those two stepchildren
who, between them, looked as though they could provide
case histories for a comprehensive text book on teenage
crisis, as well as the twins. She had a large rambling house
to look after and a garden to match. And she was married
to a man who thought that sharing the domestic load meant
changing a light bulb once a year. "She has been looking
terribly tired recently."

"Poor Julia? It's David I feel sorry for. Married to a
woman who looks like a sack of potatoes and breathes
whisky fumes over the breakfast toast."

"Oh Sybbo, that's hardly fair. Julia's under a lot of
pressure."

"Exactly. That's what's worrying me. You'll be at the
board meeting this afternoon, I suppose?"

"Of course."

"Good. Don't mention this conversation. I'll have a word
with Emily and arrange for the three of us to get together
after the meeting."

"*Three* of us?" We'd always worked as a team, a four-
some.

"It's Julia I want to discuss, Pauline. We've got to do
something about Julia."

I put the phone down and drew a few desultory lines on
my design pad. After talking to Sybilla the joy had gone
out of my armhole. I fiddled about with the drawing, took
out the peplum . . . hopeless. Cardin, circa '68, not one of
his best years. Where were all my other sketches? I un-
earthed them from under a pile of ironing. Why couldn't
George's mother do a bit of ironing if she was so eager to
help?

It was no good, I couldn't concentrate. I didn't totally
trust Sybilla. That bit about the whisky fumes over the

toast, making Julia sound like a bag-lady. I'd never noticed her drinking more than the occasional glass of wine over lunch, and how had Sybilla come by this intriguing vignette of domestic life, if not from Julia's husband?

I couldn't imagine why any woman, particularly Sybilla Bolsover, who could take her pick of attractive men (and, according to Emily, frequently did) should fancy David Mainwaring. But Clerry and I had been walking along the river bank a few weeks earlier, and I had been surprised to see the two of them, talking tensely in a parked car.

The venue was such a cliché for Sybilla, who preferred to tryst at the Ritz, that I thought maybe they were having in-depth discussions about Bolsover's. It was no secret that David was keen to do a management buy out, and Sybilla's friends were notoriously rich. And then I spotted them a second time, coming out of the Golden Pheasant, arm in arm.

"How's David getting on?" I'd asked Sybilla casually, the next day.

"David?" Sybilla reacted as though she'd never met a man with this unusual name.

"David Mainwaring. Thought I saw you chatting . . ."

"David Mainwaring? My dear, I haven't seen David for *months*."

Sybilla's view of Julia might not be entirely objective.

Until I got my Renault I used to lock myself in the bath-room when I wanted to be alone, but families bang on bathroom doors and rattle door handles. Nobody could get at me in my Renault. It was the best present I ever had; four wheels guaranteeing privacy, freedom and time to think.

People who buy themselves car telephones must be maso-chists, I thought, as I drove towards Cambridge. I wasn't looking forward to that meeting. In two years the four of us had built up a profitable business and, unlike the Bolsover board, we'd managed it without stand up rows or devious knifings in the shoulder blade area. If Julia was having some

Pauline

sort of personal crisis I'd have preferred us all to talk about
it round the table, rather than creeping off and discussing
her fatigue level or whisky consumption behind her back.
I wished I'd said that to Sybilla when she phoned. But
Sybilla had an imperious way of sweeping you along with
her ideas, and by the time you'd digested them and said,
'Hey, wait a minute, Sybbo . . .'' she was off at a tangent
with another thought.

There was a meter in Jesus Lane. That had to be a good
omen. And the second bit of good luck was the sight of
Emily Sutcliffe rounding the corner to a chorus of wolf
whistles from the workmen transforming an old barber's
shop into a vegetarian restaurant. Emily was stuck in a
'sixties time warp and it suited her. She must have been
forty plus but she still had that free loping walk girls
suddenly discovered when they put on tights, shortened
their skirts and went swinging down the King's Road.

"Hi, Pauline." She caught me up in a second. "Did you
get a phone call from Sybilla this morning?"

I nodded. 'Don't like the sound of it, do you?"

"Hate it," said Emily. "I've no intention of gossiping about Julia behind her back. Told Sybilla so this
morning."

"Thank God. I've been worrying about it all day."

"So Julia forgot to post a few cards? It doesn't make her
an alcoholic, does it? And who can blame her for taking
the odd nip, when that unlovely husband of hers is carrying
on with the lovely Sybilla?"

I was taking little runs to keep up with Emily, but my
mind was right up there with her. "You're sure?"

"'Course I'm sure. She told me so herself. Says David's
good in bed."

"Not so good out of it."

"Two of a kind, wouldn't you say? Let's try and keep
this meeting official and impersonal, stop Sybilla going
over the top."

When we arrived, Julia was sitting in the office above
the shop, looking pale and shuffling papers about. "Hullo,

you two. I'm afraid I can't find the minutes of our last meeting."

"That's because I haven't given them to you yet." Emily, efficient company secretary as well as creative accountant, foraged in her briefcase and placed a neatly clipped sheaf of papers in front of Julia.

"Right then . . ." Julia put on her spectacles, studied the minutes, took her spectacles off, pushed up her sleeves and cleared her throat nervously. She was wearing a shapeless flower-print dress which I hoped nobody thought was designed by me. She looked more like the president of the WI than the managing director of a thrusting young fashion empire, which was how the local paper described us when we opened the Primrose Hill branch. ". . . we'd better get started."

"We'll need a quorum, Julia." What on earth had got into Emily? We might not be having a jolly coffee and gossip in the Kardomah, as George liked to think, but we were not exactly shifting millions about the boardroom of ICI, either. Presumably Emily was starting as she meant to go on, official and impersonal.

"Oh dear." Julia looked vaguely round the table. "Sorry Em. Sybilla's not here yet. Does anyone know where she is?"

"I'm here, darlings." Sybilla swept in. Marvellous entrance. Totally wasted on us. "Sorry I'm late, but it took forever getting here." She laid a chocolate brown pigskin Filofax on the table and sat down. "I can't imagine why I have to come dragging down to Cambridge for these meetings now we've got the NW1 shop. So much more central."

"More central for you, Sybilla," said Emily, "but you're the only one living in London, and it's hardly practical for Pauline to go rushing about on British Rail at the moment."

"Pauline dear, I am sorry," said Sybilla, not looking it. "Those linen tents you're wearing are so adorable, I keep forgetting."

Julia cleared her throat again. "Shall we begin with the minutes of the last meeting?"

She started reading about capital expenditure (we seemed to have spent an enormous sum on inscrutable electronic sewing machines which neither I, nor Ahmet Basrawy's outworkers, understood), below the line promotional expenditure (this appeared to be the catering costs for the Primrose Hill launch), and quoted figures for pretax profits for the period February to April, which had so many noughts on the end that it sounded almost as though we *were* running ICI. "And the directors want it recorded," Julia concluded thankfully, "that if the Primrose Hill branch is successful, we should seek to acquire premises in the Covent Garden area for a third branch of Natural Sources, and to this end Emily Sutcliffe will approach major banks and finance houses with a view to raising a loan on our existing properties. The board also considered the possibility of setting up franchises, but agreed that we should consolidate our existing business before undertaking any further expansion." She looked round anxiously. "Is that all right?"

"Everyone agreed?" said Emily, briskly taking notes.

"About that launch . . ." Sybilla leant forward aggressively.

"Agreed," I said quickly.

"So, what's on the agenda for today?" Julia resumed her paper shifting.

"I have a copy here." Emily passed over a copy.

Julia studied it gloomily. "Top of the agenda, the Primrose Hill launch."

"I would like to put it on record," said Emily, "that in spite of the fact that a number of invitations were unfortunately mislaid, the launch was successful, we achieved sixty column inches in the nationals and the promise of three editorials in the monthlies . . ."

"Successful?" Sybilla's shoulder pads shook with indignation. "Without Selena? And Joanna was furious."

"It's customary to address your remarks to the chair," said Emily, very dignified.

"If the chair's in a fit condition to hear anything," said Sybilla, so nastily that even if Julia was lying on the floor, singing that Glasgow belonged to her, I'd still have called for a vote of confidence in her.

"Madam Chairman," I heard myself saying, "I'd like to propose that that last remark be struck off the record . . ."

"Seconded," said Emily, quick as a flash.

"Point of order," said Sybilla. "Oh, for God's sake, I've had enough of this absurd charade. Julia drank too much and hid my invitations in her underwear . . ."

"Sybilla," said Emily, warningly.

"All right, all right. She was overtired, emotional, call it what you will. The fact is that Julia can't cope any more. I didn't want to talk about it here, in front of her, as you both know." She glowered at me and Emily, and Julia gave us a wan grateful smile. "What I'd like to know is precisely how you came to mislay fifty invitations, Julia?"

"I'm terribly sorry," Julia said. "There seems to have been such a lot on recently, and I just put them in the drawer and . . ."

"You don't have to make any excuses, Julia," said Emily. "Sixty column inches – not counting your unfortunate outburst in the *Mail* Diary, Sybilla – is more publicity than we'd anticipated, and I doubt if we could have accommodated another fifty people. They were practically picnicking on Primrose Hill as it was."

I gave Julia an encouraging smile. "I'd like to record a vote of confidence in Julia Mainwaring as chairman and managing director of Natural Sources."

"Seconded," cried Emily.

Sybilla snatched the pigskin Filofax from the table, and thrust it into a matching briefcase. "Well, don't expect me to go along with it, or second it or whatever damn fool phrase they use in boardrooms." She rose, pushed back her chair, made for the door and turned to deliver her last line. "I must say I find it difficult to have confidence in anyone

59

who's disloyal enough to sell Bolsover shares at a time like this."

It was a weak exit, not a patch on her entrance. But then I hadn't the faintest idea what she was talking about.

Emily obviously had, though. "Three thousand preference wasn't it? I must admit Trevor and I thought it was a little . . ." I could see she was sifting through her vocabulary for an inoffensive word, ". . . unusual."

"I'm sorry." Julia blinked at us apologetically and then dropped her head on her arms and started sobbing. Emily began earnestly writing nothing very much on her pad, and I went over to Julia and put my arm around her. She was one of those locked into herself people who made you feel intrusive if you met her in the street and asked how she was feeling, and her shoulders stiffened involuntarily.

"It's not just the launch and those bloody shares," she murmured into the inlaid mahogany table (one of our earlier above-the-line expenditures). "I only sold them because Sybilla was bitching about having to put up all the money for Primrose Hill. I didn't know it would cause all this trouble. And now they're threatening to expel Simon . . . something to do with a younger boy . . . and Alex smokes like a chimney, she's only *twelve*, and David won't face up to any of it. And I never have any time these days to be with the Mels . . ."

There was a sudden stabbing pain as I stopped at the St Neots lights. And another. And another. It couldn't be? That meeting was hardly the "put up your feet and have a nice rest" Mr Eland had recommended, but the baby wasn't due for at least a week. I changed down into third, taking it slowly, just in case, and thanked God that Emily had taken Julia home, rather than me. The way she'd looked, she was the last person I would have chosen to heroically deliver my baby in the back seat of the Renault.

I drove down the High Street on automatic pilot, stopping at familiar lights and rounding accustomed corners without thought. It was more what I imagined might be going to happen than the actual pain, which wasn't really all that bad.

George's mother was drying and putting away saucepans as I stumbled into the kitchen. She took one look at me and said, "Sit down, love, I'll call an ambulance and phone for Mr Eland."

I'd never been so pleased to see anyone in my life.

Pitkin has 22.6% of Bolsover

Pitkin Industries, the Midlands-based engineering group, yesterday bought nearly 4m shares, or 7% of Bolsover's equity. These shares increased the size of Pitkin's holding to 22.6%. It is understood that Sir Jeremy Pitkin has identified Bolsover's difficulties as the shortage of senior management and lack of strategic direction. Neither David Mainwaring, Managing Director, nor Peter Bolsover, Chairman of the Board, were available for comment.

Financial Times,
6th September, 1985

L ife on the domestic front changed considerably after Tobias was born, and in my opinion, if anyone had asked it, not for the better.

It started when I took Clerihue in to the hospital to see her new little baby brother, and Mother insisted on coming too.

She took one look at the baby and went quite silly.

"Look at him, the little ruffian. And hasn't he got a look of his grandfather . . . ?" (He looked as much like that boardroom portrait of the first Peter Bolsover – or, for that matter, Mao Tse Tung – as he looked like my father, but women will always see what they want to see.) ". . . well done, dear, I knew it would be a boy. George, why don't you take Clerihue for a little walk round the gardens while Pauline and I have a chat?"

So Clerry and I went for a little walk. After one quick look at her brother, ("Why is he orange?") she wasn't all that interested anyway. And I certainly didn't want to stand around while they told each other embarrassing things about dilating.

We had gone Private, of course; I felt that the wife of a director of Bolsover's should have her own room at Addenbrookes. "Anyway," Pauline had said, "I'll need to be on the telephone a lot, Basrawy's getting awfully slack about deliveries."

As a modern father I had insisted on my right to be present at the birth. I had missed Clerihue's, because Pauline had gone and had her while I was in Lowestoft for a sales conference. Way back in May I had got Marcia to rearrange my schedule so there was no chance of missing this one.

"Have it your own way," Mr Eland, FRCS, said to me, "but I warn you, I'm there to look after mother and baby. If you have to faint, do it under the bed and don't get in my way."

Not quite the manner in which you expect to be spoken to when you've gone Private, but of course these surgeons are very autocratic.

It went quite well to start with. Pauline panted a lot in a way I considered rather unnecessary (surely Mother didn't do that when she had me?) and nothing was covered up. I didn't quite like standing around with a mask on looking at Pauly's thighs while other people were looking at them too.

"There's my clever girl," said Mr Eland, "lovely, lovely, now we're ready for the big push."

Pauline yelped, and suddenly there was a sort of nasty little . . . growth.

The next thing I knew a nurse was leaning over me and mopping my head.

"All right, Mr Jenkins. You're all right, just a little cut, you banged your head on the radiator."

"Jenks," I said. You'd think they'd know better than to have radiators sticking out into delivery rooms.

"You've got a lovely little boy, look."

The growth had turned into a little monkey with a Chinese face; you could see there was something wrong with it.

"Isn't he marvellous, darling? Look at his feet, aren't they wonderful?"

Poor Pauline, I didn't know quite what to say. Mr Eland slapped me on the back.

"A chip off the old block, eh? Congratulations, a perfect baby. Better let me have a look at that cut."

On the way out, after I'd said goodnight to Pauline and Tobias, I passed Sister's room. Mr Eland was in there, and they were both screaming with laughter.

"I had to put more stitches in the father's head than I did in the mother's perineum," he was saying, "and I can't even charge him."

"Hope it won't spoil his looks. All my nurses are in love with him."

"More fools them. That wife's worth ten of him on a bad day."

And to think I was paying for that sort of comment.

The ultimate treachery was Mother's attitude to the cat. Clerihue had christened it Stripey, and in my experience once you start giving animals names, there's no getting rid of them.

After I brought Pauline and Tobias home and settled them in ("Don't fuss, George, I know how to dilute Milton.") I went downstairs and said to Mother, "Now's my chance to get rid of that dirty little animal. Won't have it in the house with –"

"You'll do no such thing," said Mother. "Get rid of Stripey, indeed. We can't have that, can we, pussy? That wife of yours is no fool, George. Clerihue won't be jealous of the new baby if she has something of her own to look after. Pauline had it all worked out, you've got to hand it to her. Sister was telling me she's never seen such a perfect delivery. It quite took me back to when you were . . . George, I'm talking to you."

It would have been a relief to leave the house and go to work, except that work was worse than home then. Apparently Pitkin Industries had got 22.6 per cent of our shares, which didn't sound all that much to me. Where would I have been without Marcia?

"Put it this way, Mr J.," she said, nudging back her cuticles, "22.6 per cent is just under a quarter of the total stock, right? The board of directors control about 25 per cent, right? Which leaves 50 per cent in the hands of shareholders looking for a quick buck, right? Dicey, wouldn't you say?"

"Surely our shareholders will be loyal?"

"Loyal to their pockets, like we're all loyal. Anyway, what about Julia Mainwaring's 3,000 preference she sold last year? Once the board's wives start unloading, you can't expect your average punter –"

"I don't think anyone's supposed to know about that."

"Mary in the canteen doesn't know about it, she was sent home with a bad thumb. Everyone else does. You can hear everything that's said in the boardroom down in Quality Control. Something to do with the central heating pipes . . . Mr J.?"

"Yes, Marcia? You know nail varnish brings on my migraines, I have mentioned it before."

"It's nail hardener, actually. Mind if I ask you something? Do you like being sales director?"

I tried to laugh in an amused manner. "What a question, Marcia."

"Oh, I know – more bread and a bigger car and the directors' dining room and all that. But me and Rosemary from Personnel were saying the other day that when you were just another salesman and we all called you George, you seemed to laugh a lot more then."

"The cares of office, Marcia. Now, where's that letter to Geoff Farnsworth? I dictated it Monday, we really ought to –"

"Yeah, but then you told me to hold it, remember? Until we heard how his Tokyo trip had gone. It's aerobics tonight, I'll have a chat with Tracy."

"Tracy?"

"Geoff Farnsworth's secretary. I did tell you, Mr J."

Geoff Farnsworth had by then been to Tokyo twice, as I pointed out to David Mainwaring. My estimate of our chances of selling him our new freeze-drying packaging unit varied from nil to you've got to be joking.

I might as well have saved my breath.

"I've got better things to think about than Geoff Farnsworth's dried onions," he said, "anyway, isn't that your department, George?"

It was hardly surprising I didn't laugh like I used to.

Me and Roger Makepeace were neck and neck on sales figures in 1983 when old Clement Bolsover keeled over watching a suggestive film in Peterborough. Black sheep of the family, been on the board for years, I suppose they called him sales director for want of a better name. You could hardly call a member of the Bolsover family the Director in Charge of Lewd Glances.

After the funeral (it was not obligatory for members of the staff to attend . . . someone would have noticed if you hadn't), me and Roger Makepeace were having a quick pint at the Lord Salisbury.

"I can't think why they had him on the board in the first place," I said, "disgusting, really, all those women."

"Because he was Peter Bolsover's cousin and the Bolsovers stick to each other like glue. Family, don't you know, old chap? Anyway, those amazing aristocratic looks of his went down a bomb at AGMs. Let's have the other half. Your North-East figures are a bit on the impressive side, George."

"Bit of luck, really," I said modestly, "and how about those new outlets of yours in Cornwall? Cornwall, of all places."

"I know, couldn't believe it. You realise they'll be looking for a new sales director? On our performance, it's got to be either you or me."

"Bring someone in from outside, won't they? Aren't we a bit young?"

"Should think they'd be quite keen to have someone whose arteries won't seize up at the sight of a suspender belt. Anyway, may the best man win, and all that sort of rubbish."

Driving home that night I thought, there we are then. Roger Makepeace, Marlborough and Durham, at home with everyone, versus George Jenks, who trips over carpets. No contest.

The best man didn't win, as it turned out. Roger Makepeace took me out for a drink, slapped me on the back and smiled as though he was really pleased. Left two months later and joined Pitkin Industries. Funny, really, how things turn out.

And now there we were at yet another board meeting. No wonder we weren't making any money; all we seemed to do was sit round and talk about why we weren't making any money.

"It seems perfectly obvious to me," said David Mainwaring, lighting a cigar, "that all we need is an injection of capital. Played golf with Ray Whatsisname of the Nat West the other day. Struck me as being very chummy. Trevor, why don't you –?"

"Ray Brooks," said Peter, "nice chap. Far too intelligent to chuck good money after bad. Still, I suppose Trevor could go and have a word. What size of injection were you thinking of, David?"

"Half a million would get us off the hook, wouldn't it, Trevor?"

"In a manner of speaking . . . it would at least cover the wages bill, but I fear that taking the long term view . . ."

Trevor droned on. I stopped listening, because I had a rather vivid vision of Quality Control clustered round the central heating pipes. Any suggestion that wages were in jeopardy, and they'd walk out. Not that I'd care; as head of sales I had frequently had to point out that machine-tooling demands accuracy to within a hundredth of a millimetre. "I'm sure you will appreciate that valves that very nearly fit," I said, "are not an instantly saleable item." I always tried to inject a bit of humour into my rebukes, to show I was still one of the . . .

"George?"

"What? Right. Yes. Good thinking."

"You'd agree with that, would you, George?" Peter was looking patient.

"Ah. Well. In the light of present circumstances . . ."

"Trevor is talking about a white knight."

I prayed that Marcia was down there by the central heating; she would have to tell me what they were on about. My mother used to use the White Knight Laundry, but I hardly supposed . . .

"An interesting idea," I said, "very interesting indeed. Very much my line of thinking, Trevor."

"We're agreed, then, are we?" said Peter. "A loan from the bank to bridge us over, and David and Trevor will put out feelers for a white knight."

"Put the ferrets down," said David, "and see what comes to the surface."

Trevor looked glum.

"Now," said Peter, "next item. We really ought to put out some sort of statement . . . that *FT* piece today."

"Statement?" David ground out his cigar viciously. "I'll tell you what I think we should bloody say. That bloody treacherous Pitkin, last time I tell him where to buy his horses. Shared a bottle of champers with me at Doncaster, nice as pie, and now the double-dealing bastard has the nerve . . ."

When I got back to my office, Marcia and a bosomy girl who I guessed was Rosemary from Personnel were drinking something out of plastic mugs and giggling.

"Oh, excuse me, Mr Jenks," said Rosemary, "Marcia and me were just having a birthday drink, as it's nearly five. See you later, Marce." She giggled again, and left the room.

"Really, Marcia, I don't think . . . whose birthday is it, anyway?"

"Mine, Mr J. I say, that was a turn up for the book, wasn't it?"

"How much can you actually hear, down in Quality Control?"

"Enough. They'll never find a white knight for this worn out old load of rubbish. What a hoot when you said 'very much my line of thinking.' I thought Rosemary would split herself. A white knight, Mr J. is, and I quote, a friendly bidder who is prepared to offer more for a target's shares than a hostile bidder."

"Yes, well, of course I knew –"

"Bet you didn't. Did you see all that in the *FT* about shortage of senior management and lack of strategic direction?"

"Very unfortunate. Mr Mainwaring was most –"

"We all heard what Dubious Dave thought about it. I should think the whole of St Neots did. Take my advice, Mr J. Leave the sinking ship and go back to selling nuts and bolts, or cuddly toys or whatever you fancy."

I would have to speak to Marcia, but not just then, I was getting that double vision I always get before a migraine.

"Thank you, Marcia. Where are those Aitcheson Burbank invoices I asked you for?"

"On your desk, Mr J. See you in the morning."

She put on her coat, picked up her bag and left, smelling of acetone. What with one thing and another, it would be prudent to take some Neurofen. I picked up the Aitcheson Burbank invoices, which they'd returned with rather a curt note, and switched on the dictaphone.

"Letter to Leonard Ponsonby, Aitcheson Burbank, usual address, today's date. Our reference P27 stroke 0443, your reference . . . on their letter, Marcia. Dear Len, what a shame you had to miss golf last Tuesday, it was a perfect day for it. I am trying some new balls which I think you might be interested in. New paragraph. Now, about this little matter of the fan belt idlers. I am of course aware that a small percentage of our April delivery did not quite come up to scratch . . . make that did not perhaps achieve our usual high quality, but you must be aware . . . delete that. But in view of our long standing and amicable relationship, I am sure you will be as . . . as perturbed as I am when you read your accounts department's letter, copy enclosed. Make a photocopy and enclose it, Marcia. I am sure this little matter can be easily sorted out person to person, perhaps we can make lunch next week? Make a diary note, Marcia, for me to ring him on Monday. Yours, etc . . . PS. Pauline was asking about Sally and the new baby. We really ought to get together and compare notes. Tobias is already on solids!"

It was after six by the time I left the office, and my right eye was throbbing in a manner I knew only too well. As I took the short cut to the car park through the foundry I was rather surprised to see David was still there. He was talking to Jim Geraghty, the foundry shop steward, and while I was never one for eavesdropping . . . I paused to look for my car keys behind a handy air vent.

"Now look, here Geraghty . . ."

"Mr Geraghty to you, Mr Mainwaring. I'm trying to be reasonable. My lads know you've got troubles. All the newsprint in here today was pink. They usually read the *Sun* . . . lack of strategic direction, and all that. What about our jobs, that's what we want to know?"

"The wages bill will be met. There is no doubt on that score."

"So we heard. What we want to know is, is there a cash flow problem or isn't there? Are we going to be taken over, or aren't we?"

"You may tell the men that they have my personal word –"

"If it's all the same to you, Mr Mainwaring, they'd rather have Mr Bolsover's personal word. You know where you are with him."

"I'll be damned if I'm going to take that kind of impertinence from a jumped up little Irish –"

"Oh, I don't think I'd say things like that, Mr Mainwaring. They never seem to go down very well with tribunals, do they?"

Perhaps I could put things right. I found my car keys and strolled casually across the foundry.

"'Night, David. 'Night Jim. How's that boy of yours doing? Still keen on football?"

"I've just got the two girls, Mr Jenks. Goodnight, then, gentlemen."

He stomped out, fussily checking doors as he went. David grinned at me and looked younger in the process.

"Nice try, George. You won't cut much ice with Geraghty. He's a born trouble-maker. What I want to know is, where does he get his gen? Remarkably well-informed, isn't he?"

"I have heard it said . . . it has been hinted to me, just this morning, as it happens . . ."

"Yes?" David was moving purposefully towards the car park and his first drink of the evening.

"You can hear a good deal of what is said in the board-room down in Quality Control. Something to do with the central heating pipes, my informant informed me."

"What? You knew that this morning and you let us sit there this afternoon and –"

"Did I say this morning? Silly of me, slip of the tongue. No, no, it was of course after the board meeting that I heard . . ."

"The cunning blighters. No wonder I'm left with my foot in my mouth in Union negotiations. Coming for a quick one?"

I wanted to be home in time to read Clerihue her good-night story. We had just got to the bit where Mole gets lost in the Wild Wood and I'd found it quite difficult to stop reading the night before. Not often David Mainwaring asked George Jenks for a drink, though, so I followed him to the Cambridge Hunter, where he asked for His Usual. It turned out to be colourless and large. I opted for a sherry and after a short pause in which I could hear David thinking Men don't drink sherry, I added, very dry, please, though really I preferred Pale Cream.

When it came I could hardly get it down, but I did all that appreciative hissing and thinning of the lips to show I knew a really good sherry when I tasted one.

Not that David noticed; he was too busy imbibing and catching the barman's eye for another.

"Need a couple of stiff ones before I go home these days," he said.

"Your beautiful house. I pointed it out to Mother when we drove past the other day, and she said . . ."

"Looks all right on the outside, I grant you. Inside it's like some bloody office. Julia's got no sense of organisation, of course. Bits of paper everywhere, samples of material all over the bedroom. Telephone ringing all night with some little wog shouting at me about shade variations all the way from Bombay or somewhere . . . I tell you, George . . ."

"Pauline's working very hard too."

"And did you see Julia on *Look East*? What a shambles."

"I thought they were all very good. Quite a few of my contacts mentioned seeing my wife on telly."

"Oh, Pauline and Emily were all right, and Sybilla, of course, was dazzling. All Julia did was mutter and make faces."

"Your gardens were looking lovely when we passed," I said in a tactful manner.

"The *gardens*," said David sarcastically, making good use of his second drink, "of course the gardens look good. She spends all her time out there gossiping with geraniums."

"Ah."

"That's why the house looks like a pig's dinner. That's why the other three have to do all the work. That's why Sybilla never has time for . . . Christ, is it six already? Better be off."

He had gone. I gratefully left the rest of my sherry and said good night to the barman. "'Night, squire," he said, not an expression I cared for.

I got home rather late to be greeted by a scene of unattractive bustle. While I was parking the car I could see through the kitchen window that Mother was giving Tobias his bottle,

Clerihue was forging her way through a mound of tomato sandwiches, and Pauline was piling a lot of muslin-coloured clothes into boxes. None of them noticed me.

When the head of the house gets home, I thought irritably, he should be greeted by calm and peace and people asking him what they can fetch him.

I would wait for supper in front of "the box" in the sitting room. I hoped Mother had done one of her trifles. Lunch hadn't been anything to write home about, directors' dining room or no directors' dining room. I'd have done better with fish and chips from the canteen.

I put my briefcase down loudly by the hallstand. No wonder they couldn't hear me with all that jabbering.

Pauline: "I can't find those fabric swatches anywhere. Or the sample buttons for the culottes."

Mother: "Now, where did I see them? Here they are, dear, on the dresser. If you want my advice you'll sit down and have a nice glass of sherry."

Clerihue: "Stripey wants some sandwich."

Pauline: "Don't talk with your mouth full, darling. Now, have I packed everything?"

Mother: "He's had his Kit-E-Kat, you mustn't spoil him, Clerry . . ." Noise of liquid gurgling into glass. "You've got to think of yourself, Pauline, you haven't stopped today. Sit down and drink this, five minutes won't bring the world to a halt. *There's* a good boy. Now we're more comfortable, aren't we?"

Pauline: "Thank you, Gloria. I don't know where I'd be without you. Only I promised to get these toiles over to Julia's this evening. She's taking them down to the Primrose Hill shop tomorrow to show an American buyer."

Mother: "George can drive them over, after supper. Time you put your feet up, the baby's two months old and you're still looking pulled down."

Pauline: "Heavens, George's supper. I'll get some chops out of the deepfreeze and bake some potatoes."

Mother: "Nonsense. George can nip down to that fish

and chip place near Eaton Socon. I would have done one of my trifles, but if you ask me, he's getting a bit of a tummy."

Oh thank you. Thank you very much. George can do this, George can do that. George can't have his trifle. They seemed to forget I'd been at work all day. I was deciding whether to stalk into the kitchen and give them one of my looks, or go and sulk in the sitting room, when Mother darted into the hall with my son under her arm.

"Oh, there you are, dear. You're early, aren't you? I'm just going to put Tobias in his cot, and Clerry can watch telly. You've got to put your foot down, George, and insist that Pauline goes up for a rest. That girl's worn out. I know you won't mind, dear, I've told her you'll fetch some fish and chips and take those patterns over to Julia Mainwaring."

"I've got a migraine."

"Nice spin in the fresh air will soon put that right. Isn't it a lovely evening? Makes you glad to be alive. Come on, Toby, up the stairs to Bedfordshire."

On the way to Julia's (Mother had worked out a route plan for me. I had to go to Julia's near Kimbolton first, and return via the fish and chips so they would be nice and hot for us all. Oh, and while I was at it, Julia had promised us some mulberry cuttings), I started thinking about the Universe, and my place in it. That led to my nearly banging into a van which had stopped to turn right. So I thought about Julia instead.

David's second wife was what my mother called "one of the old kind". Quiet, well-dressed without pushing her shoulder-pads at you, and a really lovely smile. A force to be reckoned with in the business world, and she's brought up the twins beautifully. They were lovely kids, apart from their soppy names. I just hoped we'd be able to do as good a job with Clerihue and Tobias.

When I arrived at the Mainwarings' imposing country house, Julia was in the garden surrounded by several dogs.

She didn't look as well dressed as I'd remembered, though of course she was gardening. The dogs jumped up and left paw marks on my trousers.

"Down, Pippa," said Julia. "You really oughtn't to let her do that, George. Do look at my Alchemilla Mollis, isn't she doing well? Much better on a west wall, aren't we, lovey? Have you come to see David?"

"Got some boxes in the car for you. Pauline says you need them to take to London tomorrow."

"Tomorrow? I don't think I'm going to London tomorrow, am I? No, I can't be, because I've got to take Pippa to the vet, haven't I, precious?"

"I think they're needed in the Primrose Hill shop for some American buyers."

"Really?" said Julia vaguely. "You've got wilt, haven't you, my poor darling. What are we going to do about you?"

I gave Julia a sharp look. Girls will gossip, I know, but surely Pauline wouldn't . . . ?

"What do you think, George? Gardeners' Question Time says cut back to clean tissue. Someone else says Bordeaux Mixture, but I don't know . . ."

Somewhat to my relief, Julia was looking thoughtfully at a climbing plant with limp buds.

"Why not send for a white knight?" I said sourly.

"What? Do you think Madame Edward André or the President on that trellis?"

"I don't know what you're talking about, Julia. I've spent the last week listening to people talking about things I don't know what they're talking about."

For the first time since I arrived, Julia was looking at me as though I were a plant.

"Out of your depth, George? Join the club. How about a drink?"

"Well, that would be most . . ." I turned to go back to the house, but Julia marched into a nearby potting shed. She produced, from behind a row of containers labelled Phostrogen, Growmore, and other gardening terms, a plain bottle, and poured brown liquid from it into two plastic cups. I looked at it dubiously.

"It's all right, George, it's not fungicide. Alcoholics are never more than ten paces from a bottle, didn't you know that?"

"Julia! You're not a –"

"Oh, I think I am, don't you?" Knocked it back like John Wayne and poured another. "I'm sick of those women. Getting at me because I lose a few silly invitations. Asking me questions all the time. I was quite happy with my flower shop, you know. Now I'm supposed to be big business and I hate it. Emily talking about bridging loans –"

"I know what you mean," I said, taking a cautious sip. It did taste like whisky.

"And Sybilla, with her Oh, *darlings* and isn't it *fun* being on *Woman's Hour?* I didn't think it was fun, couldn't think of anything to say. Your Pauline's the only one worth a row of beans."

We were outside again and strolling along a herbaceous border. I took another swig and started to say something loyal about Pauly, but Julia swept on.

"Pauline writes music with her sleeves, you know."

"What?" I didn't understand again.

"She's Mozart with some of her seams. Now look at that, those bloody snails. Look what they've done to my hostas."

She went back into the shed and reappeared with a carton called Sluggit and the plain bottle. The contents of the carton were scattered on the ground and the bottle tipped into her cup. I wondered whether she ever got it the wrong way round? I didn't think she was quite well.

"Why don't you talk to David about it?" I said, looking for somewhere to put my plastic cup.

"David? I wouldn't use David as a mulch. Hang on, I've got some mulberry cuttings Pauline wanted. I doubt if they'll take, but there's no harm in trying."

★   ★   ★

I was standing in line at the fish and chip place wondering whether to get some scampi and sauce tartare as well, they did it excellently there. In front of me was an elderly lady, and in front of her were four youths off motorbikes. They were describing a football match in rather unnecessary terms. The old lady muttered "disgraceful" twice, and then said out loud, "If you don't mind, I don't want to listen to that kind of language while I'm waiting for my order." She looked at me for support. I pretended I hadn't heard; no sense in getting involved. As it happened, the boys shuffled their feet and one of them said, "Sorry, love, didn't see you were there," so I could have intervened, after all . . . anyway, I was otherwise concerned, mulling over what I'd heard that day.

Julia, that evening, saying, "David? I wouldn't use David as a mulch." And David in the pub after work, what was it exactly? "That's why Sybilla never has time for . . ."

I fished out my notebook and thumbed back to last May, when I overheard Peter and David talking in the Horse and Hare. Just as well I wrote it down. Peter definitely said, in a rather funny way, "Sybilla – as you know, David – has always done exactly what she wanted."

It seemed fairly obvious what Sybilla never has time for. I wondered what Pauly would say? I decided to get three portions of scampi as well as the cod and chips.

And that was a mistake, as I found when I got home. I should have got four scampi because Clerry liked them too, and where were the extra sachets of sauce tartare?

"Really, George," said Mother, "you know how mean those sachets are. Never mind, I will do without my scampi, Clerihue can have mine, can't you, pet?"

"Love Gan-Gan," said Clerihue, climbing onto her knee.

"I really don't want any," said Pauline loyally. "Just cod and chips will be masses for me. Oh lovely, the chips are all soggy."

"Nonsense, Pauline, you need building up . . ."

Mother and Pauline went on arguing about who would give up their scampi. By the time we got to the fish and chips they were cooling, and it didn't need Hercule Poirot to work out who gave up his scampi in the end.

"Probably just as well, dear," said Mother. "You are getting a bit of a tummy, you know."

As I'd had occasion to point out to Pauline in the past, there were many advantages to Mother living with us. One of the disadvantages was that I had less and less time alone with my wife. We were in bed before I had a chance to talk to her person to person.

"Do you know what I think?"

"What, George? Goodness, I'm tired."

"I have a suspicion that there might be something . . . going on between David and Sybilla. Nothing definite, just a few little hints I've picked up."

"David and Sybbo? Everyone knows about that, darling. They've been sneaking off for months."

We had to learn a poem at school by Rupert Browning, I think it was, about bringing some good news from Ghent to Aix. It was very long, and all I remember now is "I galloped, Dirck galloped, we galloped all three," and two of the horses collapsed.

Anyway, one of them got there in the end, and everyone stood round cheering. I wondered how he'd have felt if they'd said, "Ghent? So what's new, we heard about Ghent last week."

"You knew? Why didn't you tell me?"

"I suppose I just assumed you knew like everyone else," said Pauline, shuffling her pillows around. "Thanks for taking those boxes over to Julia, darling. Such a relief, I was really worn out."

"There's no guarantee the boxes will get to London tomorrow. Julia said she wasn't going to London, she was taking one of those dogs to the vet."

"What! But she's got to." Pauline sat up in bed, turned on the light and looked at the alarm clock. "Ten past eleven,

78

I wonder if it's too late to phone? Well, I'll just have to. Why didn't you tell me earlier, George?"

I contemplated saying, "I suppose I just assumed you knew," but that would have been a bit malicious. Anyway, she was dialling.

"Emily? I didn't wake you, did I? Oh, thank heavens. Listen, George took those toiles over to Julia this evening. You know, the ones for the American buyers. Apparently Julia told George she wasn't going to London tomorrow. What? I wish you and Sybbo would stop saying that. Of course she wasn't drunk, hold on . . ." Pauline looked at me over the phone "Was she, George? . . ."

I liked Julia much better than Emily Sutcliffe. I'd seen warmer things in the gateau section of Bejams, so I shook my head decisively.

". . . George says certainly not, sober as a judge. No, I'm not going to ring her at this time of night, Emily. You can. David's bound to answer, and you know how rude . . . good luck, ring me back when you've spoken."

Pauline put the phone down, and I cuddled her to me.

"Actually," I said, kissing her ear, "Julia's got a bottle of whisky in the potting shed, behind a spray for greenfly."

She wrenched herself away in an unfriendly manner.

"Don't you start, George. Everybody's getting at Julia these days. No wonder she looks such a wreck. She's always been very nice to me, she's the only one of that lot I'd really trust, and I won't listen . . ."

"She said some very funny things, too, when she wasn't addressing a hollyhock. She said your seams are like Mozart."

"She said that? Julia really said that?"

"I know. Honestly, Pauly, I didn't know where to look."

"Oh, George, don't you see? She meant . . . well, she meant I'm really good. How nice of her."

The phone rang, and Pauly snatched it up.

"Emily? . . . oh God, did he? Told you he'd be vile. So what's the position? I see. Can you take them down, then?

Are you? I'd forgotten that. OK, leave it with me. I'll think of something."

The something she thought of was me, (as if I didn't have enough to worry about, with a possible takeover looming) so I drove down the A1 at eight in the morning. Got up at six, drove over to Julia's to collect the silly boxes (why did I take them there in the first place, was what I wanted to know?) and of course Julia wasn't up, so I had to deal with David. It took me ages to locate him. Eventually I ran him to earth down in the stables.

He was not in a good mood, and nor were his four jodhpured children. What on earth were they all doing up at this hour?

"Dad, do come and look at Misty's hock. Isn't it a bit warm?"

"I'm bloody not wearing a Pony Club tie. Too squalidly hearty."

"You pig. You know those are Duchess's leathers. Give them back."

"Where's my hat? I can't find my hat. You've nicked it, Alex, you bastard, you lost yours when we went to Mrs Edmund's for stable management."

"I wouldn't wear your sweaty hat if it was the last hat on earth."

"The family's home for the hols, then?" I said cheerily.

Simon Mainwaring looked down his nose.

"Half term, actually," he said. "Dad, can I borrow one of your ties?"

"Going out horseback riding?" I persevered. "What fun."

The look on Simon's face was reproduced exactly on Alexandra's and the Mel who takes after David. The Mel who takes after Julia smiled nicely and said, "Actually we're going cubbing, Mr Jenks."

"If we ever get there," said David. "This tack room's a disgrace. A quid to whoever finds my spurs. Alex, where are those boxes of Julia's?"

"In the drinkies cupboard?" said Simon.

If he were my son I'd know what to do with him, I thought, and even David looked put out.

"No, you can't borrow one of my ties, Simon, and shut up. I must say, George, I think it's the outside of enough that you should waste the firm's time acting as errand boy for those women."

Nobody seemed to think that it was the outside of enough that David should waste the firm's time going cub-hunting. A sport, if you can call it that, of which I do not approve.

"I know where they are, Dad," said the Julia-Mel, "shall I get them? They're in the hall where Mum left them last night."

"Show George where they are, would you, darling?" said David, "and while you're at it you might bring my flask."

Melanie and I walked up to the house through the gardens. There were drops of dew in the middle of lupin leaves. I don't usually notice things like that.

"My mother will be so sorry to have missed you," said Melanie formally. She looked at me quickly and looked away again. "She's not up because she gets a bit tired. I think she went to bed quite late last night. She has a lot of work to do with the shops, you know."

"Melanie," I said.

"Yes, Mr Jenks?"

"Sometimes grown-ups . . ." You should never start a sentence unless you know how it's going to end. It was half past seven on a perfect autumn morning and I didn't know how to tell her it was going to be all right. I didn't even know if it was going to be all right.

"I hate Simon," Melanie said.

"Pain in the neck isn't he? So would you be if you had all those spots."

"How many do you think he's got? About fifty?"

"At a very conservative estimate," I said. I didn't say that adolescent acne was not what I would be worrying about if I were Simon's parents. Melanie giggled and tucked her hand under my arm.

"You are funny, Mr Jenks," she said, and I wondered, not for the first time, why I couldn't talk to adults in that relaxed way.

"I tell you what, Melanie," I said. "Pauline said last night . . . you know Pauline, my wife?" Melanie nodded. "And this is strictly between us . . . she said that your mother was the only person in Natural Sources that she really trusted."

"Mrs Jenks said that? She's awfully pretty, isn't she?"

"So if Mum is getting a bit tired, I shouldn't worry about it. There's so much going on, they're all overworking at the moment. Last night we had to have fish and chips for dinner."

"Lucky you. We had some yukky casserole that Dad got out of the deepfreeze, and it still had bits of iced beef in the middle."

Arriving at the Natural Sources shop in Primrose Hill, I reflected with some pleasure on blustering, loud-mouthed David Mainwaring making a cock-up out of defrosting a casserole.

There was no Sybilla in the shop. There was nobody in the shop except a fawn-like girl who put down the phone and gave every impression that she was about to flick back her ears and make for the undergrowth. She flinched as I plonked the boxes down on the counter.

"Lady Sybilla is expecting these," I said, "urgently."

"Oh, Sybbo isn't here, Mr . . . ?"

"Jenks."

"Jenks? Are you . . . you're not . . . *Pauline's* husband?" She said it in a way which made me wonder how Dennis Thatcher manages to look so good-humoured all the time.

"Pauline is my wife, yes. About these clothes. I was told they are needed urgently for American buyers, and if they aren't, I wonder why I got up at –"

The fawn relaxed. "Oh right, they're for this afternoon. I say, Mr Jenks, is Eaton Square on your way?"

"Not really, no. I'm going straight –"

"Only that was Sybbo on the phone. Throwing a fit because Caroline's dress was left behind here last night. It's got to be at Eaton Square by ten and I daren't trust a taxi."

"Well, I'm certainly not –"

"Oh, *could* you?" For a fawn-like creature she was not very good at letting people end their sentences. "Only it's absolutely vital for Natural Sources. Sybbo and Caroline are being photographed for *Vogue*, amazing publicity isn't it, and this is what Caroline is supposed to wear."

She went to a rail and took down a creamy pleated affair with lace. Last time I saw Caroline Bolsover she had been cleaning her bike in dungarees, but I supposed girls grow up quickly these days.

"There's nowhere to park in Eaton Square," I said feebly.

"You're bound to find a meter this early, oh, you are kind."

Fairly typical, I thought grimly, as I inched my way down rush-hour Park Lane, the creamy affair on my back seat ("Only you won't crush it, will you, Mr Jenks?"). I appeared to be incapable of saying no to anybody.

The fawn-like creature at Natural Sources had been right. I did find a meter in Eaton Square, though being the district it is, it only took 50p and 20p coins and I had to stop a passing woman for change.

The Bolsovers lived in a flat, but nothing like any flat I'd ever been in. The door was opened by a manservant of foreign aspect who looked at me as though I'd come to mend a telephone.

"Lady Sybilla is expecting me," I said, waving the cream dress at him.

"Ah yes, they phoned from the shop. You are Mr Mainwaring's driver?"

"Certainly not," I said. The floors were marble and pillars were scattered about. A log fire burned in a manor-house way and I didn't quite know how to explain that I was a senior executive doing a favour. I didn't have to, because Sybilla burst down some stairs into the hall.

"Pedro, you'll have to phone Primrose Hill and ask them . . . oh, thank God, George, you're here at last. That wretched girl, I told her to remind me last night. You can't trust anybody, can you?"

Sybilla was wearing a long floaty dress in blue and green that looked very nice, though Mother had always said, "Blue and green should never be seen."

"Well, I must be off," I said. "I hope the dress isn't crushed." I held it out to her, but she was already darting back up the stairs.

"Come in and have some coffee and meet everyone."

I followed her dubiously into a long dark sitting room that was crowded with cameras, people, shiny umbrellas and Caroline Bolsover in dungarees.

"Everybody, this is George, a colleague of my husband's, who has quite miraculously come to the rescue. George, Arabella Pinter-Bambury from *Vogue*, and this is Jasper Plantain, the photographer everyone's talking about. Don't look so modest, Jasper."

She didn't bother to introduce anybody else, they were only assistants. So I said "Pleased to meet you," to the room in general. I didn't think Jasper, whose name I didn't actually believe, looked modest at all.

"Caroline, darling, here's your dress at last. Thank Mr Jenks for bringing it."

I held the dress out to Caroline, who took one look at it and said, "I'll be buggered if I wear that."

There were one or two raised eyebrows. Sybilla forgot to look charming.

"*Caroline!* Where did you hear that kind of language?"

"Ernie at the garage said it when he was explaining to me about transmission fluids."

"Did he, indeed?"

Arabella Something-Something, who looked about seventeen, said, "Are you interested in engineering, Caroline?"

"I'm going to be one when I grow up, like my father."

"How marvellous to find someone of your age who knows what she's going to do. Listen, would you be photographed in that dress if you got a modelling fee?"

Caroline, whose strong Bolsover eyebrows were well in evidence, looked at her mother. "There's that Black and Decker Workmate 2," she said, "only £64, and it does –"

"There we are, then," said Arabella, taking the dress from me and handing it to Caroline, "go and put it on, love, quick as you can."

Ten minutes later I was sipping a cup of coffee and watching a photographic session.

"Lady Sybilla, could your daughter sit a bit nearer to you? Relax, Caroline, this is supposed to be fun. Cuddle into Mum a bit, OK?"

Caroline slumped bonily against Sybilla, catching her quite a nasty blow in her left breast. Sybilla winced. "Carrie, darling, do try. Think how your friends will envy you when they see . . ."

"They'll think it's puketime. When can I take this beastly dress off?"

"When we're finished. How does it look, Jasper?"

"Mmm. Bit flat. Needs an upright, something to . . ."

"How about moving that standard lamp?" said Arabella.

Jasper was looking at me in a manner I would have found quite unacceptable if there weren't so many people in the room. "Done any modelling?" he said. "Natural Sources does men's clothes, doesn't it?"

To my horror – what would Mother say? – Sybilla happened to have a sample linen suit in the flat and it happened to be my size.

"Oh, I really don't think . . ." I said.

Caroline winked at me.

"Go on, Mr Jenks, maybe you'll get a Workmate, too."

I'm not saying No again, I thought, as I changed in what I assumed was Peter Bolsover's dressing room. Why can't I ever say No? On the other hand the linen suit was very sharp indeed . . . I wondered if they'd let me keep it.

There was a knock on the door and a young woman entered without waiting for me to say "come in".

"Sit down in front of this mirror, George."

She opened a box and took out . . .

"Now wait a minute," I said, "I'm not going to . . ."

"All I'm going to do is matt out the shine. Politicians have it done all the time on telly. And perhaps just bring up those amazing cheekbones a bit."

I suddenly thought of my father, who used to make them laugh at the Dog and Fox, imitating poofters.

Nobody seemed to see anything untoward when I returned to the drawing room, and I took up my position behind the sofa on which Sybilla and Caroline were sitting.

"Now, George," said Jasper, "we want a fin de siècle look, you know the sort of thing."

"Ah."

"What Jasper means," said Sybilla, "is your clothes are from a range called Men of Empire."

"Imagine," said Arabella, "the oppressive heat of India, 1857. You are with your wife and child on a verandah. You hear the sudden cough of a tiger . . . there are shadows moving up the drive, George. Sepoys, their eyes mad with bloodlust. It is the first night of the Mutiny. What do you do?"

"I run away."

"Wouldn't we all? Seriously, 'I will die to defend my women' is what we're looking for."

"Is this all right?"

"Nice," said Jasper, "lovely, lovely, lift the jaw a bit, touch more arrogance, eyes looking *through* the lens at the Himalayas. Look at Mum, Caroline . . . er, not quite like that."

"Caroline," said Arabella, "what's so marvellous about this new workbench?"

"You can set it up anywhere, and it's got this amazing . . ."

Click click click.

Farthing Wharf
Eaton Socon

Behind the facade of a listed Victorian warehouse, a
spectacular riverside development of prestigious apartments
and town houses, each one individually designed to preserve
the original features of this superb building. Specifications
include Original Windows, Open Fireplaces, Full Gas Central
Heating, Fully Fitted Kitchen, Video Entryphones,
Luxurious Tiled Bathroom. Studio apartments from
£35,000. Three bedroomed Town Houses enjoy the benefit
of Studio and Roof Terrace, and Double Garage with Self-
Contained Flat. £75,000 to include Fully Fitted 100% Wool
Carpets and Wallcoverings of your choice.

St Neots Express,
28th November, 1985

"Where's my Nurofen?" Getting up from the breakfast
table, George started ferreting about on the dresser,
amongst neat piles of ironing (2 a.m. last night) and not so
neat piles of small garments waiting to be ironed. He had
the cross-eyed scowl of a chronic migraine sufferer who
isn't actually suffering yet, but knows that the way things
are going he very soon will be.

"It's under Toby's rattle, George." I could tell he was
going to ask for a favour because he gave me a long
reproachful look, instead of asking me why I have hidden
his Nurofen.

"A day at the golf club will do you the world of good,
Pauly," he said, "and you've always liked Sally Ponsonby.
She's just had a baby too, you know. There'll be lots for
you two girls to talk about."

Studio and roof terrace? A proper studio with space and

87

light. And, with any luck, a door with a lock on it. I dragged my eyes away from the enticing advertisement. Sally Ponsonby? "Who is Sally Ponsonby?"

"Oh really, Pauly." George took two Nurofen and washed them down with a gulp of coffee.

"You're taking far too many of those pills, George." Gloria put a plate of bacon and eggs on the table and sat down. "Don't you worry about that bit of ironing, Pauline, I'll get down to that straight after breakfast."

"Of course I'm taking too many pills." George gestured fretfully around the room. "The house is so full of kiddies' toys and ironing and bits of dressmaking there's no room to sit down, and it's not much better at work with everyone jabbering in code about white knights and leveraged buyouts. Of *course* you know Sally Ponsonby, Pauline. Married to Len. Aitcheson Burbank. Old friend of mine and he's very kindly invited us to his golf club for lunch. Promised me a few holes of golf . . ."

"Oh great. While Sally and I sit and chat." I remembered the Ponsonbys now. He, bluff, uncongenial northerner with gold cuff links so large they'd boomerang back at him if he dropped one. She, blonde, big-bosomed, as aggressively feminine as Danny La Rue. The last time we met she'd detailed her problems with au pairs – apparently she'd imported the laziest, dirtiest most ungrateful selection of girls from every country in Europe – and the grandeur of her villa in Cannes, only she pronounced it Cahn. I disliked her then and I didn't see why motherhood should transform us into soul mates. "There's no way I'm wasting my Saturday on Sally Ponsonby, George."

George bit sulkily into a piece of toast. "Len is one of my best customers, and he's being difficult about the last consignment of fanbelt idlers. Claims they were faulty. Can't afford to lose Aitcheson Burbank . . ."

Double garage with self-contained flat? George's mother out of sight, if not entirely out of mind. Even though she was being so helpful I would find her more appealing on the other side of a wall. I scanned the page for the name of the agent, decided to give them a ring. £75,000? A bit steep, but surely with George's salary and Natural Sources really taking off . . . ?

"Put down that paper, Pauly. I'm talking to you. I said I can't afford to lose Aitcheson Burbank and it's the very least you can do after I ferried those clothes back and forth."

I supposed this was not the moment to displease a Bolsover client. And he had been good about the deliveries. "Oh, very well, then."

"The trouble with you, my lad, is that you've got no consideration for others." Before Tobias was born, George could do no wrong in his mother's eyes, but she only had to take one look at Tobias to transfer all her unquestioning love from son to grandson. She pushed away her empty plate, and gave George a long critical look. "Can't you see Pauline's worn out, with the baby, and her job, and looking after this place, and now you expect her to give up her Saturdays?"

George sighed and picked up his briefcase. "What chance do I have against this monstrous regiment of women? It'll be a relaxation to discuss delivery dates with David Mainwaring. By the way, Pauly, we're out of All–Bran . . ."

"You know the way to the All–Bran shop," said his mother. "It's next door to the chemist where they sell Pampers. Bring us back half a dozen packets, will you, we're nearly out of them."

I'd never have thought I'd be pleased to see Mrs Jenks popping her head round a door, but when she arrived at the hospital, the day after I had Tobias, there was a look in her eyes which I can only describe as sisterly. I could tell by the way that George went on about Toby's dear little hands that he was alarmed by the appearance of his newly born son. And Clerry had gazed at her inanimate brother with tearful disappointment. "But he won't be able to *play*." Only Gloria Jenks had appreciated my beautiful baby.

When George and Clerry thankfully left the room, she'd bent down and kissed me. "Thank you, thank you, my dear." She was crying. I started crying, too.

"A boy," she said, fussing with my flower arrangements so I couldn't see the tears. "You are a clever girl."

I'd been smugly thinking this myself, and brooding guiltily that these primeval emotions made a nonsense of my feminist beliefs. "There's a doctor's wife in the next room," I said. "It's her fourth girl."

"So long as the baby's all right, that's what matters." We gave each other a complicit smile at the correctness of this conventional response. It was, I suppose, the first genuine smile we'd ever exchanged.

I'd left her at home with the babies, she seemed to have forgotten that she was frail. Eight hours to Toby's next feed, we were weaning him onto the bottle. That gave me plenty of time to think about stock for the proposed Covent Garden shop, take a look at the woollen shirts arriving from Bombay, even get a chance to phone that estate agent.

"I'm thinking of parking George's mother over the garage," I told Julia, showing her the ad in the *St Neots Express*.

"Good idea." She had a hand over the phone, a slightly shaky hand. Sometimes I wondered about that bottle of whisky in the potting shed. "The shirts have got as far as London Airport, Pauline. Oh, hold on a sec." She removed her hand from the mouthpiece. "I don't want to hear about climatic conditions in Bombay, Mr Basrawy." Pause. "I don't want to hear about unreasonable import restrictions, either. I want those shirts here, in my office, by tomorrow lunchtime." She put down the phone and rubbed her eyes wearily. "They'll clash with the sale if they don't get here soon. Sybilla was on the phone half an hour ago. Wants us all to be photographed for a colour supplement. Well, I'm not going to do it."

"They want to photograph us?"

"One of those features showing designers wearing their own clothes. Sybilla says the woman at the *Sunday Times* thinks it would be more amusing if all four of us were photographed lounging about in Natural Sources outfits. I don't see anything amusing about it."

Julia had been paralysed with nerves on *Look East,* from the moment when the studio manager dropped a microphone down the back of her dress, and (even I had to admit it) an embarrassment on *Woman's Hour.* The interviewer, introducing us with a light laugh to alert the listeners to the fact that this was a fashion spot rather than an in-depth sociological discussion on women's role in the 'eighties, had smiled encouragingly at Julia from behind her microphone. "And last, but certainly not least in this talented quartet – Julia Mainwaring. Julia, I believe you actually started Natural Sources?"

We'd all turned to look at Julia who rolled her eyes anxiously back at us, took a sip of her hospitality Orvieto (an unwise top-up on her lunchtime Chateauneuf du Pape) and choked. The interviewer waved her away from the round table and the eavesdropping circle of microphones, and Emily had swiftly picked up the question and fielded it while Julia coughed and spluttered in a corner of the studio.

"I'm not going to do any publicity, ever again." She looked so tense you'd think she was a national celebrity wondering how to evade searching questions about her drug problem and how long she'd been having an affair with Warren Beatty.

"You won't have to say anything, Julia. And it would be wonderful publicity for Covent Garden. It'll come out in a couple of months. Perfect timing."

"You three can do it," said Julia firmly. "Tell you what, though. I'll give Philip Johnson a ring about Farthing Wharf, if you like. He's the developer. Plays poker with David."

As it happened, I didn't have time to phone the agent or pull strings with Philip Johnson, because Emily arrived in the office after lunch with the news that Mrs Marasawa, Tokyo's token business woman, the feared and revered fashion director of Takashimaya, was seriously interested in setting up a Natural Sources shop in their Tokyo store.

"She wants an exact replica of Primrose Hill," said Emily. "I told her assistant you'd go over there and organise it."

"But I can't go to Tokyo, just like that. Toby's only four months."

"On the bottle, isn't he?" said Emily, in her crisp American way. "I had my three on the bottle by the time they were six weeks. Only way to do it if you're working."

"Well, not quite . . ." I didn't like the idea of leaving my baby so soon, and Clerry still hadn't settled down. A kitten is not, we had all discovered, a total substitute for the undivided attention of two parents and one grandmother.

"You can organise it by next week," said Emily. "It's a fantastic opportunity. If the Tokyo shop is a success she'll put Natural Sources into every Takashimaya store in Japan."

Would it be fair to ask Gloria to look after the babies? She had been looking so much better those last few weeks. And George could always help out. "I can only be away from home for a few days."

"Sure," said Emily. She agreed so swiftly that I knew I'd be off to Japan for at least a week. "You'll miss the *Sunday Times* session. Still, the three of us can make like a crowd."

"Japan?" Julia looked at us vaguely. "Tokyo? David's going there sometime soon. Can't think why."

"David and Trevor," said Emily. "Looking for a white knight. They're off in a couple of days, hoping to woo Hoshima, the Japanese competitor that's been picking up a lot of their business. I suppose they reckon they'd be better off with a hands-off management half the world away than Pitkin round the corner. They're staying at the Okura. I've booked you in there, too, Pauline."

I was thinking of remonstrating about this high-handed decision making when Julia said, "Oh, by the way, Emily, it will be two of you, two of you making like a crowd.

I've told Pauline I'm not doing any more publicity."

"Why don't we discuss it later, Julia?" said Emily, so firmly that I made a note to leave Julia the oatmeal suit with the flared jacket; the one that would conceal from the camera the fact that she'd put on three inches around the waist.

It would be simpler to drop into Sandringham for a gossip with the Queen than gain an audience with Mrs Marasawa. I'd arrived in Tokyo the previous afternoon, and was instantly over-impressed by the massed flower arrangements and food displays at Narita airport, a refreshing change from the litter motif I'd left behind at Heathrow.

A taxi had appeared instantly and whisked me to Takashimaya where I had asked for Mrs Marasawa, been shown into a large anteroom with a vast table ringed by easy chairs, and fed coffee and compliments by Mrs Marasawa's three male assistants. What an efficient country, I marvelled, no wonder they have achieved an economic miracle. Two hours later and still in the anteroom, I'd changed my mind. Working at this pace I couldn't see how they ever had two yen to rub together. .

"Please explain why you wish to see Mrs Marasawa. A little more coffee?"

"Thank you. Mrs Marasawa wishes to see me. I have an appointment with her."

"Please show letter of appointment?"

Letter of appointment unfortunately left on dresser in kitchen next to Nurofen and baby's rattle. "I'm afraid I forgot to bring the letter with me."

"Impossible to see Mrs Marasawa without letter. Mrs Marasawa very important lady."

"I, too, am very important lady." I couldn't believe it was Pauline Jenks talking like this. "Please tell Mrs Marasawa I am here."

"You are very beautiful lady," said assistant number one.

"English women all very beautiful," said assistant number two.

"Very beautiful and so young to be very important lady," said assistant number three. "Another coffee, Mrs Chenks?"

I began to think quite warmly of bluff no-nonsense Len Ponsonby who had rudely confided, over lunch on Saturday, that he fancied Sally in something with a bit of oomph to it, and couldn't imagine who bought all that ethnic rubbish we sold in Natural Sources.

"Please leave business card for Mrs Marasawa," said assistant number one, rising. Assistants two and three also rose, shook my hand courteously and bowed.

I rose as well. "I'm afraid I don't have a business card."

"No business card?" Assistant number one, shocked, took two business cards from a sheaf in his pocket and handed them to me. "Then please to write your name and company and telephone number on one card and we will endeavour to make appointment with Mrs Marasawa for tomorrow."

There was a note waiting for me in my pigeon-hole at the Okura. "8.20 p.m. Welcome to Tokyo. We're downstairs in the Teppanyaki bar. Do join us if you arrive in time. David and Trevor."

I found them sitting on high chairs around a circular hotplate, presided over by a chef in a white hat. They were wearing bibs, David, moistly sucking a large Havana, like an overweight greedy baby and Trevor, trying to give his impression of the invisible man.

"There you are, Pauline." David waved his cigar welcomingly as I came through the door, and moved to make room for me. "Come and sit down." I climbed onto the vacant seat between them. "Put on your bib. Everyone wears them, you see. Now, I've ordered the fresh prawns, Trev's going to munch on some seaweed, aren't you, Trev?"

Trevor, looking pale, was about to reply when the chef suddenly slapped a dozen live prawns onto the hotplate. I watched, with fascinated horror, as they wiggled, thrashed, sizzled and were still.

"Sadistic buggers," said David, gazing eagerly at the prawns which had been tipped onto his plate. "They only do it to upset the tourists."

"Then they've certainly succeeded in my case," said Trevor, going even paler and taking off his bib. "I don't think I'll bother with the seaweed, if you don't mind."

"Nonsense, Trev. Stay where you are. No worse than throwing live lobsters into the pot. Mustn't desert Pauline when she's only just arrived. A dozen prawns for you, my dear?" He peeled one and ate it. "I must say, they're delicious . . ."

I said I thought I'd join Trevor in the seaweed, and asked how their wooing of Hoshima was progressing.

"Splendidly, splendidly, my dear," said David.

"Not terribly well," said Trevor simultaneously.

It appeared that they had spent their first two days bowing and smiling, exchanging pleasantries and drinking coffee. "Bad form to bow lower than the boss man," said David. "Didn't know that at the beginning, of course, and Trev and I were down there on the floor, practically giving an impersonation of the Pope, until one of the little yellow chaps took Trev aside and put him in the picture."

On the third day, Mr Otsuki, the chairman of Hoshima, had politely intimated that a merger between their two great companies would be to the mutual advantage of Bolsover, Hoshima and their shareholders, not to mention forging a further link of friendship between Great Britain and Japan.

"I was cock-a-hoop, as you can imagine, Pauline. One in the eye for Jeremy Pitkin, with his bloody 22.6 per cent. So naturally, when the old boy suggested a weekend at Atami, sea view, hot springs, delightful hotel run by a *charming* geisha he knew I'd be delighted to meet . . . well, when in Rome . . . I left Trev with the paperwork and took off on the Bullet with Otsuki."

The weekend had not been a total success. "I had to keep changing my bloody shoes. There was a pair for wandering about the hotel, a pair for wearing in my room, a pair of slippers for going to the lavatory, even a special pair of wooden mules in which to fall down the steep steps into the hot spring pool. Naturally I kept putting on the wrong shoes, and this damned geisha woman insisted on crouching down and changing them."

"And was she attractive? The geisha woman?"

Trevor gave a snort of laughter.

David turned on him, dropping his last meticulously shelled prawn on the floor. "Now look what you've done, Trevor. Eighty-four if she was a day. Served bacon and eggs in my room for breakfast, and I was ready for it, I can tell you, after a night on a hard mattress on the floor. Bloody woman kept bowing to me as she laid the table, a humble crouch for each knife, fork and plate, and by the time I got to the grub – cross-legged because the table was only inches from the floor – the bacon had congealed and the egg was cold. I don't know why you find it so funny, Trevor, you weren't exactly laughing fit to burst in the karaoke bar last night."

"The karaoke bar was a fitting end to an unfortunate day," said Trevor. "After Mr Otsuki had virtually promised to acquire 32 per cent of Bolsover and, in the event of a rival offer from Pitkin, throw an extra £5 million into the war-chest, he started making provisos . . ."

"Wanted all his johnnies on our board," said David. "Wanted to democratise the canteen – can you imagine settling down to a lunchtime chop next to Geraghty? Wanted us all doing bloody gymnastics in the car park . . ."

"Now you're exaggerating," said Trevor, "but he did speak eloquently of the Japanese style of management. I rather gathered from one of his directors that it would be a loss of face if we were not to concede to some of his requests."

"And what about my loss of face?" said David. "I don't see why these Orientals should have the prerogative on face-saving."

"Yes, you did share that thought with Mr Otsuki over the saki at lunch, David," said Trevor, "with the result that he explained another intriguing facet of Japanese business . . ."

"Said he couldn't give me an answer until he'd carried out a referendum of the whole company," said David. "Have you ever heard anything so damn silly? Taking the charlady aside and saying, 'We're discussing the possible acquisiton of a 32 per cent stake in a Midlands-based light engineering firm, Mrs Faruda. Would you consider it a possible target for our area of business or can you identify an alternative sector for future expansion?'"

"I think everyone recognises that it's just a form of words," said Trevor. "The work force vote the way the president wants them to vote. And if, at the end of the day, they come out with a thumbs-down, he can pass on the bad news without any personal embarrassment."

"Without loss of face, you mean?"

"Exactly," said Trevor. He had some colour in his cheeks now, and I had the impression he'd be prepared to see the deal go down the drain, and his own job with it, for the pleasure of watching David making a pig's ear of the negotiations. "And after that, it seemed wise to accept the invitation from Mr Otsuki and his board to join them for an evening's entertainment at their favourite karaoke bar."

"A few jars after a hard day's bargaining seemed like a sound plan," said David. "Didn't realise, of course, what they got up to in those karaoke places . . ."

"More geishas?" I was enjoying this glimpse of the Bolsover directors at play.

"Simpering women behind the bar, if that's what you mean," said David. "They sing, Pauline."

"How jolly. Just like a sing-song in the pub."

"Nothing at all like a sing-song in the pub," said Trevor. "Each businessman is expected to give a solo and, like everything else in Japan, it's actually rather competitive. As a courtesy to us, Mr Otsuki who, I admit, has rather a fine voice, kicked off with 'D'ye Ken John Peel', and his board of directors followed, in order of importance, with

'Ilkley Moor B'aht 'At' and other old British favourites."

"Put us right in the soup," said David, "Trev and I having very few Japanese ditties in our repertoire. Trev produced some Polynesian love song . . ."

"Actually, a Korean folk song," said Trevor, looking rather pleased with himself.

". . . and the only thing I could think of was *The Mikado*."

"David sang 'Three Little Maids from School are We'," said Trevor. "In a Japanese accent. It was very moving."

We went to bed early. "Another day, another dollar," said David, his optimism recharged with a double Remy Martin and a lager chaser.

That was my first business trip abroad and, flying home, I decided that it had been a definite success. Mrs Marasawa, a formidable fifty-year-old with a professional smile and steely eyes, had agreed to give the Natural Sources boutique a prime position on her fashion floor. She had approved the projected shop design and the capsule collection I'd brought with me, and given me a half hour lecture on stock control which I ached to pass on to the merchandising director of every British store.

Communication had been stilted at the start of our meeting, with each word having to be translated by number one assistant.

"Please tell Mrs Marasawa that for our Spring collection we will be majoring on linen separates in gradations of yellow."

"Mrs Marasawa say yellow not suitable for Japanese. Please suggest alternative colour."

When I'd asked about sizing, Mrs Marasawa had spoken for about five minutes, with many a courteous smile and nod in my direction.

"Mrs Marasawa say Japanese lady very small," said number one assistant.

"Nonsense." Mrs Marasawa brushed him aside with a flick of the wrist. "I was explaining, Mrs Jenks, that although the average Japanese woman is much smaller than her European counterpart, we have a preponderance of sizes six and eight, the shape of her figure is intrinsically different and we would have to supply you with sample patterns."

"Pretending they don't speak English is another of their inscrutable tricks," said David, that evening. "Otsuki pulled that one on us, too. Gives them a negotiating advantage, time to think."

I'd left David and Trevor setting off for yet another meeting with Hoshima. Mr Otsuki was still waiting for the considered view of his work force. "He keeps bowing and smiling and saying 'tomollow, tomollow,'" said David. "We could damn near afford a management buy out with the money we've spent in this hotel."

George had always been discreet about Bolsover's boardroom strategies – I was not sure he totally understood the subtler financial machinations – but I'd gathered from Emily that when David and Trevor had tried to raise money for a management buy out they'd been turned down by two finance houses, three venture capital companies and David's golfing partner, Mr Ray Brooks, branch manager of the Nat West in Huntingdon.

Undeterred by this, David had phoned Emily when he heard that we were looking for a loan to capitalise the new Covent Garden branch. "Take my advice and get on to Ray Brooks in Huntingdon. Sound chap. Just mention my name."

Fortunately, Emily ignored the advice and went straight to the top, to the regional executive director at Nat West's head office, toting a folder stuffed with current and forward budgets, cash flow projections and a comprehensive business plan.

She'd returned with a substantial loan and an appealingly low interest rate. "The City's aching to give away money if you give them the right package," she'd told us at our last board meeting. "What's more, they'd be interested in backing a franchise scheme when the time's right."

Finishing my lunch – such fun, like playing shops, with all those mini packages of biscuits and cheese and butter – I put on my earphones and settled down to watch Dudley Moore being manic in a mindless American comedy. With Takashimaya practically in the bag it looked as though the time would be right any day now.

I arrived home to find Gloria, Clerry and Stripey watching television, Tobias gurgling happily in his carrycot at their side. A reassuring domestic scene. There were piles of messages – Stripey was due for a flu injection, Mr Basrawy wanted precise figures on the striped cotton shorts, Sally Ponsonby would like me to be on her charity committee (no, thank you) and, in the middle of them all, "Ring Mr Johnson re Farthing Wharf."

It was five twenty-five. He'd be closing in five minutes. I dashed into the dining room and dialled his number.

"Mrs Jenks? I'm so glad you called. Julia Mainwaring asked me to hold one of the houses for you. They're selling as fast as we can get them on the market, but as you're a friend of Julia's . . . You'll want to see it, of course."

I made an appointment to visit Farthing Wharf first thing the following morning. Early, so George could come, too. I suppose I should have waited, and talked to him first, but I was sure he wouldn't mind me mentioning it to Gloria . . .

Taking the copy of the *St Neots Express* with the ad in it into the sitting room, I waved it excitedly at the group in front of television.

"Very nice, dear," said Gloria, taking off her spectacles and holding the newspaper close to her nose.

"The thing is . . . I'm thinking of moving there. Look, there's a studio for me and you could have a self-contained flat . . ."

Gloria read slowly through the particulars, nodding approvingly at the Fully Fitted Kitchen ("That'll be handy . . .") and the Video Entryphone ("Can't be too careful these days . . .") until she got to the price. "£75,000? Isn't that rather expensive?"

"Well, I was going to . . ." Was going to ask her if she'd like to chip in . . . but maybe she was saving her house money for a nursing home?

I'd never been very good at warm gestures, but found myself sitting on the sofa between Gloria and Clerry and impulsively taking Gloria's hand.

"How *are* you, Gloria? Really?"

She withdrew her hand, looked at me doubtfully. "Never better, Pauline."

"But . . . I know you haven't been well. You probably didn't want to worry me."

"Not well?" She was affronted. "My dear Pauline, I've never had a day's illness in my life."

Something internal? A matter of months? Surely that was what George had said? Oh well, in that case . . .

"What I was going to suggest is that maybe you could spare a few thousand? From the sale of your house, I mean."

"Of course I would, my dear, but I haven't a bean."

"But . . . ?"

"Excuse me a minute, Pauline." She got up and switched off the *News*, where some Israelis and Palestinians were busy shooting each other. "*Not* a suitable programme for little minds. The money, dear? But I gave it all to George. Months ago."

LEADING LADIES

Something is happening to power dressing. Women at the top these days are saying No to Die-Nasty shoulders, the Challenging Skirt and Look-at-Me jewellery; Yes to fragile fabrics, the faint fragrance of English hedgerows and a beguiling air of helplessness. Warning to up and coming young city thrusters (male); next time she snatches that account from you, you're liable to find you're carrying her briefcase for her.

Arabella Pinter-Bambury investigated six of the steeliest brains that conceal themselves behind froth and frills. *Jasper Plantain* took the photographs.

This page: Lady Sybilla Bolsover, guiding light behind the phenomenally successful Natural Sources fashion group, pensive in her Edwardian-shadowy Eaton Square sitting room. Lady Sybilla, whose dictum is 'Good brains don't always come in pin-stripes' makes her point tellingly in swathes of palest green and blue silk, suggesting the underwater world of Ondine, (£375, Natural Sources) with silk evening slippers – these ethereal ladies wear nothing so down-to-earth as shoes – dyed to match. Her jewellery, well-bred, diffident pearls with a gleam of green jade, from a selection at Butler and Wilson, Fulham Road.

Ten year old Caroline Bolsover, who wants to be an engineer, prefers this pleated dress in silk tussore (£59.95 from Natural Sources Growing Up range) to dungarees. 'Mummy's right,' she says, 'I like to look pretty even if I am thinking about gear ratios.'

Their protective companion, every frail woman's vital accessory, sports a gentlemanly linen suit from the 'Men of Empire' project. 'Neimann Marcus is thinking of doing His and Her Natural Sources,' says Lady Sybilla wistfully. We would wager there is nothing wistful about the way she calculates profits.

Vogue, **January, 1986**

N ow that Pauline's calling Mother Gloria, and they tell each other things, Mother's attitude has not been all I could ask for.

"I am going to speak my piece, George, like it or not," she said to me in November when we first contemplated buying the warehouse development at Eaton Socon. "Pauline has spoken to me about Money."

"She shouldn't have done that, Mother. You know I take care of every –"

"Why didn't you tell her all my money was in your account?"

"I did, I think. Yes, now that you mention it, I'm sure I must have mentioned it."

"No wonder she kept on looking at me in a funny way whenever housekeeping was mentioned. How could you let her think I was living off you all this time? Anyway, I want that money back. And another thing, George, Pauline seems to be under the impression that I'm delicate. I might lose a few pounds, now that I'm going to be more involved in Pauline's business, but apart from that I'm as fit as a fiddle."

"Involved in Pauline's business? Mother, I think you should think very carefully before you invest."

"I didn't say anything about investing. I am planning to take driving lessons and buy a little car so I can help with deliveries. I won't have so much time for cooking, of course. Pauline and I were thinking we might have to get someone in. Perhaps you can help a bit more, now that you're going to lose your job."

It seemed she had joined the extensive band of people who knew more about the takeover than I did. I found her reaction rather insensitive.

Pauline, I was relieved to discover, did not fly off the handle about my little white lie in a hysterical feminine manner, though she was a bit sharp.

"Only a matter of months, your *exact words*, George. How could you? And what about the money? Remember when she bought me mushrooms for breakfast before I had Tobias? I thought, '25p out of £68 thousand, big deal.' And now I feel such a swine. Why didn't you tell me, George? Why are you so secretive about money?"

I've never thought of myself as secretive, only careful. I suppose it was how I was brought up.

"Never let the left hand know what the right hand is doing," Dad used to say, "especially where the ladies are concerned." Our house was full of silences and unanswered questions. It's different for Pauline. In her house, everything always got shouted out.

I went out and bought a copy of the *Vogue* magazine, and was gazing at my picture with some pride, when Mother and Pauline and Clerihue came in.

"I say, darling, you look marvellous. Doesn't Daddy look handsome, Clerry?"

"Why can't I have a dress like that little girl's?" said Clerry.

Mother picked up the magazine and studied it carefully. I got the impression she wasn't all that struck. I supposed she was thinking it was a bit of a come-down for a sales director to be used as an anonymous male model.

"A lot of people do it now, Mother."

"Do what?" she said sharply.

"Well, get photographed for magazines. As a matter of fact Arabella said she'd put me in touch with an agent if I wanted to do any more, and Jasper said I was a natural."

"Mmm," said Mother.

Pauline took the magazine from Mother and held it out at arm's length.

"That dress is really knock-out, though I say it myself. And I can't get over the way you look, George."

"They put something on my cheekbones."

"No, it's more than that, you look sort of . . . totally in charge. You remind me of someone, and I can't think who."

Mother closed *Vogue* briskly. "Edward Fox playing the Duke of Windsor," she said, "I saw it at once. Come on Clerry, time to help Granny lay the table."

I don't know how other people get taken over, but it all seemed a bit of an anticlimax when Bolsover's finally caved in.

Pauline flew back from Tokyo before Trevor and David.

"I'm not sure I'm very happy about all this travelling of Pauline's," I said to Mother. "Clerry and Tobias will have no sense of continuity, if this goes on."

"They've got me every day," Mother said, "and it looks as though they'll see a lot more of their father, before long."

Pauline was full of excitement after a successful deal with Madame Kama Sutra or whatever she calls herself, but apparently had found the other two rather poor company.

"Thank heavens we didn't come back on the same plane," she said. "Pair of old glooms. There I was, on my last night, trying to tell them about the Japanese franchises, and all they could talk about was *The Bridge on the River Kwai* and once a Nip, always a Nip. I gather Hoshima treated them like dust beneath their chariot wheels. George, darling, I'm afraid poor old Bolsover's have just about had it, you know."

Just because she'd been to Tokyo, she thought she knew everything about the business world.

"Of course I know," I said, "I am on the board, Pauline."

"Yes, but . . . I get the impression the board is sort of . . . pretending Pitkin isn't really there, that if they keep their eyes closed long enough the takeover will go away. Emily says it's only a matter of days, she's quite worried about what Trevor's going to do. Of course, you'll be all right, darling."

"Why will I be all right?"

"Well, I'm earning so much now, and it'll be lovely for the children to have you at home all day."

It was only a few days after that that it was all in the *FT*; Bolsover's Falls to Pitkin Bid, etc, etc.

Saves the shop floor clustering round the central heating pipes, I thought, as we gathered in the boardroom for our last meeting. I couldn't exactly see why we were having a meeting at all, until Peter Bolsover started speaking.

"I think we all knew what was going to happen," he said, "and now it has happened, I wanted to take the opportunity to thank you all for your unremitting hard work and loyalty."

Trevor and I modestly looked down our noses. David

lit a cigar. Unremitting, I thought, that's one way of putting it. The first Peter Bolsover's eyes bored into my shoulder blades. I was sitting right under his portrait, and I sort of felt that if I turned round the portrait would say something bluff and Yorkshire about sending a boy to do a man's work.

"All water under the bridge now, Peter," David said. "We did what we could, and –"

"If you wouldn't mind, David, I would like to . . . well, make a personal statement. I am very aware . . . as chairman of the board I feel . . . I suppose what I'm trying to say is I'm sorry. The responsibility lies with me."

"I think I'm speaking for the rest of us," said David, not bothering to look at me and Trevor, "when I say that, wherever our paths take us, I personally will never forget your, I think I'm not going too far in saying, your courageous admission –"

"David, do you ever stop and listen to yourself?" Trevor said. I looked at him enviously. "Light another cigar, why don't you, the company's paying. If you hurry you might be able to put another pair of Purdeys down on expenses before Pitkin's accountants start asking questions."

"Now look here, Sutcliffe –"

"Don't you Sutcliffe me, David. I'm the one who knows how the money was spent, remember. Well, most of it. Boxes at Ascot, vast great *barges* at Henley, all those seats at Wimbledon. And let's not forget how fervently we patronised the Promenade Concerts just in case some non-existent buyer from Dresden dropped in on the chance of hearing the Fourth *Brandenburg*. All so that David Mainwaring could stuff himself with smoked salmon without actually having to foot –"

"I'm not taking any more of this," said David, getting up and striding over to the window. "If you think that . . . good God, I don't believe it. Peter, isn't that . . . ? They aren't wasting any time, are they? Pretty poor form, wouldn't you say?"

We clustered round the window and watched a Rolls Royce saunter to a halt. Jeremy Pitkin got out accompanied by two men who gave the impression of regularly exceeding the speed limit on motorways.

"What a shower," said David, "look like double-glazing merchants. Suppose we'll have to have them up, Peter?"

"Since they now own the building and everything in it, we'd look rather foolish if we did anything else." He picked up the phone. "Front desk, please. Ah. Would you be good enough to show Sir Jeremy and his cohorts up to the boardroom, please? Yes, right away."

We sat down in our places. I couldn't think of anything to do while we were waiting, so I drew a really excellent picture of a horse standing in a field. I had to make the grass quite long, because I couldn't remember how their legs go at the bottom. By the time I'd drawn a tree for the horse to stand under, the Pitkin party was in the room.

"Good morning, Jeremy," said Peter, "and . . . ?"

"Morning, Peter . . . Luke Favell and Tim Wright. Only fair to warn you they're smarter than they look, ha ha. Dave! How are you? By the by, if you're thinking of selling that new grey . . ."

"No I'm not," said David, "and if I was, he's got far too good a mouth to be wasted on you."

"Always shoots from the hip, our David. Luke, Tim, I'm sure you know Peter Bolsover, David Mainwaring, Trevor . . . er, Sutcliffe and . . ." he looked enquiringly in my direction. Typical he didn't know my name.

"George Jenks. Our sales director," said Peter.

"Of course," said Sir Jeremy. "Well, Peter, no sense in prolonging the agony, is there? Keep it all amicable, that's the way. What?" He bent towards one of his cohorts, who muttered in his ear. "Really? You think that's . . . ? Oh well. Frightfully sorry, Peter, but we feel that your presence, er, not strictly according to protocol apparently. Anyway, I'm sure you'd rather –"

Peter stood up. I thought he was looking at me, at first, then I realised he was focusing over my head. If the first

Peter Bolsover looked contemptuously at me, how would he be looking at his grandson?

"Of course," Peter said, "I should have thought of that for myself. Good morning, gentlemen."

He moved towards the door. It's funny how sometimes you don't know you're going to do something until after you've done it.

There I was standing up and saying, "If Mr Bolsover is leaving, I would like to be excused, too." I gathered up my papers ("Clerry will like that drawing," I thought, "I'll show it to her tonight,") and followed Peter out of the room. I looked at David and Trevor, but they didn't catch my eye. I was rather pleased with the stand I had made; I only wished it hadn't sounded as if I was back at school asking to go to the lavatory.

I told Pauly all about it when I got home. "So I suppose you've got a jobless husband," I said. "I knew it was going to happen . . . but when it does, you feel a bit sick."

"I think it was marvellous, what you did. Trust David and Trevor to sit there, hoping they could smarm their way in. What did Peter say?"

"We looked at each other in the corridor and he said, 'I take that very kindly, George. Not that I'm surprised. Could always depend on you.'"

"Oh George. It makes me want to cry."

"Well, and then he said: 'Tell you what, I've been saving a half bottle of Cliquot. Come on let's drown our sorrows and to hell with the bastards.' So we sat there in his office knocking back champagne out of really beautiful glasses. He saw me admiring mine and said, 'Old Waterford. Another successful purchase of my grandfather's. He'd have been proud of me today, wouldn't he, George?'

'I saw you looking at his portrait,' I said. 'If it could have spoken I bet it would have said, 'My grandson's the only gentleman in the room.' We'd opened a second half bottle by then, Pauly, so I was a bit . . . Oh God, and then he started talking about Sybilla."

"Does he know about her and David?"

"Her and David, her and a ski instructor, her and Jasper Plantain –"

"*What?* That photographer?"

"Apparently. Though I must say, I wondered if he'd got it right. I thought he was a bit of a poofter, myself. Did you know Sybilla wants to sell the Hall and move permanently to London? Peter says she feels that now Natural Sources has got so big she ought to be in the centre of things."

"In the centre of things like a spider in the centre of her web. Did you notice, in that *Vogue* piece, not a word about me? I only design the clothes, that's all. Not a word about Emily, organising massive financial back-up. Not a word about Julia, who God knows is doing her best. We're all minions as far as Sybilla is concerned."

"And then at the end, Pauly, we walked down to the car park together and he said . . ."

"What, darling?"

"He said, 'Sorry to have burdened you with all that, George. Do me a favour and forget it. The trouble is . . . well, one gets a bit lonely, doesn't one?' And off he drove. Look what he gave me." I took the Waterford glass out of my pocket. "He said his grandfather would have wanted me to have it. I don't think he was quite himself, Pauline, otherwise why would he have said that?"

A week after my conversation with Peter I went into the office to clear my desk and drop off my formal letter of resignation.

"Should I take the glass with me on the off-chance of seeing Peter? I ought to give it back, oughtn't I?" I'd asked Pauline.

"I don't think you can. It would hurt his feelings."

"I wouldn't like him to think I took advantage, Pauline."

"Of course he won't, darling. Off you go and get it over with."

Peter wasn't around, anyway. Nor were a lot of other people.

Ron Taylor from the car park, for one. I wasn't all that set on him, actually, but at least he didn't wear jeans and call me Squire.

"Can't park there, Squire" said this lout, "can't you read, or what? That's Mr Makepeace's nitch. The sales director. Reps park over there in the Visitors' section."

"I'm not a rep, actually. I am an ex-member of the board."

"Unless your name's on my list you're going to have to –"

"Oh, never mind," I said, "I'll put it in the Visitors."

Marcia dropped in to see me when I was sorting out my desk.

"Brought you some cardboard boxes to put things in, George. (No more Mr Jenks, I noticed, not even Mr J. I liked George better, anyway.) Got a lot to clear, have you?"

"Most of it's junk. I don't care if I never see another Farnsworth Foods at Your Convenience calendar, for starters." I took it down and dropped it in the WPB.

"I'm working for David Mainwaring now, did you know?" said Marcia. "Right old –"

"I knew Miss Nelson had left. David won't be working here for long, will he?"

"He thinks he's going to sit on the right hand side of God. Pitkin has other ideas. Strictly between us, they're going to give David the heave-ho at the next board meeting. Hey, what's all this about old Nelly Nelson working for your wife?"

"She has taken a position with Natural Sources, yes. Pauline says she's extremely capable."

"Wonders will never cease. So what are you up to these days?"

"Taking a bit of a rest, Marcia. Seeing a lot of my children, and so forth."

"Seeing a lot of your children won't bring in the shekels."

Marcia always had a tiresome tendency to go straight to the point, especially when the point was not a particularly attractive one.

"Actually, I've got one or two things in mind . . ."

"Everyone out of work always says that."

I took down a framed photograph of myself with several flushed men at a Rotary dinner, no more of those, thank heavens, and dropped it into one of Marcia's cardboard boxes.

I hadn't seen Roger Makepeace since 1983, when I was made sales director at Bolsover's and he left for Pitkin Industries, a sharpish move as it turned out.

He was parking his car in the sales director's space that used to be mine.

"How's the world treating you, George?" he said, rather tactlessly I thought, as my arms were full of relics of my commercial life. "Have you got time for a drink?"

"All the time in the world, Roger," I said, stowing my belongings in my car.

We settled at a quiet table in the Lord Salisbury.

"Do you remember the last time we had a drink here?" he said, ordering a Bloody Mary (him) and a half of Mild (me).

"After old Clement Bolsover's funeral," I said, "long time no see, Roger."

"Sorry about Bolsover's, and all that."

"All's fair in love and war, I suppose."

"Of course, we knew all about David and Trevor toddling off to the land of the little slit-eyed men to unearth a white knight. Yellow knight, you might say . . ."

I did not smile.

". . . sorry, bad taste. Wasted their time, we could have told them. Hoshima UK were never interested in investing yet more lolly in spare parts manufacture. We're supplying them, tied the deal up months ago."

He took a swig of his Bloody Mary. "And how about you, George? Anything on the agenda?" He was kindly going to offer me a job, which I didn't really want. Nice chap, though.

"I remember you as the only salesman who was as good as me, George. Better, probably. What would you think about coming back as regional sales manager?"

Not a lot, as it happened, though it was nice of him to ask.

"Nice of you to ask, Roger. How about the other half?"

"If you insist. I don't know what you're thinking of doing, George. But you'll be wasted if you're not selling. Your legendary North-East figures . . ."

"Let me tell you something, Roger. I hate selling. Oh, I was all right on the road, unloading nuts and bolts and bits and pieces. Then they made me sales director – should have been you – and I had to sell concepts, ideas, visualisations. Couldn't do it, Roger. Didn't know what they were talking about half the time. Anyway, strictly between you and me and the gatepost, I've got something in mind."

Pauline was rather impressed when I told her that Roger Makepeace wanted me on the team.

"Really? I say, that's flattering. What as?"

"He didn't say, exactly. Something pretty high up, though. Anyway, I told him I wasn't interested. I'm thinking seriously about this modelling lark, Pauly."

"Mmm. You'd get awfully bored in the long run."

"I got awfully bored playing golf with Geoff Farnsworth. Anyway, I'm going to ring Arabella for the name of that agent."

When it came to the point, I didn't like to ring Arabella Pinter-Bambury for the name of an agent. I picked up the telephone several times – waiting until Pauline and the children were out of the house – and then put it down again. When you got down to it, what exactly was I going to say to her?

"Oh, good morning, Miss Pinter-Bambury. I don't know if you remember, but we met at Lady Sybilla Bolsover's in Eaton Square." She wouldn't remember, of course, and

I would have to say, "I was the one in the 'Men of Empire' suit . . . and I hoped it wasn't an imposition, but I would be most grateful if . . ." Anyway, I'd have to speak to her secretary first, and I could just imagine how secretaries on *Vogue* sounded.

Easier, really, to find my own agent. I looked up the yellow pages for London, W. I. in the library. All the names sounded alarming. Top Models? I surely wasn't ready for that quite yet, nor anything International. Most of them seemed to be run by women with bossy names; in the end I picked one called Reginald's, with an address near Baker Street Underground which would be quite handy if things worked out.

Reginald sounded cautious when he answered his phone.

"I only represent professionals, Mr Jenks. Unless you've done work of this kind before . . ."

"I certainly have," I said, "quite a lot, actually."

"Oh, well then. Having trouble with your present agent, are you? Who are you with?"

"I'd really rather not . . ."

"Say no more. A nod's as good as a wink to a blind horse. You won't have any problems of that kind with *us*, Mr Jenks. When can you drop in and see me?"

"I'm up in London on Thursday. Perhaps the morning?"

"Ten-thirty suit you? Right, see you then."

It was all fitting in very well, apart from the fact that I didn't quite understand everything Reginald said. Thursday afternoon I was due at an address in Spitalfields to pick up garments from one of Mr Basrawy's cousins who was in charge of Making-Up. So I could legitimately go to London without Pauline asking me why I was going. Or, for that matter, Mother asking me why. Or Clerry. The three of them sounded like the FBI sometimes.

I drove up in my office Rover, which still seemed to be at my disposal; I wondered whether I ought to mention it to anyone. "Let sleeping dogs lie," said Mother, and Pauline said, "Perhaps it's part of your golden handshake."

I was relieved to find that Reginald's office was in a very
respectable street, and surprised to find that there were no
very big glossy photographs of models in his waiting room.
It was a bit like waiting for the dentist, reading "How to
Improve your Word-Power" in old *Reader's Digests*. I was
just about to switch to *Country Life*'s description of the East
of England Show of 1981, when a young woman came in,
looked me up and down in a pert manner, and said that
Reggie would see me now.

Reggie was very affable.

He threw himself back in his chair and looked at me
through narrowed eyes. His face was rather sallow.

"Yes," he said, "oh yes. You're what . . . six foot?"

"Six two, actually."

"You've no idea how difficult it is to get tall men these
days. You'd think with the Health Service and wheatgerm
bread we'd be breeding giants. You'd be wrong. The
number of shrimps I have to turn away, nice boys, nothing
wrong with them, but you can't look masterful if your
eyes only come up to her elbows. Look at me as though I
was a woman."

"Er . . . couldn't I look at your secretary as though she
were a woman?"

Reginald laughed merrily.

"Quite right. Never put up with imitations when the
real thing is to hand." He pressed his intercom. "Susannah,
lovekins, spare us a moment of your valuable time, would
you?"

I looked at Susannah as though she was a woman, and
Reginald became even more affable.

"I like it," he said, "that damn-your-eyes upper-class
look, it speaks to me. Modern version of the duke and the
dairymaid. Tell you what, Suze, he'd work well with
Daisy."

"Thinking just that myself," said Susannah.

"Right," said Reginald, "a short talk about terms."

He mentioned some figures which sounded quite flattering. Even when you took into account his commission,

which as far as I could make out was twenty-five per cent.

"Possibly a wee mite higher than some other agencies," said Reginald, "but you will appreciate . . ."

"Oh, well of course," I said urbanely.

"Well, that seems to be that. Except for the sixty-four thousand dollar question, but we're all boys here, aren't we? The old equipment . . . in full working order, and all that?"

"The old equipment?" I said, "Do you mean . . . do I have to bring my own cardigans?"

"Your own cardigans," said Reginald, "your own *cardigans*!"

He looked at Susannah. "Does he have to bring his own cardigans, Suze?"

"I suppose it's a variation," Susannah said. "When you get down to it, riding breeches are getting quite run-of-the-mill. Cardigans. How about the absent-minded professor and the new young laboratory assistant? Daise in a white coat and spectacles, I can see it."

"I just thought that in this game," I said, congratulating myself on sounding quite knowledgeable, "you sort of started with knitting patterns and worked your way up."

Reginald sighed and looked at Susannah.

"Mr Jenks," he said, "I think it might save us both a certain amount of time if I showed you some stills of the kind of work my clients regularly undertake."

Reginald showed me some stills of the kind of work his clients regularly undertook, and I left.

"Could I speak to Arabella Pinter-Bambury, please?"

"Hang on. Chloe, is Bells around? Hang on, she's here somewhere. I do wish you wouldn't put your coffee mug on my schedules, Dave; they're all brown rings – it's so unprofessional. Phone for you, Bellsie."

"Hullo?"

"Oh, er, Miss Pinter-Bambury, you won't remember

me, but we met when you were interviewing Sybilla Bolsover."

"George! How are you?"

"Well, not really very –"

"You were going to ring me for the name of an agent. I've mentioned you to one or two people and they're rather interested. Where are you?"

"Baker Street. I've just had the most terrible . . . I picked an agent from the yellow pages, Arabella . . . we seemed to be at cross purposes, rather . . ."

"Tell you what. I'm just nipping out for cottage cheese on rye, yuk, but it keeps the arteries happy. Join me, why not? The Granary in Albermarle Street in twenty minutes suit you?"

It took me twenty-five minutes to look up Albemarle Street in the A to Z, (I had prudently parked my car in an underground warren before my appointment with that dreadful man), get myself onto the Jubilee Line, and arrive at Green Park. Platforms a disgrace, I noticed, and only one of the ticket machines worked. Also there were young men in the corridors playing musical instruments in a sullen way. And no station staff moving them on. My father would have had a fit.

Cottage cheese and rye, I realised when I joined Arabella, was a mere figure of speech. She was standing in front of a counter loaded with steaming dishes.

"You look harassed, George," she said, giving me a quick kiss as though we'd known each other for ages. "Help me decide . . . lasagne or paella? And do look at that moussaka, heavenly. Why do you make life so difficult?" she said sternly to the young man behind the counter.

He grinned. "I think you had the paella last time."

"Right. It's the moussaka, then. What about you, George?"

"Paella, please, it's never the same when you make it at home."

I tried to pay for us both, but Arabella said that we'd go

halves; "Why should you buy me lunch? I'm the one who's working at the moment."

Why wasn't I offended, like I was when Mother and Marcia talked to me about not earning?

We went downstairs and sat at a table for four, opposite two girls. Between them they probably weighed about fourteen stone and were busily putting away vast portions of a sweet that looked exceptionally fattening.

"Now," said Arabella, lunging eagerly at her moussaka, "mmm, gorgeous . . . now what happened with this agent you went to? You sounded a bit hassled on the phone."

"It was all rather unfortunate. I had no idea, of course."

"What? Noisy in here, isn't it? Which agent did you try?"

I lowered my voice. "Called Reginald's. Really quite disgraceful these places should be allowed to –"

"Reginald's?" Arabella's voiced trilled effortlessly over the surrounding conversation. "Porn videos? Whatever made you go there, George?"

The girls opposite stopped saying "I wasn't going to have any of *that*, thank you very much," to each other, and stared at me.

"I didn't know, did I? I told you – just picked him out of the yellow pages."

"What a hoot," said Arabella. "What did he say, exactly?"

"It wasn't a hoot at the time. The degradation . . . I feel quite soiled. Offering me money to take my clothes off."

Arabella put down her fork and gave me a forthright gaze. "Do you ever look at Page 3 girls, George?"

"We take the *Guardian*, actually. But of course I do occasionally . . . what man doesn't?"

"And you don't think that's degrading?"

"Quite different. That's just being normal."

"You've got a right one there," said the girl opposite Arabella.

"Not his fault, brainwashed from birth like the rest of

them. So it's morally OK, is it, for you to say, 'Nice pair of Bristols?'" I did wish she'd lower her voice, "but morally degrading for you to drop your –"

I jumped in desperately. "It's only natural for men to want to look at –"

"You know what my boss said to me today?" said the girl opposite me, "'Like your dress, Mandy, certainly shows you off to advantage.' Don't have to tell you where he was looking." I looked there myself, and hastily dropped my eyes to my paella. "I've just about had it with the old goat and his, 'If only I were twenty again', he should be so lucky. So I said, 'more than I can say for your trousers, Mr Framlingham; you ought to speak to your tailor.' And he gave me one of those looks."

The other two nodded knowledgeably.

"Like you'd just told him Jesus Christ cheats at cards," said Arabella.

"Right. So he said, 'We don't care for personal remarks of that nature round here, Mandy.' So I said, 'Just as long as we all remember that, Mr Framlingham. If you want those letters to catch the lunchtime post, hadn't you better start dictating?'"

"But," I said, "won't he fire you for answering him back like that? Not that I can't see your point," I added hastily, wishing I hadn't put it quite like that. The three girls looked at me as though I were mad.

"Can't, can he? She'd have him at a tribunal for sexual harassment, wouldn't she?"

"I seem to have found myself in quite a little nest of feminists," I said jovially. But apparently that was wrong, too.

One thing you can say for Spitalfields, I thought when I eventually found it (miles from anywhere I'd ever been before, and looked like a suburb of Calcutta), the women do seem submissive and feminine in their saris. Not like that trio of viragos I'd found myself lunching with.

"Really, George," said Arabella when the other two had

flounced off, "it's time you realised that one doesn't have to be Betty Friedan to resent being a sex-object."

"I don't see why it's rude to call people feminists," I said, toying with the idea of asking who Betty Friedan was, and deciding not to bother.

"Conjures up such a humourless vision, that's why. Like my ghastly sister. Hey, don't you live in St Neots?" I nodded. "Coincidence. That's where she's currently shacked up. Avoid her like the plague."

"I'm sure any sister of yours . . ." I said gallantly.

"Divorced, two hideous brats, boy not potty trained at three in case he develops guilt feelings about the urino-genital tract . . ." I looked round uneasily, but nearly everybody else had gone by now, ". . . and a girl of six who learnt with her alphabet that All Men are Rapists. Not that she's actually learnt the ABC, of course, far too middle-class ritualistic. God help the children Amanda teaches, is all I can say."

"She's a teacher, is she?"

"Not really, but that's what she calls herself. Must go. I've written down numbers for two agencies. Mention my name. See you, George."

I didn't have time to ring the agencies before I embarked on the long trail to Spitalfields; I'd have to do it from home when everybody was out, I thought, as I rang a grubby doorbell with "Basrawy" on a card next to it.

Nothing happened, so I pushed open the door and found myself on the threshold of a vast long room, filled with women and children rattling away on sewing machines. The loop of my macintosh caught on the doorhandle in a way which never happens to Cary Grant, and by the time I'd unhooked it and turned round again, the room seemed emptier. Out of the corner of my eye I saw two children slide out through a side door. A plump young Indian man forged towards me between the rows of sewing machines.

"Oh, really, is this quite fair?" he said. "I told your colleague last week that we were putting in motion all his requirements. But Rome wasn't built in a day, you know. You must give me more time."

"I don't know what you're talking about," I said.

"You are not, then, from the Department of Health and Social Security?"

"Certainly not," I said coldly. "I am here to collect some garments for Natural Sources."

"My dear chap," he clapped me on the shoulder, "I cannot apologise enough. A natural mistake, you will be the first to admit. Ahmet Basrawy, how do you do? They are like vultures, these DHSS people. Do you know how many square feet of working space a textile machinist must, by law, have?"

"No."

"Nor do I. They keep on sending me letters telling me. If I read them all I wouldn't have time to earn an honest living. Fire-escapes . . . they are obsessed with fire-escapes; I suppose their cousins manufacture them. Look for yourself. Doesn't my work force seem a happy one?"

"It's very hot in here," I said. "Didn't I see some children working the machines? Surely –"

Mr Basrawy's eyes glittered.

"You *are* from the DHSS. You are a spy, pretending –"

"My name is Jenks. I am Pauline Jenks's husband, and if you would be good enough to hand over the garments . . ."

Mr Basrawy kissed his fingertips and blew the kiss away in a manner which made me want to strike him. "Ah, the divine Pauline, so talented. You must tell her I have been a clever boy with the culottes. By taking out four inches of the gathers I have saved, overall, nearly five hundred metres of cotton."

Pauline won't like that, I thought as I drove wearily through St Neots. Nearly home. What a day it had been. Mistaken for a porn actor in the morning and a DHSS inspector in the afternoon, must be some kind of a – I braked sharply as one of those lunatic women drivers shot out of a side road and turned left in an erratic manner. I followed her for a few hundred yards until she turned right, in the very teeth of a lorry whose driver hooted and flashed his lights. The two girls in the back looked out of the window with their mouths open. Julia's twins.

"Hello, darling, what kind of a day?" said Pauline when I got home.

"Patchy," I said. "I say, Pauly, I nearly just got crashed into by Julia Mainwaring. Had the twins with her. You should have seen the way she was driving. If you want my opinion she was as tight as –"

"How can you be so mean, George? Julia's the last person to drink drive with the children on board."

Fashion Group director banned for drink driving

Julia Mainwaring, 47, managing director of Natural Sources, the Cambridge based fashion group, whose husband, David Mainwaring, recently retired as managing director of Bolsover Engineering (St. Neots) Ltd, appeared before the Cambridge City Magistrates Court on Thursday, March 11th on a drink driving charge.

Mr. John Earsby, prosecuting, told magistrates that Mainwaring was driving erratically down the High Street at 8.30 a.m. and failed to halt at a red light. When stopped by police Mainwaring said she had taken an aspirin and a glass of brandy before leaving home because she had toothache. An intoximeter breath test machine gave a reading of 70 micrograms of alcohol per 100 millilitres of breath. The legal limit is 35 micrograms. Mainwaring was charged with driving with excess alcohol and admitted the offence. She was fined £300, her licence was endorsed and she was disqualified from driving for eighteen months.

Cambridge Evening News, **13th March, 1986**

Things certainly changed for the better when we moved to Farthing Wharf. Gloria had her granny flat, George had his study (which he insisted on calling his den, as though he were some sort of wild forest creature), the children had a large sunny playroom and I had the best view in Cambridgeshire. And a lock on my door.

I also gave up cooking. It was not a wilful feminist decision ("You've got nothing to do all day, George, why don't you get the dinner for a change?") but an admission of feminine weakness. The new kitchen was banked with electronic controls like a space station, and all the equipment was hidden discreetly behind panelled doors, so that I kept opening the dishwasher to get out the milk and putting the dirty washing in the fridge.

A couple of weeks after we moved in, I decided to roast a joint of beef; and then decided to go out and buy a take-away chicken when the instruction manual, instead of issuing instructions about roasting on Number 4 for twenty minutes to the pound, started babbling about the unique benefits of combining Infra technology and Turbo technology.

"Let me look at it, Pauline." George took the manual firmly out of my hands. "The trouble with you is that you don't bother to read the instructions properly." He studied it intently. "I say, this oven is amazing. Do you realise you can bake and roast simultaneously on six different levels?"

I couldn't see why I'd want to perform this culinary feat, any more than I understood why the ceramic hob needed two heat zones to boil an egg or what the microwave thought about in its two-stage memory.

Once he'd mastered all the masculine stuff about thermostatically controlled variable oven heat and 0.80 cu. ft usable capacity microwave space, George opened his first cookery book surreptitiously, as though it was called *100 Amusing Ways with Whips and Manacles* rather than *The Good Housekeeping Infra Turbo Cookbook*. He didn't go so far as to conceal it in a plain wrapper but shyly hid the cover with his arms if anyone, particularly his mother, came into the kitchen and caught him with it. I noticed that he read *The Art of French Cookery* with far more concentration than he ever gave to *The Engineer*.

When Gloria rather tactlessly told him that now he had nothing much to do he could help out a bit more around the house (something I'd never have dreamed of saying, since I felt permanently guilty about having a wonderful job when George was out of work) she probably expected him to push the Hoover about once a week and produce the occasional steak and crinkle chip to rapturous applause from the womenfolk. But George, while doing very little Hoover-pushing, plunged right in at the Cordon Bleu end of cookery, marinating meat in wine and herbs, grilling fish over fennel twigs, baking his own bread.

Proudly bearing his first batch of bread, covered with a damp tea towel, up the stairs to the airing cupboard to raise the dough, he had bumped into Gloria putting away the freshly ironed laundry.

"Let me do that, George," she said, attempting to take the tin from him, but George hung on grimly.

"Leave me alone, Mother. It's wholemeal and I'm going to put cracked wheat on it."

"I suppose it's all right," she said, bringing me a cup of coffee in the studio and reporting the incident, "but it's not very manly, is it – cooking?"

I realised she had come up to be reassured that George was not about to spring out of his closet. "The best chefs in the world are men."

"That's true." She sipped her coffee reflectively. "But they don't go modelling clothes in their spare time, do they?"

"I'm sure he won't make a habit of it," I said. There seemed to be no point in worrying Gloria by telling her that George was rather taken with the idea.

He'd told me, in bed one night, (the only time and place we seemed to have time to talk to each other), that since Sybilla's fashion pictures had turned out so well he was thinking of getting an agent. "It's money for nothing, Pauly, you just stand there and look relaxed."

"And is it that easy?" I had always found it most unrelaxing being told to relax in front of cameras for our publicity pictures.

"Easier than trying to sell out-of-date freeze-drying packaging units to people who don't want to buy them," he said, taking me in his arms. "I hated it, you know, Pauly. Why are you going so stiff?"

"I'm not going stiff. I'm just a bit tired, that's all."

"You've been a bit tired ever since I left Bolsover's. Is it because I'm not a director any more, because I haven't got a job?"

"Of course it isn't."

"Well, what is it, then?" He rolled away from me. I suppose he'd had enough rejection from his clients without risking it in his own bed.

"It's nothing. There's just so much to do." I couldn't tell his dejected back that part of me had gone cold when I

124

found out about Gloria and her money. He'd paid her back, of course. The Bolsover directors, with unaccustomed efficiency, had provided themselves with healthy index-linked pensions and a spectacular lump sum when they left the firm. It was the deviousness I hated. All that lying to get 6½ per cent interest on his mother's nest egg.

I had two babies to look after, and three shops to worry about (not counting the Takashimaya boutique and Mrs Marasawa's meticulous demands). It was a relief that George had taken to the new kitchen technology with such enthusiasm.

One evening, when he had taken the children to Waitrose to hunt down sweetbreads, the front door bell went. I assumed it was Gloria. She used to barge in and out of rooms without so much as a discreet cough, but the moment she moved in to the granny flat she started behaving like a neighbour. Sometimes she even came on the telephone to ask if it was a convenient moment for her to pop round and do my ironing.

I thought I'd ask her to join us for dinner. It seemed a bit mean to let her go back to a lonely chop, when she'd kindly offered to put Clerry and Tobias to bed while I checked a vital pattern.

"Fancy Sweetbreads à la Financière for dinner tonight?" I said, throwing open the front door. But it wasn't Gloria.

"That sounds delicious," said Peter Bolsover, "but are you quite sure it's a serious invitation?"

So, of course, I had to say how delighted George and I would be if he joined us for dinner, which was true so far as I was concerned, although I wasn't sure how delighted George would be to find himself cooking dinner for his ex-chairman. In George's family real men didn't eat quiche and they certainly never cooked it. The most liberated gesture his father ever made was to put his beer glass in the sink with a "*There* you are, Gloria."

★　　★　　★

"You've seen the evening paper, of course." Peter sat on the edge of the new cream sofa, twirling his gin and tonic glass despondently.

"Not another Bolsover story?"

Ever since Sir Jeremy strode into the boardroom there had been headlines in the local papers about machine room reorganisations, departmental closures, Bolsover staff redundancies. Miss Nelson, David's loyal secretary, had been quickly displaced by Marcia, a sharp girl who always seemed to be in mid-manicure whenever I went into George's office. I couldn't think why he hadn't got rid of her years ago.

It was Julia's idea to bring Miss Nelson into Natural Sources. Within a week she'd sorted out our VAT returns, and within three weeks she'd organised Ahmet Basrawy's delivery dates, always the most enigmatic area of our business.

"It's about Julia, I'm afraid." Peter handed me a rolled up copy of the *Cambridge Evening News*. "David phoned me at lunchtime when he saw it had got into the paper. Happened a few days ago; she was driving the Mels to school when they picked her up."

So everyone was right about Julia, except me. I supposed that was why she'd been so absent-minded in the office. Miss Nelson had obviously summed up the situation on her first day when she seized piles of unfiled letters and folders from Julia's desk and said firmly: "You'd better let me deal with this little lot, Mrs Mainwaring."

"I don't understand about micrograms and millilitres. Had she had much to drink?"

"Certainly more than a medicinal tot of brandy," Peter said. "Upsetting for the twins. They were taken to the police station. David had to go and collect them."

"And Julia?"

"In the Mount Vernon Nursing Home. That's why I dropped in to see you, Pauline."

"Is she . . ." for a moment I couldn't remember the right phrase, ". . . drying out?"

"I gather from David it's rather more serious than that. Dr Barker said something to him about a breakdown." Peter looked gloomily into his glass. Suddenly gin seemed inappropriate and neither of us touched our drinks. "She refuses to see him. Sybilla's in London, as usual, and I gather Emily's at a conference . . ."

"USM '86. The Junior Markets Exhibition." (I'd never heard of the USM and Sybilla said it sounded like a Scottish football team to her. "Unlisted Securities Market. A sort of junior Stock Market," said Julia, "David doesn't think we're ready for it yet." "In that case," Emily had said, "I'd better go and check out this exhibition.")

"So I was wondering if you, Pauline . . . ?"

"Why, of course." I jumped up and looked around for my handbag. "I'll go now."

"I knew you'd say that." Peter looked relieved. "I'd go myself, only I think she'd rather see another woman. Better leave it till tomorrow, though, give her a chance to settle in, and perhaps you should have a word with David first . . . ?"

"I'll call in and see him in the morning and then go on to Julia."

The front door opened and George called up the stairs. "We're back, Pauly." Clerry came running into the room and clambered all over Peter.

"Darling . . ." I said, warningly.

"It's all right, Pauline." Peter put down his drink and hugged Clerihue. "She reminds me of Caroline when she was young enough to love everyone indiscriminately."

"And doesn't she now?"

"They grow up early these days." He looked wistfully at Clerry.

"But surely Caroline's only eleven?"

"Going on twenty-one," said Peter. "I'm probably being foolish and old-fashioned, Pauline, so don't take any notice of me, but I do hate her being displayed at smart London parties as though she were this month's key accessory, or dressed up like a doll for fashion pictures."

What he was saying was that he didn't approve of Sybilla's style of motherhood and I had no intention of getting involved in that particular discussion. "You'd rather she stayed in the country and remained a little engineer, you mean?"

"Just so," said Peter, as George came in with a Waitrose carrier.

"I've got the sweetbreads, Pauly. Peter! What a surprise!"

"Looks like work for you, Pauline," said Peter, rising to shake George's free hand.

"On the contrary, Peter," said George stiffly. "Work for me. I've rather taken to the culinary arts, quite a precise science these days, you know."

"A splendid relaxation," said Peter. "I feel just the same about gardening." He started telling George about the Stranvaesia Davidiana he'd just planted in the shrubbery and stopped suddenly. "That carrier's leaking, George."

Later, after I'd mopped the carpet (pale gold, to client's choice), I cornered George in the kitchen and told him about Julia, and that Peter was staying for dinner.

"What ever made you invite him?" George chopped onions agressively with a sharp knife. "I've only bought enough for two."

"Well, you'll have to stretch it to three." How typical, I thought sadly, that George was more worried about his catering arrangements than about Julia. I had to remind myself that he was a kind and loving father.

Dinner was a stilted occasion. We were just settling down to something fancy, involving prawns and fennel, when Gloria appeared.

"I'm just off. They're both tucked up in bed and I've read Clerry a chapter of *Little Grey Rabbit*. Why, Sir Peter . . . ?"

Peter rose and courteously pulled out a chair. "Mrs Jenks. How very nice to see you again."

George also rose, pushed the chair back firmly under the table, and taking his mother's arm, propelled her out of the door. "What a pity you can't stay and dine with us, Mother."

"Well . . ." Gloria looked back hopefully at the unwelcoming chair.

I found myself thinking unkindly of George again, but realised he would have to perform a loaves and fishes feat to turn dinner for two into dinner for four.

"Not *Sir* Peter, Mother. Just plain Mr Bolsover."

Plain Mr Bolsover, who could hear this reprimand from the other side of the door as clearly as I could, started making polite noises about the food. In fact, the whole meal became a Gourmet Evening, with George wondering if there was, perhaps, too much coriander in the prawns and were the sweetbreads quite au point. "They could have done with another ten minutes." He munched reflectively. "How're yours, Peter?"

"Absolutely delicious, George. Absolutely delicious."

"And the wine is to your taste, I trust?"

"Oh, quite perfect, Really."

Waitrose basic red, £3.99 a litre, decanted into cut glass. I wished George wouldn't go on so.

We were at the apple charlotte meringue stage ("An excellent recipe if you have to come up with an instant pudding, Peter . . ."), before we got around to discussing Julia.

"I imagine it would be difficult not to drink if you were married to David," said Peter.

"See what you mean, Peter," said George. "Not the easiest of men to live with."

Peter smiled, sipped his Waitrose red. "True. But I actually meant that David is an assiduous social drinker, as you may have noticed, George."

"Indeed, indeed. That was what I was trying to say." George's eager desire to say the right thing was embarrassing. I wondered if he'd been like that at board meetings.

"And in these last few months Julia has been matching him, glass for glass."

"She's got a lot of worries," I said, defensively.

Peter nodded. "And I don't suppose that insurance business helped. David must have told Julia about it."

"Almost certainly, I should say." George had that shifty look again. He hadn't told me about that insurance business, and as Peter revealed the full story, I saw why. In Bolsover's final months, David, desperate for ready cash to pay the wages, had been banking his employees' PAYE and National Insurance deductions. Cheating your staff of their pension rights was not, after all, so very different from cheating your mother of her interest rate.

"But surely Trevor must have known?" I couldn't imagine Trevor Sutcliffe going in for fraud.

"Didn't spot it at first," said Peter. "None of us did. He came to me the moment he realised what was going on."

"Peter paid back the money out of his own pocket," said George.

"Least I could do. Some of the people at Bolsover had been with us for thirty years. Just imagine how I'd have felt if they'd turned up at the DHSS and been told they weren't entitled to their social security payments."

I phoned David Mainwaring the next morning, to say I wanted to come over and talk to him about Julia.

He reacted much as I expected. "Talk about Julia? Whatever for? Fighting off the toothache, that's all. Bit of bad luck the police were lurking about."

"But David . . . the nursing home?"

"Oh that. A couple of good nights' sleep will soon put her right. Drop in and have a chat, by all means. Haven't seen you since we tackled those prawns together in Tokyo."

The Mainwarings' drive was very long. By the time I'd reached the third bend of the spinney I was wishing I'd gone straight to the nursing home.

One look at Julia would probably tell me more about why she was there than any amount of dissembling chat from David. And, after hearing about that trick with the wage packets, it was going to be difficult to be civil to him, let alone sympathetic.

Simon Mainwaring appeared round the side of the house as I got out of my lovely Renault. It was brand new, with leather upholstery, and had been waiting for me outside the office when I returned from the successful Tokyo trip.

"It's beautiful," I said to Emily, "but leather seats cost at least an extra £1,000."

"This is an office car, Pauline," she said. "It would look pretty silly for a director of Natural Sources to drive around with plastic seats."

"Pauline, I've been waiting for you." Simon looked pale, not his usual immaculately groomed self. He'd moved to a tutorial college in Cambridge, was retaking his O levels and wanted to go to art college. Discovering that I had been at St Martin's, he'd taken to dropping in at my studio to talk about art and life, and the most effective cure for acne.

"That business at school," he'd said, on one of his visits. "It wasn't what everyone thought, you know."

"I know very little about it," I said quickly, in case he thought we were all gossiping avidly about him. All Julia had said, after that outburst in the office on the day Toby was born, was that David had brought Simon home and told him he didn't want a bloody queer for a son.

"I was very fond of Henry, that's all. And just because he's three years younger . . . everyone's got such filthy minds."

"How beastly for you. I am sorry."

Looking at Simon's worried face that morning, it occurred to me that it was bad enough being sixteen and unsure of your own feelings, without having to cope with the inadequacies of the adults around you, as well.

"I don't want Father to see me talking to you." He looked nervously over his shoulder and led me behind a rampant rose bush.

"I say, Simon, this is like something out of John le Carré."

"I'm sorry, but Father's impossible. He'll tell you that there's nothing wrong with Julia. He won't admit the truth, even to himself. She does drink a lot, you know. I thought it was quite funny at first. The bottles disguised as Liquinure or whatever that stuff is she feeds to the plants, but it isn't funny at all."

"I know." I gave his hand a reassuring squeeze. "I'd better go and talk to your father, I suppose."

"Before you go." Simon grabbed my arm again. "There's something I want to tell you. Julia was sitting by the swimming pool on Saturday. It was sunny, the Mels had some friends over and they were messing about in the pool. She should have been so happy. But she was just sitting there, staring into space, with the tears rolling down her cheeks. Father, pretty predictably, told her to pull herself together."

Just about the worst thing he could say, I thought, as David, booming social noises, answered the front door.

"Don't know what all this fuss is about, Pauline." He led me into his study. "Damn stupid of Julia to get caught, but all this nonsense about nursing homes . . ."

He didn't ask me to sit down, but I sat down anyway.

". . . she's got everything any woman could possibly want. Beautiful home, plenty of money, interesting job. I told her she ought to pull herself together."

"Perhaps she can't."

"That's what that fool Barker said. Insisted on carting her off to the funny farm."

"Perhaps your carrying on with Sybilla Bolsover has something to do with it?" I was surprised to hear myself speaking so frankly.

"Sybilla?" David thought about denying it, saw my expression (which, according to George, can be quite frightening when I'm cross) and decided against it. "That was just a bit of fun. All over now. Julia knows she's got nothing to worry about so far as Syb is concerned."

He went in for a few diversionary tactics, lighting a cigarette, pouring himself another cup of coffee, changing the conversation. "Fill you up?"

"Not for me, thank you."

"So how's old George getting on? British Steel and Unilever vying for his services, are they?"

"He's had one or two offers." I was certainly not going to mention cookery or modelling to David Mainwaring. "And you?"

"Never better, never better," he said, too quickly. "Got the feelers out for the odd non-executive directorships, of course, and meanwhile I'm enjoying all the things I haven't had time to do these last twenty years."

I looked courteously questioning.

"Had a marvellous day's hunting the other week."

"I thought you always went hunting."

"Yes. Well, I managed to fit it in occasionally." He poured another cup of coffee, looked round his study and focused on *Sporting Life*. "Been able to catch up on my reading. I'm doing a lot of reading."

"Give my love to Julia," he said, as I was leaving. "Bloody doctors won't let me see her, for some damn fool reason or other."

The television set was on. One of those programmes where they give you a patio set if you know the Christian names of the Beatles or who was the first man to run a mile under five minutes. Julia was not watching it. She was sitting up in bed, staring at the wall. She didn't see me at first.

"Julia . . ."

She turned. "Pauline. What are you doing here?"

"Wanted to see you . . . find out how you are."

"I'm all right, I think. I don't want to see David."

"He's at home. Sends his love."

"Too late for that. And the Mels? I shouldn't have been driving." She began crying, the tears drifting messily down her cheeks.

"They're fine. At school." I passed her a Kleenex which she rolled into a tight ball. "David told them you weren't well, that you'd be home soon."

"He's been having an affair with Sybilla. Did you know that?"

"Yes."

"I suppose everybody did except me. Have you got a

133

Kleenex?" I passed her another and she dabbed at her face, reminding me of the first time we met, when she was patting on rouge, just as ineffectively. "Can't stop crying, isn't it silly?"

"I'm sorry." I didn't want to encourage her to say anything she'd regret having told me later. "No wonder you're miserable."

"Oh, it isn't David. Sybilla isn't the first, you know." She lay back on the pillow and shut her eyes. "There's a psychiatrist here who keeps asking me what I'm thinking."

"And do you tell him?"

"Her. I don't know what I'm thinking." She opened her eyes and gave me a wan smile. "I make things up so she'll go away."

"Would you like me to go away?"

"I would, really. But thank you for coming, Pauline. You will come again, won't you?"

"Of course I will. Is there anything I can bring you?"

She managed another wan smile. "A bottle of vodka, perhaps?"

It was, I realised, Julia's way of admitting she had a drink problem.

There was a van parked inconsiderately across our double garage. Taking a sheaf of designs in one hand and a shopping bag in the other, I stormed into the house, intent on writing a "To whom it may concern. Will you please move your vehicle" note.

Gloria was giving the children their tea. Clerry was eating a boiled egg and Tobias was throwing cereal on the floor.

Dumping the designs and the shopping on the table, I kissed both children, who put their arms around my neck and egg and Farex on my shirt, which somehow didn't matter.

"There's a van plonked right in front of the garages. Has anyone seen the note pad?"

"It's Gan-Gan's," said Clerry.

I turned to Gloria. "Gan-Gan's?"

"It's a delivery van, Pauline. Clerihue and I went into Huntingdon this morning and bought it. Does forty-five miles to the gallon, so the man tells me."

I knew Gloria had been taking driving lessons, of course, but presumed she was going to treat herself to a little runabout. "A delivery van, Gloria?"

She bit into her toast, looking pleased with herself.

"Surely you could afford a proper car?"

"Oh, nothing to do with money, Pauline. There'll be no ice cream until you've eaten up that egg, Clerry."

Clerry turned her egg upside down in the chicken egg cup. "All gone."

Briskly turning the egg right side up, Gloria looked inside it. "Eat up the white, darling. I'm going to give you a hand, Pauline. You're wasting a fortune on those delivery firms, George can hardly find his way to Spitalfields, and now that Julia's lost her licence . . ."

George entered on cue, with a smallish white bowl covered with a damp cloth. He seemed to spend a lot of time, in those days, walking around the house carrying bowls covered in damp cloths.

"Somebody's taken my yogurt out of the airing cupboard. Hullo Pauly, good day?"

"Beastly. I went to see David . . . and Julia . . ."

"I was just telling Pauline that I'm going to help out with the deliveries for her business," said Gloria. "I took that muck out of the airing cupboard, George. It was heaving about all over the children's vests and knickers."

"You've ruined it, Mother. Now I'll have to start again." He went over to the fridge, took out a milk bottle and started pouring milk into a saucepan.

"Excuse me, you two." I sat down at the table and looked at my husband and my mother-in-law, the cook and the driver. "If Gloria's going to work for Natural Sources . . ."

"Just part-time, dear."

"Even part-time, Gloria. If you're out delivering, or

whatever, we'll need to get someone reliable to look after Clerry and Toby and help in the house."

"Don't like the idea of having children and then giving them to someone else to look after," said George, testing the milk with his finger.

"Quite." Gloria nodded approvingly in George's direction. "You can look after Clerry and Toby when we're busy, can't you, George?"

"Well . . ." said George, looking at us both doubtfully.

"Of course you can, George. They are your children, after all."

"Well," said George again, "I don't know . . ."

There was a nasty noise behind him. It was the milk boiling over.

Going into the office next day I found Emily at her desk, surrounded by bits of important-looking paper and Miss Nelson, behind Julia's desk, word processing the accounts.

"Hi, Pauline," said Emily. "Today's news is that Bloomingdale's have been on about the hand-knitted sweaters, four days late on delivery, and I don't think the time is right to launch ourselves on the USM."

Sitting down at my desk, I reached for my post, to find that Miss Nelson had already opened it and divided it into relevant piles.

"Sent eight sweaters back to the knitters yesterday, Em. Wrong tension. They'll be with us Friday. What's the problem with the USM? I thought we were going to raise money and make a fortune."

"Could lose everything," said Emily. "Nobody can touch us now, but once we're on the market we're open to grabs."

"Open to grabs? But who would want us?"

Miss Nelson looked up from her accounts. "That's what Mr Mainwaring said three months before Bolsover's was taken over."

"But we're hardly in the same league . . . ?"

"Annual pre-tax profits of nearly a million on the three shops," said Miss Nelson. "£55,000 from Tokyo last month. You're doing very nicely, Mrs Jenks."

"Listen to what Miss Nelson is saying," said Emily, "she's a wise woman."

Miss Nelson looked pleased. I felt sure David Mainwaring had never said she was a wise woman.

"How about a nice cup of coffee?" she said.

I told Emily about my visit to Julia, while Miss Nelson made the coffee.

"Poor Julia," said Emily. "I'll go and see her this evening on my way home. So the Sybilla/David thing is over, is it?"

"So David says."

"I expect they'll both find someone else to make miserable," said Emily. "Isn't it a pity Sybilla's such a bitch? She really is the most brilliant saleswoman."

"What's she sold now? Twenty Tips on Seducing your Best Friend's Husband?"

"It's a feature for *Woman*. One of the July issues."

"We won't have to be photographed and interviewed again?"

"Not us, exactly," says Emily. "It's about older women going back to work. You know the sort of thing . . . ?"

"But who . . . ?" The only older woman around Natural Sources was Miss Nelson and she'd been working all her life. "Surely not Miss Nelson?"

"Sybilla was thinking of Gloria. Quite a good story, mother-in-law of the designer and so on."

"Sybilla's certainly a quick mover, but a bit too quick off the mark this time. Gloria only took delivery of her van yesterday."

"That's all right. She'll have been driving around for months by July."

I remembered Gloria's purse-lipped reaction to George's fashion spread.

"She won't do it, Emily," I said. "Not a chance."

What have Kate, Gloria, Tigger and Coral got in common?

The honey from Kate's bees goes to prestige West End grocers . . . Gloria runs a top-notch delivery service . . . Tigger's domestic help agency makes life that much easier for women executives . . . Coral wrote a book called "Sexual Harassment – Don't Knock It", which shot into the best-selling lists and is currently being adapted for a TV sitcom . . .

So they're all working women, what's new about that?

These are working women with a difference. Their children have had children. We're talking about the new breed of Go-Ahead Grannies, women who've surged into a career when traditionally they should be picking up the crochet hook.

"Not that it's been easy," says Gloria Jenks. "My son is a little on the old-fashioned side, like most men. It was my daughter-in-law who gave me all the support I needed. Of course, Pauline knows all about the problems of working women. She's the genius behind Natural Sources, *and* she's bringing up two children."

Gloria remembers the day when Pauline stormed into the house complaining that someone had parked a van across their drive. "We still laugh about the look on her face when I said it was mine, and I'd bought it to help her out. She has partners in Natural Sources, of course, but as designer and project originator the brunt naturally falls on her shoulders."

Woman, 9th July, 1986

It was getting quite difficult to fit everything in. I had to resort to making lists, and I was thinking of buying a Filofax to make them in. In the meantime I was making do with a plastic looseleaf from Ryman's. That morning's list was by no means atypical:

1 Ring Sally re poss. Burberry ad series.

Unfortunately they wanted me in Inverness in the middle of September, and it seemed to be possible that Pauline would be in India then with that poisonous Basrawy. In better days Mother would have taken over the children, but by then, of course, she was spending all her time on the M25 shouting at lorry drivers.

2 Speak to playgroup organiser about Clerry and her "aggression problem".

I had not yet encountered the playgroup organiser, and couldn't imagine what fault she could possibly find in Clerry; I intended to be extremely firm.

3 Raspberry vinegar.

4 Ring Trevor back.

He had apparently called while I was out; Mother said he sounded funny, whatever that meant.

5 Ring Julia re twins' dentist appointment.

It seemed I was the only person in the entire world who was available to take them into Cambridge. What was their father doing, that's what I wanted to know? Drinking and leering at Emily Sutcliffe was my guess.

6 Ring laundry re missing shirt.

7 I didn't actually write 7 down, but what I had to do was talk to Mother about that frightful article in *Woman*. How could she have said all that?

"How could she have said all that, Pauly?"

"Wasn't she marvellous? What a pro. Did you notice none of the others got a word in about their projects? I loved the bit about the brunt falling on my shoulders, didn't you? So much for Sybilla. What are you doing with those raspberries?"

"Making raspberry vinegar; I can cross that off my list. I can see from your point the article was quite . . ."

"Amazing. Mentioned the Covent Garden shop,

mentioned our turnover, didn't mention Sybilla, you'd think Gloria had been in PR for years."

"But . . . that bit towards the end, about her marriage. Pauly, didn't it seem to you that Mother was, sort of hinting that she hadn't been happy?"

Pauline unscrewed a bottle of Dufrais Red Wine Vinegar and dropped some raspberries in. "Is this right? George, you must have known she wasn't happy."

"Never seemed unhappy to me."

"Don't you remember . . . when we were watching that programme about battered wives a couple of months ago?"

"All I remember thinking is that some women seem to ask for it. Didn't Mother go to bed early that night?"

"You didn't wonder why? You sat there saying, 'Some women ask for it, don't they?' and Gloria went to bed. Work it out, George."

"Work what out? Father would never have raised his hand to a woman. Out of the question. Anyway, I'd have known, wouldn't I, Pauly?"

"You did know, didn't you . . . George?"

"Shut up," I shouted. "Bloody shut up. Anyway, what could I have done about it? It was their business. I heard them, sometimes. One minute you're worrying about Geography homework, the next he's saying, 'I'm going to have to admonish you, Gloria.' You're supposed to look up to your father, aren't you? Admonish, what a disgusting word, I hated it. 'Your gentleman friend can't help you now,' he kept on saying, 'quite the Upper Crust but not around when he's needed' . . . and then those thuds. And next morning it would be Kelloggs and marmalade and Mother in long sleeves even when it was hot."

"George, I really am so sorry."

"I suppose you all knew about it, next door?"

"I didn't have the faintest idea. Mum and Dad did. That's why . . . um —"

"That's why they didn't want you to marry me? Thought I might be a chip off the old block?"

"Mum was a bit worried. Dad stood up for you, the old love. 'George wouldn't hurt a kitten,' he said. Anyway, darling, it's all in the past."

"I could never understand it. Dad seemed quite hen-pecked most of the time . . . oh well, at least Mother is happy now."

"And didn't she look terrific in the *Woman* picture? George . . . what did your father mean . . . 'Your gentleman friend'?"

"I don't know," I said, but I was beginning to think I did.

"Sally? About the Scottish shoot. How early in September could it possibly be?"

"George, I have told you. I can't expect Patrick Lichfield to rearrange his schedules to suit one model, can I? I don't have to remind you that there are other men around who can wear clothes and stand up straight, do I?"

"No, no . . . it's just, there's a faint possibility that my wife might be going to India about then, and I don't know who will look after the children."

"Tell her to go some other time. This is quite a chance for you, George."

"Oh, I don't think I could say that. She's going on business, you see."

"So is this business. Come back to me tomorrow with yes or no, George. And try and remember that reliability and availability are as important, in this game, as pretty hair."

She sounded distinctly sour. Probably the best thing was for me to ring and say yes, I can do it, and then not mention it to Pauline until much nearer the time. There was no point in having an argument until I absolutely had to.

My life, I thought as I drove into St Neots to collect Clerry from her playgroup, is full of women telling me what to do. And when I tried to come back at them, they attacked me with their species of logic. What happened to the good old days when men were the head of the family and their womenfolk did as they were told? It all seemed to have slipped away while I wasn't looking.

The playgroup was run in a village hall on the western outskirts of St Neots. When I arrived the children were out in a grassy, muddy space in front. "There'll be a lot of washing machines at full hum tonight," I thought, as I watched small boys pour buckets of wet sand over small girls.

I couldn't see our Clerry anywhere. I approached the woman who was, presumably, in charge, if that's what she called reading a book while people kicked each other.

"I am looking for Clerihue Jenks," I said.

"Clerihue?" She threw down the book (*Sexual Harassment – Don't Knock It*, I noticed). "Load of cloacal claptrap. Clerihue? Oh yes, the trouble-maker. She's over there, behind the slide. She is totally without peer-compatability, you do realise that?"

I looked at the small girl huddled behind the slide, and realised it was my Clerry wearing jeans and a silly T-shirt about Greenham Common.

"That's not what she got dressed in this morning. She doesn't look happy. I thought playgroups were supposed to be fun?"

"She was wearing a gingham dress with frills, Jenks. If that isn't Role Tyranny, I'd like to know what is."

"She chose it herself, at Mothercare."

"Striving to please in a way she instinctively knows is wrong."

"Shouldn't you do something about that boy over there? He is lying on top of that girl in a way which I consider most unsuitable."

"Exploration is important to young minds."

"I dare say. I don't think the little girl . . . she's making a lot of noise, isn't she?"

"Then she should do something about it. Kick him where it hurts, Priscilla, I've told you often enough."

"Is this place licensed?" I said. What on earth could Pauline be about, leaving my child in the charge of this madwoman? A girl of about six and a younger boy wandered up. They were not at all prepossessing. I supposed it was sexist to blow your nose. The boy was clutching a teddy bear which I recognised as Clerry's.

"Amanda," said the girl, "Clerihue pinched Jake when he borrowed her teddy bear. I told her property is theft and she said I smelt nasty."

"We must try and remember, Canvey, that Clerihue is a very trammelled person."

"I'll have that teddy bear, if you don't mind," I said, snatching it from Jake. I must remember to disinfect it, I thought. Jake screamed, and aimed a kick at my leg. "Mummy, make that nasty man go away," he said.

"I've told you not to call me that, Jake. My name is Amanda. I don't call you Sonny, do I?"

"Are these your children?" Something was beginning to nibble at the back of my mind.

"Certainly not. Mine was the womb that nourished them. Now they belong to themselves."

"Oh. Unusual name, Canvey."

"Canvey Island is where the rape that resulted in her conception took place."

Should the child be listening to this? "I say, how dreadful. I am most awfully –"

"A rape that had the full backing of macho-dominated church and state."

"You mean . . . you were married to . . ." the nibble had become a certainty. "Are you by any chance Arabella Pinter-Bambury's sister?"

"All my sisters are my sisters."

"Did you happen to be nourished by the same womb, is what I suppose I meant." I'd never met anyone who made such a performance out of a simple conversation. I suddenly thought fondly of David Mainwaring; a bastard, but at least you occasionally knew what he was talking about.

"Our mother," said Amanda, "always preferred Arabella to me. You know why, don't you?"

Yes, but I could hardly say so.

143

"Well, perhaps she –"

"Don't you patronise me with any of your phallocentric tact. Arabella conforms to the pressures of society, but of course Mother refuses to admit –"

"Why do you call her Mother?"

"What?"

"Aren't you rather imposing a stereotypical role-model? Come along, Clerry, time to go home."

I was extremely pleased with my exit line, but my good humour waned rapidly. It took me quite a long time to get Clerry into the car. She wouldn't leave without her gingham dress, which I eventually found under some poster paints (I doubted even Biotex would get the marks out) and her teddy bear, which that little swine Jake had managed to lay his hands on again.

"Don't worry, darling," I said as we drove away, "you're never going back to that place again."

"Why not, Daddy? I like it."

"Of course you don't like it. That little monster Jake, trying to steal dear old Mr Teddy."

"I stood on his hand when Amanda wasn't looking. I must go back, Daddy, next week we're going to see some nasty Americans. We made a banner today, saying Go Home Warmingers."

"What Americans? . . . warmingers?"

"The ones who live with the bomb. We've all got to bring sandwiches and a raincoat, and fifty pee for the collection."

I couldn't even park properly when I got home; one of Mother's vans was in my space. She had two by then, resprayed white with We Go For It in large navy blue letters on the side, with my telephone number underneath. It really was time she got her own line. I was appalled when she told me in May that she was thinking of buying another van. She didn't put it like that, of course; she was into all the jargon, hardly recognisable as the woman who ran the house in Hammersmith for Dad and me.

"I really feel the time is ripe to consolidate my expansion plans," she said. "Not a day passes without my turning away a job."

"I thought you bought the van to help Pauline out?" I said.

"Well, of course I did, originally. But you've no idea, George, the number of small local businesses that are looking for really reliable delivery on the dot. That nice Mr Brooks at the Nat West estimated I should be able to pay back the loan by September at the latest, when I showed him my books."

"Pay back? You're surely never going to *borrow*, Mother, when you've got all that money in the bank?"

Mother gave me a pitying smile.

"You don't know the first thing about fiscal arrangements, do you, dear?"

"Anyway, who's going to drive this second van? Have you any idea of the kind of wages you'd have to pay?"

"I went into all that with Mr Brooks. I've got Marcia Blake lined up and raring to go."

"Marcia? My old secretary?"

"Can't wait to leave Bolsover's, or Pitkin Consolidated or whatever it calls itself now. Dreadful atmosphere, apparently, and they've repainted the Ladies Room a terrible green."

"Oh, well, if they've painted the Ladies Room green," I said sarcastically, "I quite see . . ."

Mother wasn't listening. She went ahead and bought the van, and Mr Brooks of Nat West gave her a glass of sherry to celebrate. I hadn't borrowed a penny from him, and he never offered me a glass of sherry when I dropped in for a new chequebook. I thought I might move my account to Lloyds, you had to laugh at those commercials with Rumpole of the Bailey in them.

Not only was Mother's van taking up my space, Marcia was sitting in it, with Mother and Pauline idling their time away gossiping to her.

"You'll do the parsley pots job at Buckden tomorrow, then, Marcia?" said Mother. "That'll leave me free to collect that shipment of Hunza apricots for the health food shop at St Ives. If it goes on like this I'm going to have to get another van, Pauline. When do you want the Afghan jerseys at Covent Garden?"

"Monday, at the latest," said Pauline. "Clerry! Did you have a lovely time at the playgroup, darling?"

"She most certainly did not," I said. "Really, Pauline, I am very angry. That woman! How could you commit our child to her care?"

"I know," said Pauline agreeably, "doesn't she talk a load of rubbish? Beneath all the gibberish she actually runs a very sound playgroup."

"Over my dead body will Clerry go back there. And to cap it all I'm supposed to donate 50p to some bunch of militants."

"They're not militants, Daddy," said Clerry. "They're women against the bomb. I want to go back, I love it there."

"Why was no one talking to you when I picked you up?"

"It was my turn to be the ethnic minority."

"The what?"

"Every day one of us is the ethnic minority and nobody talks to us, so we know what it's like."

"To think my taxes are paying for that pernicious left-wing –"

"Sounds rather sensible to me. Didn't they do a film once where somebody turned black for a day in the deep south?" said Marcia. "If you'll let me have those invoices, Gloria, I'll be off."

I hadn't actually seen Julia, when I came to think of it, since that time I collected some stuff from her and she had bottles hidden all over the garden. She had sounded perfectly coherent on the phone.

"This is awfully kind of you, George, are you sure you

don't mind? Only David has to be up in London and I'm
. . ." rueful laugh, ". . . still off the road. Their appointment's at ten tomorrow, and it's this side of Cambridge,
so shouldn't take you more than half an hour . . ."

"I'll pick them up at nine-fifteen to be on the safe side.
See you tomorrow, then."

Looking at my watch as I turned into Julia's gate, I saw
it was only just nine. I hoped she wouldn't think I'd arrived
early to get a cup of coffee.

"George, how nice you're early. Plenty of time for some
coffee."

"No really, I —"

"Well, I'm having some. Milk and sugar?"

She led me through the hall and into the kitchen, bellow-
ing up the stairs, "George is here, darlings, leaving in fifteen
minutes."

"Julia, you look, you look so well."

"I'm on the way, George, not quite there, but nearly.
That first psychiatrist was a disaster. Vast and dressed to
make the worst of it. I sat there looking at her and thinking,
'If that's all you can do for yourself, there's not a hell of a
lot you can do for me.'"

"I don't suppose anyone can help you if you don't like
them."

"Exactly. This new man . . . oh George, he looked at
me and said, 'You're so normal you're practically typical.
Doing far too much, what you've got to do is get a bit
selfish.'"

"I can't imagine you as selfish, exactly, Julia."

"Well, I'm jolly going to be. Apparently, in layman's
terms, I'd used up the chemical which makes for happiness
. . . well, something like that, and I'm taking pills to put
it back."

"And they're working?"

"Like a dream. The only thing is, there's a whole lot of
food I can't eat while I'm taking them. No cheese, no game,
nothing fermented, but so what?"

"Come and have dinner soon, Julia. Pauline and Mother

would like that, and you must give me the list so I know what not to cook."

"I'd love to, George. And don't worry about not putting wine in the sauce. I'm not an alcoholic, it turns out."

"Really?" I couldn't help recalling the first conversation I had with Julia, when she was the MD's wife and I was a new young salesman. "Very nice for the time of year," was about all I could manage. Now we were into intimate details.

"I was just using drink as a temporary crutch. Now I can take it or leave it. Mostly I leave it. For one thing I must lose some weight. There you are, darlings. Don't look so glum, it's only a checkup."

"If Mummy says it's all right, we'll get some ice cream to eat on the way back," I said, shepherding the Mels into the car.

I'd always liked the Julia-Mel, and even the David-Mel was beginning to show signs of improvement.

They were both very chipper in the car on the way home, what with having had no fillings and eating several choc ices. I listened unashamedly as they talked about their father.

"Hope Dad comes back from London in a better mood than he went."

"Certainly couldn't be crappier."

"Well, the poor old thing is trying to get a job, not much cop at his age."

"Can't happen too soon. If I was Mum I'd go mad, with him hanging about all the time comparing loo paper prices at Waitrose and the Co-op."

"Here we are home, safe and sound," I said. Julia was in the garden, as usual.

"Hello darlings, all well? Thank you so much, George. Time for a drink?"

"I've got to get back and give Tobias his lunch . . ." the twins rushed off into the house, ". . . I gather David's turned into a price-comparison expert?"

"Oh, don't talk about it. I can't wait for him to find something real to fill his time. I've got better things to do than trudge round Huntingdon unearthing the all-time bargain in paper towels."

Typical, when you're in a hurry. Police go-slow accident signs on the A45. I was going to be late home for lunch because some idiot hadn't looked where he was going. Two lanes merging into one. I courteously waved in a lorry loaded with hay. He'd have cut in anyway, so I might as well be gracious about it.

One of those men who make it their business to know everything was striding about.

"What's going on?" I said, winding down my window.

"Two ambulances and a fire-engine. Some poor bastard's had it."

It was very close that day. Luckily I had some cartons of Boots Fresh Pressed English Apple Juice in the glove compartment. I had tried them all, and Boots was easily the best. I turned on my cassette-player . . . "Bye bye, Miss American pie . . ."

We moved a few yards forward, now I was in the shade of some trees, it was so boring, sitting there.

". . . drove my chevvy to the levee but the levee was dry . . ."

I was up to the accident, and I tried not to look as I drove past. Oh God, nobody could have come alive out of that. A jack-knifed juggernaut, French registration. They think they can come over here and drive on the wrong side of the road. A white van, crumpled. Oil all over the place. A young police constable, trying to look as though he'd seen it all before. And navy blue letters saying 860 . . . my telephone number.

Obeying the Highway Code, I glanced in my mirror and signified that I was coming to a halt. I drew in to a convenient lay-by, got out, and locked the car. Walked back towards the accident. Must remember and get some fish for supper, I thought. Mother does like . . .

"Excuse me, sir, if you don't mind."

"The driver of that van. I don't want to be a nuisance, Constable. My mother has a van like that. We Go For It, it says on the side. She's all right, isn't she?"

It's a funny thing about policemen. When they nick you for speeding they're forty-five years old. On occasions like this they're nineteen and don't know where to look.

"Just a minute, sir . . . Sarge, this gentleman thinks . . ." he drew him aside and whispered. Not Mother it couldn't be. I did hope it was Marcia. What a rotten thing to think.

"Ah, Mr . . . er?"

"Jenks. George Jenks."

"I understand . . . my constable tells me . . . the lady driving the van . . ."

"Is she all right?"

"Everything's being done. In very good hands. If we could have the name of the lady in question? Your mother? I'm sorry, sir, but we have to –"

"I'm not sure. Could I sit down? I don't know, it depends what the load is."

Someone gave me a plastic mug of tea. Not enough sugar.

"You were saying, sir, the load?"

"If it's . . . let me get this right. If it's parsley pots it's Marcia, Marcia Blake. If it's dried apricots . . . surely Mother wouldn't come this way for St Ives, would she?"

There was nowhere to put the mug, so I took it with me as we walked towards the remains of the van. Lots of cardboard boxes burst open. "Store in a cool dry place" it said on the packet I picked up. "Caution: Hunza apricots do contain a stone."

It seemed appropriate to have rain at the funeral ("Heaven's crying for Gan-Gan," Clerry remarked cheerfully at breakfast, "and for Stripey," she added, bursting into tears), but somehow it didn't seem quite reverent, huddling under an umbrella.

"Cometh up, and is cut down, like a flower . . ." It was

hardly raining at all now. Perhaps, as chief mourner, I should put down my umbrella. But I couldn't, because he was throwing the earth, and it wouldn't look right. I wished they did that after we'd gone. It was the worst noise I'd ever heard.

"Our sister here departed . . ."

Peter Bolsover was there, of course, and Sybilla was not, equally of course. There were the Sutcliffes. David Mainwaring was present, much to my surprise (I hadn't forgiven him for saying "that frightful mother". I would get him for that one day, even if he was looking as pi as if he really cared.) Julia hadn't come because she was looking after Clerry and Tobias. I bet she'd look after the children like a shot, I thought, when I go to Scotland in September. Shan't mention it to Pauline, though, she's bound to put up some silly objection. Pauline was dressed in black this time. I still didn't think grey was right for my father's funeral. She looked as though she'd been up all night.

"In sure and certain hope of the Resurrection . . ."

That must be nearly the end. "Why don't you all come back to me, afterwards?" Julia had suggested, when she offered to take the children. "I can get everything ready while you're at the . . . for when you get back."

We all got into the cars, with everyone hanging back to look polite. Pauly and I ended up taking Marcia, who kept on saying, "If only I'd taken the apricots, I'll never forgive myself."

I was quite short with her, and Pauly gave me a look.

We drove along the A45, just like I had after the accident.

A policeman had driven me to Addenbrookes in one of their cars. I hadn't known they did that.

I sat in the back, remembering hot socks. When I was small and came home with wet feet Mother always had a pair of socks warming on the radiator. She used to rub my feet, her hands always made me feel safe.

"Try not to worry, sir, I'm sure everything will be all right."

"We always had ham and chips on Saturdays. Can't you go any faster?"

"Nearly there. Just passing the American Cemetery."

I caught his eye in the rear-view mirror. I could see he was wishing we'd been passing somewhere else.

Last time I was in Addenbrookes was when Tobias was born. The Intensive Care Unit isn't much like Maternity. Well, it wouldn't be, would it?

"Mr Jenks, if you'd like to wait here a moment, Dr Lamb will have a word with you."

"Is she all right?"

"Dr Lamb will be here in a moment."

Dr Lamb, when he arrived, looked old enough to buy cigarettes, too young to buy drink, and too tired to think straight.

"Mr Jenks. I wish there was an easy way to say this."

"Is she?"

"No. But, only a matter of time. I promise you we've done everything possible, but the injuries . . . would you like to sit with her?"

I sat there for hours. It turned out later it was forty-five minutes. I thought there'd be tubes, like there are on television, but there were just a lot of bandages round her head, and her hands lying on the bedspread.

She opened her eyes and looked at me, just like she used to when my feet were cold.

"There you are, Boo," she said. "I missed you, last Wednesday."

"I'm not Boo, Mother, I'm George."

She smiled at me like a girl, and then she went.

"Come and have a cup of tea, Mr Jenks," said a nurse, "she didn't suffer at all, you know."

I suppose they're trained to talk comforting nonsense.

The same policeman drove me back to my car.

"I just hope someone beats the hell out of that French lorry-driver," I said. "Sometimes they fall down the stairs to the cells, don't they?"

"He's in Intensive Care, Mr Jenks. Got a wife and five

children, I understand. According to witnesses, your mother was distracted by some animal jumping about in the van. Drove straight into the lorry's path."

I should have phoned Pauline from the hospital, I thought, as I parked. Should have told her. I went into the kitchen to find Clerry crying and Pauline on the phone. Tobias wasn't there. Mother was probably putting him down for his nap. No, of course she wasn't, but I couldn't stop thinking that the door would open, and there she'd be.

"I'll ring you back." Pauline slammed down the phone. "George, you're frightfully late. Where *have* you been? So selfish, just disappearing when you feel like it. Stripey's disappeared, Clerry is frantic. Gloria's let me down, it's not like her, swore she'd be back in time to . . . George? *Now* what's the matter?"

It was no use remembering all that now. I had to be practical. Julia provided a really excellent tea, and everyone tucked in, in the furtive manner of people eating after funerals. There must be some way of making money out of the granny flat, I thought, no point in leaving it empty. When I'd mentioned something of the kind to Pauline the day before, she'd started crying again and said how could I? Anyone would have thought Mother was her mother, the way she'd been going on. David came over with a glass in his hand. He didn't look at all well, not that I cared.

"Bad business, old chap," he said, "no need to tell you how we all feel. When you're up to it, there's something I want to have a serious talk about. On the QT, of course. Mentioned it to Trev, he's very keen."

He shambled off in the direction of the drinks, stuffing a couple of smoked salmon rolls into his mouth as he went. Where was Trevor? Over there by himself looking out at the garden. I would just have a word with him . . .

"Trevor, I never got round to phoning you back. It's just, there's been so much to organise. By the by, I'd like a word of advice from you on Capital Transfer Tax. Quite a nice sum of money involved, as it happens, and I want to be certain to minimalise –"

"Anything I can do," said Trevor rather coldly. Did he expect me to pay him for a bit of friendly advice? "At a more appropriate moment, perhaps, George?"

"Of course, of course, naturally I wouldn't . . . what did you telephone me about last week? Mother said you sounded funny."

"Can't talk now. Wondered what you thought of this idea of David's? I was appalled at first, of course . . . but now I've had time to think it over . . ."

Professionals' marriages worst hit by redundancy

Middle-class professionals suffer more marital problems because of loss of status and income than those of other classes, when they are made redundant or forced to take early retirement, according to the Institute of Marital Studies. Marriages are also threatened when a man loses a job that helped him to bolster his masculinity or which he used to sublimate aggression, greed and envy, research shows. One 53-year-old executive, made redundant from his job as managing director of a Midlands' light engineering firm, took his management style into the home. 'He insists on supervising his wife's shopping. When she chooses something in the supermarket, he puts it back on the shelf and chooses something else,' an ex-colleague told *Victoria Phillips*. 'The competitive spirit and envy that had helped him to reach the top in his career is destroying his marriage.'

The Times, 2nd September, 1986

"Our Covent Garden figures look a bit murky," said Julia.

It was good to have her back in the office. Slimmer, more confident, and with Rose's Lime Juice in the drawer where she used to keep the Smirnoff.

"Pilferage problems," said Emily. "The sooner we get into franchising the better. It's really uneconomic to run our own shops unless one of us is there to keep an eye on the stock."

"Customers or staff?" said Julia.

"Both, I suspect. There's a woman who's nicked herself a complete wardrobe at the Covent Garden shop, only we can't catch her actually at it. And I've had to fire that little dark girl who does three afternoons a week at Primrose Hill."

"Maisie?" said Julia. "I took her on, daughter of a friend of mine. Surely not?"

"Caught her leaving on Friday wearing three sweaters and two skirts under the duster coat we let her have at cost price." Emily picked up *The Times*. "Have you read this bit about marriage and redundancy? I must say Trevor doesn't behave like that. He acts as though he's permanently on holiday."

Julia skimmed through the article. "It sounds *exactly* like David. Nice to know I'm not the only woman whose husband won't buy a bottle of olive oil without checking the price in four different shops."

Reading it over her shoulder, I felt a moment of unease. The characters seemed curiously familiar.

"Does David really monitor the supermarket trolley?" I said. "He doesn't seem the type to me."

"Actually," said Julia, "he's getting rather bored with the financial aspects of Fibrebran. He's started to move back into his executive mode . . ."

"David's landed a job?" said Emily, with what I thought was rather unflattering surprise.

"Not unless you count running the children and me as though we were British Steel," said Julia. "Breakfast in our house is like a board meeting. The MD takes the chair and fills us in on our tasks for the day. 'Alexandra – large granary loaf, health food shop behind the church. Simon – change library books, order new Dick Francis. Julia – dry cleaning to Sketchley in High Street. Tell them stain on tie is Stilton cheese.'"

"How exhausting," I said, "enough to drive you to drink." Then I hastily added, "Sorry, but you know what I mean . . ." which made it worse.

"Of course I know what you mean," said Julia, sympathetically, "but there's no fear of that. David's the one with the bottle now, only it's whisky and he doesn't bother to hide it. When Dr Barker came round to see me the other day he ended up lecturing David about eating, drinking and smoking too much. Said he was heading for a heart attack if he didn't cut back."

"And is he cutting back?"

"Of course not. But he is making an effort to be nice, Pauline. I suppose it's because I've been ill. These days he really seems to be taking an interest in what I'm doing.

Last night at dinner he actually asked me about Natural
Sources. Were we on target for the end of this financial year?
Was there too much money outstanding with creditors? He
even suggested the different kinds of franchise schemes we
should be looking into."

"He kept phoning me and offering advice when you
were in hospital," said Emily. "I suppose he hasn't got
enough to do. I've heard from Ahmet, by the way. He
has booked two seats for Bombay next Wednesday." She
looked at both of us. "Julia? Ahmet's been awfully good
about holding up the trip, hoping you'd be well
enough . . ."

"I really don't think . . . get your priorities right, the
doctor said, and with the Mels home from school, Simon's
exams . . ."

Julia had that stressful squint at the back of the eyes again,
the way she used to look before reaching down to her
bottom right hand drawer. I'd have to manage it, somehow.

"I'll go," I said. I thought quickly. George could look
after the children; Clerry was at playschool in the mornings,
anyway, and I'd already shown the autumn collection to
press and buyers. "It is my area, after all."

"True," said Emily. "I don't know my weft from my
warp. And Sybilla's hopelessly impractical. She's the one
who okayed those skimpy culottes that didn't fit anyone.
Ahmet sold her some tale about saving money on
fabric."

I hated parking under the dead windows of the granny flat.
If only Stripey hadn't hidden himself away in Gloria's van
that day. I did miss her. And not just for her help with the
children, either. She had been so happy in those last few
months, proudly knocking seconds off her delivery routes:
"If I nip up through the Savoy garage and cross over into
Southampton Street I miss all the traffic on the Embank-
ment and in the Strand, Pauline."

Gloria was a doer, not a thinker. She needed to be busy,

and for most of her life she had nothing to do except store up imagined grievances against her neighbours, fill her days with fattening snacks and unload her resentment on Arthur, when he came home from work in the evening. You could almost feel her frustration beating against the walls of the small terraced house next door.

"For God's sake stop nagging, woman," Arthur would say.

"Don't shout, Arthur, they'll hear us . . ."

Then there'd be a thud on the other side of the thin partition wall (Sanderson's "Bamboo" our side, Fads "Floral" theirs) followed by a sob, and the slam of the front door as Arthur left for the Windsor Castle.

"Shouldn't we do something about it, Brian?"

"I don't think we should interfere, dear," Dad would say, turning *Panorama* up a bit louder.

"Do something about what, Mum?"

"Never you mind, love." I was grown up and engaged to George before she answered that question and I realised what the noises next door really meant.

It had been terrible tidying away the remnants of Gloria's life.

"Will you do it, Pauly?" George had said. "I can't face going in there."

I'd given the clothes to Oxfam, everything except the simulated mink coat Arthur bought her for George's christening. She treasured that coat. When she put it on, for special occasions, it flared out and ballooned down to her ankles in ugly sausage shaped panels. "Looks just like the real thing, doesn't it?" she used to say, swaying this way and that like a model, to show off the fullness. I wrapped it carefully in tissue and mothballs and packed it into a box. I didn't want some laughing young girl foraging through a stall in Portobello Market and holding up Gloria's best coat. "Hey look at this wonderfully kitsch item . . . I've just got to have it. Only five quid."

I found the photograph at the back of a small drawer of

the dressing table, with a pearl necklace, the turquoise clasp in an antique gold setting. I'll keep that for Clerry, I thought, at the same time as another part of my mind was recognising the young couple in the picture, leaning against a Jaguar XK 120, their arms around each other, smiling confidently at the camera. The girl was unmistakably Gloria, young and pretty in a printed cotton frock. The young man looked familiar and rather grand, as though he'd just stepped through a Rattigan french window.

I held the photograph up to the light and studied it carefully. So this was the upper crust boyfriend? He looked kind, a sweet face, and he reminded me of somebody.

It hit me as I was turning the picture over. Of course. Tobias. On the other side of the photograph, Gloria had printed in neat small letters "Boo and me, The Compleat Angler, 1954."

What had she said the first time she saw Toby? "He's the image of his grandfather."

When I got home George was upstairs putting the children to bed. Although the cooker was still a mystery, I'd almost mastered the microwave, and was just extracting two Marks & Spencer duck à l'oranges, when he came into the kitchen wearing his best Jaeger grey flannel suit and a pink and white striped shirt. He looked very handsome.

"I've put the children to bed, Pauly." He took a plate and sat down at the table. "Thought we could dispense with baths tonight, as it's rather late." He chewed the duckling reflectively. "This is very good. A little too much orange, perhaps?"

"Tell M and S."

"Aha, ready prepared, is it? I'll do a proper meal for us tomorrow. I say, Pauly, I had a piece of very good news today."

It seemed a pity to spoil his cheery mood by quibbling over whether expensively purchased duckling à l'orange was proper food or not. "Don't say Pitkin have upped their offer?"

"Pitkin? Lord no. I told Roger Makepeace ages ago that I wasn't interested. This is much more exciting." He held up his chin and gave me his left profile. "Do I look like a member of the landed gentry? A country squire, perhaps, or the younger son of an earl?"

"You look very nice, darling. I was just thinking, as you came in . . ."

"I got the Burberry assignment. Went in to see Sally this morning, and it's all signed and sealed."

"The Burberry assignment?" I had a vague memory at the back of my mind of George going up to London with his portfolio of photographs. But that had been months ago . . .

"You remember, Pauly. Lord Lichfield. A series of advertisements for Burberry. He's going to photograph me standing around in lochs, wearing the classic mac and casting flies or whatever it is they do up there. I'm to fly up to Scotland with him next week."

"Next week? But you can't possibly go to Scotland next week."

"Why ever not? And, I have to tell you, Pauly, it's serious money. More in one week than I earned in three months hard slog at Bolsover."

"But you can't go to Scotland next week. I'm going to India. Julia isn't up to it, you knew I might have to go, I told you . . ."

"Did you?" George narrowed his eyes, pursed his lips, trying to recall the conversation. Lord Lichfield would not have been impressed by this piece of acting. "Anyway, it's out of the question, Pauline. You'll have to postpone India until I get back."

"Ahmet has booked the tickets, made the arrangements, it's all fixed . . ."

"You've only just got back from Japan, Pauline. You can't spend your time whirling round the world, not when you've got a family to look after."

"It's my job, George. And I thought it was your job to look after the children. You're the one who wouldn't have a nanny . . ."

"It wasn't easy to land this assignment. Sally says there were at least half a dozen men up for it. Evidently Patrick was most impressed with my portfolio. Told Sally I had a look of Edward Fox . . ."

"Playing the Duke of Windsor, I suppose."

"How did you know? Said he liked my supercilious sneer." George gave me a petulant look which was more Toby refusing to eat his Farex than the Duke of Windsor subjugating Stanley Baldwin. "I'm not giving this up, Pauline. It's my big chance."

It was his big chance when he joined Bolsover's and I had to leave my job in London, too. "You'll soon find something to do, Pauly," he'd said.

"There'll be other ads, George. I'm going to India next week."

"But Pauline, this is work."

"Mine's work too, and one of us has to stay behind and look after Clerry and Toby . . ."

I was beginning to feel hot and hysterical, boiling up to saying something I'd regret later, like "who's bringing in the money, anyway?" when Clerry came into the kitchen, crying.

"I miss Gan-Gan," she said, pushing a story book towards my knee. "She used to read me this story. When's she coming back?"

"Gan-Gan's not coming back, Clerihue," said George, scooping up Clerry, settling her on his knee, and opening the book. 'Now, let's see. Once upon a time . . .'

"Why isn't Gan-Gan coming back?"

"Because Gan-Gan's gone to heaven," said George, looking up at the Edwardian rise-and-fall light over the table.

"Has Stripey gone to heaven, too?"

"Yes," said George, "Stripey and Gan-Gan are looking after each other in heaven."

"We'll get two new kittens when I get back from India,"

I said, as Clerry began sobbing again. "One for you and one for Toby."

"Ginger kittens? Like Stripey?" Clerry cheered up instantly. If only it was as easy to replace grandmothers. "Where's India?"

"A long way away, darling," said George meanly.

"Only a few hours on an aeroplane, precious, and Mummy's only going for a week."

Clerry jumped off George's knee. "I'm going to tell Toby about the kittens."

"And then get into bed, my love. It's way past your bedtime." As Clerry ran upstairs, I looked at George, placidly eating on the other side of the table. Had I been beastly about insisting on going to India? That article in *The Times* today . . . was I being insensitive?

"George, do you mind being a househusband?"

"What could be more important than bringing up children?"

"I know, only there was an article in *The Times* today . . ."

George's face lit up. "You saw it, did you? One in the eye for David Mainwaring."

"David Mainwaring? You can't mean . . . I don't believe it, George . . . surely you weren't the ex-colleague they quoted?"

"And why not?" said George, defiantly cutting a piece of cheese. "Victoria Phillips phoned me up about it, day before yesterday. Arabella Pinter-Bambury, that nice girl at *Vogue*, put her on to me."

"Never mind about Arabella. What made you talk to the newspapers about David?"

"I had my own reasons for giving the interview, Pauline."

"Quite. I just wondered what they were . . ."

"It'll be excellent publicity, my picture in the paper. The *Mail on Sunday* has asked Victoria to broaden out the news story for a feature with interviews and pictures. Naturally, I was as helpful as possible. Gave her that bit about David for *The Times* piece and told her I'd be prepared to give an in-depth interview, and could probably supply a few interesting case histories. David, Peter, Trevor . . ."

"They'll love that."

"Do you think so? I thought they might be a bit difficult about it, so I told Victoria the case histories would have to be anonymous. 'Mr T.S., forty-six-year-old finance director . . .' You know the kind of thing. I thought I'd invite them round for a game of bridge and ask a few subtle questions. And, would you believe it, David actually phoned up this morning and suggested a meeting? Said he had something important he wanted to discuss."

"Convenient. You'll be able to have your game of bridge and collect your thirty pieces of silver." There was a delicate flush to George's cheeks which, I suspected, had more to do with the excitement of getting his name in the papers than shame about shopping his ex-colleagues. "No wonder you're going pink."

"I'm not going pink. And anyway, I shan't have time to organise anything, with going to Scotland next week."

"But you're not going to Scotland," I said firmly.

"When Lady Sybilla visited us she was staying at the Hilton," Ahmet said, as we sipped champagne and circled above Bombay, "but it would be a great honour to me and to my family, if you would consent to stay in my brother's house. It is in a most pleasant suburb, only a few miles outside Ahmadabad, and really quite convenient for Chikmagur, where my workers are situated."

"That would be very kind, Ahmet. So long as I can phone my husband, when I arrive, and give him my number . . ."

I was amazed when George agreed to sacrifice the Burberry experience to stay at home and look after the children.

"I do see that your work is more important than one little ad, even a series of ads," he'd said. We were in bed at the time, so I couldn't see his expression. I thought it might be ironic and was very slightly worried.

"You're sure? Clerry and Toby will be all right?"

"Of course, darling." He'd snuggled closer, kissed my right ear. "Don't you worry about a thing."

A shorter, fatter, younger version of Ahmet was at the airport to meet us. He sprang out of an old Ford and embraced Ahmet warmly.

"May I present my brother Ashok, Mrs Jenks." Ahmet gazed at his brother proudly. "Mrs Jenks is a very famous designer in London, Ashok."

Ashok said he was charmed and ushered me into the Ford. "It is an exceedingly long journey to Ahmadabad, Mrs Jenks, but we will stop on the way for refreshments. I did not want you taking the public transport. Sheela was most insistent that I welcome you to India myself."

Five years ago abroad meant Majorca to me. Now I could recognise that the Bombay skyline looked rather like Manhattan. But even a tough New York cop would have given up on the traffic. A man was leisurely pulling a cart of dried fish, and half a dozen cows wandered idly in the road. Taxis hooted, car engines boiled and seized up, and the buses pulling up alongside us had limbs protruding from every window. I was not quite sure whether I was experiencing culture shock, jet lag or the pressing need for an iced Perrier with a slice of lemon in it.

Ashok flung himself enthusiastically into the traffic, and didn't take his hand off the horn until we stopped at a small roadside hotel for lunch.

The vegetable curry was delicious, with piles of chapatis to scoop up the juice. The lime drink with it was not delicious at all.

"Nimbopani," said Ashok. "I think you'll find it most refreshing."

"A bottle of wine would not come amiss," said Ahmet, noticing my involuntary grimace.

A television beamed relentlessly from a corner of the restaurant. The manageress, dressed in sari and dupatta, with red pigment in her hair parting, watched impassively as Paul Hogan tickled his taste buds with a tube of Fosters, a lithe young man poured himself into skin-tight jeans and yogurt cartons bounced over the English countryside.

"Very latest advertising video from London," Ashok said. "My children watch them all the time. "I bet he drinks Carling Black Label! You know that one, Mrs Jenks?" He put down his fork, stuck out his chest. "*I'm* with the Woolwich!"

Driving through the state of Gujerat towards Ahmedabad, the roads grew dustier, the earth browner. In the villages men and children sat outside their houses weaving, cooking, washing. A silent graceful army of women, balancing pots on their heads, walked towards distant wells.

"For five years now we have had a very serious drought in Gujerat," said Ashok. "Sometimes it is many miles to the nearest well, so the men are having to do women's work."

An hour later, Ashok slammed on the brakes outside a square concrete box in an estate of concrete boxes, and his wife, Sheela, came out to greet us. She was wearing a sari in shiny vivid Polyester, her jewelled hands were exquisitely manicured and she was wobbling unsteadily on high-heeled Charles Jourdan sling-backs. No water-carrier she. The Basrawys, I discovered, were Sindis; nouveaux riches shopkeepers, businessmen, minor professionals.

"This is a great honour for us, Mrs Jenks." She took my hand in both of hers and ushered me inside. "Come. You will want to make yourself comfortable." She led the way upstairs. "I have put you in our bedroom. No, no, I insist," as I started to protest. "Our bedroom has an en suite bathroom."

I was so tired that the double bed, covered with a garish nylon eiderdown, looked infinitely appealing. The teak tables on each side of the bed supported table lamps with frilly shades. No wonder Sybilla had insisted on the Hilton, I thought ungratefully. It seemed I had crossed the globe to get to Ealing.

"Put Mrs Jenks's cases on the table, Ashok," she said, and taking my arm, led me through a doorway into a tiled bathroom, with shower and lavatory. "The en suite bathroom, Mrs Jenks."

"It is splendid, thank you, Mrs Basrawy."

As she turned to leave the bathroom, Mrs Basrawy's eyes fell on a water jug standing next to the lavatory. The same kind of water jug I had met in the primitive toilet at the hotel en route, and rightly presumed was for sluicing purposes. Mrs Basrawy clapped a hand to her mouth in dismay, dashed out of the bathroom screaming something at her ayah, and returned, triumphantly holding a lilac toilet roll.

"These servants. All the same. They would forget their heads if they were not attached to their bodies. A toilet roll, Mrs Jenks, like the one in the advertisement, with the sweet puppy dog."

I was up early the next day, eager to visit the villages and factories where our cloth was woven and made up into my designs, and to search the markets for antique saris, which I could already see transformed into embroidered silk and organza evening dresses.

"Ashok and I have many business matters to attend to," said Ahmet, over breakfast. "I will leave you in Sheela's good hands, Mrs Jenks . . ."

"But Ahmet . . ."

He raised an imperious hand. "We shall meet you ladies at the Gymkhana Club this evening. Sheela is at your service, Mrs Jenks. Please enjoy yourself, have a good day."

I did not have a good day. In England I was a valued customer and Ahmet was anxious to please. In India I was merely a woman; which meant, in the Basrawy household, sitting around eating chocolates – I had bought Sheela Basrawy a mega-sized box of Cadbury's Dairy Milk at Ahmet's suggestion – peeking through the net curtains at the neighbours, and discussing the shortcomings of the servants.

Sheela's servant seemed to spend most of the day sweeping dust into corners, and she wore the most beautiful soft cotton sari. I wondered if I could ask her where she bought it?

"Poor woman," Sheela popped a soft centre into her mouth and gestured disparagingly at the ayah, "she wears the same old-fashioned sari every day. I have one hundred and ten saris in my wardrobe, all new, the very best. Come, I will show them to you." She gave my cool and simple linen shift a kindly sideways glance. "You will be wanting to change for the Gymkhana Club, I expect?"

I'd vaguely imagined that the Gymkhana Club would be full of chubby children pinning rosettes onto Thelwell ponies, but it was more like the seedy hotel in *Staying On*, where Celia Johnson and Trevor Howard lived out their days dining on doubtful rissoles and memories of the Raj. The Lloyd Loom chairs with sagging seats, the magnificent plaster ceiling rose framing a rigidly ugly stainless steel chandelier, the dusty patina of a St James's club before the committee let in the ladies to pay for refurbishment. And the members of the Gymkhana Club, ranged around a small raised dance floor enjoying well-bred sandwiches with a disconcerting side serving of chips and tomato ketchup, had the same complacent expressions as members of Boodles, supremely confident that they were the right people in the right place.

"Mr Jenks is fighting fit, I trust?" said Ahmet, as we moved decorously together, fighting the rhythm of "Wake Me Up Before you Go-Go." "And the charming children?"

"They are well, thank you." No need to mention that Mr Jenks would be far from fighting fit once I got hold of him.

I'd phoned home just before lunch and there was no reply. Funny, I thought. Seven-thirty in the morning, George should be boiling a kettle for his morning tea, waking Toby and Clerry. After three more attempts, I caught Emily leaving for the office. George, she said, was in Scotland, taking photographs or something.

"What?" I screamed, "but Emily . . . where are the children?"

"They're with Julia, of course. I thought you knew."

A quick call to Julia confirmed George's duplicity. "Nothing to worry about, Pauline. They're having a wonderful time with the Mels, and Alex and Simon are fairly coining it in baby-sitting fees."

Before executing a final stately turn of the floor I vented my displeasure on Ahmet, pointing out that I had not come all the way to India to admire his sister-in-law's saris. I made authoritative noises about late delivery dates, shoddy workmanship, redesigned pared-down culottes. And, as we twirled gracefully up to our table, briskly dropped a hint that there were, after all, other suppliers.

We left for Chikmagur first thing next morning. I'd often wondered why our prints were more predictable than the ethnic bales on the stalls in Birmingham market, and the answer turned out to be that Ashok chose the designs. I also discovered that the Basrawys were weaving the wrong width of fabric for my patterns.

"This is a primitive design, not good enough for Natural Sources, Mrs Jenks." He gestured towards an old man hand-blocking an enchanting jumble of white animals onto the palest yellow cotton. "Now this," he held up a length of silk which I swore I'd disliked in Harrods a few weeks previously, "this is an absolutely exact copy of Seker fabric."

It was going to be easier to standardise the fabric widths than modify Ashok's taste. As I went through their designs with the villagers, he and Ahmet stood at my side contradicting each other.

"That one is no good. Throw it out, please."

"No, no," I said, "the pattern is wonderful, it is almost perfect . . . without the squiggly line, perhaps?"

"A splendid design. Take out the squiggly line, please."

"The colour in this fabric is all washed out. Re-dye, please."

"It's the washed-out look I'm after," I said.

"Colour excellent. Remember in future, all fabric to be washed out."

In the workrooms at Ahmedabad I found that Ashok's machinists, crowded into rickety warrens, were using antique sewing machines well below the standard of Ahmet's London equipment.

"No problem," said Ashok. "We do the basic work here, the finish is supplied in London."

I realised why we had delivery problems. "But that's a waste of time and resources. You'll have to update your machines, Ashok."

"Impossible!" Ashok showed me into a small office and hissed figures at me. "Already I am having to pay women extra money. Before, I paid very fair wage straight to husbands. Now the women demand more money and I have to give it to them direct."

"Before?"

"Before SEWO, Self-Employed Women's Organisation. You know who set them up to this, Mrs Jenks? Middle-class trouble-makers, Communists, all of them. They will be the ruin of me."

Going through the figures I observed that Ashok's profits would bring a gleam of triumph to the eye of any British manufacturer, but I agreed to share the cost of modernising his machinery and his workrooms. I didn't tell the Basrawys, but I looked upon this investment as a gesture of solidarity with SEWO.

I'd travelled out with two suitcases and I came home with six, bursting with incredible colourful cloth, the delicate remains of antique saris.

"There is a very fine market in Bombay, all the latest merchandise," Sheela had said, as Ahmet and I were leaving Ahmedabad. "You will find many beautiful saris there, not like Chadori Chowk . . ." She gave a small shudder of disgust. "That is awful old-fashioned bazaar, nothing new at all."

"Straight to Chadori Chowk, Ahmet," I said, when we arrived in Bombay.

Stepping fastidiously through a thronged bazaar, heavily scented with sweat and fish, he led me into a rickety

Pauline

building, up a staircase, along a long narrow corridor. On each side, through the cracks of partially open doors, I could see people sewing, smoking, sorting cloth, writing. He stopped and tapped at one of the doors.

"Dinesh?"

Dinesh, an elderly Indian, ushered us into a room with shelves on each side holding bundle upon bundle of rags. He made us tea and then pulled down the bundles and untied the rags, spilling out incredible cloth in myriads of colours. A mish-mash of vivid organzas and silks, Chinese embroidery, hand-blocked gold elephants. I bought as much cloth as I could carry and arranged for Dinesh to send regular parcels to Ahmet in Spitalfields.

"If you'd paid attention to the game, partner, instead of chattering like an old woman, you could have dropped your clubs and trumped that queen . . ."

David Mainwaring was downstairs being nasty to George over the bridge table. Served him right. I hadn't forgiven him for lying about Scotland and I didn't think I ever would.

Tucking Clerry into bed, with Toby vulnerably asleep in his cot, I wondered bleakly about our future as a family. George was honest and open when I married him, at least I thought he was. Now, he was sneakily prepared to off-load our children for the sake of a few photographs.

"And how was Scotland?" I'd asked him, when I got home from India. "Was Patrick Lichfield impressed by your Edward Fox profile?"

"Scotland?" George was fussing about at the stove so he didn't have to look at me. "How do you mean . . . Scotland?"

He turned round then and saw it was no use continuing the charade. "I didn't want to worry you, Pauly. I knew Clerry and Toby would be all right with Julia."

"That's not the point, George." The point, I thought, is that I don't trust you any more. But I was too tired to say anything so important.

David Mainwaring was still dissecting the last hand. As I kissed Clerry goodnight, his voice drifted up the staircase, ". . . I called three diamonds to your hearts, if you remember, so why in God's name did we end up with four spades? How about another whisky?"

"As I was saying, Trev . . ." That was George, making rather heavy weather of digging copy out of his ex-colleagues. "Are you finding time hanging on your hands since you left Bolsover?"

"Not at all," replied Trevor. "Watched the Nat West Trophy this morning; brilliant innings by Gower. And I've bought myself rather a neat little PC, with a graphics adapter and a Megabyte of ram . . ."

"What on earth's a ram got to do with computers?" David again. I could almost smell the whisky fumes.

"Dear me, David. Don't tell me computerisation never reached the MD's office. I'm talking random access memory here."

"So, you're doing a bit of work on the computer, Trevor?" Peter Bolsover's voice.

"I'm not working, Peter." Trevor said the word as though it was something unpleasant. "Just playing around, really. You can buy these adventure games, you see. This morning I damn near beat the dragon to the treasure."

"Dragons?" said George. "Treasure?" Clearly, Mr T.S., forty-six-year-old finance director, was contributing some intriguing quotes for Victoria Phillips.

"That's right. It's got these jolly graphics. When you tell the machine to go north, you actually see a figure walking up the screen. It's very clever."

"Sounds damn silly to me," said David. "Another top up, if I may, George."

"Coming up. And how about you, David? Keeping busy?"

"One or two non-executive directorships in the offing. But there's been a lot to do at home with Julia out of action, and then your two adding to the menagerie. I was going to Twickers last week. Had to call it off. Royal Command from Miss Bulstrode, the twins' headmistress, and Julia was caught up in some damn meeting or other. These schools want you to do all their work for them. 'Don't tell me that Melanie is overshadowed by her sister and isn't achieving her full potential,' I said. 'That's your part of ship. I just pay the fees.' And I missed a fantastic try by Williams.''

"It isn't easy for any of us," said George. "Hard on the girls, too."

"That's very true, George," David said, "I've been thinking along those lines myself . . ." He lowered his voice.

Clerry and Toby were both asleep. I crept out of their room and closed the door quietly. The bridge party downstairs had abandoned their game. David was talking about price-earnings ratios and interim pretax profits. "The development potential is there," he was saying, "and I, for one, would be prepared to work for less than I'm worth for an equity stake in the company."

What company? Were the Bolsover board getting together again?

POST-EXECUTIVE DISTRESS: FACT OR FICTION?

There *is* life after redundancy, *Victoria Phillips* discovered when she investigated one man who cheerfully refuses to relax on the scrap-heap.

It is a fairly typical morning in the Jenks household. Pauline, head designer of Natural Sources, is already at her drawing board upstairs. George, who last year lost his job as Sales Director of an engineering firm, is getting breakfast for 4 year old Clerihue and Tobias, who is two. George is rather a perfectionist about breakfasts; 'Any nutritionist will tell you it's the most important meal of the day . . . no bought muesli in this house, I make it up myself. Free-range eggs, of course, though not more than three a week.' And the marmalade? George looks hurt. 'Home-made, what else?'

Does he find the role of house-husband just a little bit demeaning? 'I'm one of the lucky ones. I've turned down several very flattering offers because, well, because this is where I'm needed at the moment – at the heart of the family.'

Do all men deal with redundancy this well? George removes some muesli from Tobias's jersey. 'Three of my friends are in much the same position as I. Sadly, two of them have had difficulty in adapting. Derek plays chess all day on his computer, I gather his family eat a lot of packaged foods, so expensive and no fibre content to speak of. And Paul . . . alcohol is no answer to frustration, of course, but some people are their own worst enemies, aren't they? On the other hand, Gregory has adapted splendidly.'

You, 8th March, 1987

We were well into phase one of the takeover, and as far as I could make out, the girls hadn't the faintest idea of what was going on. They thought we were being helpful. Typical of women, not to notice what's going on under their noses; my father certainly had a point.

I first began to realise what David was up to when Trevor dropped in a few days after my bridge party. We were a bit chaotic at the time, what with Pauline being behind on some designs for the January showings, and the Indesit man in to repair the washing machine.

"Come and look at our new kittens, Mr Sutcliffe," said Clerry, dragging him into the kitchen, "they're called Mindy and Mork."

Pauline stopped talking to the Indesit man. "Trevor!

How nice. Coffee? This gentleman says, George, that we have omitted to clean the outlet filter, otherwise there's nothing wrong."

"It says nothing in the instructions about servicing the filter."

"Yes it does, mate, on page nine. Nice pair of kittens you've got there. The wife breeds Burmese. Any particular type, those two?"

"How much do I owe you?" I intervened, before Pauline could fall into conversation. She'd gone and given him a cup of coffee, always a mistake with tradesmen. Call-out charges are quite high enough, they'll take any excuse to stay in the house over the hour.

I paid the Indesit man (I would have preferred to bargain a bit about the cost, but I didn't like to with Trevor standing there listening) and took Trevor through to the den.

"I'm thinking of putting up some more shelves," I said. "Quite soon I'll be calling this room the library," I added humorously.

Trevor strolled over to look at my bookshelf; that'll impress him, I thought, I'm building up quite a nice little collection. The *Reader's Digest* DIY manual, *Jane Austen Retold as Short Stories*, two Jeffrey Archers, and the *Anthology of Seafaring Tales*, which I inherited from my grandfather. And, of course, all Stephen King in paperback.

"Quite," said Trevor. Two marks out of ten for enthusiasm, but then these mathematical types don't go in much for reading.

"Anyway, George, what do you think?"

"What do I think about what?"

"This idea of David's. As I told you when I first heard about it, I thought it was a bit, well, sharp. But I can see his point, can't you?"

"Not really. He's a bit difficult to understand when he's been drinking."

I hoped Trevor would go soon. There was a new recipe for monkfish I wanted to try out, from the *Financial Times* weekend section. Such a relief not to have to read the financial part any more; anyway, Pauline always bagged it and took it up to her studio. I don't suppose she understood any of it, probably thought it looked good lying around.

"I can see what David's getting at," Trevor droned on, "ripe for a takeover, when you stand back and have a good look."

The trouble is you've got to marinate it first, and monkfish takes such a long time to prepare, with all those slippery bits to remove.

"Who's ripe for a takeover, Trevor?"

He lowered his voice and looked at the door. "Emily and the others, of course, Natural Sources."

"Take over Natural Sources? Is that what David was going on about? Who's going to take them over?"

"For heavens' sake keep your voice down. We are, of course."

The monkfish would have to wait. This was getting a bit dodgy.

"Who's we? You and David and me?"

"Logical, when you think about it. Julia's always ill, Sybilla spends her time being photographed, Pauline is overworked, and Emily . . ."

"I had the impression Emily was doing a very good job."

"I never see her," Trevor said fretfully, "and when I do see her she says haven't I got anything better to do than play silly computer games. Silly! Some of those games require considerable skill, George. There's a new chess one that –"

"Anyway, I don't think the girls would like it."

"I'm sure they would, once they got used to the idea. Be honest, George, do you like sitting around doing nothing?"

"Doing nothing? Running a house, bringing up two children? *Nothing?*"

"It's not exactly what we were trained for, is it? David says we're not achieving our potential, and I think he's right."

"Anyway, we can't, can we? Natural Sources isn't a

public company. Their shares aren't on the open market, so how can we buy them out?"

"That's the beauty of David's plan. We don't buy them out, we infiltrate. He's been making a point, recently, of taking an interest in Julia's work. Made a few suggestions about streamlining, franchising, that kind of thing . . ." He caught my eye. ". . . I know what you're thinking, but I really believe he's learned his lesson, George. Got some very shrewd ideas about pilferage, for instance."

I imagined David Mainwaring's ideas on pilferage wouldn't be all that dissimilar to what went on in Saudi Arabia. I used to work at Natural Sources, now I'm left-handed, kind of thing. Something else occurred to me.

"You haven't mentioned Peter. What's his reaction?"

Trevor wandered over to my bookshelf, picked up *Jane Austen Retold as Short Stories*, and riffled casually through it.

"Peter? Bit premature to give him the full picture, David thinks." He shuddered slightly, and put the book down.

"Not too cold in here for you, is it? Why not give him the full picture?"

"Well . . . you know Peter. Playing fields of Eton, and all that stuff."

"I say, do borrow that book if you'd like to, Trevor. It makes quite a good read with all the boring bits cut out. It's all right, it's got my bookplate in it. Playing fields of Eton?"

"Straight bat, doing the decent thing."

"You mean you and David think that Peter wouldn't think it was quite above board, for us to worm our way into Natural Sources?"

"Not worm our way. David feels we could really be of help."

"If Peter doesn't have anything to do with it, neither will I. I'll just find you a carrier bag."

"What?"

"For the book. It's deluxe leatherette, I wouldn't want it to get wet. No, no, I insist."

I bustled him towards the door. Potato salad would be rather good with the monkfish, high time I started supper. Trevor stopped and looked thoughtfully at me.

"George, aren't you tired of having dish-washing hands?"

"Boots do an extremely good cream. It's their Traditional Hand Conditioning Cream, I can personally recommend it."

"Oh, really, George, do listen to yourself. Do you honestly think you were put into the world to tell another man what kind of handcream to use?"

Put like that, I thought, after he'd gone . . . and when you got down to it, wasn't Pauline taking rather a lot for granted, these days? Don't forget this, and have you done that. And to cap it all, I'd made a real effort with Lamb Polo for supper the night before, and all she'd done was push it round her plate.

"Actually, George, I had lamb for lunch at the Connaught. This is delicious of course, very interesting. Oh, you haven't done a pudding, have you? If only I'd known, I wouldn't have eaten all those profiteroles."

I was approached again a week or so later. This time by David, ringing me up to thank me for a dinner party I'd given the night before. Since he never thanked anyone for anything, I guessed he wanted something.

"Bloody good parsley dumplings, George. How do you do them?"

I had to laugh. David Mainwaring, ex-Marlborough, ex-Oxford, and particularly ex-the managing director's office of Bolsover Engineering Ltd. What a come-down to have to phone George Jenks to grovel for a recipe for parsley dumplings.

"Well, actually, David, I just made them up as I went along . . ."

Page 57 of *Poor Cook*, as it happens, but he could find that out for himself. I wasn't the head of his sales force any more, and I'd got better things to do with my life than dictate recipes for parsley dumplings. It was nearly time I gave my two their lunch, actually.

". . . a bit of this, a bit of that, you know the form."

"Smashing dinner last night, George. Julia was saying on the way home that we ought to get your recipe for Chocolate Marquise. She's got those American buyers over next week, you know, and she wants us to give them something a bit out of the ordinary . . . so I wondered . . . ?"

The way he was talking, anyone would think he actually did some cooking himself. We all knew all he did around the house was tell Julia she paid too much for fabric softener. He'd taken the credit for other people's work at Bolsover's, too.

". . . anyway, I'll be round your way after lunch. Got to get Alexandra some pot plants to take back to school, so we'll be dropping by the garden centre this afternoon . . ."

Alexandra went to some swept-up girls' school in the Home Counties where as far as I could make out it was considered rather working-class to get more than four O levels, and one of them had to be Art; I could just imagine what she'd think of George Jenks and his dish-washing hands.

"Look forward to seeing you," I said untruthfully. I put the phone down and tiptoed up to Pauline's studio. I would really have enjoyed giving it a good tidy.

Bolts of cotton everywhere, drawings, old mugs with paintbrushes stuck in them, a pie-dish full of pastels and crayons and charcoal. I didn't know how she worked in all that clutter, but all she ever said was, "Leave it alone, George, I know where everything is."

I opened the door quietly and put my head round. Pauline didn't like to be disturbed when she was creating something, but I'd done brains in black butter and baby carrots for Clerry and Toby. It would do her good to have a break and eat with the rest of us like a family.

Pauline looked round at me with that quick smile that meant Now What?

"Not interrupting you, am I? Only I've done the brains a new way; there's masses if you'd like some. How are you getting on?"

I picked up one of her sketches and looked at it admiringly.

"The old hand hasn't lost its skill, has it? I do like the way you've draped that cross-over."

Pauline took the sketch from me, scrunched it up and chucked it vaguely in the direction of the Lord Roberts' Workshop logbasket which she used as a rubbish bin. It missed and I went over and picked it up.

"It was a reject, actually. Do leave it alone, George, I'll tidy everything up later."

"You look tired. Come and have some lunch. Come on. You've been at it all morning. Honestly, Pauly, those three don't half take advantage of you. Where would they be without you?"

That didn't go down very well.

"I hate it when you say that, George. I really hate it. They work just as hard as I do, only differently. Who was that on the phone? I was expecting Julia to ring about the antique saris . . ."

"Actually it was David. Wants to drop round later with that frightful Alexandra. Wants my recipe for parsley dumplings, actually."

"Not surprised, they were delicious. David? According to Julia, he can't find his way to the kitchen."

"And what did you tell Julia about me? What a light hand I've got with pastry? How I always seem to have a headache at bedtime? I don't like you talking about me behind my back."

"George. What on earth are you on about? I don't talk about you, just listen to the others talking about their husbands. I'm starving, let's go and attack those brains of yours. What time is David coming? I'll stay upstairs, if you don't mind."

* * *

"Trevor tells me you're a bit iffy about Peter's attitude," said David after we'd persuaded Alexandra to read to Clerry and Toby in the garden.

"If you think he'd think it was underhanded, then I think I'd think that too." And anyway I don't like you very much, I added mentally.

"As a matter of fact, old Trev may have overplayed the, er, the takeover aspect rather. Don't get me wrong, we don't want to do the girls out of anything, just help them along a bit. Put it this way; they're doing very well, in their way, by themselves. Think how much better Natural Sources would do with our shoulders to the wheel."

"With a bit of luck it might even do as well as Bolsover's," I said sourly.

"Bolsover's. Yes, well, don't you see, that's rather why we're keeping a bit mum as far as Peter's concerned. Salt of the earth, and all that, but even his best friend . . ." and that certainly isn't you, I thought, ". . . wouldn't call him a businessman. You heard him yourself at our last board meeting, admitting that –"

"He's always been very nice to me," I said.

"Puts up a good front, I'll grant you. But behind your back, George . . . don't mind admitting I had to go out on a limb for you, once or twice. Very glad to do it, of course, you know where my loyalties lie. Didn't think the way he was talking was quite the done thing. Anyway, think it over."

Think what over? I thought, as I stirred a bechamel that night. It's all a bit of a muddle. Whatever David said today, he and Trevor obviously plan to take over from the women. David to replace Julia, Trevor, I supposed, to be finance director instead of Emily. And if I did agree to go in, where would that put me? I couldn't design clothes instead of Pauline, even if I had the time (though I wouldn't be surprised if it wasn't a lot easier than she makes out). I didn't see why I should be expected to run the house and have a career as well; I wouldn't have a minute to myself. Why trust David anyway? Of course he was lying when he implied Peter had said things behind my back; he'd never do that. Not about me, with our special relationship.

The biggest question of all was why did David and Trevor want me at all? They'd never thought much of me at Bolsover's.

I'd quite made up my mind, by the following morning, that I'd have nothing to do with their furtive plans. I decided, as I shaved, that I'd tell Pauline all about it. Forewarned is forearmed, I thought.

It turned out when I got downstairs that I had forgotten to make Clerry a horse hat for the playgroup Entertainment. I'd also forgotten to tell Pauline that the Entertainment was that afternoon.

"I've got to look like a horse by after lunch," wailed Clerry.

"Really, George, how could you have forgotten to tell me? Of course Mummy's coming to see you be a horse, darling. Damn, I'll have to phone Emily and get her to . . . what kind of horse, Clerry?"

"A night," snuffled Clerry.

"A night horse? Do you mean a nightmare, darling?"

"No, Mummy, a night for chess."

"Oh, that kind of knight," said Pauline. "Don't worry, darling, I'll soon make one for you."

"I was going to," I said stiffly.

"Yes, but you didn't, did you? And look at this kitchen . . . go up to my studio, Clerihue, and find some horse-coloured cotton in the bin under my table . . . really, George, do I have to do everything round here? Work all day, empty the dishwasher at night, and you can't even get round to making a horse's head."

She flounced out and I started tidying up the kitchen. Empty the dishwasher? She did it once last week. If that was the way she wanted to play it . . . I picked up the telephone.

"Trevor? Can't say much at the moment, but I'm with you all the way . . ." Pauline walked back into the kitchen. ". . . boil them first, do you? That's a very good wrinkle,

Trevor, I must write that one down." Pauline snatched up some scissors, glared at me, and flounced out again. "Sorry about that, one of the opposition. When do we meet?"

After I'd put the phone down, I went upstairs to speak firmly to Pauline.

Waitrose was opening its St Neots branch. We had all been watching the building go up with some excitement; ("Modern architecture at its best," said Trevor. I don't know what he thinks he knows about it; anyone can see it's roomy and light and looks welcoming, without being pompous about modern architecture.)

"I don't think I'll go in the morning," I said to Pauly, "there's bound to be a crush. Masses of parking, though, they've really thought it out very –"

"Who cares when you go?" said Pauline. She had taken to a rather moody manner since I had to admonish her about the horse's head last September, but Christmas cheered her up no end, and anyway one has to put one's foot down sometimes.

To pass the time until I went shopping I got Sunday's *You* magazine out from under the settee. A really excellent photo of yours truly, very good publicity for my modelling career, if I chose to go on with it. Unfortunately Amanda Braithwaite didn't approve of modelling. Nothing Better than Prostitution, she called it, and while I thought that was going a little far, I was beginning to see her point.

I had given a lot of information about husbands adapting to redundancy and house roles to Victoria. Perhaps rather too much, I thought, as I reread the article for about the fifteenth time.

Of course I had insisted on changing all the names, but they'd have no difficulty in identifying themselves; only "Gregory" would be pleased. Peter would really appreciate being described as "a gentleman of the old school . . . content to potter about his beautiful garden and take the dogs for walks."

"Paul" and "Derek", though, perhaps I was a bit . . .

Pauline sauntered in.

"I thought you were going to Waitrose? What's that you're reading?"

"I did tell you, Pauline, I'm going this afternoon. Actually . . ." I supposed I would have to show it to her sooner or later, might as well get it over with, ". . . it's that article I was helping with for *You Magazine*."

"And you've had it since Sunday? Why didn't you show it to me? Let's have a look."

"Would you like some coffee, dear?"

"Love some, thanks."

By the time I got back with the coffee, she was deep into it.

"Pretty good photo of me, don't you think?"

"Oh, George."

"What? I don't expect they'll recognise themselves, do you?"

"'A gentleman of the old school.' Peter will *die*. And all that about the other two, I don't suppose any of them will speak to you again."

"Clerihue and Tobias are making a lot of noise in the garden, aren't they?"

"Never mind about them, they're just playing. How on earth are you going to face Peter and David and Trevor? And how am I going to face their wives?"

I parked outside Waitrose full of anticipation. I couldn't believe it was only a year since Bolsover's was taken over. Those were the days when I hardly knew my way round supermarkets, couldn't have made pesto if you'd paid me, didn't know how to switch on the Hoover. Didn't know where the Hoover was kept, if we were going to be honest.

The parking facilities were quite extensive, I noted. But when I got to the PAY HERE machine, I also noted that the machine didn't give change, so my 15p's worth actually cost me 20. Disgraceful, really, I would make a point of writing to the council about it.

Inside it was quite festive, more like going to a party

than doing the shopping. All the employees were beaming, and when I asked a young assistant where the taramasalata was, he didn't just tell me, he took me there. Trevor and Emily Sutcliffe were also buying taramasalata. I kissed Emily on the cheek, and then wondered whether it was Etiquette to kiss an acquaintance near the packeted delicatessen.

"Hello, George," she said, "everyone seems to be here. Have you seen Peter? Pondering the Laphroaig. And David's over by the fish. Pricing the plaice, probably."

"Quite a gala occasion," I said. "I didn't know they did cartons of custard, did you? And have you seen the bread section?"

"Well, must get on," said Trevor; he seemed restive. Probably afraid I would talk about Natural Sources in a tactless way. He might have given me credit for some sense.

I pushed my trolley, laden with aubergines, peppers and courgettes (ratatouille tonight) not to mention cat food and litter, towards the wine section, hoping to see Peter. I hadn't liked to display my ignorance in front of the Sutcliffes, but Laphroaig sounded to me like a French wine. Disappointingly, he wasn't there, but I busied myself choosing sherry.

"George. I can't believe what I'm seeing. Et tu, Brute?"

It was Amanda Braithwaite. As well as organising the playgroup, she was currently editing a fact sheet on inequality. I didn't know what she lived on, as the playgroup work was voluntary, and the fact sheet was handed out free in the streets to people who dropped it in the gutter. Amanda was looking at my trolley as though it contained cut-price chastity belts.

I knew perfectly well what et tu Brute meant, we did Julius Caesar for O levels, but I couldn't quite see what Amanda found treacherous in my trolley. I quickly ran through the causes she supported . . . kangaroos in the cat food, perhaps? Or did the aubergines come from somewhere morally unacceptable? I thought they were Spanish. Surely Spain was all right since Franco had gone?

"South African sherry, George, how could you?"

I should have remembered that Amanda's background is very County; early standards die hard.

"Not going to drink it, of course, Amanda, this is for cooking . . . not bad at all for cooking."

"I'm not talking about how it tastes, George. I'm talking about the heel of tyranny the men and women who picked these grapes toil under. You can't possibly support it."

"No, well, I don't, of course, but –"

Amanda took the South African sherry (actually it was delicious) out of my trolley and replaced it with Amontillado, Produce of Spain. At least I knew my aubergines were ethical, but I couldn't help noticing the new bottle was a pound dearer than my first choice. Taking a Stand on the Moral High Ground does nothing for one's budget.

"It makes you cringe, doesn't it . . . ?" said Amanda, gazing round Waitrose. It was full of cheerful people, piling their trolleys with good food. ". . . do you think any of these yuppies ever consider taking a stance on Nicaragua? Do they realise they are cramming their bellies with nutrition that belongs by rights to the Third World? Degrading, isn't it, to live in a country that spends more on its pets than a Bengali family does on its children?"

I pushed some onions over the Whiskas, and wished Amanda would lower her voice. Perhaps there was something else we could chat about.

"I was thinking, Amanda, whether your living accommodation is satisfactory? You did say, the other day, that one or two of the other ladies, persons, in the commune were proving a bit . . ."

"Hopelessly bourgeois values. I have better things to do with my time than polishing bath taps."

"Quite. Only our granny flat has been empty now since . . . since July, and I thought you might like to –"

"What kind of rent are you asking? I might be very interested, George, and then we could have our discussion group in your sitting room. Much more space than we've got now." She turned to a young assistant. "I'd like to see the manager of the wine department, please."

"I'll just get him, if you'll wait a moment."

Amanda turned back to me.

"I am going to challenge him about the South African sherry. Quite often it's just ignorance, you know. When you point out to them that they're wilfully supporting apartheid, they are sometimes quite reasonable."

"I must go and find a leg of lamb," I said, not wishing to be part of the ensuing conversation.

We met again in the car park when we'd both finished our shopping.

"How did your conversation with the wine manager go?"

"We may well have to picket, George. Let's have a meeting at your house about it. Would Pauline be interested in carrying a banner, do you think?"

I got home to find Pauline was on the irritable side, so I didn't mention the banners. I'd left the children with her while I went shopping, not an unreasonable arrangement, I would have thought; but apparently Clerihue had spilt poster paint on some tussore, Mindy had bitten a piece out of Mork's ear, ". . . and Tobias is eating cat food again . . . you'd think, after all the fuss you make about nutritive values . . ."

I sometimes think Pauly doesn't quite realise the demands of looking after two toddlers. Toby was doing exactly what he should as a two-year-old, exploring his little environment and experimenting with tastes and textures. Amanda had said only recently at the Mums and Toddlers discussion group that Young Minds should never be Trammelled. "They should roam like free spirits, questing, questioning, querying. Never say No to a Small Child. That is like slamming the door of experience in its face."

Unfortunately Toby always seemed to do his questing when Pauly was about.

"Did you hear what I said, Clerihue? For the last time, No, Mum is not going to take you to feed the quack-quacks. I'm busy, that's why."

I could see this was not the moment to point out to

Pauline that she had just slammed the door of experience in Clerry's face, and that Amanda considered baby talk to be regressive. We did not refer to quack-quacks and choo-choos; we talked about trumpeter swans, if that's what they were, and Inter-City 125s.

"Come on, Clerihue and Tobias, upstairs. Dad will take you to feed the trumpeter swans after your nap."

"Want to feed the quack-quacks with Mum," droned Clerihue. "I rove my Mummy. Don't rove Daddy. Don't want a nap."

"Love, Clerihue, not rove. Daddy give you a piggy-back? Up the stairs to Bedfordshire."

"We're already in Bedfordshire, silly Daddy. Mummy, give me a piggy-back."

"Actually we're in Cambridgeshire."

One should always tell children the truth, even when they're being particularly tiresome. I would have been quite hurt if Amanda hadn't warned us. "The parent-figure that has, by necessity, to set the parameters of what passes as sociably acceptable behaviour is not necessarily the one who appears, to rebellious young minds, the most attractive."

"Clerihue. Tobias," said Pauline, "go upstairs at once and get into bed or I will eat you both up for my tea."

Both children screamed with laughter and went upstairs.

"Pauly . . . darling . . . should you? Threats of violence, who knows what effect on the receptive young mind. Amanda Braithwaite says –"

"Rubbish. They know I wouldn't lay a finger on them. I can't remember what Mrs Braithwaite looks like. Isn't she frizzy-haired and ethnic?"

"Amanda Braithwaite is, as it happens, a very attractive woman."

"Not attractive enough to persuade the father of her children to stick with her, apparently . . ."

(Considering Pauline had an artistic temperament, her views on one-parented families were a shade old-fashioned. I was not going to get into an argument with her on this issue, and I would have to be a little more tactful in my references to Amanda. I could see that Pauline, stuck up in her loft designing all day, was just a wee bit green-eyed about my new friends.)

". . . and her views on children are hopelessly out-dated. Discipline is the thing, nowadays. You really ought to be a bit firmer with them, George. This place looks as though Jemima Puddleduck does the cleaning."

I'd managed to put Pauline in one of her moods, and for the life of me I couldn't tell you why. And who was Jemima Puddleduck? Some children's book character that everyone knew about except George Jenks, I supposed.

We'd had quite an interesting session about Books and the Awakening perception at the Mums and Toddlers. We'd all agreed that reading matter for little minds must reflect life as it is; rabbits do not wear coats and trousers, and bears do not have friends who are kangaroos.

"A. A. Milne," said Amanda, "has a lot to answer for."

I was sure she was right, but didn't quite like the idea of teaching Clerihue to read *Jenny Lives with Eric and Jeremy*, or whatever it was called.

It was obviously not a propitious time to broach my idea about Amanda taking over the granny flat.

Magistrate lashes out at local 'sweatshop'

Fining Mr. Ahmet Basrawy, proprietor of a clothing factory in Paradise Walk, Brick Lane, E1, £1,500 at Old Street Magistrates Court yesterday, magistrate Mr. Philip Johnson said the conditions in his Brick Lane factory were as bad as those in the Indian sub-continent. 'It is a disgrace that we should be replicating some of the conditions these people have left behind,' he said.

Basrawy was forced to close down his factory when Factory Inspector John Hopkins and Senior Fire Prevention Officer Derek Hubbard issued a Prohibition Notice earlier this week. They told magistrates that when they visited Basrawy's premises they found faulty wiring, no running hot water, fire exits blocked by bundles of rags and children as young as 14 working in the factory.

Basrawy, of Oakley Avenue, Rainham, Essex, pleaded guilty to failing to register his factory with the Health and Safety Executive and to offences under the Health and Safety at Work Act and the Children and Young Persons' Act 1933. He was not available for comment yesterday.

East London Advertiser,
17th June, 1987

The speedometer read 80, irresponsibly speedy when you've got two children belted in behind you, your palms are sweating, your mind is in a turmoil and you're exhibiting all the symptoms of panic. Or was I having a nervous breakdown as I bypassed Biggleswade?

"How fast are we going, Mummy?"

"Too fast, darling." My Renault was equipped with Turbo technology like the cooker and had a mettlesome way of racing over the speed limit if I touched the accelerator.

"I like going fast," said Clerry. "Are we nearly at Gran's?"

"Gan-Gan's in heaven," said Toby.

"Not Gan-Gan, stupid, Gran."

I wasn't leaving George . . . I didn't think I was, anyway. Just going to my mother for a few days. I hadn't seen enough of her since Dad died. It was time she saw the grandchildren . . . better slow down, that BMW was over-taking blind. I was fooling myself, of course. What I really meant was that after that second time, I had to get away . . .

And then we were on the motorway, and I had plenty of time to think about what I've been trying to forget.

It started with that stupid horse's head. Maybe I did go a bit over the top, but there was so much to do that week. We were setting up the franchises, standardising shopfronts, interviewing retailers, choosing the key distributor for each area, sitting through endless presentations from advertising agencies.

When George first started at Bolsover's and was whey-faced with anxiety about not achieving his sales targets, I'd transformed into an obliging mixture of Claire Rayner and Deborah Kerr, offering bracing encouragement one moment, solicitous sherry and sympathy the next. Surely, now that I was the one under pressure, it wasn't asking too much for George to cope with a horse's head?

He'd come into the studio as I was kneeling on the floor, cutting out the horse-coloured fabric; thank God Clerry wasn't there; she'd sulked off to the nursery to put on a pair of white leotards after I'd vetoed her new tartan dress as being an unsuitable outfit for a white knight.

"Pauline . . ."

"What is it now?" I said impatiently.

"Don't ever speak to me like that again, Pauline," he said.

"What on earth are you talking about?" I turned and looked up at him. A cold stranger was standing over me with a clenched fist. I started to rise.

I think he was as surprised as I was when he thumped me on the shoulder.

I rubbed my shoulder. "Hey, George, that hurt . . ."

"I'm not your servant, Pauline."

"But you *hit* me."

"I had to, Pauline," he said. "It's no good talking to you any more; you never listen."

He left the room after that, and acted afterwards as though nothing had happened. I tried to do the same. He was unhappy, he didn't mean it, I reassured myself. In spite of all the bravado in that embarrassing *Mail on Sunday* article about wanting to be where he was most needed, the plain fact was that in two years George had turned from a director of a public company into someone whose most pressing decision of the day was finding an amusing new way to cook monkfish.

We went to the playgroup Entertainment that afternoon, sitting close in the small car, isolated from each other. As I drove the Renault straight into a vacant parking spot I expected George to say, "Reverse in, Pauline," the way he always did. But he didn't say anything.

"Ten out of ten to the Jenks family for originality and presentation." One of the other mothers came up to us after the rousing "Ten Green Bottles" finale. "That was an exceptionally fine horse's head."

"All Pauly's doing." George put an arm around me, a convincing performance of the proud, affectionate husband. It hurt when he touched my shoulder.

"I'll be home late tonight," I told George the following morning.

"I will keep something in the oven for your supper," he answered politely. They were the first words we'd exchanged since the playgroup Entertainment.

I had a long day ahead; we had to approve an advertising campaign, and agree a standard shop design for the franchises.

"Let's choose the first one that doesn't give us a slide show of all their previous brilliant campaigns," said Sybilla.

"Or the one that's actually bothered to find out what Natural Sources is all about, instead of giving us their interpretation of what they think we ought to be doing," said Emily.

The advertising agency fielded half a dozen bright young experts who sat across the table from Julia, Sybilla, Emily and me, lecturing us earnestly about area consumer profiles (from what I could gather everyone in Area J drove around in Porsches while the unfortunate residents in Area K still stumbled down the garden to the outside toilet), market share (they were going to give us more of it), future sales projects (hopeful if we signed on the dotted line with them) and the estimated CPT (I didn't like to ask what that was).

"CPT?" said Julia.

"Cost per thousand," said Emily.

Then they showed us the ads they intended to plaster over poster sites across the country, and put into magazines with the right target audience.

"Not a hard enough sell," said Emily, studying scenes of such rural purity they made the Hovis ads look unwholesome.

"Nonsense," said Sybilla. "We're not flogging merchandise here, Emily, we're creating an image."

The six young experts smiled at her gratefully and turned to Julia and me.

"I like it," said Julia.

"Me too," I said, wondering why I always seemed to be the last voice in the Greek chorus.

There was more evocative imagery after lunch when we were presented with "a new shopping concept", as the head of the design team put it. "It's like you walk into your neighbour's house, see this great jacket slung across the back of a chair and you've just got to have it."

"Another soft sell," said Emily, gazing gloomily at shop interiors designed to look like rustic log cabins with stripped pine floors, sheaves of wheat in the fireplace and garments strewn artlessly over antique screens and cretonne-covered chairs.

"Very clever," said Sybilla, "though I must say it doesn't look like *my* neighbour's house."

"We can't afford to build replicas of Eaton Square in every suburban High Street," said Emily tartly. She studied the drawings more closely. "Where's the merchandise? What about pricing?"

The head of the design team tapped the old pine cupboards and chests, doors and drawers invitingly open, with his Mont Blanc fountain pen.

"These will take at least two garments of your complete range in every size." He picked up an embroidered sweater, a best seller last season, and a linen skirt, my favourite design in the current collection, and flipped over the hems to reveal colourful price tickets. "Each price tag is colour coordinated to the size," he said, "and attached to the bottom of the garment for easy consumer access."

"No more fumbling around necklines looking for the price and the elusive size twelve, and finding incomprehensible pictures telling you how to do your washing," said Emily. "I'll go for that."

"It's got a friendly, unintimidating look to it," said Julia, "not the kind of shop you have to dress up for. I like it."

"Me too," I said again.

It all went so quickly that I was home by half past four, thinking how lovely, I'd have a couple of relaxed hours with the children before they went to bed. Toby was in his cot, fast asleep and very wet. Clerry and George were nowhere to be seen.

Where was George? Why was Toby in bed already? And shouldn't he be dry by twenty-one months, anyway? I lifted him from the cot. He was warm and damp and he entwined his arms beguilingly around my neck.

We chatted happily as I changed him.

"Who's the best baby in the world, then?"

"Toby . . ."

"Who loves Toby?"

"Mummy . . ."

I cuddled him and brooded over the dilemma of being an absentee mother. When I had Clerry there was time to gossip with the other mothers at the clinic about all the things that mattered. "Is yours on solids yet?" . . . "You can't beat Zinc and Castor Oil Ointment for nappy rash,'' . . . "What do you think about the whooping cough vaccine?"

But my view of Toby's babyhood had been mostly through George's eyes and sometimes it was a bit of a blurred picture.

"The nurse at the antenatal clinic says he's doing splendidly," George had reported a few weeks ago. "Just the occasional loss of sphincter control."

"You mean there's something wrong . . . ?" My voice rose hysterically.

"Nothing at all," said George, lowering his voice reprovingly as Clerry came into the room. "Perfectly normal. I didn't tell you because I knew you'd fuss."

I'd just settled Toby back into his cot, was making myself a cup of tea and reflecting on this curious change of attitude, when George and Clerry and Amanda Braithwaite walked into the kitchen.

"*There* you are, George," I said, slamming down the kettle. "Where have you been?"

"Careful with that hob, Pauline," he picked up the kettle, inspecting the ceramic surface for a stray scratch, "and I don't have to tell you where I am every minute of the day. Amanda's here."

I gave Amanda a brisk nod of acknowledgement. "You most certainly do, George, when Toby's left all alone in the house."

"Only for a minute, Pauline. I was next door, showing Amanda the granny flat."

"Granny flat!" Amanda Braithwaite smirked unpleasantly, and settled herself at the kitchen table. "What a bourgeois concept."

I'd had enough of advertising concepts and design concepts that day and didn't intend discussing bourgeois ones with Ms Braithwaite. "A cup of tea, Mrs Braithwaite?"

I could see that she was considering a polemic about the derogatory sexist connotations of the appellation "Mrs", but decided against it. There was an anxious-to-please look about her as she said, "I like the flat. It has peaceful vibrations."

"Gloria was always very happy there," I passed her a cup of tea. "Milk? Sugar?"

She peered suspiciously into the cup. "Is it a tisane?"

"P.G. Tips," I said.

"Oh. No thank you. Yes, the flat will be a good environment for Jake and Canvey."

Jake and Canvey? I looked over at George who was still studying the ceramic hob with determined concentration.

"Jake and Canvey?" I said to George, when Amanda Braithwaite had left. "They sound like a couple of 'sixties folk singers."

"They are Amanda's children," George turned and gave me a rather appealing grin. "Or, as she prefers to put it, her womb nourished them."

"Sounds disgusting." I realised I was smiling back in a friendly sort of way. If I wasn't careful I'd find myself nodding agreeably as Amanda Braithwaite, and her no doubt frightful children, took root above the garage.

I put my cup of tea down firmly on the table. "They're not coming here, George," I said, which started it all.

Evidently George had offered Amanda the flat after she had an ideological disagreement with the other members of her Cambridge commune about cleaning the bath, and was asked to leave. "She has nowhere else to go, Pauline, and she'll pay a fair rent; she's already fixed it with the council."

"The council? You mean £10 a week and she's a sitting tenant for life. May I point out who put down most of the money for this house and who pays the mortgage?"

There was a tug at my skirt. "I don't like Jake. He hurt my teddy bear." I'd forgotten Clerry was still in the room.

"Up to bed, darling. I bet you 5p you can't get undressed and tucked up before I get there." Clerry raced off upstairs.

I lost my 5p, as it turned out.

"How dare you taunt me about money?" George said as he hit me, "and in front of the child, too."

He lashed out again, but I was too fast for him. I did a quick dodge and he hit his fist on the fridge.

Later I went in to see Clerry. She was fast asleep in bed with her arms around her teddy bear. "He won't hurt your teddy again," I whispered fiercely, "I won't let Jake hurt teddy."

Clerry opened her eyes. "You owe me 5p, Mum." she said.

I slept in the studio that night.

"Coffee for you, Pauly?" He'd pushed the coffee pot towards me at breakfast the next morning, munching his filthy home-made muesli as though we were a normal happily married couple. Then he went off early to some meeting with David Mainwaring.

Apparently the old Bolsover board were in the process of taking over another company, although I couldn't imagine where they'd got the money. Nor, for that matter, how they could work together after slinging all that mud at each other last time.

I dressed the children, packed a couple of cases, and left a note on the mantelpiece, the way they always do in television plays, saying that I had gone to my mother's.

"Are we nearly at Gran's now, Mummy?"

"Nearly, darling. But we've got to cross London, first."

Clerry pressed her face against the window, leaving a moist mark on the glass. "I don't like London."

Down Cricklewood Lane, across Willesden to Acton . . . Gloria would have appreciated this subtle route. It was warm in the car but I'd better not roll up my shirt sleeves or Mum would start asking questions. Something clicked in the back of my mind. The memory of Gloria Jenks walking up our street on a blazingly hot August day, wearing a blue dress with long sleeves.

Mum's sitting room was smaller than I remembered it, and there were dozens of little tables, loaded with precious possessions for Clerry and Toby to knock over. Overawed by the strange surroundings, they were sitting together on the sofa, eating biscuits (not chocolate ones, I was relieved to see), like well-behaved children in a Victorian photograph. I didn't like to think of the chaos they'd create in this ordered home once they relaxed into being themselves.

I was out of my chair and across the room just in time to field Clerry's tea plate, one of mother's best Coalport, as it slid off the sofa towards the pale green carpet.

"Don't fuss, darling," said Mother. "You've been on tenterhooks ever since you arrived. Now, I've put the children in your old room and you can have Daddy's and my room."

"But what about you, love?"

"Oh, I'll be quite happy down here, on the sofa."

Since the sofa was barely big enough for two small children, and tautly covered in shiny cretonne, I thought that happiness was not spending a night on it. I began to wonder if the flight to Hammersmith was going to be more upsetting for my poor mother than for George.

"And to what do I owe the pleasure of this visit?" Mother said, when Clerry and Toby were in bed, and we were sharing companionable baked beans on toast in the kitchen.

"I don't have to have a special reason for visiting you, darling, and it's ages since you've seen Clerry and Toby . . ."

"Hmm." Mother gave me that same clear look she used when I was a child, which meant, "I know you're not telling me the truth, but I'll find it out in my own good time."

"If you'd given me a bit more warning, love, I'd have got in some chops or done a nice roast."

"This is perfect, Mum. Much nicer than mousse d'asperges au jus de cerfeuil."

"Mousse de what?"

"Asparagus mousse. George made it on Saturday night."

"Sounds high-falutin to me," said Mother. "You'd think George would have something better to do with his time than mess about with fancy recipes."

I told her that George had taken over the home front;

cooking, shopping, and looking after the children. "No good with the laundry, though. I have to sort that. George still puts the socks in with the whites."

"Men have got no idea about washing." Mother got up and put on the kettle. "Daddy always used to leave Kleenex in his pyjama pocket, made a terrible mess in the machine. But then, your father couldn't have changed a nappy or turned his hand to mousse de whatnot, either. Does George enjoy all this domesticity?"

"Yes . . ." I put my hand up to my left arm, I could feel the bruise. "I think so . . ."

Mother put a cup of tea in front of me and sat down opposite, giving me that clear look again. "And how about you, darling? I've kept all the cuttings about your business, and weren't you good on *Woman's Hour*?"

"It's big business now, Mother. We're taking on franchises all over the country . . ."

"Like those Body Shops, you mean?"

". . . running shops is impossible, the staff and the customers help themselves to the stock . . ."

"Mrs Jenkinson put four scouring pads and a tin of Ardennes Paté into her coat pocket in BuyLate because she was having the menopause."

"Exactly, shoplifting. Our franchisees will own their own shops, they won't be paying us fees or royalties or anything, but they'll have to agree to buy only our clothes, follow agreed sales levels, price mark-ups and merchandising rules and adopt our standard shop layout." I was terribly impressed when I heard myself saying all this; I sounded just like Emily.

"Goodness . . ." Mother put down her teacup. "I don't understand a word of all that, dear, but it all sounds wonderful. I wish Daddy was still alive to see it, he'd have been so proud of you."

"Oh, it isn't just me. I only do the designing."

"*Only* do the designing? You mustn't underestimate yourself, Pauline. Daddy always said you were too modest for your own good."

I stayed at Mother's for five days. "You get on with your work, I know you've got a lot to do," she'd said the morning after we'd arrived, already looking hollow-eyed after a night on the sofa. "Clerry and Toby and I are going to see the sights together; it's time I got to know my grandchildren."

They went to the zoo and to Madame Tussaud's ("Spooky," said Clerry) and the Tower of London ("Spooky," said Clerry. It was her new word), and sampled hamburgers in just about every McDonald's in London. After four days mother had a wan look as she erected the pushchair and set off on yet another arduous outing to the Science Museum.

"Tobias is partial to the Stegosaurus," she said.

It was helpful to spend time in the two London shops, watching the customers, seeing them snatch excitedly at pelmet-short skirts which stayed on the rails in Cambridge and reject the loose blazer jackets which were best sellers in the Kite.

I lunched with Sybilla at the Caprice as Mother slogged round the Science Museum. "It'll do you good to get your eye in on what Londoners are wearing," Sybilla said, as though I'd just arrived from Omsk. The women were mostly dressed in tight mini dresses and had dumped their capacious executive shoulder bags in favour of small purses. I wondered where they put their make-up and their cigarettes and then realised that they wore expensive tans instead of Lancôme, and very few seemed to be smoking.

We went back to Eaton Square after lunch. "I've got an idea I want to try out on you," Sybilla said.

Laid out on her bed were six of my colourful sari evening dresses, glinting exotic streaks of gold under the chandelier. "Look at these dresses," she said, as though she'd just run them cleverly to earth in Harrods. "Can you imagine anything more glamorous?"

I was about to remark sharply that I had designed the dresses with glamour in mind, when I noticed a silver framed wedding photograph on the bureau. Sybilla and Peter. Men do tend to look the same when they are dressed up in morning suits, but the profile of the bridegroom gazing adoringly at Sybilla could have been George smiling down proudly at me in the wedding photograph on my dressing table.

"Has it ever occurred to you, Sybilla," I said, "that Peter and George are very alike?"

"Both boring men, if that's what you mean." Sybilla unwillingly switched her gaze from frocks to photograph. "Look at that bow tie coming adrift from his shirt. Typical Peter. But I haven't brought you up here to look at family snaps, Pauline. How many of these dresses can we make in the next three months?"

"Depends whether Dinesh has managed to find me enough antique saris. They're old silk threaded with real gold. They'll be expensive."

"So we'll have to do what Emily would call a hard sell on them," said Sybilla. "Photograph them on the least likely women, demonstrate that anyone can be transformed into a sex object by slipping into a Natural Sources evening gown. Look at this . . ." She opened a magazine at a feature headlined "Woman in a Man's World" which told how Annette Corrigan from County Kildare joined the WRNS and became Vice Admiral Corrigan, i/c Naval Headquarters, Plymouth. The portrait of Vice Admiral Corrigan showed a homely woman constrained in navy blue serge. "We'll get the top women in the Services and photograph them in their uniforms and then in our dresses." She slammed the magazine down on the bed triumphantly. "What do you think of that?"

I had to hand it to Sybilla. She may not have a lovely character but her enthusiasm was irresistible. "It's brilliant. If they'll do it . . ."

"Of course they'll do it, if I ask them." She looked up irritably as there was a tentative knock at the door. "What is it?"

Pedro, the butler, tiptoed into the room. "Apologies for

disturbing you m'lady, but there is an Indian gentleman at the door. Says his name is Basrawy and you know him."

"Whatever is Ahmet doing here?" said Sybilla. "Show him into the drawing room, Pedro."

Ahmet was sitting on the edge of one of Sybilla's white sofas, looking as out of place as I had felt that first time I came to Eaton Square. He rose as we came in. "Lady Sybilla, something appalling has occurred . . . Pauline, I have been endeavouring to contact you all this morning; your husband told me you were in London . . ." He clutched his cheeks with both hands. "I am ruined, ruined . . ."

"Sit down and relax, Ahmet." Sybilla waved a hand at the butler. "Some coffee, if you please, Pedro. Now, what's all this about, Ahmet?"

"Government officials have been to my factory," said Ahmet. "They have pasted a notice on my door saying I am to close down . . ."

"Of course you can't close down," said Sybilla, "you haven't delivered the bulk of our summer range yet."

"I know, I know," Ahmet moaned. "They spoke of faulty wiring. How do I know the wiring is faulty? They say we have no hot water for hand-washing and there are rags blocking the fire exits. Rags! These are the antique saris Dinesh sent you from India, Pauline . . ."

"The saris!" cried Sybilla, "but they've got to be made up in the next few weeks to back up my editorial . . ."

"And children," Ahmet ignored Sybilla's interruption. "I let them come to the workrooms out of the kindness of my heart, to be with their mothers, and now I learn I am infringing some silly law about young persons . . . no," he waved Pedro away excitedly, "no, I don't take coffee, thank you. Tomorrow I have to go to court and I shall be ruined." He slumped back on the sofa, closed his eyes. "Who would do this to me? Who could deprive me of my livelihood?"

"Presumably," I said, "there are inspectors doing regular checks."

"Only if you are registered with the Health and Safety people. I am not, and that is another offence; they are throwing the complete book in my direction. Somebody, some evil rival has spoken against me. 'We are acting on information received,' one of the officers said."

"I'll get on to Philip Smedley," said Sybilla. "Friend of Peter's. Best solicitor in London, has factory law at his fingertips. He'll know what has to be done to get you going again, Ahmet."

We phoned Julia and Emily before I left Sybilla's and arranged to meet them on Saturday to try and sort out the Basrawy problem.

"I hadn't realised," I said, "that Ahmet was running a sweatshop. I've only seen the ground floor. Isn't it dreadful to think we've made our money out of all those Bangladeshis crowded into the upstairs rooms and the whole place likely to go up in flames any minute . . ."

"It would be more to the point if you worried about them being thrown out of work." Sybilla was searching through the S–Z directory. "Here we are, Smedley Parkinson Cohen. Half of Golders Green founded their fortunes in Brick Lane, Pauline. There have always been immigrant communities willing to work their guts out to succeed in a new country."

I was muttering about how the fact that it had always happened didn't make it right as Sybilla picked up the phone.

"Oh, by the way," she dialled a number. "Have you heard about Emily and David?"

"Emily and David? Surely not?" Difficult to say why would Emily, married to an attractive man like Trevor, bother with the ghastly David, when Sybilla, married to an even more attractive man, had obviously found David an appealing bedfellow.

"That's what I hear. Smedley Parkinson Cohen? Put me through to Philip Smedley, will you. It's Lady Sybilla Bolsover."

She clapped a hand over the mouthpiece and waved me towards the door. "I'll sort out the legal end with Philip. See you in Cambridge tomorrow."

I told Mother, when I got back to Hammersmith, that I'd have to go home the next day. I hadn't told her why I was in London; I suppose I didn't want to admit that she had been right about George.

"Everything's going well, is it, between you and George?" she asked tentatively.

"Don't worry, Mum."

"Well, if ever . . . you know, darling, there's always room for you here, if ever . . ."

"I know, Mum." I hugged her. "And thank you."

George had phoned twice, asking me when I was coming back.

"I'm sorry about what happened," he said, the second time. "I don't know what came over me, Pauly."

He didn't mention Amanda Braithwaite or the granny flat. I'd so enjoyed seeing Mother again, and the children loved being with her. "I'm going to ask Mother if she'd like to come and live in Gloria's flat," I said.

"Anything you like, Pauline," he said.

"Oh no, dear, I'd really rather not," she said when I suggested it. "I feel closer to Daddy here, in our home. But I tell you what, why don't I come back and stay with you for a few days . . . ?"

We've never had to spell things out to each other in our family. "It would be wonderful," I said.

As I drove home with Mother and Clerry and Toby at my side, I felt as though I was returning with my support troops. Damn George. I was surrounded by the people I loved best, I'd be all right.

If it ever happened again, I'd be ready with the raised knee. Or I'd leave him. I'd thought of that, of course, thought of little else those last few days. But it wasn't simple to walk out of a marriage when you had two small children; they loved their father and George doted on them. I had to give him another chance.

He opened the front door as the car drew up. The children rushed at him excitedly as Mother and I took the cases out of the car. It was such an ordinary family reunion, that I found myself automatically pecking George affectionately on the cheek as he came to help with the bags.

"Let me do that. Sarah, what a delightful surprise. I'm so pleased to hear we're to have another granny in the granny flat."

"That's very civil of you, George, but I fear it will only be for a few days."

I'd never noticed it before, but George and Mother didn't sound like themselves when they were talking to each other.

George led the way into the kitchen. "I expect you could do with a cup of tea after your journey?"

"A cup of tea never comes amiss," said Mother, sitting down at the kitchen table and rising again quickly to intercept a fistful of Rabbit Whiskas midway between the kittens' plastic feeding bowl and Toby's mouth. "No, darling. Dirty."

George poured out the tea. "Milk and sugar for you, Sarah?"

"Thank you kindly, George."

"Mum, can I take Gran over and show her the flat?" said Clerry.

I wasn't ready to be alone with George yet. "In a minute, darling, give Gran a chance to have her tea."

"I can finish it when I get back," said my mother, rising and taking Clerry's hand.

"And Toby . . ." Running after them, Toby reached for Mother's other hand.

"And Toby," said Mother. "You can both show me my room."

George and I were alone together in a vast silence.

"I'm glad you came back, Pauly," he said at the same moment as I said, "I had to come back, George . . ."

"Oh, Pauly." He was coming towards me, about to put his arms around me.

"I had to come back for an important meeting."

He stopped instantly, and sat down, pretending he was heading for his tea rather than me. "Oh?"

"Ahmet Basrawy. They've closed down his factory."

"That's why you came back?"

That was the moment when I could have thrown myself in his arms sobbing, "no, no, George, I came back because I couldn't bear to be apart from you any longer," but it wouldn't have been true. The bruise on my arm was still sore.

"I've arranged to meet Julia, Emily and Sybilla at the office tomorrow . . ."

"But it's Saturday. You know I like to do the weekly shop on Saturday morning."

"You'll have to do it by yourself, then. Or enlist Mother's help. There's half our summer collection locked up inside Ahmet's factory and we've got to rethink all our production and delivery dates."

"Ahmet told me on the phone that he'd had a visit from the factory inspector." George looked at me over the top of his teacup. "As a matter of fact, Pauline, I'm surprised you condone such appalling conditions . . . Work, work, work, in poverty, hunger and dirt, as the poem has it . . ."

I was as shocked as George when I learned about Ahmet's factory, but I was not in a mood to have ethical verse quoted at me. "There may be a certain amount of dirt in Paradise Walk, George, but I think poverty and hunger would be rather overstating the case."

"I told Basrawy when he phoned that he was nothing but a lackey for the capitalist bosses . . ."

"Julia, Emily, Sybilla and me, you mean?"

"No, of course I don't mean you. I see the closing down of Basrawy's factory as an important move in the proletariat's fight for equality . . ."

"I think the man from the Health and Safety Executive

was more interested in blocked fire escapes than fighting for equality, George."

"But don't you realise, Pauline, that this is just another example of the way our degenerate society exploits the Third World?"

George's interest in the Third World has never extended further than Madhur Jaffrey's vegetable curry, and I was wondering where he'd picked up the Marxist jargon, when Mother walked into the kitchen.

"I shall be most comfortable there, my dears." She sat down as George poured her out another cup of tea. "Thank you, George. I must say, Pauline, Gloria certainly widened her range of interests since the days when we lived next door to each other."

"Oh, she did, Mum." I began telling her about the delivery vans.

"Yes, dear. I knew she'd turned into quite an entrepreneur. But I found the most curious pamphlets on the bedside table. Look . . ." In one hand Mother held a leaflet headed *Lesbian Linkline Newsletter*, in the other a leaflet labelled *Black Women Against Housework*. "I never realised Gloria felt so deeply about dusting."

Sybilla lit her third cigarette in five minutes and tapped her elegant crocodile shoe impatiently. "Julia's late, as usual."

"Give her another five minutes, and then I'll phone her," said Emily. "I spoke to her yesterday, she knows about the meeting."

"Really, it's too bad of her. Pauline and I come dashing up here from London and Julia can't be bothered to drive round the corner. Don't you find it inconsiderate, Pauline?"

"Mmm?" I found it difficult to concentrate on anything except the irritating fact that in my absence Amanda Braithwaite had obviously been living in the granny flat. "I expect she's busy."

"Typical of you, Pauline, to be so understanding," said Sybilla, not intending a compliment.

The phone went. "I'll get it," said Emily. "I expect it's Julia."

"Philip's been on to the Health and Safety Executive," said Sybilla, as Emily made shocked sympathetic noises into the phone. "He's agreed the improvements that have to be made to the premises before Ahmet can reopen. Says they shouldn't take more than two or three weeks, but it'll cost. We may have to inject some capital . . ." She turned as Emily put down the phone. "Julia?"

"Yes," said Emily. "She's waiting for the doctor. David has had a heart attack."

Call for
clampdown
on
Molesworth
militants

POLICE were called to the American Air
Force base at Molesworth in the early hours
of Sunday morning to deal with an out-
break of violence amongst the anti-nuclear
demonstrators camping there. Amongst
those detained were Mr. George Jenks,
husband of Pauline Jenks, the well-known
clothes designer. St. Neots resident Mr.
Jenks (32), whose two small children were
present at the incident, said, 'I am proud of
what I did.' Ms. Amanda Braithwaite, who
runs a St. Neots playgroup, was also taken
into custody. . . .

St Neots Express,
23rd July, 1987

There was a small secret glow about Pauline that summer, and I was sure it was caused by Ahmet Basrawy.
I'd been leafing through one of those women's magazines,
waiting for Clerry to come out of the dentist's surgery
("I'm grown-up now, Daddy," she'd said, "I'm old enough
to go in by myself." She was quite a little madam in her

way) when I came across an article entitled "How you can tell it's the Real Thing." It was all about being in love. You've got to laugh at the things these women write about, but I suppose they have to fill in the pages with something. It turned out quite interesting, in a shallow way. "Answer these questions – honestly, remember! – to discover if your man of the moment is really meant for you. Say 'Yes' to more than five, and you might just be heading for the altar!"

Some of the questions seemed pretty daft to me: "a) Do you get up earlier than necessary because you can't wait to start another wonderful day? b) Do you wash your hair every night so that it will feel extra silky? c) Does your face look better without make-up than with? d) Have you lost a couple of pounds?" It occurred to me that if Pauline were answering the questions, she'd have ticked just about all of them.

It didn't take much brain power to work out why. She'd been strange ever since that Indian trip. She could hardly be bothered to speak to me, let alone . . . how could she so demean herself as to have an affair with an Indian? But the clues were all there. I decided to face her with it before she flew off to New York, and was determined to put my foot down about her taking yet another foreign trip with that snake Basrawy:

"How do you think I feel when you go off on these jaunts, Pauline?"

She was packing, and scarcely bothered to look up. "Hardly a jaunt, George. It's very hard work."

"Working?" I said sardonically. "Is that what you call it?"

"I call it working because that's what it is, George."

I noticed some glamorous new undies seemed necessary for her "working" trip. "I didn't know you had a black petticoat, Pauline. And you've changed your hairstyle. Everyone knows what that means."

Pauline looked at me in an insultingly weary manner. "I can't be bothered playing games, George. You tell me what it means."

"It's Basrawy, isn't it? You're having an affair."

"*Ahmet?* Don't be so absurd, George. You've been reading too many steamy novels about the glamour of international travel. I can assure you that Ahmet and I shared no moonlit romantic nights on the veranda of the Gymkhana Club."

"No need to be facetious, Pauline, and don't try to deny it. I heard you, on the phone . . ."

"You've been listening to my telephone conversations?"

"I just happened to pick up the extension. You were whispering. 'I'll do it, Ahmet,' you said, 'but nobody must ever know.' Perhaps you'd care to explain exactly what it is that nobody must ever know?"

She didn't even try to deny it. "I see no need to explain anything," she said, as bold as you please.

I went towards her then. I wasn't going to touch her, just remonstrate, but she moved quickly to the other side of the bed as though I was some kind of maniac. "Don't you lay a finger on me, George Jenks," she said. "What would Amanda say?"

"There's no need to bring Amanda into this," I said, with as much dignity as I could muster.

"Isn't there? If we are talking about adultery . . ." Pauline raised her voice like a fishwife, ". . . shouldn't we be discussing you and Amanda?"

"Me and Amanda?" I hoped that Pauline was talking about the fact that I'd allowed Amanda and Jake and Canvey to stay in the granny flat while she was at her mother's. Admittedly it wasn't very clever of Amanda to leave those pamphlets lying about for that silly smiling mother of Pauline's to find; but after all, it was originally *my* mother's flat, and when Mrs Browne went home to Hammersmith, Pauline had finally agreed that Amanda could move back. Just for a month.

Deciding it might be wiser not to prolong the conversation I turned on my heel and left the room.

I was surprised Ahmet Basrawy was still in business, after being fined for running a sweatshop; but there he was, flying to America with other people's wives as though nothing had happened. Apparently Sybilla Bolsover had some lap dog solicitor in tow who sorted the whole thing out for them.

Typical, after all the trouble I'd been to.

I had started with the DHSS.

"May I speak to your complaints department?"

"What kind of complaint would that be?"

"Well, it's a bit difficult to describe, exactly . . ."

"The new pension rates don't come into commission until September, you know. If you have not yet received your pink form . . ."

"Nothing to do with pensions, as it happens, it is to do with children. I happen to be in possession of information—"

"No, you need our other number for child benefit, the Stoke Newington one."

"Could you please listen, Miss? I'm not interested in benefit. It's child cruelty I'm after."

"Sandra, I've got one of those on the line. Says he's after child cruelty, would you believe it?"

A new voice came on the line and made the kind of suggestion one does not expect to hear from civil servants.

In the end I rang the local council. At least they had the courtesy to listen.

"Paradise Walk, Brick Lane, you say? And what would you estimate the children's age to be? Dear, dear, not a totally unfamiliar situation. We will set matters in motion, Mr . . . ? You need not, of course, give your name if you . . ."

"Mainwaring, David Mainwaring."

"If you care to leave us your telephone number, Mr Mainwaring, in complete confidence, of course, in case we need to get back to you?"

I gave them David's telephone number. That way, if it did leak out that somebody had informed on that frightful little wog, they wouldn't know it was me. I couldn't help laughing when I thought of the look on David's face if Tower Hamlets actually did ring back; with any luck the shock would complete the good work his heart attack started last month.

It was shortly after Pauline's return from her hysterical flight to her mother, that she'd come back from a board meeting (what a way to describe a lot of women gossiping) saying, "Oh, poor Julia. David's had a heart attack."

"Oh dear," I'd said in a bored manner, "fatal, I trust?"

Pauline looked at me coldly and left the room. I suppose she thought I was being insensitive. She didn't know what I'd had to put up with from David pleased-with-himself Mainwaring. Only the week before, he'd made me accompany him on one of his devious visits to the Cambridge branch of Natural Sources. The ignominy of following him around, pretending to be interested in batiste Bermuda shorts, while Julia looked at us as though we were rodent operators. I could only be grateful the other girls weren't there to hear the way he spoke to me.

"Look like Marks & Spencer boxers, don't they, George?" And when I'd tried to defend them for Pauline's sake, he'd given me one of those disparaging looks of his. "Don't bother, George, I can't hang about here all afternoon while you think of something to say."

Pauline went on that New York trip, of course, in spite of anything I could say. It was a perfect July morning, the day after she got back; Clerihue had put some roses in a jar on the breakfast table, Toby had got his favourite bib on, and I had hidden the *St Neots Express*.

For the children's sake I would try and be pleasant to Pauline when she came down, even if she had insisted on sleeping in her studio again. It was rather unfortunate that she suspected about me and Amanda, as it didn't give me much of a leg to stand on about Basrawy. Not that I hadn't the right to do what I wanted with my life, of course, but I'd just as soon not argue about it.

I looked across the courtyard and smiled to myself. The sound of kiddies' voices came from the granny flat, which I thought of as the Amanda flat. This time she was here to stay, whatever Pauline said. I couldn't do without Amanda, not since . . . it was quite a revelation. Amanda was so much more . . . knowledgeable than Pauline had ever been, sometimes I was quite glad the light was off. But as Amanda said, we should welcome our instincts, not flee from them.

"Mummy, Mummy," Clerry screeched, when Pauline came down to breakfast, "why didn't you wake me up last night? I stayed up as long as I could to give you a big hug."

"Give me one now, darling. Oh, it's so lovely to see you again, my angel. Tobias? How's my great big little boy? How about a kiss for your poor old mum? Good morning, George. What's that ghastly racket coming from Gloria's flat? I understood that Braithwaite woman would be gone by the time I got back."

"It hasn't been Gloria's flat for a year now, Pauline. Throwing money down the drain, leaving it empty. Amanda Braithwaite is paying a very satisfactory rent."

"Ten pounds a week doesn't satisfy me."

Amanda was actually paying fifteen pounds a week. I kept the extra five to pad out the housekeeping.

"The poor girl has so little to live on, and she faces life so gallantly that I feel I must do what I can to help."

"Gallant? How can you be so naive?"

"What on earth do you mean? Amanda's on Social Security."

"Social Security wouldn't buy her a single dab of that scent she covers herself with. George, I thought I made it quite clear . . . Clerry, darling, hadn't you and Toby better go and clean your teeth? There's my clevers, and then I'll come up and show you what I brought back from New York for you."

She waited until they left the room, and then turned on me.

"I thought I told you I wasn't having that woman as a permanent fixture in my flat that I pay the mortgage on? The place will be a pigsty if her housekeeping's anything like her hair . . ." She walked over to the window and peered out through it, ". . . and look, who's that extraordinary hulk taking in the milk? That's not Amanda, though she's bloody nearly the same size."

"Amanda is a very giving person. There's no need to look like that, Pauline. She has invited a friend to stay, until she gets things sorted out."

"And who's that child with the hulk? That's not Canvey."

"A friend *and* her child. They are undergoing problems in the marital environment."

"She's got a black eye, George. *George*. Is that Braithwaite cow turning my flat into a battered wives refuge? I must admit, I can see the amusing side."

"I can't see anything particularly amusing –"

"It's certainly practical. I won't have far to go, will I? Just a couple of steps across the garden, and Amanda will be on my side."

"I don't know what you are talking about."

"Oh, shut up, it's so boring when you stand there and lie; you've hit me twice, George, because you took me by surprise and I couldn't believe what was happening. But let me warn you here and now: try it just once more and you'll get everything from a knee where it hurts to being reported to Amanda Hippo-Hips over there."

She left the room before I had time to say anything in my own defence. Typical of Pauline to exaggerate a couple of taps into wife-battering.

That first time when she talked to me as if I was a scullery maid, I went to her studio with the intention of putting my position firmly but reasonably. It was only when I saw the impertinent and unrepentant look on her face that I lifted my hand to slap her. And as clearly as if he were standing in the room, I could hear my old dad say, "Not where it shows, lad." So I tapped her on the shoulder, just to show who was in charge. As far as I was concerned, that was the end of that. We'd had a very pleasant time at the playgroup Entertainment that afternoon, which proved, I thought, that women like to know their place.

And that other time, when she implied in her arrogant way that I was no longer the breadwinner. I couldn't stand for that, could I? And when I scraped my wrist on the fridge, she couldn't even be bothered to find the Elastoplast.

I had finished clearing up the kitchen (I trusted her ladyship would approve) and was sitting at the table writing my shopping list, when Pauline whirled back in like a hurricane. Clerry and Toby had followed her downstairs, but prudently stayed in the hall, peering in at us.

"Can this possibly be true, what Clerihue's been telling me? My children *arrested*? Where is the *Express*, give it to me at once. My God, can't I turn my back for *one second* without something going wrong?"

I took the *Express* out of the drawer where I kept the string and carrier bags, and gave it to her.

"I should have thought, Pauline, that you would be proud that our children are learning early about commitment . . ."

Clerry interrupted; she was getting quite a tone of her mother, and I had to sit there while she prattled on about the midnight picnic and the naughty airmen's bombs and the great big van Daddy was pushed into, in a way that made me sound like a buffoon.

I needed some advice. George Jenks had plainly come to a turning point, and I didn't quite know where to turn. It seemed only a few months ago that we were a normal family; father breadwinner, mother with her bits of part-time sewing, two children, a mortgage. And suddenly we'd turned from *The Archers* into *Dynasty*. Pauline jet-setting around on lustful trips with a known criminal; me, not surprisingly in the circumstances, turning for solace to Another Woman; Clerihue and Tobias entertained by a wpc with hot chocolate and biscuits just because their father stood up for his rights to a very impudent young constable who was too big for his boots.

"I think I ought to inform you," I'd said to the sergeant at the police station, "that I intend taking matters further. I don't know if you know who I am —"

"I will as soon as you give me your name, sir."

"I am not one of your blacks you can push around as you like, you know."

"I can see you're not black, sir. We're trained in observation in the force."

"George, do shut up," said Amanda.

"I will not be silenced. This isn't Russia, Sergeant."

"Another piece of information we were issued with in basic training. Now sir, if I might have your name and address?"

"I don't have to tell you that."

"Yes, you do, George," said Amanda. "I am Amanda Braithwaite. This is George Jenks. Those two children are his."

"Jenny, take them up to the canteen and feed them cocoa, would you? Do you really think it's responsible, sir, to bring two young children on this sort of lark?"

"Lark?" said Amanda. "Do you realise, Sergeant, that we are fighting for your life, amongst others?"

"Very kind of you, I'm sure. Twenty officers on overtime, and two of them in casualty with cuts and bruises. Do me a favour, miss, next time you get the urge, go and defend freedom in someone else's manor."

Amanda always says the police are fascist pigs, but every time I remembered that degrading episode, I couldn't help thinking that he sounded like that nice man in *The Bill*, and I sounded silly. And another thing; if what we were doing was all that important to Future Generations, why didn't Amanda bring her two?

Advice. I did what I should have done weeks before. There was only one person I could trust, and I trusted him for the best possible reason. Though I did think he might have told me himself, instead of leaving me to work it out. I picked up the phone.

"George! How nice to hear from you . . . of course you

can come and see me. This afternoon? Why not? About
three?"

When I arrived, Peter was in his study, telephoning. He
gestured to me to sit down, and made encouraging "I won't
be long" signs.

". . . in principle I'm very interested indeed. The figures
are in the post, you say? Quite frankly, what appeals to me
is the chance to inject some money into local craftsmanship.
Quite. I'll wait to hear from you, then."

He put the phone down. "Sorry about that. Funny you
should ring, I was going to get in touch with you. George,
this idea of David's that we should help out in Natural
Sources –"

"And Trevor's."

"And Trevor's, yes, though I don't think he's got his
heart in it. Do you get the feeling there's something a bit
weird about it all? Of course I'll help Sybilla all I can, not
that she's around much to help these days. But when you
get down to it, do the girls really need any help? They're
doing brilliantly. I dropped into the Cambridge office the
other day, and David was there, buzzing about and making
suggestions about throughput and stat sheets and so on. I
got the impression they wished he'd go away and let them
get on with it."

"He hasn't told you, then?"

"I don't think so."

"David intends that the four of us should take over
Natural Sources."

"What an extraordinary idea. Why?"

"Well, I suppose . . . well, we could help them to make
more money."

"On our record we could help them to go broke."

"Anyway, David and Trevor don't like housework
very much. If you want my opinion, Peter, they're not
prepared to put their shoulders to the wheel. Trevor
seems quite proud of the fact that he can't make may-
onnaise, and David couldn't find a duster if you paid
him."

George

"You've taken to it like a duck to water, haven't you, George?"

"Up to a point. I rather pride myself on my cooking –"

Peter grinned. "But scrubbing saucepans is out? Join the club. I'm frankly pretty helpless in the kitchen, but I've rather fallen on my feet. Mrs Orchard, my old nanny, has moved in. I haven't been so well looked after since I was in the nursery, and I've got one or two business irons in the fire that might heat up very satisfactorily. Anyway, I will take no part in David's plan. Now that you've explained it to me, I find it very distasteful indeed."

"My viewpoint exactly. Quite a long time ago, I said to David that if you didn't approve, I wouldn't touch it with a bargepole. Peter?"

"Yes, George?"

"I've got to talk to you."

"Problems? If I can help at all you know you've only to –"

"Pauline is having an affair with Ahmet Basrawy."

"*Pauline?* George, of course she isn't. You've always struck me as being the most happy pair. Whatever gave you the idea?"

"I challenged her with it, and she didn't deny it."

"But, my dear boy . . ." I loved it when he said that, ". . . on what evidence? She probably didn't deny it because she was angry, furious because you didn't trust her. Anyway, Ahmet's devoted to his wife. I should know, he cornered me at some Natural Sources office do and showed me 175 photographs of his Amelia and their three sons. Honestly, George, I do think you're on the wrong tack."

"I heard her on the phone to him. She said, 'I'll do it, Ahmet, but you're not to tell a soul.' And she flies all over the world with him."

"Business, George, not pleasure. And I think you'll find, if you ask her, that what she was agreeing to do was finance the purchase of some advanced sewing machines. She asked my advice and I told her I thought it was, on the whole, a sound investment. I honestly promise I don't think you've got a thing to worry about. Go home now –"

"I know I've got something to worry about. If it isn't Basrawy, then it's somebody else. Pauline is in love with someone, and if I ever find out who it is . . ."

"I'm sure she isn't. But I am very flattered that you felt you could talk to me about it."

"Of course I came to you. Who else would I come to, but my real father?"

I stopped at a lay-by on the way home. I turned the engine off, and switched on Alistair Cooke, and I cringed, and I hummed. Who was more embarrassed, Peter or me? Oh God, how could I have made such a silly mistake?

"Your . . . real father?" Peter said. "George, I . . . what on earth do you think . . . do you know how old I am?"

"Er . . . ?"

"I would have been about twelve when you were conceived. Whatever made you think . . . ?"

"It was when I was photographed for that *Vogue* article last year. When my mother saw the pictures, she went a bit funny . . . and Pauline said they reminded her of someone. And when I took another look at them, I looked like you. And why did I get that seat on the board? Roger Makepeace said the Bolsovers always stick together. Look at me, Peter, I know I'm a Bolsover."

"Dear God," said Peter, "the sins of the fathers. Yes, George, you are a Bolsover. I always thought you should have been told, but your mother wouldn't have it. Your father was Clement Bolsover."

"Clement? That old . . . ?"

"I gather it was really rather romantic. Your mother and Clement sat next to each other in a cinema one afternoon, and it went on from there. Bit like *Brief Encounter*. Don't blame her, George. I gather she wasn't happily married."

"They got on very well," I said stiffly. I didn't like the idea of Peter knowing about the admonishments. "So how did I first get the salesman's job at Bolsover's?"

"Your mother wrote to Clement. A very reasonable letter. No demands, no threats, no blackmail. She'd be very grateful if Bolsover's could give her son a job. If they couldn't she would quite understand. She was a nice woman, your mother. So Clement came to me, and naturally we took you on. Very glad to, your qualifications were excellent."

"And I don't suppose Clement paid her a penny."

"Offered to, offered to pay for your education, but the only thing she ever accepted from him was a small piece of jewellery. I got to know her quite well after she moved up here. We used to meet for coffee now and then . . ." he smiled, ". . . she used to call me 'Sir Peter', bit of a joke, I don't know how it started. Oh, well."

"Do David and Trevor know?"

"Certainly not. Makepeace was right, we Bolsovers stick together. I remember looking across at you at Clement's funeral, and thinking, 'it's like a Greek tragedy. That young man doesn't know he's mourning the loins that fathered him.'"

I didn't quite care for words like loins in conjunction with my mother, but I supposed that's what they teach you in private education.

"I didn't mourn much at Dad's funeral. Looking back, I don't think anyone did. I remember Pauline wearing grey, and saying Mother would be glad to live alone. I thought she was being a bit cynical."

"Just realistic, perhaps," said Peter.

"When Toby was born, Mother said he looked just like his grandfather, and then when you gave me that Waterford glass, after our last board meeting, you said your grandfather would have wanted me to have it."

"I was a bit maudlin that day, I'm afraid."

Something occurred to me.

"Why didn't Clement leave me any money? I bet he was worth a packet. It doesn't seem quite fair."

Peter's face flinched, the way people's faces flinch when George Jenks says "Pardon", or starts to tell a joke.

"George, he only left debts. The family trust paid them off."

That's what you say, I thought. It might be worth checking with the solicitor.

"And what about his clothes? He had some very nice suits, I seem to remember."

Peter looked as though someone had poured tomato ketchup over his smoked salmon.

"I'm afraid it didn't occur to me. They went to Oxfam. Anyway, it would have looked rather strange if I'd given Clement's clothes to one of our salesmen, George."

"You could have kept them."

"I had no way of knowing you would ever find out. Your mother absolutely insisted, as I told you –"

"Very convenient . . ." I could see Peter was finding my manner more and more distasteful, but what did I care, now that he was no longer my father? "Quite frankly, I don't think I've been properly treated."

The phone rang, and Peter picked it up.

"Hello? Oh, good afternoon, Sybilla . . . Oh, won't you? Well, I didn't actually think you'd get here when you gave me your solemn word that you would. How's Caroline going to get down? . . . No, Sybilla, she cannot travel on the train by herself, not at her age . . . I simply won't have it, that's why not. I suppose I'll have to come up and fetch her . . . I don't really understand, no, but then I haven't understood you for a long time now."

He put the phone down, and sighed. "I'd be grateful if you would forget you heard all that, George. Is that the time?"

Knowing that his class always says, "Is that the time?" when they want you to go away, I got up and moved towards the door.

"If you took my advice, Peter," I said, "you'd show Lady Sybilla who is boss."

I got home to find the kitchen was full of my children and Amanda's. Where was Amanda, and why wasn't she

keeping an eye on them? Pauline, of course, was off somewhere being important.

Jake and Canvey had much improved since they came to
live in the flat; I could only put it down to the influence of
a father figure.

The four of them were sitting round the table drawing.
There was a lot of water about, and someone had trodden
a crayon into the Vinyl. Really, where was Amanda?

"Look, Daddy," said Clerry, "I've drawn a lovely picture
of Mork and Mindy. Uncle David rang up. He said he'd
been to the market and bought some more shares. Do they
sell shares at St Neots market, Daddy?"

"Never mind that now. Where is Amanda?"

"She's on the telephone," said Canvey, "talking to her
stockbroker."

Emily Sutcliffe of Natural Sources is Business Woman of the Year

At a reception at the Savoy Hotel yesterday, HRH The Princess Royal presented Boston-born Emily Sutcliffe, financial dynamo of the international fashion group, Natural Sources, with the 1987 Business Woman of the Year Award.

Emily Sutcliffe, 41, came to England 18 years ago and, in 1983, was one of the four co-founders of Natural Sources. She was primarily responsible for setting up worldwide franchises for the company and, last month, successfully floated Natural Sources on the Unlisted Securities Market.

Emily met her husband, English mathematician Trevor Sutcliffe, when she was taking a degree in Business Studies at Harvard and he was a post graduate student at the Massachusetts Institute of Technology. They were married a year later and have two daughters, 17-year old Lucy, 15-year old Alice, and a 5-year old son, Thomas.

Accepting the Award, Emily Sutcliffe paid tribute to her husband, who retired as Finance Director of a leading Midlands' engineering firm early last year. 'Behind every successful woman there's a man who doesn't mind peeling the potatoes and listening to the details of your terrible day,' she said.

Evening Standard, 7th October, 1987

George and Amanda. I'd found out that they were having an affair in the most unpleasant way. George and I were in bed together, a couple of days before my New York trip. He moved tentatively towards me, and I moved firmly away.

"What's the matter, Pauly?"

"Nothing . . ." a pantomime of shivering. "Just a bit cold, that's all." I'd made up my mind to try and make the marriage work; I could hardly tell him that I went cold every time he came near me.

"Come here then, and let me warm you up."

Warm and sleepy and in the dark, sex was occasionally bearable, even satisfying, the basic pleasure of drinking a long cold glass of water when you're thirsty. Sometimes I'd see George's profile in the half light and imagine he was somebody else . . .

George rolled on top of me. He was heavy, and I was just trying to remember who it was that said a gentleman always takes the weight on his elbows, when I got a whiff of the unmistakable scent of Giorgio, Amanda's perfume. The strongest and about the most expensive scent on the perfumery counter. Lurking exotically on my husband's skin, it sent out a clear signal that he had not, as I had naively supposed, spent the afternoon with Amanda dissecting the political content of a tin of pineapple.

"Not now, George," I pushed him away. "I'm tired."

"You're always tired these days, Pauline," he said.

I wanted to walk out on him then, but what about the children? What about the cats? What about New York? When you read dramatic stories about the breakdown of a marriage nobody ever mentions the domestic details which make leaving home so difficult.

"Promise me one thing," I said to George, just before I left for the airport. "I don't want that woman to have anything to do with my children."

"Why?" said George. "You're happy enough for them to go to her playgroup."

"I mean here, at home. You know perfectly well what I mean."

"Oh, all right," said George, "you're going to miss your plane if you don't hurry."

Did I mind about Amanda? I found myself wondering about that at the airport, waiting for the fog to lift. At one end of the emotional scale, somewhere between vanity and self-esteem, I minded very much. Amanda Braithwaite, grubby, fuzzy hair, hideous clothes and, worst of all, humourless. He might, at least, have swapped me for a quality model. But where it should have mattered, it didn't. George's infidelity was unimportant. I knew I didn't love him any more and when I cried it was for Dad saying: "Remember, sweetheart, you're marrying George, not the Jenks family." I cried for my father.

After Amanda had been blackballed from the commune I'd reluctantly agreed to let her stay in the granny flat for a month, until she found somewhere else. Over a month had passed and she was still there. There'd been so much going on at work, I hadn't the energy to fight with George about it. Besides, I'd grown quite fond of Canvey and Jake. They spent more and more time in our house, seeming to find the organised routine and discipline a pleasantly diverting novelty.

Amanda threw wholewheat crackers, cottage cheese and politically irreprochable nuts at them when the mood took her. They'd only been in the flat for a couple of weeks when Jake and Canvey began dropping in at our regular mealtimes. The first time they appeared at the kitchen table, with grubby hands and faces, I made them go into the cloakroom and wash.

"Really, Pauline," George gave me a reproving look. "Jake and Canvey don't understand your suburban values. A little dirt never hurt anybody."

"It hurts me," I said. "I'm going to have difficulty choking down this stew if I have to look at those faces."

They returned to the table clean and shining. "Look, Mrs Jenks," Canvey spread out her hands for inspection. "Clean."

"Not Mrs Jenks, Canvey," said George. "Pauline."

"I like Mrs Jenks better," said Canvey. "It sounds more like a proper mummy." She slid the bread basket over the table, and Jake grabbed the biggest piece, crammed it into his mouth and showered us with damp crumbs as he launched into a boastful tale about how he ran much faster than Adrian Smethwick.

"You must be very good at running," I said, "but don't talk with your mouth full."

"Adrian Smethwick is creepy," said Clerry.

"I don't think we should be encouraging the competitive

spirit," said George, sounding just like Amanda. I should have realised then that there was something between them.

I suppose I was flattered that Amanda's children were so happy in my house. They started begging their mother for scented soap ("like Mrs Jenks has . . ."), and lamb chops (Amanda was, of course, vegetarian), and clean clothes "I want a pretty dress like Clerry, 'Manda . . .") and I somehow had the idea that if I pushed Amanda out of the granny flat I'd be failing her children.

Too bad, I thought, when I should have been concentrating on Bloomingdale's razor-sharp buyers. Amanda Braithwaite would have to go.

The day after that revealing whiff of Giorgio, she had barged confidently into my studio in the breezy way of someone who wouldn't dream of sleeping with another woman's husband.

"Pauline, I'm not interrupting you?"

"You are, as it happens." I didn't see any reason to observe social niceties with Amanda. In fact I was about to tell her to get the hell out of my granny flat and my life . . .

"I was looking for a copy of the *Financial Times*," she said.

"It's here somewhere." When I'd identified her scent on George, I thought I'd want to hit her next time I saw her. Now that she was actually standing there, all I felt was irritation.

I passed her the *FT*. "I should have thought the *Morning Star* was more your idea of a good read, Amanda."

"I prefer the ideological integrity of the *Socialist Worker Review*," she said, grabbing the paper from me and expertly flicking through to the share prices.

"ICI are up 3p," she cried excitedly and then moaned, "Oh God, Glaxo are down again . . ."

I watched her avidly scanning the "Top One Hundred". "I thought you didn't have any money, Amanda?"

"Oh, I don't have any *money*. When he died, Daddy left Arabella and me quite interesting share portfolios."

I certainly felt like hitting her then. Amanda Braithwaite,

paying me a fixed rent of £10 a week, while sneering at my bourgeois values and sleeping with my husband, was practically funding British industry. When I got back from America I was definitely going to do something about Ms Braithwaite.

"And have you been good while I've been away?"

Clerry and Toby were opening the presents I'd bought them in New York; expensive guilt gifts because I'd been in America instead of reading bedtime stories to my children.

"'Course we've been good." Clerry looked up, her face suddenly alight with the pleasure of imparting news. "We had a lovely time, Mummy. We had a picnic *in the middle of the night*. Amanda made banana sandwiches, and we sang songs with lots of other people, and then guess what happened?"

A midnight feast? A sing-song? Surely, Clerry must be making this up? "I don't know, darling, tell me."

"We had a ride in a police car."

I raced downstairs, followed closely by Clerry and Toby. George was in the kitchen, clearing up the breakfast.

"Can this possibly be true, George? My children arrested . . . ?"

George complacently handed me the local paper and made a pompous speech about commitment. There, midway down the front page, I read the full story of my husband's irresponsibility.

"St Neots resident Mr Jenks said, 'I am proud of what I did.' Proud? My God, George . . ."

"Not now, Pauline," he gave me an irritating not-in-front-of-the-children signal. As if I could possibly tell him what I thought of him in front of Clerry and Toby. And then he added, unforgivably, "Go and get ready for school now, Clerihue, or Mummy will be cross again."

It was October by the time I got Amanda out of the flat.

At first she'd been belligerent. "I'm going to the rent tribunal, you know."

"Drop in there, by all means," I said, "but when I tell them that you've broken the terms of your contract by taking in lodgers I don't think you'll find them very sympathetic."

Then she tried pathos. "Don't put me out on the street, Pauline. Don't turn me into a bag-lady."

Since the only bags I'd ever seen in her flat were Kenzo and Justin de Blank, I didn't bother to answer that one.

I would never have got rid of her if I hadn't called in one day when George was there. He spent a lot of time in Amanda's flat. I used to see him when I came home from work, sprinting back across the yard to get into the kitchen before I came in.

They were drinking a tisane as I walked into the sitting room, which I found more irritating than if I'd discovered them romping round the bed together. The front door was open, ready, I presumed, for George's quick getaway.

"There you are, George."

He gave a guilty start. "Pauline . . ."

Ignoring George, I gave Amanda the ultimatum I'd been rehearsing in the car. "If you're not off these premises by next Friday, Mrs Braithwaite, I am getting a court order and having you thrown out."

"You can't do that." Amanda put down her mug with Fat is a Feminist Issue sloganed around the rim. "This is my home."

"And failing that," I said, "I shall file for divorce and name you as co-respondent."

"You wouldn't?" Amanda looked shattered. Having an affair was one thing, but getting involved in a suburban domestic drama with somebody called George Jenks was obviously not a scenario that appealed to her.

"Leave this to me, Amanda." George rose and came slowly towards me.

I dodged as he struck out, and Amanda, leaping up from the sofa, took a flying tackle and brought him down on the carpet. She was a big woman and he lay there, winded, with Amanda towering over him.

"You coward, George Jenks." She gave him a prod with the toe of her boot. "How dare you hit a defenceless woman."

George gazed fearfully at Amanda's boot, as she sympathetically took my hand. "Are you hurt, sister?"

"I'm not hurt, thank you." I withdrew my hand, grateful but confused by the fact that my husband's mistress had suddenly turned into my sister.

She left the following Friday. "I've no wish to stay here anyway, Pauline," she gestured at St Neots through the window. "I've outgrown this provincial backwater." She clamped the brass locks on her antique kelim bag. "Arabella has introduced me to one or two people. I'm going into journalism. I have done a bit of writing, you know."

I remembered the pamphlets littering the streets of this provincial backwater. "With the *Socialist Worker Review*?"

"With *Tatler*, actually." At least she had the grace to grin. "I intend to subvert the class structure from within. And if you'll be good enough to forward any correspondence, this is my address." She handed me a piece of paper. "I've bought a worker's cottage in Battersea."

I knew the road, it was the one with all the pale peach and green ruched blinds, £250,000 worth of upwardly mobile chic.

Canvey and Jake kissed me goodbye. "You will come and see us, won't you, Mrs Jenks?"

There was no sign of George. He'd been unusually subdued since Amanda's rugby tackle.

"I made a mistake about George, as you probably did," said Amanda, getting into the taxi. "He's nothing but a facist oppressor, like the rest of them. If you ever need anyone to give evidence of his violent tendencies in a court of law, you can count on me. And there's another thing," she said, through the window, "I'd watch out for those shares of yours, if I were you. I don't like the look of the market. I went liquid a couple of days ago."

I found George lurking in the kitchen. "Well, she's gone

then," he said. "I suppose we ought to think about letting the granny flat."

"Why don't you live there?" I didn't realise until I said it what a brilliant idea it was.

George's placatory expression faded. "Why should I move out of my house? I've never heard such an absurd idea in my life. And what about the children?"

"You wouldn't be moving to Battersea, George, just across the yard."

"No," said George, though his eyes glazed at the mention of Battersea.

"Yes," I said, "or I'll call Amanda. She's prepared to give evidence in court that you've hit me more than once."

"You wouldn't? Amanda wouldn't . . ."

"Oh yes, we would."

The arrangement worked surprisingly well. George continued to run the house and look after Clerry and Toby when I was out, and disappeared across the courtyard when I came home, a reversal of the procedure he had followed when Amanda lived in the flat.

The children didn't seem to think it was odd, to have Mummy and Daddy on different sides of a courtyard. "It's boring in the granny flat, now that Amanda and Jake and Canvey have gone," said Clerry, as she cut out a doll's dress on my studio floor.

As Emily threaded her way back to our table, through the hostile stares of women who had invested in expensive new outfits (some of them mine, I was pleased to see) in the hope of winning the Businesswoman of the Year Award, we rose and clapped her to her seat.

"What an appalling thing to say," David Mainwaring had remained slumped in his seat. "Made Trevor sound the most unutterable wimp."

"*Trevor* peeling potatoes?" muttered George. "That'll be the day."

Peter Bolsover gave a congratulatory clap in the direction of Trevor, who was looking pink and pleased.

"Get up, David." Julia gave him a wifely yank. "Here's Emily." As he wavered unsteadily to his feet, she swiftly swapped his brandy for her Perrier.

"Where's my brandy?" David lurched for his glass, knocking over the Perrier as Emily kissed Trevor and sat down, flushed and trembling.

"What a ghastly experience. Did I sound all right?"

"You sounded wonderful." Julia laid her napkin across the wet tablecloth.

"Where on earth did Princess Anne, or whatever she's called now, find that extraordinary grey garment?" Sybilla, as usual, succeeded in striking a sour note. "She looks like a headmistress on prize day."

"I thought she looked marvellous." I waved my glass of champagne at Emily. "Well done, Em."

"This calls for another drink." David waved at the waiter. "Drinks all round. A double Remy Martin for me, waiter."

"I feel awful about getting this . . ." Emily gestured at her statuette. "We should all have won it."

"Heaven forbid," Sybilla took a look at the statuette and shuddered. "Though I must say, darling, that citation thing they read out; it did rather sound as though you'd done the whole thing single-handed."

"That's hardly fair, Sybilla," said Peter. "Emily couldn't have made it clearer that Natural Sources is a team effort."

"Like one of those gushing Oscar tributes, you mean?" Sybilla gave Peter one of her more chilling smiles. "Thanking everyone down to the gofer. Nobody takes any notice of all that rubbish."

"Julia Mainwaring started the business, Pauline Jenks created the clothes and Sybilla Bolsover sold Natural Sources to the public," Emily had said in her speech, "I just do the sums." Surely even Sybilla must have realised that it was Emily's sums that turned us from a cottage industry into an international business. And it was Emily who raised money on the USM last month to launch the franchises.

*   *   *

She'd put up the idea at a board meeting back in August.

"But I thought it was dodgy to float the company?" I wasn't at all sure what exactly it was we were floating or why, but according to Emily it was going to make us a lot of money. "I thought you said it laid us open to a takeover."

"Not if we only release 36 per cent," said Emily. "That will leave us holding 16 per cent each and with 64 per cent among us we're in an unassailable position."

"Anyway, the only people who seem interested in Natural Sources are our husbands," said Julia. "David's always hanging round the office, offering his expertise, as he puts it."

"The expertise that led Bolsover's into disaster," said Emily frankly.

"Exactly," said Julia. "You know, I honestly believe he thought we'd just step aside and hand him our business."

"There's no doubt he's up to something," said Emily. "I've had lunch with him twice, and his intentions are strictly dishonourable. He keeps asking me personal questions about my net assets." She looked round the table.

"David isn't the only one who's been trying to interfere. When Trevor offered to help me out with the flotation I told him firmly that he was far more useful at home, looking after Thomas. He seemed quite relieved."

"Yes, and I've overheard George on the telephone, muttering about 'the other side', and 'the opposition'," I said.

"Like a character in an Enid Blyton adventure planning a coup with his chums," said Sybilla. "How pathetic."

"How about Peter?" said Emily.

"Peter?" Sybilla lit a cigarette languidly. "I hardly ever see Peter, as you all probably know. He buries himself in his shrubberies and I'm mostly in London. But it doesn't sound like Peter. He is totally incapable of deception," she said, as though this were a major character defect. I wished I could say the same about George.

(This chat about our husbands was tactfully translated into the Minutes by Miss Nelson as: "After agreeing to float off 36 per cent of Natural Sources on the Unlisted Securities Market, the directors unanimously agreed to counter any infiltration of the company by sundry interested parties . . .")

After that Emily had spoken fluently about net assets, convertible rights issues, pretax profits of £1.8 million and our estimated 1988 earnings. "We have barely scratched the surface in the United States, and this flotation will give us the necessary financial strength to develop our business there," she said.

"Absolutely," I said, "when I was there in July, all the major stores were interested in setting up in-store franchise outlets."

"What about Bloomingdale's?" said Sybilla. "That's the one that matters."

"It was all in Pauline's excellent report, Sybilla," said Julia.

The Bloomingdale buyers had vied flatteringly with each other to have us in their departments.

"Natural Sources is all about mix 'n match," said Separates.

"Really? I see it as mainly dresses," said Formal and Evening.

"I'd have said it was strictly casual," said Active Sportswear.

Even the buyer for the Oriental Room got in on the act, on account of Dinesh's antique saris.

I settled it by asking for the prime position in the Designer Mall, and I got it.

I supposed, to the outside world, George and I still looked like a couple, as we stood on the steps of the Savoy with the Businesswoman of the Year, making social noises about what a wonderful evening we'd had and how we must all get together more often.

Kissing me goodbye, Emily said, "Thank you, Pauline. It was you and me really, wasn't it?"

I hugged her. "Mostly you."

Julia and David were staying at the hotel, a wise precaution, and Julia was trying to stop David from getting
into a taxi.

"Come on, David," Peter grabbed David's elbow and
propelled him back inside. "Can you manage on the other
side, Julia?"

The two of them supported David into the lift.

"Well, I'm off to Annabel's, darlings." Sybilla blew a
series of kisses vaguely in our direction. "Promised to meet
some chums. Tell Peter, will you?"

Why would anyone want to go to Annabel's when they
could go home with Peter Bolsover?

"Come *on*, Pauly." George was having difficulty finding
the sleeves in his coat.

I slotted his arms into the appropriate holes. "Hang on
a minute, George, we'll have to wait for Peter . . ."

"Don't want to wait for Peter Bolsover. I'm always
waiting for people like Peter bloody Bolsover."

Peter appeared. "David has passed out on the bed, I don't
think Julia will hear any more from him until the morning."
He gave George a worried glance. "You'll be all right,
Pauline?"

"Of course she'll be all right," George slurred.

"I'll be fine Peter, thank you." I kissed him goodbye and
he put his arms around me for a moment. Then he held
me at arm's length, looking seriously at me. "You're quite
sure?"

"Yes, really. Peter, I'm afraid Sybilla's gone to
Annabel's."

"Good. I'm going to Eaton Square." Not quite the
reaction I'd expected, but somehow rather pleasing.
"Where are you parked?"

Down in the car park George fumbled with his keys.
"Something wrong with the damn lock . . ."

"You'd better let me drive, George."

"What for?" He got the car door open, and was strug-
gling out of his coat.

"You'll be stopped by the police, breathalysed . . ."

"You're trying to castrate me, Pauline," he said, but he did hand over the keys.

"Of course I'm not trying to castrate you." I switched on the ignition. "I just don't want us to get killed, that's all."

As I drove out of the car park I saw Peter. He waved, and then turned and hailed a taxi. Almost as though he was waiting to see if I was all right.

"Bloody bossy women," said George, as we rounded Marble Arch. "Bloody bossy, all of you. You just wait, Pauline, you and that bloody bitch Sybilla – 'I'm off to Annabel's' – didn't ask us, did she? And that smug Emily Sutcliffe, so pleased with herself – 'I just did the sums.' Well, she didn't do them right, did she? Silly cow. You don't know what's coming to you, all of you . . ."

Emily was on the phone from the London office next morning.

"Pauline? The word in the City is that someone's buying up our shares through a nominee. Simax Holdings. I've asked around and nobody's heard of them."

"Didn't they come in at the last minute, when we went public, and buy 15 per cent?" I was rather pleased with myself for remembering that.

"That's right. And now they've got a buying order out to pick up any Natural Sources shares that come on the market."

"It's all that brilliant hyping you did to the brokers and analysts."

I heard a tsk of irritation down the line. "That was *quite* different, Pauline. Then I was trying to get a good price for the flotation. What's happening now is that this company is showing an unhealthy interest in us."

"Unhealthy? I thought we wanted people to buy our shares."

Emily spelt it out patiently. "We don't want one company buying so many."

"But we're all right . . . if we've got 64 per cent?"

"We certainly should be," Emily said doubtfully, "but I still don't like it. We've got a board meeting on the 18th. I'll see what I can find out before then."

"Time for school now, darlings," I kissed the children goodbye. "Off you go, I mustn't be late for the board meeting."

"I don't like school now that Amanda's gone," said Clerry. "Miss Bembridge won't let us do finger painting; she says fingers are for counting on. She makes us learn horrid tables."

"Good for Miss Bembridge. You'll grow up to be clever like Emily."

"Don't want to be like Emily," said Clerry, "want to be like you."

As George left with the children, the phone went.

"Pauline? It's me. Cancel everything." If it wasn't cool, calm Emily, I'd say there was a note of hysteria in her voice.

"What's happened?"

"Just got word. The Nikkei has dropped like a stone . . ."

"The Nikkei?"

"Tokyo Stock Exchange index. Too early to say whether London and New York will follow, but everyone in the City's going mad. I'll keep in touch."

"Black Monday" screamed the newspaper headlines next day, "Stock Market Crash", "Shares Tumble". "Is this 1929 all over again?" they asked, making Emily's reaction seem positively laid back.

It was the first time I'd ever read the *Financial Times* properly. Usually it ended up, still neatly folded, in the cats' tray. Our shares had dropped from 200p to 125p but a quick glance down the page showed we were no worse than anyone else.

Julia phoned while I was reading the *FT*. "Is it serious, do you think? The one time I could really do with some expertise from David, and he's gone off to London."

George was also in London. Some modelling assign-ment, I assumed but didn't bother to ask, so I was just getting ready to collect the children, when Emily phoned again.

"It's worse than I thought, Pauline. Everyone's selling under pressure to cut their losses and Simax Holdings are offering a 10 per cent premium on our market price. They're buying at 137.50p. Can you get hold of Julia and Sybilla? We ought to meet this afternoon."

I put down the phone and picked it up again. Yes, Adrian Smethwick's mother would take over the school run and look after my two until I got back. Yes, Julia could make the meeting. "What a ridiculous waste of time," said Sybilla. "I'm meant to be having my hair done."

When Emily walked into the office I was not sure whether to read exhaustion or defeat in the slump of her shoulders. She sat down heavily and fumbled in her bag. "Has anyone got a cigarette?"

Julia threw over a packet of Silk Cut. "I didn't know you smoked."

"I do now." She lit a cigarette and inhaled deeply. "I've just heard. Simax Holdings have taken over Natural Sources. They've got 52 per cent."

"But they can't have . . ." I looked round the table. ". . . can they? Between us we've got 64 per cent."

"Not any more," said Emily. "One of us has sold out." She looked across the table at Julia. I suppose, like me, she was remembering Julia's Bolsover sellout.

"It certainly wasn't me," said Julia.

Sybilla glanced at her watch. "Well, in that case there's nothing to be done, is there? I'm late, as it is." She collected her things and started to rise. "Do we actually know who is behind Simax Holdings?"

"Yes," said Emily. "I'm sorry, Julia. It's David."

Death of distinguished local resident

Mr. David Mainwaring, 58, until recently the Managing Director of Bolsover's Engineering (St. Neots) Ltd, died last Wednesday evening at his home near Sandy. Mr. Mainwaring, who suffered a minor heart attack last year, was found ailing by his wife, Mrs. Julia Mainwaring, and a close family friend and ex-colleague of Mr. Mainwaring's, Mr. George Jenks.

Said Mr. Jenks, 'This is a grievous blow to all of us, and particularly we who counted ourselves fortunate to be numbered among David's friends.'

Mr. Mainwaring was found in distress in his study when his wife and Mr. Jenks returned to the house after collecting her twin daughters from school. Their efforts to revive him were not successful. 'We did everything we could, but alas, it was not to be,' said Mr. Jenks. 'Why did it have to happen at such a happy time for David? Everything was going for him. He and his wife were revelling in the opportunity to work together.'

Last October Mr. Mainwaring acquired a 52% holding in Natural Sources, the international fashion group of which Julia Mainwaring is Managing Director.

Mr. Mainwaring leaves, as well as twin daughters by his present marriage, a son and daughter by his first marriage.

St Neots Express, 11th February, 1988

While Pauline was away I stayed in the house; as soon as she got back I had to retire to the granny flat like a dog that's no longer needed on guard duty. Not that there's anything to complain of in the accommodation; a commodious bedsitting room, with its own little bathroom and kitchen. But I really must get round to redecorating it, if this split living is going to be a permanent factor. Jake and Canvey seem to have Expressed Themselves Visually all over the walls, and although I am in heartfelt agreement with the principles of CND, I do not necessarily wish to have its logo stencilled all over my bathroom. And I will have to change the curtains if I am to get rid of the smell. Amanda must have used Giorgio as an air-freshener.

I was very disappointed with Amanda. I might have found it in myself to forgive her for the disgraceful way she tackled me that day like an All Black, flinging me to the ground and ticking me off in front of Pauline, but what had happened to her principles?

I'd dropped in at the Granary when I was up in London to see Sally, my agent, about the possibility of future modelling assignments.

"I thought you'd decided to give up, George?" Sally said.

"Only temporarily." I smiled at her in the way which always works. "Now I'm available again. But only, of course, for really prestigious –"

"Younger men are coming along all the time. Pity you dropped out the last few months; this is a very immediate business, you know. See what I can do. Would you accept knitting pattern assignments?"

So I was quite put out when I went into the Granary, but cheered up at once when I saw their moussaka.

I cheered up even more when I went downstairs and saw Arabella Pinter-Bambury sitting at a table with one of her smart friends. I slid into a chair opposite.

"Hello, George," said Arabella, "I haven't seen you for absolute yonks."

"Good God, George, you look pretty hang-dog," said her friend. I took another look.

"Amanda! What have you done to yourself?"

Her frizzy hair had turned into a shining cap, she had lost masses of weight, and her clothes were not the kind one associates with the Struggles of the Proletariat. She looked quite different from when she sat on me threateningly; I decided not to mention that demeaning occasion.

"Oh, well, working on *Tatler*, one really couldn't go round looking like a jelly bag. Bella took me in hand." The sisters grinned at each other.

"Oh," I said, reflecting that calling it *Tatler* without the "The" made it sound even more Sloane, "and where are Jake and Canvey?"

"At Wetherby and Lady Eden's. Worth every penny, you've got to start thinking about Common Entrance so early these days."

"Common Entrance?"

"If Jake's going to make it to Eton, he's got a lot of hard work ahead of him."

"Eton? The bastion of middle-class prejudice? The breeding ground of arrogance and privilege?" I was quoting the old Amanda word for word, but she seemed to have forgotten all that.

"You don't want to believe all you see in the media," she said. "Now, what are we going to do about you, George?"

Both the sisters looked at me in a brooding manner.

"Do about me?"

"It's high time you took over your life, George, instead of maundering about accepting what comes," said Amanda, "not to mention knocking defenceless women about."

"Don't exaggerate. I merely –"

"You merely hit your wife. Now, what are you going to do with yourself?"

"My life is very full, actually. I was thinking of going back to modelling." I had no intention of letting these bossy women organise me.

"Modelling?" said Arabella. "Not exactly a long-term career, is it? How old are you, George?"

I remembered what my agent had said about younger men.

"Still in my early thirties," I said curtly, wanting to add, "if it's any business of yours," but not quite liking to. I had, after all, loved Amanda (had I? Or was it just when the light was out?) and Arabella was an extremely nice woman, if a shade on the dictatorial side.

I compared them to the other women I knew. Sybilla, that selfish bitch, how much longer was Peter going to put up with her? Emily Sutcliffe, as cold as cucumber, but with a business brain you could only admire. Julia, well over her illness now, but vague and inclined to lapse into horticultural lingo. And Pauline, cool and distant, still taking it out on me because I had been slightly unfaithful to her. None of them thought of me as a person. As far as they were concerned I was Mr Pauline Jenks, always available to take children to the dentist or chauffeur clothes from one place to another.

It occurred to me, as I ate my moussaka (not quite as good as mine, but excellent, nevertheless) that Amanda and Arabella were the only women I knew who didn't treat me as a househusband.

The other lot even treated me as a househusband at that board meeting. I'm surprised I wasn't expected to make the coffee.

It was at the end of October, right after David had nefariously acquired a majority holding in Natural Sources. You could have cut the atmosphere with a knife.

Present (as Miss Nelson's notes probably put it) were Julia Mainwaring, Pauline Jenks, Emily Sutcliffe, David Mainwaring, and last and certainly least, George Jenks. No Sybilla, of course, she had perfidiously sold her shares to David, and anyway she was in Barbados. And no Peter; he had refused to have anything to do with the takeover plan. Peter was not in Barbados. Trevor was absent, probably because Emily had told him to stay away. I suspected there was no real reason for him to be there, anyway; as far as I could gather he had, after his initial interest, contributed neither money nor enthusiasm to the scheme. The only reason I was there was that I had lent David £20,000 towards buying the stock, and I was beginning to wish I hadn't. Pauline didn't know about the loan, but she was giving me dagger glances, Julia was looking at me as though I had Dutch Elm disease, and Emily behaved towards me as she normally behaved towards me; that is to say as though I were not there at all.

David had been very cheerful on the telephone. "I'm going to need you at the meeting, George," he had said, "to watch my back with all those women. Trevor has opted out, ought to have known he'd never stand the pace, and of course poor old Peter was never really in it at all . . ." "Poor old Peter" is in fact nearly twenty years younger than David, but I thought it would be infelicitous to point it out ". . . we're going to have to have our wits about us, just follow my lead, old chap. Know I can count on you."

If you know that you don't know much, I thought sourly. On the other hand, the women were getting insufferable, what with Women of the Year awards and telephones in their cars. I had discovered that Pauline went to the hairdresser every single week; I tried to remember how often Mother went, back in those good old days at Hammersmith. Twice a year for a perm, if I recollected correctly, and my father unfailingly said, "Off beautifying yourself again, Gloria? You'll have me in the poorhouse before you've finished."

I only wished hairdressing was the only sign of Pauline's extravagance. Going through her papers when she was out one day (since she hardly ever spoke to me, it was the only way I could keep up to date), I found a photograph of a tumbledown cottage attached to a roneoed description. Apparently it was an old mas, whatever that might be, Mess was more the word for it, near Draguignan in the hills of Provençe. It was surrounded by several hectares of orchard (why the French can't have acres like everyone else is beyond me) and was for sale at eight hundred and fifty thousand francs. Pinned to it was a note saying, "It's a snip. Go for it *now*, love Emily."

I didn't know how much eight hundred and fifty thousand francs was in real money, but it didn't sound like a snip to me. And anyway, what was Pauline doing, going into property deals without my cognisance?

David had got to the meeting early and bagged the chair at the head of the table. The women clustered hostilely at the other end, and I sat in the middle, wishing I was a smoker.

"Now," said David in a bluff manner, "I suggest we sink our differences and work together as a team. As I see it, the future –"

"Point of order," said Emily. "As Julia Mainwaring is managing director of Natural Sources, should she not be in the chair?"

"As majority shareholder," said David genially, "I naturally take the chair."

"You haven't even been voted onto the board, yet."

"I don't have to be voted, I own the bloody thing, or as good as, anyway."

"I once told someone I wouldn't use David as a mulch," said Julia. "I would like it put on record, Miss Nelson, that I wouldn't even consider him for compost. Though there are aspects of his behaviour that would work quite well as fertiliser."

"No need to be offensive, Julia," said David.

"Yes there is, there's every need. Despicable, disloyal, underhand, sneaky, treacherous. The adjectives are endless, just take your pick."

"Perfectly ordinary business practice, it happens all the –"

"I would also like it on record that I am filing for divorce. Heaven knows the women are as endless as the adjectives."

"Well done, Julia," said Pauline. I didn't quite like the sound of that.

"Quite," said Emily, "but I really think we ought to talk about the future, if there's going to be one, of Natural Sources."

"The future," said David, "*exactly*. I've always admired your brain, Emily, straight to the point as usual."

"It wasn't my brain you were trying to get your hands on, that time we had lunch and you made your pathetic attempt to worm information about the company out of me. Did you really think a pat on the thigh would make me reveal all?"

"Water over the dam," said David. "All's fair, etc. You ladies may have noticed I've been taking a close interest in your working methods over the last few months . . ."

"We certainly noticed you were hanging round the office and getting in our way," said Pauline. I did wish she wouldn't be quite so pert.

". . . and I have here," David rattled a sheaf of papers, "a number of well-considered suggestions on how we will upgrade profits. I think you will find them quite interesting. Miss Nelson, circulate these, will you?"

Miss Nelson looked at Julia. "Would you like me to circulate them, Mrs Mainwaring?" she said.

"Certainly not. They won't be worth reading, anyway."

I stood up, collected the papers from in front of David, and passed them to the women.

"What exactly are you doing here, George?" said Emily.

"He put some money behind the takeover," said David, (oh God, I wished he hadn't) "every right to be here. Anyway, he'll soon be heading our sales force."

"Oh George," said Julia, not unkindly, "how silly of you."

"*Brushed nylon?*" screamed Pauline, who had been looking at David's memo. "Are you out of your mind, or what?"

"He's not heading any sales force that I have anything to do with," said Emily.

"If that's how you feel," said David, throwing me a look which I think meant Now we're getting somewhere, "then the board will, reluctantly, of course, accept your resignation."

"I thought you said you admired Emily's brain," said Julia. "If you are going to replace it with your own, I think we should warn the franchisees."

"Polyester," said Pauline, "Julia, he's actually suggesting 40 per cent cotton and 60 per cent –"

David lit a cigar. "I'm sure you'll find them extremely challenging to work with, Pauline. Non-iron, too, you will note. And look at the cost comparison with all that

George

old-fashioned linen you insist on using. Yes, I thought that would make you think. That Ahmet fellow, Bas what's his name, he assures me that with his contacts he can get us –"

"You'll have to rename the firm, of course," said Emily. "How about Unnatural Rubbish? Well, I'm not having anything to do with it."

Pauline, in between giving me terrible looks, was still reading the memo.

"David, seriously . . . this bit about Maximum Yardage Per Garment . . ."

"Done quite a bit of homework," said David complacently.

". . . culottes, one and five eighth yards, full skirts two and two thirds yards, shirts . . . David, they'll be hopelessly skimpy. I couldn't work on that basis, I really couldn't."

"You will when you see the profit margins. You girls, very talented in your own way, don't think I'm putting you down, but no idea of reading a profit and loss sheet. You weren't charging enough."

"What it boils down to," said Emily, "is over-priced cheap tat. I suppose it's useless to remind you, David, that Japan and the US can't get enough of Pauline's designs, that Julia has been the mainstay of our organisation, and that I did actually win the Business Woman of the Year award? You will have my formal letter of resignation in the morning."

Pauline and Julia looked at each other.

"And mine," they both said.

"Not so fast," said David, "the trouble with women is they never read the small print. Read them the relevant clause, George. Oh, do get on with it," he added, as I searched through my papers. What was I doing, allied to this unpleasant man, making me look like a fool? I found the Articles of Agreement and read them the relevant clause.

"I don't remember signing anything that said we had to give two years' notice," said Pauline.

Emily took the contract from me without so much as a by your leave.

245

"Mmm. When we first set up the company . . . it's here, all right, the lawyer made us put it in. I do actually remember him saying, 'You can't count on good will, you've got to have it down in black and white.' Oh, *bugger*."

"Read on," said David complacently. ". . . 'unless a majority shareholding sees fit to accept such a resignation.' Well, I'll accept yours, Emily, and I'll certainly accept yours, Julia; you can go back to your delphiniums and your Drambuie. But I need your name, Pauline. I'm afraid you're stuck with me."

It really got quite unpleasant after that. The women, typically, I'm afraid, lost their tempers. Julia said that if Pauline had to stay on, then she'd stay on too, to back her up. Emily said that she was awfully sorry, but she wouldn't. David said tough cheese, Julia had resigned and that was that. Miss Nelson, whose pencil had been flying over the pages of her notebook, cleared her throat in that demure way she has, and said that she thought she ought to mention that she had no record in her minutes of Mrs Mainwaring tendering her resignation. David told Miss Nelson she was fired, and Julia told David that he was a bastard and that she was still in charge of hiring and firing.

David left shortly after that, blustering about they'd soon see who was boss round here and there'd be some changes made, mark his words. He snapped his fingers at me as though I were a puppy dog.

"Come on, George, no sense in wasting time with this lot."

I toyed with the idea of staying behind in an independent manner, but took a look at the women's faces and decided that discretion was the better part of valour.

"Well, then," I said, "good morning, ladies." What made me add, "parting in such sweet sorrow," I will never know, nerves probably, and when I picked up my sheaf of papers several of them naturally slipped onto the floor. None of them helped me to pick them up. Even Miss Nelson, who in better days was, after all, my subordinate, sat and watched me scrabbling.

By the time I'd shut the door behind me, David had left. Gone to have a quick one, probably, or more likely a quick four or five. No thought for anyone else; I could have done with a drink, too.

I hadn't shut the door properly, and it clicked open again. I could hear them quite clearly.

"Nice one about the minutes, Nelly," said Pauline.

"Nice one about the divorce, Julia," said Emily.

"I've been thinking about it for ages. Putting it off, you know, because what about the children and all that . . . I'm actually grateful that he's made up my mind for me."

"Have you made any plans?" said Pauline. "Where will you live? If you need a temporary roof, you can always move in with me. Masses of room, now that Geroge is in the granny flat."

Really, had her indiscretion no bounds?

"Oh, Pauline, that is kind. But I own the house, actually. My father gave it to us for a wedding present. David was rather shirty, at the time, that Dad insisted on it being in my name. I can see why, now. I suppose Dad guessed David would turn out to be rubbish. I say, have you heard about Sybilla? I bet there'll be a divorce there, too."

"The Argentinian polo player?" said Emily.

"The *what!*" said Pauline. "Oh, I don't believe it, what a cliché."

"She's gone too far this time. I really think the worm will turn."

There was a small silence, and then Pauline said, "I wouldn't exactly describe Peter as a worm, Emily."

"You must admit he's pretty wormlike as far as Sybilla is concerned," said Julia. "I saw him last week at a Horticultural Show, and I thought he was crosser about Sybilla selling out to David than about her infidelities."

"Have we ever discovered why she sold?"

"Partly boredom, I suspect," said Emily. "Sybbo is one of those people who loves starting things. As soon as they're a success, she loses interest, and moves on to something new. No doubt Luigi, or whatever he's called, had come on the scene and she wanted to clear the decks for action."

"Do you remember how she rushed off to Annabel's after your award?" said Julia. "'To see a few chums,' she said? One chum, I bet. Emily, what are you going to do? You're far too clever to do nothing."

"Trevor and I are going into property together. Which reminds me, I must dash; there's a man in Spain I've got to phone, and they keep such weird office hours."

I moved away from the door, sat down at the other end of the room, and pretended to be doing *The Times* crossword puzzle. Property indeed, what did Emily Sutcliffe know about property? Then I remembered that silly note about a French farmhouse; had she been practising dealing on Pauline?

The day after David passed on, our doctor dropped in to see how Clerihue and Tobe's chickenpox was progressing.

"Don't worry, young woman," he said to Clerry, "there won't be a mark on that pretty face of yours. As long as you promise not to scratch. I know it's itchy, I'll give you something for it." He looked across at me. "And look what you've done to your father."

I had come out in a nasty prickly rash round my eyebrows (stress, I assumed) which worried me rather, as I had contemplated taking up my modelling again. And I was not feeling on top of the world, which I had put down to the fact that looking after sick children is very monotonous. They were thirsty all the time, especially when I was downstairs cooking, and they weren't just thirsty for water; it had to be some lemon barley stuff they'd seen on television. Pauline, conveniently for her, was away rushing round the country, no doubt with some man. "Calming down the franchisees," as she put it, "they are worried sick about the takeover, and who can blame them?"

"Shingles. Often happens," said the doctor, "same virus,

you see. With the younger members of the family it's chickenpox, we oldsters get shingles. If I've seen it once, I've seen it a –"

"No doubt," I said coldly, irritated by his reference to oldsters. "When will this rash go away?"

"Oh, give it a few days. Now that the rash has come out, you're probably not infectious, but I should be a bit careful . . ." he scribbled on a pad, ". . . get your wife to have this prescription filled out. Where is Mrs Jenks, by the way?"

"I think it's Edinburgh, today. I'm afraid, Doctor . . . when it's a choice between career and family –"

"Mummy only went away the day before yesterday, when we started getting better," said Clerihue.

"My mummy wings me every night before I go to bed," said Tobias.

"Rings, not wings," said Clerihue officiously, sounding more like Pauline than ever. "Mummy, Mummy," she screamed.

Pauline put down her case and hugged the children. Typical of her that she hadn't apprised me that she intended an early return.

"How are your horrid spots, darlings?"

"Mine have nearly gone and Toby's are still awful," said Clerihue. "You said you weren't coming back till next week. Did you come back early to see me?"

"To see both of you, darling. Good morning, Dr Bingley. How are the patients?"

"No problems at all, doing very nicely. I'm afraid they've given your husband shingles."

"What a nuisance," said Pauline. "The first thing I must do is phone poor Julia."

I wondered if he noticed how uncaring she seemed about my plight? I did think, in front of outsiders, she might at least pretend.

"Julia Mainwaring, would that be?" said Dr Bingley. "The Mainwarings are my partner's patients. What a shock, no reason why he shouldn't have gone on for years, so long as he took care. You must be very upset, Mrs Jenks."

"Not particularly," said Pauline with what I thought was disastrous frankness, "I really didn't like him very much, and he was trying to ruin our business."

"I'm sure the doctor is far too busy to listen to business chatter, Pauline. He has more important things on his mind than your little affairs." I moved towards the door and threw it open in a suggestive manner. Unfortunately Dr Bingley showed every sign of being fascinated by Pauline's ill-timed revelations.

"I did rather wonder," he said, "how Mrs Mainwaring reacted to that takeover. Done with the best of intentions, of course, but . . ."

"Best of intentions, my foot," said Pauline. "Oh well, I suppose I'd better get on. Thank you so much for looking after the children so well, Dr Bingley. Such a relief to know we've got a real family doctor who really takes an interest."

"I must be off. Call if you have any worries at all. I've left a prescription for your husband. The rash isn't half as bad as it looks, so don't spoil him. Activity will take his mind off his itches."

What a way for a doctor to talk.

Oh well, another day, another funeral, as they say. I certainly shouldn't have been at this one. I was not looking at my best and the shingles pain was exquisite. Also I kept on wanting to scratch.

I still don't know, I thought as I shifted my feet, whether Pauline has bought the farmhouse. I hadn't quite liked to ask her because I would have had to admit I had riffled through her papers.

It seemed to be a very long funeral. St Neots in February could not be described as balmy; the wind off the fens was biting through my charcoal worsted, and the snow was staining my Gucci loafers.

Why had Peter Bolsover been asked to stand with the immediate mourners, and not me? I had had to ask him for a lift to the funeral (Pauline, of course, had filled up her ridiculous German sports car with Julia and the children, no thought of how I was going to manage) and had got the impression, during the drive, that there was more than met the eye about his relationship with Natural Sources.

"I wonder who will manage the firm now that David has gone?" I said casually. Naturally the obvious person was me, though I didn't quite like to say so. I expected that was what David meant about me being in the will. I had been his right-hand man, after all, and put in £20,000 towards the takeover. I was rather looking forward to the will reading; I hoped David had had the forethought to leave me a decent block of shares.

"The person who has been managing it, to all intents and purposes, while he was there, I suppose," said Peter.

"Do you really think so?" Useful to have his support, I thought.

"Who else? Emily and Sybilla have gone, and Julia is aching to get back to her garden. It was Pauline's designs that took Natural Sources to the top. Once she gets over her lack of self-confidence, she'll make a first-class MD."

"*Pauline!* I thought you meant – lack of self-confidence?" She had far too much confidence, if you asked me, bossing me about and buying farmhouses behind my back.

"Totally confident about her work, of course. But . . . she's always struck me as being a very diffident person. Gentle."

That was quite enough of that. "Gentle? I'm afraid that's not quite the word where the children are concerned. That is, if she bothers to see them at all."

"Oh really, George. Pauline is an exemplary mother. I simply won't listen . . . anyway, here we are at the church."

Julia looked very good in black; at least she wouldn't have to go through with the divorce proceedings, though I didn't suppose it would be quite the thing to say so. Simon and Alexandra and the two Mels looked awful; young people shouldn't have to deal with death, they don't understand it. I thought back to the last funeral I went to. Mother's, with David looking sanctimonious as though he'd cared, and me thinking, "I'll get back at you one day for what you said about Mother."

Well, I had, in a way, hadn't I? And it had all been so easy.

Naturally, when Julia's car broke down that Wednesday, it was Muggins she phoned for help.

"Oh George, it's so tiresome. I've only had my licence back for a few months, and now the garage says the car needs a new carburettor or something, allow a week for spare parts, you know the sort of thing. I've got to collect the twins at four. George, you couldn't, could you?"

"If I pick you up at half past three?" Julia had at least continued to speak to me after the revelation of my putting money into the takeover. She was about the only woman I knew, including my wife, who appeared to recognise my existence. Except for Amanda and Arabella, of course; they'd come up with rather an intriguing idea. Pauline might be in for quite a surprise, I thought complacently.

We collected the twins and I drove carefully towards the Mainwaring house.

"Looks as though there'll be more snow tonight," I said.

The Mels squeaked. "Enough to stop us going to school?" said one of them.

"It'll be jolly cold for Pauline in Edinburgh," said Julia. "Have you heard how she's getting on, George?"

"We don't discuss business, much." Or anything else, I thought.

"You can hardly blame her. David's ruining Natural Sources, you do realise that, don't you? Why on earth did you support him, George?"

"If you look at the balance sheets, profits are going up hand over fist."

"Of course they are. Selling shoddy stuff at high prices on the strength of a first class reputation, you can't help making money. Short-term money. It won't last."

"David seems to think it's all going very well."

"Do you know what I'd like to do to David?" She looked

over her shoulder, but both the twins had Walkmans on, and were clicking and twitching. "I could cheerfully kill him."

"But you're still letting him live in your house."

"Only for another week; my solicitor says he's got to move out. Can't wait to see the last of him." She drew up in front of the house and turned off the engine. "Mels . . . those wretched trannies . . . *Mels*. Take those things off and go upstairs and do your homework. Time for coffee, George?"

"That would be very nice," I said, following her into the house.

"There's a fire in the library. I won't be a sec with the coffee."

"Or an instant," I said, but Julia disappeared towards the kitchen without seeing the joke.

I switched on the lights in the library. David was slumped in an armchair by the fire, his face an unhealthy shade of grey.

"Julia," he said in a slurred way.

"It's not Julia, it's George," I explained patiently. Really, what a time of day to be drunk, I thought, how fortunate that the Mels had gone straight upstairs.

"Bloody fool. Get Julia. Quick."

"She won't be a moment, she's just getting some coffee. If you don't mind my saying so, David, you could do with some black coffee yourself."

"Julia. Now." He was breathing in a funny fast shallow way and looked unattractively sweaty; typical that he should expect Julia to run round after him as soon as she got home.

"She'll come as soon as she's ready. The roads are getting quite tricky, more snow forecast. I doubt if the Mels will get to school tomorrow. By the way, I've got the updated sales figures with me. I think you're going to be very pleased."

"Heart. Don't you understa . . . heart."

"Heart of what? I must say, old man, if I were you I'd think seriously about taking more water with it."

He gave me a really malevolent look, perhaps I shouldn't have called him Old Man. I never had before, but something emboldened me to, that day.

"Here we are, coffee at last." Julia came in with a tray, much to my relief. "Sorry to have been so long, but . . . oh, there you are, David. You might have turned on the dishwasher, not a single clean mug in the place. David? *David*. Oh God, George, he's having another attack."

"I don't think so. We were chatting about sales figures. Take it from one who knows, Julia, it's merely a slight case of lifting the elbowitis."

Julia had dumped the tray on a table and was searching through David's pockets.

"His pills, his pills, he's supposed to carry them on him. David, listen to me. Where . . . are . . . your . . . pills?"

David stopped glaring at me and looked upwards.

"In your bedroom? Right. Where . . . bedside table? Get them, George, would you? He's in the spare room, second on left at the top of the stairs. Quick."

There were two pill bottles on the bedside table. One had little blue pills in it and the label said something about angina. The others were pink and marked Indigestion Relief. I picked them both up, to be on the safe side.

The view from the spare room was really beautiful, far superior to the view from most people's master bedroom. My eye was caught by a couple of wild ducks sliding on a little frozen lake. If only I could paint, I thought, what a perfect Christmas card that would make . . .

"George! Have you found them?" Julia's panicky voice from the hall. I jumped guiltily.

"Can't quite see . . ." I called. ". . . oh yes, here they are." I thought she was rather going over the top, it wasn't as if she even liked the man. Only a few minutes ago she'd talked about killing him, and now here she was, behaving like Florence Nightingale. When I got downstairs she was waiting with a glass of water, and snatched the blue pills from me.

"Here we are, David, take this and you'll be fine. George, ambulance."

"Well," I said, moving towards the door, "if you're absolutely sure it's an emergency, Julia. They don't like being called out unless –"

"Just get it, George."

David knocked the glass out of her hand. "Bloody woman. Wrong pill. Trying kill me."

"It's the blue pills for angina, David. Isn't it George? You look."

I nodded. "The pink pills are for tummy-ache. Says so on the label."

"Bloody lie," said David. "After money, both you. Give me pink."

"George," said Julia, "get a blue pill into him. I'll go and phone. And loosen his tie."

She rushed out and I took another blue pill from the bottle.

"Open your mouth, David, and swallow. Soon be better."

"Don't let Julia finish me. Pink's right. You're in will, you know. I'll double it, just give me bloody pink."

Naturally, when Julia came back from phoning, I told her I'd been successful with a blue pill.

No point in stirring up trouble.

BED AND BOARDROOM

Maureen Harris looks at the advantages and disadvantages of the 24-hour marriage.

Could you work with your husband? More and more couples are deciding to live and work together and some of them met at the Institute of Directors in London yesterday to discuss the problems and pleasures of sharing bed and boardroom.

'It's important to have complementary characters and an equal regard for each other's talent,' said guest speaker Renate Olins, Director of London Marriage Guidance. 'The couples who come unstuck are the ones who fight over who's going to be boss.'

As Renate Olins pointed out, the couples who run a 24-hour marriage are putting all their eggs in one basket with a vengeance. 'If your marriage goes, so does your business and it can work the other way, too.'

Nobody is more aware of this than the four successful women who founded Natural Sources and made a fortune by persuading us all into pure natural fabrics. Their husbands joined the company last October and now, six months later, there have been resignations and ructions in the boardroom and only Emily Sutcliffe, last year's Business Woman of the Year, is still with the man she married. The other three marriages have all disintegrated.

Julia Mainwaring was already in the process of divorcing her husband, David, when he tragically died of a heart attack in February. Lady Sybilla Bolsover, who handled the publicity for Natural Sources, has left her husband, and Pauline Jenks, the team's designer, is living apart from her husband, sales director George Jenks.

Unchastened by the Natural Sources experience, Emily and Trevor Sutcliffe have now started a property company. 'We don't have arguments about who gets the corporate car and who gets to do the dirty dishes,' Emily Sutcliffe told the conference, 'because we are equal partners. Trevor has the financial flair, and I'm responsible for the day to day running of the company . . .

Daily Telegraph, **29th April, 1988**

G eorge arrived on my doorstep a couple of days after David's funeral. "You'll have to look after Clerry and Toby today," he said, "or are you off getting your hair done again?"

"Once a month, George," I said, "for a trim." It was

getting harder to slot even a twenty-minute hair appointment into my diary. With David making a mess of the
business and Emily out of it, I was doing the work of three
and hardly had time to pick up a pencil or think about
patterns and shapes and the new line for '89. I was relying
heavily on reruns of earlier classics. Goodness knows we
needed a bit of classicism after David's polyester patio
pants.

To add to the workload, George kept taking off for
London, leaving me with the children. If he hadn't insisted
that he wanted to look after Clerry and Toby himself, I'd
have been prepared with a nanny or instant baby-sitter. As
it was, all I could do when George suddenly disappeared,
and I had to charm a buyer in Boston on Monday and
mollify a franchisee in Middlesbrough on Friday, was to
cry out for help and hope someone would come leaping to
my aid. Usually it was Julia, who kept a couple of bunk
beds at the ready in the Mels' old nursery; sometimes it
was Marcia Blake, the girl who used to manicure her
nails in George's office and who now made so much money
as a freelance advertisement rep that she could afford to
take a day off and look after my children.

"London again, is it?" I said to George.

Clerry appeared at my side, in her nightdress. "Are
you going to London, Daddy? Can Toby and I come,
too?"

"No, you can't, Clerihue. And don't interrupt. Your
mother and I are talking."

"There's no need to snap," I said, as Clerry's mouth
trembled. I picked her up, and smoothing down her curls,
looked over her head at her father. George had spent a lot
of time on his appearance. Exquisitely cut suit, shining
Gucci loafers, a Turnbull and Asser shirt if I wasn't much
mistaken, an aura of something that would have held its
own with Giorgio in Kew Gardens, and only a hint of a
spot, cunningly concealed by Erace. There was nothing in
his eyes, nothing for me, anyway. "You're looking very
smart."

"It's the reading of the will," he said. "I feel one should be appropriately attired for such an occasion."

"David's will? Surely you're not expecting a legacy from David Mainwaring?"

George's self-satisfied smile didn't extend to his eyes. "David and I had an understanding, Pauline. Practically his last words were, 'You're in the will, you know . . .' And Mr Baverstock, the solicitor, phoned yesterday. Said he particularly wanted me to be present."

"Perhaps David has left you his golf clubs." I knew George hated golf.

"I think it will be rather more than *golf clubs*, Pauline. I think you'll find David has entrusted me with his shares, the major share-holding in Natural Sources."

George was back within two hours. I heard his car coming round the corner as I was bringing some of the children's toys in from the yard. He slammed on the brakes, jumped out, banged the door shut, took a kick at it and then bent, with a licked handkerchief, to repair the damage to his door and his Guccis.

"No golf clubs?" I said.

"That bastard." I could see he was quite keen to kick something else and prudently stayed on my side of the yard. "That double-crossing bastard."

"You weren't named in the will?"

"I was named, all right," said George. "As joint executor, with her stepmother, for that snobbish, swept-up Alexandra Mainwaring."

"That's quite an honour." I was overwhelmed with relief that George had not inherited the chairman's seat and I would not, after all, have to resign from my job as well as my marriage. "And you'll be paid, I presume, out of the estate?"

"Typical David. He didn't even put in a charging clause," said George. "I questioned Mr Baverstock very closely about it. 'But don't I get anything for doing all this work?' 'Only if the deceased stipulates a charge against the estate,' he said."

"Well, at least you'll be able to collect the children from school," I said, "I've got a myriad things to do at the office."

"I also have some important work to undertake in London," said George, "so you'll have to collect them yourself."

As he got into the car he said the unforgivably unfair thing that made me finally decide to divorce him. "You can't negate responsibility for the children for ever, you know, Pauline."

I called my mother.

"You need help?" she said. "I'll be there this evening."

She arrived at six, and had marshalled Marmite soldiers and cocoa onto the kitchen table by half past.

I'd told her, on the phone, that George and I had been separated for some time and I was thinking seriously about divorce.

"I suppose you know what you're doing . . . about George?" she said, as we packed the dishwasher.

"I think so, Mum."

"That's all right, then." She didn't add that she'd never liked George much herself or that she had warned me not to marry him, which was nice of her.

So there we were, a week later, sitting around the board-room table again, with yet another change of cast. Julia, Emily, George, me. And Simon and Alexandra Mainwaring, hands neatly folded in their laps, as politely serious as bright sixth-formers facing up to an A-level Oral.

Simon and Alexandra. *Simax*. How could we have been so dim? And David Mainwaring, who had not been planning to relinquish the chairman's seat for at least a decade or two, had not left his guilefully gained share of the company to George, but to an eighteen-year-old and a fifteen-year-old.

Julia patted the chair next to her. "Come and sit down here, darlings." Simon and Alex rose and moved round the table. Alexandra took the chair next to Julia and George grudgingly moved down the table, making a lot of fuss with briefcase and notes, to make room for Simon. "Now, this isn't going to be a proper board meeting, but I thought it would be a good idea if we all got together and decided what we were going to do about Natural Sources."

George cleared his throat. "An excellent plan, Julia. Perhaps I, as the senior board member present, as well as the executor for this charming young lady . . ." He favoured Alexandra with the winsome smile he practised in the mirror before modelling assignments, ". . . should take the chair."

Alexandra gazed stonily back at him and Julia said, "I don't think we want any nonsense about chairs. This is just an informal meeting. And do bear in mind, George, that David named you and me joint executors to act on Alexandra's behalf. Simon, of course, is old enough to speak for himself."

"I'll go along with anything you and Pauline decide," said Simon.

"Splendid," said Julia. "Pauline and I have been discussing the future of the company and, as we see it, we might as well call in the liquidators tomorrow if we continue the disastrous policies initiated by my late husband and his misguided colleagues . . ."

She looked pointedly at George who cleared his throat again, shuffled a few papers about. "Profits for the three-month period November to January are up 5 per cent," he said. "Nothing disastrous about that."

"Well, of course they are," said Julia. "Reflecting the work we did before you and David started interfering . . ."

"And the cutback on quality," said Emily. "A very short-sighted immediate benefit, if I may say so."

"I don't think you may," said George. "I seem to remember that you resigned from Natural Sources several months ago."

"This is not a board meeting, George," said Julia, "and Emily still has a 16 per cent stake in the company. As I see it, now that Sybilla and Emily have left, we're short on management skills . . ."

George gave a little cough. Julia looked at him and then looked away again quickly. ". . . and I really don't want to go back to running the company . . ."

"You're resigning?" said George. "In that case, may I offer my expertise . . . ?"

"No, I'm not resigning," said Julia. "I intend staying on the board as a non-executive director. And the rest of the time," she smiled round at us, "I shall at last have time to enjoy my children and my garden."

"Then who . . . ?" George began.

"I've been talking to Emily and to Alex and Simon," said Julia, "and we decided to ask Peter Bolsover to help us out as non-executive chairman . . ."

"Peter?" said George. "This is all most irregular. Anyway, Simon isn't even on the board."

"That's quite true," said Simon, "but I do have 26 per cent of the shares . . . don't I, Julia?"

"Of course you do, dear," said Julia. "And when you've finished at College I'm sure there'll be a place for you in the company."

"We're not running a kindergarten," said George. "You'll be putting in the Mels as finance director and chief accountant next."

"Don't be silly, George," said Julia.

"Well, I only have a few shares myself," said George, "but as executor for Miss Mainwaring, I shall certainly vote against the appointment of an outside chairman."

"As co-executor," said Julia.

"Excuse me." Alexandra put up her hand and looked round the room. "Excuse me. I'm not frightfully good at sums, but Julia has explained what Natural Sources was all about before Daddy took it over, and I think she and Emily and Pauline and Sybilla were doing the right thing and if Mr Bolsover is planning to continue their policy . . ."

"You don't know anything about it, young lady," said George.

"I do know that if you're thinking of your own interests instead of acting in the best interests of the beneficiary – that's me – I can sue you when I'm eighteen," said Alexandra, with a glint of her old sharpness. "Mr Baverstock told me."

"Right on, Alex," said Simon.

"So you'll be looking for a managing director?" George turned his back on Alexandra and Simon and fixed Julia with his charming smile. "You'll be wanting somebody with marketing skills who understands this highly competitive and specialised business?"

I was thinking that myself, and wondering why Julia and Emily hadn't included me in their discussions, when Julia said: "Exactly. That's why we've decided to ask Pauline if she'll be our managing director."

"Pauline?" said George.

"But I couldn't . . ." I said.

"We knew you'd say that," said Julia, "so we decided to enlist Peter first . . ." She looked up as Peter Bolsover came in. "Perfect timing, Peter."

"Only sorry I'm late," said Peter. "Bit of a problem with Caroline's pony. I had to wait and see the vet." He sat down next to George, as Nelly Nelson circulated coffee.

"This is a private meeting of Natural Sources." George didn't look at Peter as he said it. "I don't recall inviting Peter Bolsover to join us."

"Of course you don't," said Julia. "I invited him."

Peter smiled at me across the table. "I think Julia and Emily had a notion that I might be able to persuade you to consider the idea," he said. "They feel, and I agree with them, that you have a unique and total grasp of what Natural Sources is all about. You know the suppliers and the buyers, you're the one who has been liaising with the franchise outlets . . ."

"But I'm a designer. I don't know about business . . ."

"Of course you do," said Julia. "You built up the business, you and Emily."

"Naturally," said Peter, "you'd need a skilled team."

"I've suggested," said Emily, "that you call on Nellie

Nelson for financial advice . . . do put down those biscuits, Nellie, and join us . . ."

"Well, it's very gratifying, I must say," said Miss Nelson, taking a seat as though she'd been lobbing round board-room tables all her life, which of course she had.

"Miss Nelson?" said George. "David's secretary?"

"And my right hand," said Emily. "She and I have been working on forward budgeting plans and P and L accounts for the past two years. She knows as much about the company's finances as I do."

"And I was thinking, Pauline," said Julia, "that you might find Marcia Blake helpful on the sales and market-ing side. She seems to know a surprising amount about it . . ."

"Marcia?" said George. "Now I've heard everything." He began ramming papers into his case, snapping the locks noisily and purposefully.

"We're not planning to put Miss Nelson on the board or make Miss Blake sales director," said Peter. "Not yet . . ." he gave Nellie a courteous nod, "but I think you'll find they'll be a splendid support as you build up your team."

I felt a surge of pleasure that Peter and Julia obviously thought I was clever enough to build teams and run companies. I hardly noticed George leaving the room and slamming the door. "You mean . . ." I said, "that I'd be taking over . . . everything?"

I'd had lunch with Peter Bolsover after the meeting, at Bertorelli's, just around the corner from our Covent Garden office.

"You look as though you could do with a drink," he said. "What'll it be?"

We both looked at my hand, which was shaking in an embarrassing way. "A glass of white wine?"

"It's all a bit of a shock, isn't it?" said Peter. He put his hand on mine, briefly, causing a further tremor. "No wonder you're shaky."

I wasn't absolutely certain why I was so nervous. Was it the thought of running Natural Sources, or was it Peter? "Yes, it is a bit of a shock."

We ate very good pasta and talked about the company. "I hope you don't mind having me foisted on you," he said. "Naturally, I won't interfere . . ."

"Oh, please. I'm sure I'll need any amount of interference." Oh God, I thought, I hope he doesn't think I'm being suggestive. I felt so jumpy that I was having difficulty digesting the tagliatelle, so I had another glass of wine instead.

I didn't remember much about the rest of that lunch, except that I had the feeling that my life had totally changed in a few hours, and I drank too much Verdicchio.

But I remembered Peter's words as he put me in a taxi. "I'll be there when you need me," he said.

Mother handed me a piece of paper when I arrived home. She and Clerry were watching a domestic drama on television, badly acted in Australian accents.

"What is it?" I looked at the paper. Thirty-three Belmont Crescent, Battersea, S.W.11. "It's an address."

"I can see we didn't waste money on your education," said Mother. She was wiggling an eyebrow at me, a signal I recalled from my childhood, which meant Not in Front of Pauline. Now, I presumed it meant Not in Front of Clerry.

We went into the kitchen, and Mother closed the door conspiratorially.

"George came back a couple of hours ago, dear, in a very nasty temper. He riffled through the kitchen cupboards, made an awful mess. 'What are you looking for, George?' I said. 'Can I help?' He was quite rude, told me to mind my own business and said he wasn't leaving without his dill weed . . ."

"George leaving?" I looked out of the window at the granny flat which had that empty look again.

"I think so, darling. That's his address. Said you could

get him there in an emergency, and his solicitor would be contacting your solicitor."

I studied the piece of paper more carefully. "He's moved in with Amanda." I told Mother about Amanda Braithwaite, social mole and rugby tackler. "It was her pamphlets you found in Gloria's flat."

"All that humourless stuff. Serves him right. You're not upset are you, darling?"

"I stopped being upset about anything George did years ago," I said without thinking, and then realised it was true. I was upset for Clerihue and Toby, though, and determined that however aggressive and devious George's solicitor and my solicitor became with each other, I'd try and be pleasant to George for the children's sake.

"How did your meeting go?" Mother was always more at ease discussing general issues than personal problems. "Will Natural Sources be all right?"

"They want me to run it." It sounded unbelievable, said aloud.

"Quite right, too. You're the obvious choice."

"But I don't know anything about running a business. I'm a designer."

"Accountants run large companies, so I'm told," said Mother, "why shouldn't designers? You're nobody's fool, Pauline."

Mother was right. Designs went out to Ahmet, were returned to us, checked, and despatched to our customers. There were frequent meetings with colleagues and suppliers and customers. After an initial setback, due to David's patio pants and brushed nylon, profits started climbing again and we looked as though we'd be on target at the end of the financial year. But I didn't have time for the things I enjoyed most. My children. The chores that I used to take for granted – the hair-washing, the school run, teaching Clerry to read from Ladybird books – were now rare treats.

"I suppose you couldn't spare a few days a week, to help out in the office?" I asked Peter, over dinner one evening.

"I long to get back to the drawing board. The design team are working well but they're just not getting enough back-up. I ought to spend more time with them."

"Poor love," said Peter. "You're trying to do too much. But I really can't fit in more than one day a week. I've got one or two other irons in the fire and I like to keep at least a couple of free days for Caroline. Sybilla hasn't phoned her once since she left, you know."

"How sad," I said, and then thought how wonderful, he called me love. Well, he called me poor love, and that's almost the same.

"What about your two?" said Peter. "How are they adjusting to life with a full-time working mother?"

"They're fine," I said quickly. It wasn't quite true. Mother was still with us, running the house and looking after the children. I'd put an ad in the *Lady* for a housekeeper and Mother had been interviewing applicants and turning them all down for one good reason or another. "I'm not leaving until we find the right person," she said. "I saw a woman today with superb references, but the type who wouldn't stop loading the dishwasher for a kiss and a cuddle. And a nice motherly soul came to see me yesterday and gave the children a box of Dairy Milk, *before their lunch*."

The truth was that Clerry and Toby seemed totally happy, but I was miserable. I didn't see enough of them.

"I don't suppose you see enough of them," said Peter, as though he was reading my mind. "I hope you don't feel we've pushed you into this job, and you're missing their childhood."

"Of course not." He'd spoken so seriously, almost as if I were undergoing some sort of test; I didn't want Peter to think I was one of those unprofessional women who take time off every time a child sneezes or bring their children into the office to play with the word processors. "Natural Sources comes first."

Peter called for the bill and he didn't look at me as we stood on the pavement outside the restaurant. He didn't kiss me good night, either. "You've got your car, have you?" he said.

I didn't see him again until Easter Sunday, the day of Julia's egg hunt. She'd invited all the children and they were racing around the garden in the spring drizzle while the assorted adults drank champagne and watched from the library windows.

Emily wandered over. "How's the farmhouse, Pauline?"

"Signed and sealed and utterly beautiful," I said. I'd managed to get over there for a weekend just before George left. The moment I saw the comforting old stone house, surrounded by gnarled bent heavily laden apple trees, with a view sweeping down to the valley, I wanted it. It was a safe refuge, somewhere I could go if life and George became unbearable. "I'm hoping to get over there in September, after the August collection."

"Splendid," said Emily. "Is there much to do?"

"The inside needs painting, but the surveyor said it was structurally okay. There's an extremely nice woman down the hill, who used to work for the people who lived there before. She's taking care of it for me." Marianne had appeared in the garden, like magic, just after I'd signed the contracts. Her husband was a builder – a good one, according to the surveyor – and she'd offered to look after the house and do the cooking and cleaning whenever I wanted her. "Why does it always seem so easy to organise domestic crises in distant places and impossible to even get the washing machine fixed at home?"

"A holiday home isn't real life," said Emily. "It's like playing houses. Talking of which, Trev and I are on the move. We've sold the house at three times the amount we paid for it, no capital gains tax, and we've bought the old priory just outside Caxton . . ."

"But it's a wreck."

"Won't be when Trev and I have done it up," said Emily. "A couple of years and we can take the money and move on."

"But won't it be awfully disruptive for the children?"

"Less disruptive than having their mother working a 24-hour day," said Em. "And we're not leaving the area; they're still at the same schools."

I sipped my champagne reflectively. Clever Em. "Why haven't I organised my life as efficiently?"

"You're doing a brilliant job," said Emily.

"I feel such a fraud when I have to meet all those other managing directors and chairmen and presidents of this and that."

"Well, you shouldn't. One of the things you realise when you start mixing with heads of industry is that they're no brighter than you are." She looked up as Peter came over to join us.

"How's the property tycoon?"

"Buying and selling, Peter, in the manner of property tycoons."

Peter grinned at Emily and then he turned to me. "I've been talking to Julia, Pauline, while we were secreting eggs around the garden, and we've had an idea . . ."

"I'll go and find Trevor," said Emily.

Peter put a hand on her arm. "No, don't go, Emily. I'd like your view. Ahmet and Nellie . . ."

"A curious couple," said Emily.

"But good managers, both of them," said Peter. "I was talking to Ahmet on Thursday. His brother, Ashok, is over here now, working with him. I had the distinct impression that Ahmet was finding his Spitalfields factory too small for two Basrawys, and would like to expand into something new . . ."

"But Ahmet wouldn't leave his business?" I said.

"No need," said Peter, "he could remain chairman of his company and take over the wholesale side of Natural Sources. We're 95 per cent of his business as it is."

"And Nellie?" said Emily.

"Responsible for the retail side," said Peter. "There's nothing you can tell Nellie Nelson about distribution and delivery dates, and she's worked out an excellent new scheme for computerising stock control."

"We worked it out together," I said and wished I hadn't. It sounded petty.

"Well, whoever did it, it works," said Peter. "We'd have to find a finance director, of course."

"I can help you there," said Emily. "There's a good man at Ibcon, old friend of mine, I know he's looking for another job . . ."

"Perhaps you'd like to see him, Pauline," said Peter. "If you're happy with the whole idea. It would give you more time for designing."

"It sounds wonderful," I said.

"It's what you need," said Emily. "And you'd have more time for Clerry and Toby."

"That would be even more wonderful."

Peter was talking to Julia. I heard him say, "Pauline and Emily are in favour of our idea, let's meet up and discuss it next week . . . I say, Julia, this is an excellent party, the children are having the time of their lives . . ." And then I heard a car coming up the drive. George's car.

I hadn't seen George since he walked out of my life with his dill weed. I knew he was involved in setting up some sort of business with Amanda, because he'd taken himself and his £20,000 out of Natural Sources. To put it into a Well Woman Clinic or an Alternative Bookshop, perhaps? I hadn't asked. And I didn't fancy talking to him now.

"Let's go and join in the egg hunt," I said to Emily.

Emily had also seen George. "What a good idea," she said.

I found Clerry and Toby in the shrubbery. Clerry waved an egg triumphantly.

"Aren't you clever, darling? How many?"

"I've found four," Clerry said. "Toby's only found two."

I knelt down and Toby clambered into my arms. "It's not fair, Mummy."

Clerry put her arms around my neck and one of her eggs, unwrapped and half eaten, fell down the back of my shirt.

"Right," I began tickling her. "Revenge!"

The children squealed with delight, and we were rolling around the ground together when I looked up and saw Peter Bolsover.

"Hey, two against one isn't fair." He picked up Tobias, and I heard him whisper, "Don't let's tell Mummy and Clerry, but I happen to know there are three eggs under that log."

Tobias ran off, followed by Clerry, and Peter and I smiled at each other. Everything was all right again. And then I saw George watching us from the terrace.

Two weeks after the Easter egg hunt I'd arranged to meet Ahmet at Brown's Hotel, to talk about his work for Natural Sources.

We'd nearly finished our smoked salmon sandwiches and champagne when I heard a familiar voice.

"Darling!"

Ahmet took one look and stood up, leaving his sandwich unfinished. "Lady Sybilla! I fear I am about to make tracks. Thank you for the luncheon, Pauline. Delightful. I will talk to you tomorrow."

Sybilla slipped into his vacant chair. "Champagne. How delicious." She called over a waiter and ordered another bottle. "Put it on my bill. Room 86."

"I thought you were in Buenos Aires," I said, wishing she was.

"Got a flat there, darling, but we could hardly *live* there," said Sybilla. "Luis has a rather charming brownstone in Manhattan, and we're dossing down here while we find a suitable pied-à-terre in London."

"You should speak to Emily and Trevor. They're in the property business now."

"Emily certainly is," said Sybilla. "Trevor's still playing with his computers."

"Uncharitable, as usual."

"I'll admit he's a useful back-up," said Sybilla. "If you offer Emily less than she wants she says she'll have to consult her husband, and it turns out that Trevor wouldn't dream of accepting anything less than £500,000 for an attic in Fulham."

I wondered how Sybilla had the nerve to sit and chat about property when she'd let us all down by dumping her shares. "Why did you do it, Sybilla?"

"Do what, Pauline?" She looked at me over her champagne glass, raised it in a salute and took a sip.

"Sell out on us."

"Getaway money, darling. What else? I'm the one with the title, Peter's the one with the cash. I wanted Luis, and there wasn't time to sit around waiting for the lawyers to carve everything in half."

I looked at her, glossy and self-satisfied with an emerald the size of a traffic light on her left hand. "You always get what you want, don't you, Sybilla?"

"Who's talking?" said Sybilla. "Little Miss Meek, who sat on my sofa all those years ago with a predatory gleam in her eye. I've watched you, darling, scheming and manipulating to get where you are . . ."

I hadn't schemed and manipulated. I'd worked hard. "Uncharitable, again."

". . . and who you want," said Sybilla.

"I don't know what you mean." I picked up my bag and my coat and stood up. "I won't pretend it was a pleasure to see you again."

Sybilla poured out another glass of champagne, and smiled nastily. "I hear that you and Peter are like that." She held up two fingers, elegantly entwined.

I stood outside Brown's, trembling. I couldn't remember where I'd put my car and then I realised that I'd gone in through the Dover Street entrance and I'd come out of the Albemarle Street exit. Damn Sybilla Bolsover. I wasn't going back through the hotel, I might bump into her again. I walked slowly round the block. Peter Bolsover and I weren't like *that*. We weren't anything. I hadn't spoken to him outside the boardroom since that happy day at the egg hunt.

He had avoided me since then, and I didn't know why. How silly . . . I was crying in Albemarle Street.

PEARL JUSTIN ON NEW RESTAURANTS

Investigating my suspicion that tacky restaurants with off-hand service think they can charge West End prices, merely because they are across the river and thinner on the ground, I drove across Battersea bridge in search of NIGHT AND DAY NURSERY, which opened a couple of months ago. The good news first; this place is not tacky, and the service, though inexperienced, is willing and cheerful. The bad news is that I should have made a reservation. Though I have to admit my hour's wait in one of the most comfortable bars in London was no hardship. Downstairs in the cellar dining room (seats 40, no squashing), my friend and I cast an approving look at the décor (refreshingly, almost non-existent) and the menu. Chef George Jenks, who runs NURSERY in partnership with sisters Amanda Braithwaite and Arabella Pinter-Bambury, is a firm believer in generous helpings of mostly English food. I opted for a first-class moussaka (when I suggested to the waiter that it didn't sound like nursery food to me, he answered, reasonably enough, that they probably had nurseries in Greece, too). My friend's Lancashire Hot Pot was eaten with nostalgic reverence. We both opted for Sussex Pond Pudding, a delicious combination of suet pudding and lemon, which I personally have never eaten anywhere else. Expect to spend £25–£30 a head, not including wine, and don't go unless you're hungry.

Time Out, 17th–24th August, 1988

"What are you doing with those mushrooms, Grenville?" I said sharply. Really, had one got to do everything oneself?

"Chopping them, Mr Jenks, for the Sweetbreads Financière."

I would have been the first to say that, in theory, there is a lot to be said for the Youth Training Scheme. Quite apart from the fact that you don't have to pay them all that much, though I rather played down that side when talking to my partners; Amanda still had one or two token principles left. Grenville was keen and eager to learn, and Keith was very popular with the customers (or punters, as I was learning to call them) but neither of them knew one thing about vegetable preparation.

"In Haute Cuisine we do not chop, we slice," I explained, "all the same thickness, so they cook evenly. I have told you, Grenville."

"Sorry, Mr J."

"And look at that hollandaise. What do you imagine the Roux brothers would say if they saw it?"

"Mon Dieu?"

"Yes, well, it's separated, hasn't it? You must keep stirring, Grenville. Where is Keith?"

"Nipped out to give the dustmen a sweetener."

There was more to running a restaurant than cooking, I had found that out very quickly. We opened in June, which was a bit speedy, I thought, because I had only come to Battersea in March; Amanda had rung me in the granny flat, just after I'd returned from an extremely demeaning Natural Sources board meeting. I should have been warned, I suppose, from what Peter had said in the car going to David's funeral. But actually having to sit and listen to them all talking as though Pauline knew anything about business . . .

"George?" Amanda sounded very urgent. "We've found perfect premises just round the corner from our house. Just come on the market, failed wine bar. When can you come?"

"Today," I said.

Pauline's mother had turned up the week before, in her flat-footed way, making Marmite soldiers as though the kitchen belonged to her.

I had cornered Pauline as soon as I could.

"How long is your mother staying?" I said.

"Since it's my house, I don't think that's any of your business. Oh George, why don't I say what we're both thinking? Irretrievable Breakdown."

There was no point in pretending I didn't understand her.

"Through no fault of mine, I'd like to point out. You're

the one who kept on deserting the family home, going off with all sorts of people."

"I was working, George, I told you a thousand times. I never went off, as you put it, with anyone. And *I'd* like to point out that you're the one who hit me, and you're the one who slept with Amanda Braithwaite."

"You can't cite Amanda."

"Why not? People who sleep with other people's husbands should be grown up enough to face the consequences."

"Anyway, you can't prove it."

"I can, as it happens. George . . . I know how you feel about the children. Of course you'll have all the access you want, you do know that, don't you? Do let's try and keep it amicable."

And how amicable was Amanda going to be, I thought, when she found out she was going to be in the papers as the Other Woman? She just might be cross enough to cancel our restaurant plans, which were still in a vague stage then.

"Pauline . . . if you're absolutely set on a divorce . . ."

"I'm sorry, George, but yes, I am."

"Very well, then." I squared my shoulders, caught a glimpse of myself in the hall mirror, and lifted my jaw a trifle. "If you insist, I will not stand in your way. Surely the solicitors can arrange something without bringing a third person in? I only want what's best for you, Pauline."

She put out a hand, and patted me on the arm. "I don't quite know where we went wrong, do you? When I walked down that aisle, I thought we were going to be so happy."

I knew where it all went wrong, I thought, as I watched Grenville slicing mushrooms two eighths of an inch thick. It went wrong when the women had money and power, and we didn't. The only marriage that had survived was Emily and Trevor's, and if you asked me it was pretty obvious who wore the trousers in that direction.

As it happened, things had turned out very well for me;

even though August was supposed to be a slack month, we were booked out every night, and not just by your hoi polloi, either. The mushrooms that Grenville was meticulously slicing might well be eaten by . . . my knees had actually shivered when that actress phoned up, and I wondered whether it was a practical joke. But it wasn't, and someone from *Eastenders* would be dining in my restaurant that evening at 9.30, with a small party of five. *Eastenders* today, minor royalty tomorrow. I thought, what a change in my life since Amanda rang up in March.

It had been quite late when I'd arrived at Amanda's little workman's house in Battersea with my suitcases and some plastic bags containing vital things like dill weed and my frozen home-made pesto. Arabella was there too, because it turned out that she had bought the house next door, and they planned to throw the two houses together and turn the top floor into a self-contained flat.

"Yours, George, if it suits you," said Amanda. "Rather convenient as we're all going into partnership together. A controlled rent, of course, and no nipping downstairs when you feel like it. That aspect of our relationship is over and done with."

"Really, Amanda," I said, glancing uneasily at Arabella, who was busying herself with pouring coffee, "of course there's no question of anything like –"

"Just wanted to set the ground rules, that's all. We've made an appointment with the estate agent for ten tomorrow. There are bound to be other people after it."

"Just wait till you see it, George," said Arabella, handing me a cup and sitting down, "you'll absolutely love it. It's got this absolutely wonderful –"

"Don't tell him, Bellsie, I want to see his face when he sees it. Are you excited, George?"

"A bit breathless," I said.

Only a few weeks ago, it seemed, they had vaguely been talking about putting money into a restaurant. "Tell you what, George," said Amanda, "you could handle the cooking side."

"Me? A chef?"

"Why not? That time when I stayed with you it was night after night of Lucullus. I must have put on half a stone."

"Only you'll have to learn about marketing, George," said Arabella seriously.

So I had got hold of some books and was just beginning to get to grips with the subject when Amanda hauled me down to inspect possible premises.

Breathless didn't begin to describe it.

"You'll get over it," said Amanda. "What are we going to call this caff?"

"It must be something absolutely *now*," said Arabella. "How about Trough?"

"Too pedestrian," said Amanda, (not to mention too disgusting, I thought) "Piggy's?"

"Someone else has thought of that." They both gazed reflectively into the fire. I cleared my throat.

"I had rather thought of . . . Chez Georges . . . cosmopolitan, you know."

They both gave me that kindly, George-has-said-something-silly look that I seemed to have been on the receiving end of practically since birth.

"It doesn't actually tell the punter anything, you see," said Arabella. "What kind of food are you planning to specialise in? Maybe that would give us an idea."

Now I was on my home ground. "Certainly not Cuisine Minceur," I said firmly, "that's right out."

Arabella nodded. "Pity, though," she said regretfully, "the profits they must have raked in on a slice of raw duck and some fanned-out fennel."

"I'm thinking of much more substantial food . . . good old-fashioned stuff. Shepherd's Pie, Lancashire Hot Pot, Sussex Pond Pudding, you know the sort of thing."

"Hah! *Nursery food*," said Arabella. She got up and walked about. "Ssh, I'm thinking . . . how about . . . Day

Nursery for lunch, and Night Nursery for dinner?"

"Brill," said Amanda, "absolutely spot on."

"But what would it be under in the telephone directory?"
I said sullenly. Nursery food indeed.

"No probs," said Arabella, "Nursery, Day, and Nursery, Night. Now we've done the christening, I'm going to bed."

Amanda and I also went to bed – separately – with me wondering what kind of partnership this was going to be. The kind where George Jenks did as he was told, it looked like. The usual kind.

Next day we walked round the corner and met the estate agent outside a big old house with For Sale notices on the ground floor and basement. We entered, to find the ground floor was one large room with an old-fashioned mahogany bar across a corner. That would have to go, I rather fancied a Provençal ambience. On the other hand, we wouldn't have to spend much on redecorating, the walls were covered in a very nice dark red flock paper. Red, I'd read somewhere, stimulates the appetite.

"Can you believe this wallpaper?" said Amanda.

"Indian restaurant, circa '72," said Arabella. "Lovely bar, though, just right for our theme."

"The vendors might be prepared," said the agent, riffling through his papers, "to negotiate a price for these bar stools."

"We might be quite interested," I said, it was high time I put my oar in, "leatherette is always practical."

"I don't think so," said Amanda. "Tell you what, Bellsie, we want the kind of bentwood furniture they've got at Brown's, in Cambridge."

"Wonder where they got it from? I'll give them a ring."

We had to pass the cloakrooms, labelled Ladies and Gentlemen, to get to the cellar, and I had a brainwave.

"We could call these Boys and Girls," I said, "sort of following on the nursery theme."

Amanda and Arabella exchanged a look.

"Come on," said Arabella, "the cellar's the exciting bit."

There were two cellars, a big one in front, a smaller one at the back, with a door into an overgrown garden. Dusty, musty, with low beams that were probably riddled with woodworm. Broken crates and mouldering cardboard boxes everywhere, and a nasty pile of rags. Oh well, I thought, there were always other places.

"I take it the price includes the garden?" said Amanda. The agent nodded. "I say, Bellsie. Summer."

"I know, can't you just see it? Well, I think in principle we are extremely interested, aren't we, partners? Of course the price is a bit on the silly side, but I'm sure we can come to an agreement."

"But, but, wait," I said, "what are we going to do with these dirty cellars? Storage? I quite see the ground floor could be a perfect dining room, but –"

They gave me that look again.

"The ground floor would be reception and bar, George. And of course they'd eat down here. Kitchen in the back cellar, corridor through to outdoor eating in the summer . . ."

"Divine wrought-iron furniture . . ."

". . . and inside, all cream with those gorgeous old beams . . ."

"Oh well, if you think so," I said. "Personally I think those gorgeous old beams are on their deathbed. And what about that smell? It's either dry rot, or tramps. Cost a fortune to get this place right."

"I can see the gentleman knows what he's talking about," said the agent, "the asking price is, don't quote me, but I think I can assure you, negotiable."

"It'll have to be very negotiable indeed," I said, sticking my thumb into a beam and waving it under his eyes. How could the girls imagine I could create Haute Cuisine under these conditions?

"You'll come back to us, then?" said Arabella.

"By tomorrow morning at the latest."

We said goodbye to the agent and walked back to Amanda's house. What a waste of a morning, I thought.

"I say, wasn't George brilliant?" Arabella linked her arm in mine.

"You cunning swine, George," Amanda linked into my other arm, "making those ghastly suggestions and pretending you hated it. If we don't get ten grand off the asking price . . ."

We actually got eight and a half grand off the asking price, largely, I suspected, because we were the only idiots who wanted it. The three of us opened a bottle of champagne when we'd finally exchanged contracts (it all went through very quickly; the Pinter-Bambury family solicitor knew his way around).

"It would be nice to open in June, beginning of the Season;" said Amanda, "you've got a tame decorator, haven't you, Bellsie?"

"I'll get on to him. The only thing that worries me . . . George, have you done any research into buying? That's the make and break area, isn't it?"

"Oh, everyone knows about that," said Amanda airily. "Meat from Smithfield, fruit and veg from Covent Garden . . ."

I allowed a pitying smile to flicker across my lips. It was, at last, my turn to look superior.

The last few weeks in the granny flat had been pretty lonely, and I had got into the habit of driving off into the country for dinner at a really excellent little pub. I'd got onto quite friendly terms with the manager – it turned out his wife had deserted him, too. One night I asked him to have a Remy Martin with me after the last guests had gone.

"I'd like to ask your advice," I said. "I'm thinking of starting a restaurant."

He put down his glass and looked at me in a sharp manner. "Where?"

"My partners and I are looking for premises in Battersea."

He picked up his glass again.

"Battersea? Very nice. How can I help you?"

"It's buying the ingredients that's worrying me. I've read quite a lot about it, but a bit of practical advice from someone who knows what he's doing . . ."

"I get you. How about the other half . . . no? Probably right, the way the police are now . . . Battersea, you've certainly picked a good area for supply. Hang on a mo."

He went into his office and came back with some papers.

"I suppose it's Smithfield for meat, is it?" I said.

"Na. Unless you want to cart home sides of beef and whole lambs and chop them up yourself. Good trade butcher is what you want. Here we are, Feltwell and Parson, old-established family firm, they'll see you straight. Mention my name."

"And fish? Billingsgate's somewhere in the City, isn't it?"

"Moved to the Isle of Dogs. And the New Covent Garden, for your fruit and veg, that's at Nine Elms, just round the corner from you. Always have cash on you, and you won't have any problems. You know where the power station used to be?"

"I think so."

"Excellent Cash and Carry there, for your dry goods, flour and stuff. And butter. How classy are you going to aim?"

I thought of Arabella and Amanda.

"Pretty up-market."

"Then you'll need a good French cheese supplier. Try this one," he handed me a card.

"I really do not know how to express my gratitude for your help," I said as I left.

"Think nothing of it. We're in the same boat, aren't we? *Women*."

I was able to pass on all this information to my partners in an effortless manner; I could see they were rather impressed.

"You have been doing your homework, George," said Arabella.

* * *

As soon as contracts were exchanged, Arabella swept her "tame decorators" into action. The foreman was a middle-aged man called Mr Bell. He seemed respectable and hard-working, but didn't pay quite as much attention to my suggestions as I would have wished. It was quite interesting to observe how these upper-class girls dealt with a member of the working classes; they didn't give orders, they asked questions.

"Oh, Mr Bell, wouldn't it be wonderful if the electrics were finished by next week?"

"Did you know the ballcock in one of the loos has conked out, Mr Bell?"

"A slightly lighter shade of cream, don't you think? We don't want to look gloomy, do we?"

Only their questions managed to sound like orders, and Mr Bell trotted round after them saying, "Exactly, Miss Pinter-Bambury," and, "You're the boss, Mrs Braithwaite." He never said, "You're the boss" to me, because I obviously wasn't. When I suggested that the plaster mouldings on the ground floor be picked out in gold to give a welcoming atmosphere, he asked me if I'd cleared it with the young ladies. "They never mentioned anything about gold to me. If you want my opinion, it would be a bit on the flashy side."

So I left them all to it, only reigning supreme in the cellar that was going to be the kitchen.

I had to admit, when all the rubbish was cleared out, the walls painted cream (not just any cream, it had to be "Nursery cream", whatever that meant) and the woodwork revived, that it did have a rather homey atmosphere. And they certainly weren't sparing any money on the kitchen equipment; the latest this and the newest that was the order of the day.

I had removed my £20,000 from Natural Sources and put it into the restaurant partnership, on the principle that it would give me more say in things if I had a financial stake. So when Arabella said she'd heard about this marvellous new commercial dishwasher from Germany, and mentioned a sum that made my jaw drop, I thought it was time to put an oar in.

"Wouldn't it be cheaper to buy an ordinary English model?" I said. "You can get reconditioned ones at half the price."

"You have to spend money to make it. The Maggendorf cycle is twice as quick, and it's much quieter. Don't *worry*, George, we'll be coining it, you'll see."

But would we, I wondered? We seemed to be spending money hand over fist. And did I really know enough about cooking to run a restaurant? The most I had ever cooked for before was a lunch party for twelve, when Pauline had some Americans to entertain. I expressed my doubts to Arabella.

"You won't be cooking for forty overnight," she said, "until we get known the numbers will be quite low. You'll be able to work up to it gradually, you'll see."

They kept on saying, "You'll see" to me. I only hoped I would.

To complicate the issue, Pauline was for ever ringing me up and asking when I wanted the children for a weekend. I had to find a variety of excuses; what with one thing and another I really hadn't got any time to spare, and anyway, how would Clerry and Toby fit in with the new Canvey and Jake? Spotlessly clean, clearing the table without being asked, I hardly recognised them. The old Amanda would have described them as "hopelessly trammelled", but now she was quite brisk with them. She actually said things like, "Because it's my house and what I say goes". I could see even Arabella thought it was quite a turn-up for the book.

It was the middle of April when Pauline finally put her foot down. She rang up, sounding rather depressed and listless.

"George, you really must see the children. Clerihue asked yesterday if you still love her, it's simply not fair to them."

"Of course I'll see them, Pauline. Have you got a cold?"

"No, why?"

"Your voice sounds funny."

"No, I'm fine," she said wearily. "Look, what about next weekend? I could drive them up on Thursday, and you could drive them back on Monday, or whenever you want."

"What about school?"

"It's the middle of the holidays. That's settled, then?"

"No, it isn't," I said, "it would be most inconvenient."

"Can you hear yourself, George? You're talking about your children as though they were a delivery of, of wine, or something. Since you left in March, you've seen them once, at Julia's Easter egg hunt, and that was only for about ten minutes. I'm bringing them up on Thursday, and that's that."

She put the phone down, as bossy as ever. The Easter egg hunt. I knew something about the Easter egg hunt she didn't know. The thought of it quite cheered me up.

When I rather hesitantly broached the possibility of having the children in Battersea for a few days, the girls responded in a very bracing manner.

"How lovely," said Arabella, "you must be missing them terribly. Are they as good-looking as you, George?"

"Nice to see them again," said Amanda; "that time at the playgroup seems years ago. God, Bellsie, you can't imagine what a bore I was."

"Yes I can," said Arabella, and they both screamed with laughter. "I remember warning George about you when we had lunch once."

Amanda stopped laughing. "Hang about. We're going to Gien next weekend, to get the plates and things."

(Why it was necessary to drive halfway across France to buy crockery was something else that was beyond me, but as usual my feeble remonstrations were cheerfully stamped under.

"The most beautiful china," said one, "and you can buy it at the Boutique d'Usine."

"And four days of French food," sighed the other, "I

can't wait." Rather tactless, as I'd taken to doing the cooking.)

"I'd forgotten about that," I said, reaching for the phone, "I'll just call Pauline and tell her –"

"We wouldn't dream of your making such a sacrifice, would we, Amanda? We're borrowing Dad's Passat, plenty of room."

"You mean . . . take them to France with us?"

"Super fun," said Amanda.

"But where will we put all the plates? And what about Jake and Canvey? Won't they be jealous?"

"Most of what we buy will be shipped back commercially. We'll just bring one crate to see how it looks in the dining room. Jake and Canvey are okay. They're going to my mother's for the weekend."

It was rather a rough crossing to Le Havre. As soon as we boarded, I took the children down to our cabin and tucked them in on the bottom bunk. Then I tucked them in again on the top bunk, because they'd discovered the ladder. Tobias spent most of the night being sick, and Clerry spent all night saying she was going to be. Not that I could really blame them; quite apart from the motion, which was most upsetting, all we'd been able to find in Portsmouth were some rather disreputable hamburgers.

We ate them in the car, and Clerry said, "Wouldn't it be lovely if Mum was with us?" And Toby cried and said, "Why isn't Mum with us?"

At two o'clock – I knew because I checked my watch in disbelief – there was a bang on our cabin door. When I opened it, Amanda and Arabella fell in, giggling. They were in a very poor state of repair.

"Just came to see how you are," said Arabella. "I say, isn't this *fun*! What's that smell?"

"Sick," I said coldly.

"Oh, poor *babies*. Did we bring any Kwells, Amanda?"

"Tobias has got nothing left to be sick with," said Clerry,

"the hamburger and chips went ages ago. And some tomatoes, and now he's just –"

"You should have let them stay up a bit longer, George," said Amanda. "We've had a lovely time in the bar, haven't we, Bellsie?"

"Just as long as we don't meet that French lorry-driver again. The one you promised to have lunch with outside Versailles."

"I didn't, did I?"

"In faultless French, what's more. I was quite impressed."

"You should have stopped me."

Tobias heaved. "Where's Mummy? I want my Mummy."

The sisters were not giggling next morning when we met at the mustering point for car passengers. One of them had a migraine and the other had lost a contact lens. Which meant that yours truly not only had to drive on the right, something I've never held with, but navigate as well. The trouble with France is that a lot of bits of it look exactly like a lot of other bits. They started feeling better at lunch, which one of them had found in the Michelin under Value for Money.

"Boudin and hot potato salad, how scrummy," said Arabella.

"I want a hamburger," said Tobias.

"You should have thought of that last night," said Clerry, "then we could have –"

"*No*, Clerihue," I said.

"I wonder if I could face a drink?" said Amanda. "Yes, I think I probably can."

"I shouldn't if I were you," I said. "If your migraine's better you can do some driving."

It was with a certain amount of relief that I delivered the children back to St Neots; it had been very nice to see them, of course (though a French weekend is not necessarily the ideal venue for parenting), but my life had broadened so much since I left Pauline. The prattle of little ones did not seem to have quite its old enchantment. I had to point out to Clerihue quite sharply that it was illogical to expect Marmite soldiers in a hotel on the Loire, and Tobias broke a milk jug in the china factory.

The actress from *Eastenders* wasn't the only "celebrity" in my restaurant that night. I popped my head discreetly through the little hatch to see what the Front of House, as we call it, was looking like, and saw to my gloom that Sybilla Bolsover was ensconced at a table for two with a man whose hair reflected the light. Luis, I assumed, the wealthy polo player who had featured in all the gossip columns with Sybilla recently.

I withdrew my head sharply, I certainly didn't want her awful upper-class voice shouting, "*George!* What *do* you look like in that hat!" or some such demeaning comment.

"The sweetbreads are going down a treat, Mr J.," said Keith, swooping in with piles of dirty plates.

"It's the way you slice the mushrooms," said Grenville smugly.

"Two oxtails for table eight, two mashed potatoes, one spinach, one cauliflower cheese. I told the punter it doesn't really go with oxtail. He said he didn't care, he couldn't resist them. I say, Mr J., that loud lady at table eight . . ."

"The one with the wop gigolo?" said Keith. "I'm surprised he's got a hand to spare for eating."

"Yeah, that one. She says she knows you, Mr J., and she's going to pop in after her pudding to express her appreciation to the chef."

"Oh God."

"In fact, here she comes now."

I finished smoothing off the mashed potato in the serving dish (I did wish my partners had allowed me to call it Pommes Purée), scattered chopped chives over it, and handed it to Grenville.

"George! I can't believe it! Your little caff – the dernier cri!" Sybilla had left Luis in the dining room, one thing to be grateful for. "When Arabella told me your plan I gave you a fortnight, but just look at it! Luis adored your roly-poly, he went to Harrow, you know. I say, what about my ex-husband and your wife? Not that I give a hoot, of course . . ." she gave me a sideways glint to see if it was worth twisting the knife a bit. ". . . and you seem to be taking it very calmly."

"Pauline and I are divorcing, actually. We have agreed to go our separate ways."

"Well, we all know which way she's going. Good luck to her, with that old stick. He's bought some boring shoe factory, did you know? Must love you and leave you, Luis gets so impatient when we're apart, even for a minute."

Off she wafted, scattering "Too perfects" and "Amazings" over the bemused Keith and Grenville.

"Cor, what a cracker," said Keith. "The lady at table three said the summer pudding was the best thing she's ever eaten."

"Good," I said absentmindedly. Whatever Sybilla thought, there was never going to be anything between Pauline and Peter. I'd seen to that, very neatly, at the Easter egg hunt.

My mood, as I stood on that terrace, was irritable anyway. I had driven down to have a quiet word with Julia about backing out of being an executor (what was the point, if I wasn't going to get paid?), and of course nobody had told George Jenks there was going to be a party. I did think Julia could have asked me, even if only for the children's sake.

I did not at all care for the sight of Peter Bolsover romping, that was the only word for it, with my children. Toby should have been laughing up into my face, not his. And then Toby and Clerry ran off, and Peter and Pauline looked at each other.

I instantly started humming under my breath, remembering that time when I'd confided in Peter, *Peter* about my doubts of Pauly's fidelity. And there he was, as blatant as anything, smiling into Pauline's eyes. What a fool I'd been, I thought bitterly.

I'd already had some success, after David's funeral, with hinting to Peter that Pauline wasn't a good mother. I knew that would influence him strongly, he was always going on about Caroline and how Sybilla neglected her. But of course, then I was only trying to discredit her out of being a managing director. But now . . . I hated them both, looking at each other like teenagers.

My opportunity came towards the end of the party, when I found Peter and Caroline strolling down one of Julia's endless herbaceous borders.

"Oh Dad, what a marvellous idea." Caroline was jumping up and down excitedly. "Is it a secret, or can I . . . ?"

"No, no, not a word. I just wanted to, sort of sound you out, darling. You do promise me you wouldn't mind?"

"*Course* not. Hello, Mr Jenks."

"George, how nice to see you," said Peter, looking slightly ill-at-ease.

"Peter, I wondered if I could have a private word with you? I wouldn't bother you, but there's something . . . I'm very worried."

"Yes, of course. Caro darling, could you . . . ?"

"I'll go and pig some more Easter eggs. See you."

Peter watched her run off. "Don't they grow up quickly?" We strolled towards the house. "George, you are happy now, aren't you, with all these restaurant plans?"

Wants to have a clear conscience before he makes off with my wife, I thought.

"In myself, yes, I am very happy. But . . . oh God, Peter, I've got to confide in someone."

"Confide? Look, George, if it's anything financial, I'm sure I could . . ."

And make your conscience even sweeter, I thought.

"I wish it was money. I wondered whether I should tell a priest, in confession, but somehow I couldn't. Or the police? I can't go to the police, Peter, can I? About David's death?"

"About what?"

"I knew they'd do anything to get back control of Natural Sources, but I never thought they'd do that."

"Who?"

"Julia and Pauline. That's why I'm divorcing her, of course, I could never live with a woman who . . ."

"Who what?" Peter's face was quite still.

The look in his eyes was quite different now, and I relished it. "Perhaps this is a mistake, perhaps I shouldn't tell anyone, even you."

"I'm afraid you'll have to, now."

"Pauline got back from Edinburgh early, and came with me and Julia to collect the children. When we got back to the house, we found David . . ."

"It didn't mention Pauline was there in the *St Neots Express*."

"I dealt with the press. I thought it better, under the circumstances, not to mention Pauline."

"George, for God's sake, what are you saying?"

"There were two pill bottles, you see. Blue for heart, pink for indigestion. They looked at each other and sent me away to phone for an ambulance, and when I came back . . . Julia was putting the top back on the pink ones. And Pauline was smiling."

Confident outlook as Natural Sources and Shuttleworth merge

Peter Bolsover, non-executive chairman of Natural Sources, one of the country's leading fashion groups, plans a merger between N.S., and his recently acquired Northamptonshire shoe company. 'With 1992 in sight, Europe will be a vital target for Natural Sources,' he said in London yesterday. 'Shuttleworth will extend Natural Sources' already buoyant business with a wide range of top quality leather accessories.'

Mr. Bolsover intends initially to increase productivity at Shuttleworth by 25% and is forecasting a 45% increase to £4.3 million in pre-tax profits for the merged group for the six months to end March.

Financial Times, **24th September, 1988**

N early time for my bourride. I shan't bother to change, it's not all that much fun eating by yourself.

Clerry will phone soon, she rings me every evening at about seven. I'd wanted to bring the children, of course, and show them our lovely new house; "Don't be so self-indulgent, Pauline," Mother had said, "There's been enough change in their lives recently without you taking them out of school. You know they're safe with me."

But when the phone goes it isn't Clerry. My happy "Darling!" is answered by Emily, who laughs.

"Who were you expecting? Sorry it's only me, but I had to tell you how pleased I was about the news. Brilliant idea."

"Brilliant?"

"In the *FT* today. Natural Sources and Shuttleworth. That's what I call a really personal merger. How's Peter?"

"Oh, it's announced, is it?" We'd been discussing it, in stilted boardroom language, before I left. "Does it mention me?"

"Funnily enough," says Emily, "it doesn't . . . anyway, give him my love."

So that's it. He doesn't even want to work with me any more.

"Peter isn't here, Emily. I can't think why you think he would be."

"Sorry." Emily sounds unusually awkward. "I just thought, that's all . . ."

"We haven't talked about anything more personal than pretax profits since April."

Another newspaper cutting to add to my collection, I think sadly, as I put down the phone.

"Mummy?" This time it is Clerry. "When are you coming home?"

"Soon, darling." As soon as possible. Whatever made me think it would be any easier to make sense of my life in the middle of the French countryside? "Will you come and meet me at the airport?"

"Yes, please." I can hear her calling my mother. "Granny, can we go and meet Mummy's aeroplane?"

"When are you coming back, love?" My mother's voice.

"Not quite sure, Mum. I'll ring first . . ."

"You're all right, darling? You're having a wonderful time? Lots of rest?"

"Lots and lots of rest."

"Pauline? I've been trying to get through to you for ages." Oh dear. She sounds like she sounded two years ago.

"Julia? Oh, Julia, you haven't been . . ."

"Drinking? I certainly have. Went straight to the bottle as soon as Peter left. And so will you when you hear."

"You've seen Peter?"

"He met Dr Bingley, you see, at some party. Came roaring round here in his car first thing this morning. Well, he would, wouldn't he?"

"Is that what you called to say, Julia? Why don't you put the phone down, have a cup of coffee and call me back when you're feeling . . . better."

"No listen, why I'm ringing is . . . you're not going to

believe this, Pauline. That bloody George, and I always tried to be nice to him."

"What's George got to do with Dr Bingley? And Peter?"

"Dr Bingley told Peter that you got back from Edinburgh the day after David died."

"That's right, the children had chickenpox."

"So you couldn't have, could you? Given David the wrong pill?"

"Julia," I say wearily, "I've never given David any pills. You know that. What's all this about, anyway?"

"Remember the Easter egg hunt? George turning up unexpectedly? He told Peter that we gave David the wrong pill. Are you still there? *On purpose*. This is a rotten line."

"Julia, have I got it right? Are you seriously telling me that Peter thinks we . . . we had something to do with David's death?"

"Thought, not thinks. I put him right, I can tell you. George was the one who gave him the pill, I said."

I'm shaking so much, I can hardly dial the number. How could Peter think that Julia and I . . . ? Why did he believe George? . . . 0480 . . . finger's slipped, start again . . . but then I had, hadn't I? I'd believed him for years.

"Caroline? It's Pauline, is your father there?"

"Sorry," Caroline says cheerfully, "he's gone away. Terrific fuss about his passport, racing round the house, singing. In his drawer all the time, of course. Nanny found it."

"Where's he gone?"

"He wouldn't say. He kept grinning, and Nanny told him he was behaving like a four-year-old."

"Caroline, it's important. If he calls ask him to ring me." I give her my number slowly and carefully, and ask her to write it down.

"Hello? Oh, hello, Toby, darling." I've never been disappointed to hear the voice of one of my children before. We have a conversation about Mork and Mindy, who are, apparently, very well, and he tells me about his latest drawing, which Miss Bembridge is going to pin up on the wall tomorrow. He didn't like his supper very much, and Granny wouldn't let him leave any. Clerry has been mean to him. She won't let him play with her pram, and . . .

Marianne bustles in.

"Toby, I must go now, it's time for my supper . . . yes, of course I'll eat it all up. Good night, darling."

"Madame, Madame, c'est impossible!"

"Is something wrong, Marianne? The bourride?"

Marianne is affronted. "My bourride is never wrong, Madame. But how can I serve it if you are going to have visitors? There is this madman in my kitchen, demanding to see you. 'Ask her if she'll forgive me,' he keeps saying." She stops and gives me a shrewd look. "Tiens! I see exactly how it is. And what is to become of my bourride?"

"Oh, Marianne, is there enough for two?"

SHIRLEY LOWE & ANGELA INCE

SWAPPING

Felicia was an attractive and successful actress, revelling in the pace and glitter of London. Ann loved the country, doting on her children, her garden, her 18th-century house. Then Felicia fell in love with Ann's husband. Without really intending to, each woman took over the other's house – lock, stock, and lovelife.

'A fine comic fantasy . . . and there is enough truth . . . to make the story sparkle like very good champagne'
Nina Bawden in the *Daily Telegraph*

'Had me laughing aloud'
Kati Nicholl in *Best*

'A perfect dollop of enjoyable escapist fiction'
The Lady

'A novel I'd recommend to anyone. I took it on the train and I laughed and bubbled all the way home. It's like a glass of champagne'

Peter Giddy of *Hatchards*

Post·A·Book

A Royal Mail service in association with the Book Marketing Council & The Booksellers Association.

Post-A-Book is a Post Office trademark.

FAY WELDON

THE FAT WOMAN'S JOKE

A novel of love, greed and cream eclairs from this major contemporary writer.

She is monumental and she is magnificent and her name is Esther and she's one side of every woman who ever lived, breathed, loved, lost and ate!

'Delightfully witty and wicked'
New York Times Book Review

HODDER AND STOUGHTON PAPERBACKS

MAVIS CHEEK

PAUSE BETWEEN ACTS

Joan's answer to life-after-divorce is simple: happy seclusion: a citadel of perfect peace and sanity, which takes a little madness to maintain . . .

To stop her parents knowing about the divorce she invents a woman lodger from Nigeria . . .

To keep her ex-husband at bay she invents an affair between herself and the imaginary lodger . . .

Meanwhile she must hold off the dog-like devotion and persistent advances of the young PT teacher from school . . .

Enter, then, the roguishly theatrical Finbar Flynn and despite herself, the walls of her citadel look set to come tumbling down . . .

HODDER AND STOUGHTON PAPERBACKS

MAVIS CHEEK

PARLOUR GAMES

As Celia prepares her fortieth-birthday dinner party she reflects contentedly on how painlessly she has reached that milestone. Marriage to high-flying Alex, good children, secure friendships and life in one of London's best suburbs where Neighbourhood Watch and agonising over the right school reign supreme: could she ask for more?

As the dinner party and its parlour games unfold Celia begins to feel that she could. While Alex is peculiarly distant, her best friend's husband is anything but, and the behaviour of her other guests does little to rectify her planned perfection.

Perhaps the next forty years are not going to be quite as easy as she thought? And when she decides to surprise Alex by dropping in on his next business conference she sparks a chain of events which proves, once and for all, that life for Celia has only just begun.

Games – everyone seems to be playing them – so why shouldn't Celia play some too?

'Mavis Cheek has a sharp ear and a wicked eye for the discreet lack of charm of the bourgeoisie'

The Times

'Spry continuation of the sharp urban satire of her first . . . a most agreeable read indeed'

The Observer

HODDER AND STOUGHTON PAPERBACKS

CHRISTIE DICKASON

THE DRAGON RIDERS

Spanning forty turbulent years, from the defeat of the French to the arrival of the Americans – an extraordinary saga of struggle, passion and violence.

Saigon between the wars: the most exotic city on earth; decadent, seductive, corrupt and exciting – a city where the cultures of East and West collide.

Typical of the time and place is the improbable and doomed marriage of Ariane and Luoc. She, the innocent French girl sent East to satisfy her adolescent restlessness. He, already a killer, executioner of the man who had killed his own father.

Nina, beautiful, mysterious and determined, is the offspring of this heady alliance. A woman with the blood of two races in her veins, who will triumph over every obstacle to keep the man she loves, and to win control of a business – an empire of opium-trading – that symbolises the violence and the dreams of a society in turmoil.

HODDER AND STOUGHTON PAPERBACKS

MORE FICTION TITLES AVAILABLE FROM
CORONET BOOKS